THE GOD GAME

DANNY TOBEY

This paperback first published in Great Britain in 2020 by Gollancz

First published in Great Britain in 2020 by Gollancz
an imprint of The Orion Publishing Group Ltd
Carmelite House, 50 Victoria Embankment
London EC4Y 0DZ

An Hachette UK Company

1 3 5 7 9 10 8 6 4 2

Copyright © Danny Tobey 2020

A CIP catalogue record for this book is
available from the British Library.

ISBN (Mass Market Paperback) 978 1 473 22449 0
ISBN (eBook) 978 1 473 22450 6

Printed in Great Britain by Clays Ltd, Elcograf S.p.A

www.gollancz.co.uk

For my parents

dox
verb
1. search for and publish private or identifying information on the internet, typically with malicious intent.

doxology
noun
1. a liturgical formula of praise to God.

Men loved darkness more than light,
because their deeds were evil.

—John 3:19

1 THE GAME

The blue light of the computer screen was flickering on Charlie's and Peter's faces, making them look like astronauts lit by the cosmos.

"Say something."

"No."

"Seriously. Go for it."

"This is stupid."

"Don't you want to meet God?"

There was a knock on the door. Charlie's father.

Peter rushed to snub out the joint. He blew a tuft of smoke out the window.

"Tell him to go away," Peter said.

"You're the idiot who brought pot."

"Yeah, well, you'll go down, too, if he catches me."

Another knock.

"Tell him you're masturbating. That always gets my dad to leave."

"You're insane. You know that?"

In a way, it was true. Peter was smart, handsome, charming, and had been thrown out of the most expensive private school in town, meaning he was both rich and reckless. But there was something more. A dangerousness was just below the surface. Almost a nihilism, and more than the usual teenage morbid curiosities. It was what drew Charlie to him, but enough of the honor student was still left in

Charlie to listen to that voice in the back of his head saying, *Get into trouble, sure, but do you really want to go* there? Charlie's father hated Peter and had no idea Peter was here now.

"Charlie, come on, I want to talk to you."

"Not now, Dad."

"Come on. Open up." He tried the doorknob.

"Dad, we can talk later. Okay?"

"I got a call from the school."

"Later. I promise. I'm busy."

Charlie could imagine his dad weighing his next moves. The shadow shifted under the door.

"Fine. Tonight, okay? Not tomorrow. Tonight."

"Okay. I promise."

Charlie held his breath and watched the shadow under the door. It hesitated, then moved away.

Charlie let out a breath. He gave Peter a harsh look and said, glancing at the half-smoked joint, "Throw that thing away."

"Um, nope." Peter tucked it into his shirt pocket.

They looked back at the computer screen.

The same prompt was there, flashing, alone on the black screen.

Hello.

"Say something," Peter barked.

Charlie shook his head. Finally, he typed:

Hello.

No response. The cursor just blinked.

They gave it a while. Nothing.

Peter said, "Try something else."

Charlie shrugged.

Who is this?

The cursor blinked a few times, then the letters tapped out:

This is God.

Peter laughed. "This is awesome."

"Awesome? Huh."

"You can ask it anything. Watch."

Peter grabbed the keyboard.

Are you a man or a woman?

After a moment, it said:

I am what I am.

"Wow," Charlie said sarcastically.

"Don't blame the machine. Ask better questions."

Charlie knew what question he wanted to ask:

Why did my mom die?

But there was no way he was going to ask a stupid computer program *that*, even one that claimed to be God.

Charlie sighed and typed:

Why is there war?

A pause, then:

Because killing feels good.

Well, that was charming. Charlie asked:

To whom?

Another pause. Charlie figured he was about to get a lecture about man's dark desires, the hidden death urge, humanity's subconscious bloodlust under the thin veneer of civilization. Then the program said:

To me.

So said God, or at least the first artificial intelligence bot claiming to inhabit the persona of God. That was the story anyway. According to Peter, who had his share of crazy stories from 4chan and other bizarre corners of the Web, computer scientists had loaded up an AI with every religious text known to man, from antiquity to the present day, weighted by number of adherents, donations, historical longevity, and every other factoid they could pour in, all coursing through a deep-learning neural network. What came out, on the other end, was supposedly the sum total of human conceptions of the divine come alive, able to express itself and answer questions and spout new proverbs and instructions. It was a joke. A lark, by a bunch of overbright CS guys. Yet another time-wasting diversion on the internet, like cat videos and MMOs. But this was interesting now, to Charlie. Apparently the meta-god was an angry one. Old Testament–style.

> You like killing?
>> Yes.
> But you're God.
>> Yes.
> Aren't you supposed to be kind and loving?
>> Yes.
> So . . . isn't that a contradiction?

Charlie let that hang.
Then God answered.

> Anyone is a murderer under the right conditions.

Peter was watching, his dangerous eyes twinkling. "I told you this was cool."

Charlie shivered, despite himself. "What should I say?"

"Tell it to go fuck itself."

"Um, no. I'm not looking to get struck by lightning."

"It's just a chatbot. Don't get all superstitious on me."

"I'm not, but, you know. Even if it's a chatbot, what's the point of being a dick?"

"Well, for one thing, it's fun. For another, it's funny. And where else do you get to tell God to go fuck himself? Like, via direct message? What could be more daring? Feel like rolling the dice?"

The idea did send a thrill down Charlie's spine. He wasn't religious. He was an atheist or at best a serious agnostic. When his mom died, he buried any religious sentiment he'd had in the ground with her. Those prayers were not answered. They withered, with great suffering, and then one day . . . poof. So the idea of telling God—or even his computer surrogate—to take a long walk off a short plank was titillating and intriguing. But it still felt wrong to him. Reckless.

"Do you know Pascal's Wager?" Charlie asked.

"Is that when you bet against a triangle?"

"You smoke too much weed."

"Probably." Peter fingered the joint in his pocket longingly.

"Pascal's Wager. You should believe in God because if you're wrong, nothing happens. But if you bet against his existence and you're wrong, you go to hell—infinite loss. So the smart bet is to believe."

"Right. Okay. That assumes you can fake belief and fool the guy."

"Fine. But think about that here. You want to tell a computer program that thinks it's God to fuck off."

"Yeah."

"And what if there's a real God, watching?"

"Um, there's not."

"Okay, but say there's a one-in-a-billion chance there is. If so, he's probably going to be pissed. If it's just a computer program, you don't gain anything by cursing it. But if there is something more . . ."

"I think *you* sound like the pothead." Peter snatched the keyboard and typed in:

Go fuck yourself.

Charlie tried to grab his hand, but Peter hit Enter, laughing and stiff-arming Charlie.

Once the horse was out of the barn, they both stopped fighting and watched. A sense of excitement filled Charlie. He couldn't stop the message now, and he wouldn't have said it himself, but, hey. What's done is done. He was curious what the sum total of all human religious information, dumped into a neural net, would come up with in response.

The cursor blinked for a long time.

God didn't answer.

2 THE VINDICATORS

Charlie's mom died when he was almost seventeen, after a long battle with cancer that left the rest of his small family—Dad, Charlie, that's it—ragged. Picturing his dad alone in that master bedroom, pressing his face into Mom's old pillow, it was too much to bear. So when Charlie came downstairs, dressed for school, and noticed his dad was cooking, something he hadn't done in a long time—bacon and eggs sizzling on the stove—Charlie couldn't believe it. A stack of pancakes was ready, soaked with butter.

Charlie's dad used to cook. He was an accountant, but his passion had always been cooking. He'd make huge dinners and delicious breakfasts while Mom played with Charlie or read curled up in an overstuffed chair. When she got sick, all that had stopped.

But now, nearly a year after her death, Dad was hovering over the stove, the smell of pancakes and bacon wafting through the house.

"Hungry?" Dad asked. It was jovial, but cautiously so. Almost as if he were trying on a new shirt for the first time and didn't know whether people would laugh.

Charlie realized he felt torn. Deep down, there was something—a burst of hope. Charlie's father had fallen apart over the last couple years. He'd tried to shield Charlie from everything. The lab tests, the surgeries, the chemo, the false hopes. It worked for a while, but then his dad had broken down, and his mom was too weak, and no one was left but Charlie to hold her while she puked or to bring her cool washcloths for her forehead. As he reflected on that, the old anger surged and stamped out the hope, and a voice in his head said, *Why does he get to feel better when I still feel like I'm in a billion pieces scattered on the floor?*

"No," Charlie said, walking to the door and grabbing his backpack off the hook. "Not hungry." He felt awful as soon as he said it, but also a little powerful, in a world where he had no power left, not to save his mom, not to do anything.

When he saw the smile drop a little on his dad's face, still there but not real now, just fake for Charlie's benefit, his heart broke again, but it was too late to fix it, so he left.

Charlie parked in the student lot and passed the cliques of jocks and rich kids hanging out, passed the gym, where students congregated like cattle packed into a pen before first period, and headed to the basement to the Tech Lab, where his real friends were, the small group of bright misfits who called themselves the Vindicators.

The Tech Lab was a treasure trove for young gamers and gearheads: sixteen networked computers they could play on at lunch, a 3-D printer, a robotics station, a circuit lab. Charlie had kick-started their group one day freshman year when he noticed the same three students were showing up at lunch to play vintage *Bolo* with each other—Vanhi, Kenny, Alex. He invited them over to his house to watch *Blade Runner* and play a little *Cyberpunk*. After another all-night marathon of polyhedral dice and tabletop gaming at Kenny's house, they pulled their first prank, putting the anatomy skeleton in the cafeteria with a sign that read I ATE THE FOOD. Bleary-eyed and laughing at 7:00 A.M., someone said, "We need a name." With zero hours of sleep, this made a lot of sense to everyone, even if it was ridiculous. They didn't care.

"What should it be?" Kenny asked.

"Something tight, we're a tight group," Charlie said.

"Something fierce," Vanhi said. "We watch each other's backs."

Her name meant "fire" in Hindi, and that was appropriate, because she was full of a burning intellect, and charm, and goodness. She stood up to bullies and didn't take shit from anyone. *She* was fierce.

"It's us against the world," Kenny added. "One for all, and all for one."

Kenny was the most tightly wound of the group. He was a state-ranked cellist and vice editor of the school paper. His parents were both doctors. They told him being black was a gift, and the gift was he'd always have to work twice as hard for the same respect. No pressure. The Vindicators were his little secret from his parents, from his church—it was his escape valve.

"The Disrupters," Alex said.

"Too dark," Charlie answered.

"The Terminators!" Kenny tried.

"Jesus, we're not murderers." Vanhi laughed.

Charlie snapped his fingers. "The Vindicators."

It fit. They swore on it.

Only Peter transcended their social status. He'd come sophomore year, with his blond hair and sparkling blue eyes, after getting expelled from St. Luke's, an exclusive private school in Austin. The FBI had busted him for hacking into phone companies and creating free cell accounts for his friends. With his good looks and money, Peter could've been elite, rolling with the high caste in khakis and salmon shirts. He was naturally athletic and ran track, so he was okay with the jocks, too. His dark side also made him popular with the burners and Goths, yet he chose to hang out in the computer lab, and while the other Vindicators wouldn't admit it out loud, it secretly delighted them. *That great enigma, Peter Quine, chose us!*

"Where's Alex?" Charlie asked, setting his bag on the table. But he knew what the answer would be.

"He's not here," Vanhi said.

"Again," Kenny added.

"Maybe he's got new friends," Peter said not unkindly. Only Peter could imagine friendships outside the safe space of the Vindicators.

"I saw him sitting by himself by the portables the other day," Charlie said.

"Hmm," Vanhi said. "I don't like it."

Alex Dinh had always been an odd duck, with a flop of hair over his eyes and a goofy grin that seemed mischievous and yet halfway in another world, daydreaming. In middle school, he hung out by himself, telling people he was from Mars. By freshman year, he'd grown out of that into a lanky, soft-spoken kid who lit up when pulling pranks. They'd all been affable goofs back then, the tricksters the teachers liked because they were smart and good-natured at heart. But as time went on, Alex had gone down a different path, so slowly they barely noticed at first. Once, when they were leaving a convenience store, a security guard came running out after them. They were baffled when he told them to empty their pockets—theft wasn't exactly in the Vindicators' repertoire—but sure enough, Alex had slipped a deck of cards into his back pocket on the way out, for no reason at all. He spent the night in jail over $2.08. The whole experience had just made him squirrelier, as if jail had suited him.

"Give him some space," Kenny said. "Maybe he just needs some time alone."

"You don't want him in the group anymore," Vanhi snapped.

"I didn't say that." But then Kenny complained, "He nearly got us all *arrested*."

"That's when he needs us most," Vanhi shot back. "Charlie, what do you think?"

Charlie looked at them, but no words came out. He shrugged.

A moment later, the door to the Tech Lab swung open, and Alex came in. He looked tired, with circles under his eyes and his hair a little more tussled than usual. The conversation came to a dead stop, and everyone was looking at him.

"What?" He had a hand still on his backpack, as if he hadn't decided whether to stay.

"Nothing," Peter said affably, always the one to smooth the situation. "Just sittin' here pulling our dicks."

"Yep," Vanhi said sarcastically, "just people with dicks, pulling them. Story of my life."

Alex looked them over skeptically, then threw his bag down and walked to the back row of terminals. When the first bell rang, Charlie realized he hadn't finished his calculus homework and cursed under his breath.

On the way out, Vanhi caught his arm. "What's the matter with you? I remember when you would have gone ballistic if someone talked about kicking one of us out."

"I didn't say anything."

"That's my point. You didn't say *anything*."

"Sorry."

"Charlie, I get it. You've had the shit kicked out of you slowly for two long years. But it's a new start. Senior year. You have to come back. You were class president! You had straight A's. Look at you now. I want the old Charlie back. My best friend."

Charlie put a hand on her shoulders. "I'm afraid you're stuck with this guy."

He knew she was trying to help. Everyone tried to help. But none of them had experienced what he had, except Peter, whose own mother died long ago. Peter was the only one who didn't treat him like a delicate freak. Peter understood: compassion was a *reminder*.

"Vanhi, I'm okay. I promise."

As she left, frowning, Charlie felt his phone buzz in his pocket. A strange text was waiting for him:

GFY!

Charlie knew what that could mean. It was code for "good for you." Or "go fuck yourself."

There was no return number.

He remembered his and Peter's exchange with the chatbot last night, the so-called God AI.

Tell it to go fuck itself.

And so they had.

And now this back: *Go fuck yourself!*

But they'd been surfing anonymously, through Tor. There was no way that site knew Charlie's name, much less his cell phone. So it had to be a coincidence.

Charlie typed back:

> Who is this?

This time, there was no pause. He phone buzzed almost instantly, a fraction of a second after he hit Send. There wasn't even time for a person to type.

> It's your Daddy, God.
> Mommy says hi.
> I have a job for you.

3 CLASS OVER

Everything was slipping away for Tim Fletcher. Of course, it didn't seem that way on the outside. He was the captain of the football team. The players followed him around like dumb animals and did his bidding. And the girls, well. Duh. He could pick anyone, and so he picked Mary Clark, because she was Mary Clark, perfection, a female version of Tim. Tim's father owned a bank, so they were rich. They belonged to the best country club. Everything was exactly as it should be. Exactly as it had always been. He was a walking cliché and fucking proud of it.

And yet . . .

He could feel it. He wasn't smart, not like the nerds with their faces in books, but he wasn't dumb either. He had inherited a Waspy understanding of power.

He could feel the power shifting. In his dad's day, you'd graduate, play ball in college, inherit your dad's bank, and marry a girl that looked like mom. The nerds would become your doctors and lawyers and accountants. They'd do well, but not too well. You would chat with them as they did your books or listened to your lungs, and then they'd go home to the suburbs and you'd hit the links at Oak Haven.

But now, his dad's finances were hurting. Generations of alcoholism and mistresses had shrunk the family fortune, and they were riding on fumes. His parents kept up appearances, but through the walls he heard them fighting. At school, he was still king. Yet he saw the world change around him. At home in Austin. In Silicon Valley. The same kind of kids he dominated at Turner High were squeezing his dad's bank with apps made in college dorm rooms. The old ways weren't working anymore. Everything was disrupted. Where the hell did that leave him?

He watched Mary do her homework. She didn't know he checked her phone when she wasn't there. Why the hell was she googling Charlie Lake, that loser? They hadn't been on student council together in years, since he flamed out. Even still, Tim had always viewed their friendship warily.

"You have nothing to worry about," Mary would say, putting a carefully manicured hand on each of his broad shoulders. "I'm with *you*."

So what was she doing now?

What Tim wanted, no, *needed,* was control.

He slid the silver box across the table to Mary.

"What's this?"

"Open it."

She laughed nervously and untied the red bow.

Inside was a rose-gold bracelet. It cost a small fortune.

"Put it on."

"Tim, this is crazy. It's not even our—"

"Put it on." His voice was a little less warm.

Mary tried to clasp the bracelet around her wrist, but her fingers shook a little.

"Let me." His thumb dug a little into the space under the bone in her delicate wrist.

She winced.

"Sorry." Tim held his palms up to her, open. "Big hands." As the bell rang, he smiled broadly and stood up. "It looks great on you."

He walked to the door, past the STD poster showing how sex with one person was really sex with everyone. "You'll always be mine." He gave her his handsomest grin.

4 NEXT LEVEL

Charlie showed him the text.

Peter's eyes went wide. "Do you know what this means?"

"Yeah, some freaky AI chatbot is cyberstalking me. Or you're pranking me."

"I wouldn't mention your mom like that."

For once, no irony was in Peter's voice. He was devilish, Charlie thought, but he wasn't cruel.

"So then what the fuck?"

Peter read it again:

> It's your Daddy, God.
> Mommy says hi.
> I have a job for you.

The word *job* was a link.

"It's like the one I got. But different."

"You got one, too?"

"Yeah." Peter fished out his phone.

They were standing by the lockers outside the room of the counselor, Mrs. Fleck, with its gaudy posters about feelings and perseverance. Mrs. Fleck was the rumored owner of many cats.

Peter opened his texts.

You got ballz.
Fuck me? No—Fuck YOU!
Do you BElieve in me? I BElieve in you.
Now . . . SHOW ME.

The *SHOW* was a link, too.

"Did you click on it?" Peter asked.

"No. Did you?"

"Not yet. I wanted to do it together."

"Fine, let's use your phone," Charlie said. "I'm not looking to download some rootkit."

"I don't think that's what's going on here."

Charlie raised his eyebrows. "We insulted it. And now it wants us to click a link? No thanks."

"Look, I found the site, right?"

"Right."

"I told you about it."

"True."

"Well, maybe I didn't tell you everything I read."

"Oh, shit."

Peter gave that easy smile. "It's all good, I promise." His excitement was contagious and hard to resist. "This chatbot, it's more than that."

"More than a chatbot?"

"The people who talk about it, they're the best in the world. The most exclusive coders. Think of the chatbot as a kind of gatekeeper."

"Gatekeeper to what?"

"Well, I don't know exactly. They made him. And he stands watch. And it's hard enough just getting to the website to talk to him. But if he likes you . . ."

"Then . . ."

"Then you get invited."

"Invited to *what*?"

"Well, that's what we're going to find out."

"And you think this is our invitation?"

"No. I think this is our test to see if we *should* be invited. 'I have a job for you.' 'I believe in you.' 'Show me.' So let's show them."

"So we click the link, and then . . ."

"We see what it wants. If it's out of bounds, we don't do it."

"And if it does give us malware?"

"Look, if these people wanted to hack us, we're already hacked. Besides, like you said, we can use my phone."

Charlie was running out of excuses, or more to the point, he was running out of easy problems for Peter to bat down. If Charlie wanted to, he could think of a million good reasons not to click the link. The truth was, he didn't want to think of them.

But one thing did bother him.

"What about the reference to my mom? 'Mommy says hi.' That's just sick. And how did they even know?"

"It's all over your social media. It would take about two seconds for a bot to figure that out about you. And honestly I think it's just riffing, not being cruel. Look, think about it like an AI. *God* equals *father*, then it links *father* to *mother*. It's just connecting dots. No malice, just typical natural language processing. You know, bullshit."

Charlie sighed. "At least test the link first."

"That's fair."

Peter checked the pop-up over the link. Instead of a Web address, it showed a random string:

R29kIGlzIGdyZWF0Lg==

"It's gibberish," Charlie said. "They're masking the URL."

"Maybe, but it's not gibberish. It's encoded text. Probably base64."

"How can you tell?"

"Educated guess. Multiple of four, all the characters are A to Z or zero to nine. And that last part, Lg==. You see that sequence repeated all the time. It's a period."

"So what does it say?"

Peter googled *base64 decoder,* then pasted the string in and hit Decode.

In the text box below, the decoded text appeared:

God is great.

"That's funny," Peter said. "So they masked the Web address and hid a pass phrase in the mask. They've given us the door and the key. These people aren't trying to give us a virus. They're trying to test us. The only question now is, Do we have the guts to go stick it in?"

Charlie sighed because he knew Peter was baiting him, yet Charlie was going to do it anyway. He was curious. He went back to the original text—*I have a job for you!*—and clicked *job*.

For a moment, his screen went black.

Then, the archangel Michael appeared, in the form of a text prompt.

> You have arrived at the 12th Gate
> of New Jerusalem.
> Archangel Michael>> Password,
> please.

"Well, we already know that," Peter said. "Better lucky than smart. You want the honors?"

"Sure." Charlie typed:

God is great.

> God is great.
> Archangel Michael>> This way,
> please.

Then, in white font on a black screen, instructions appeared. It told them what to do, but not how.

"Oh," Peter said.

"Huh. That's not so bad."

"No. Kinda fun."

"And doable."

"Very doable. Very Vindicatory."

"True, but . . . do we really want to drag them into this?"

Peter looked at Charlie, surprised. "Sure. They'd love it. You want to hog this just for us?"

Charlie shook his head defensively. Why *did* he want to hog it, just for them? Because Peter had become his best friend? Because the Vindicators seemed uncool by comparison? Because being around Peter made him feel mysterious and special and—for those wild distracted moments—free from the pain that sat in his gut like a rock?

Or D, all of the above?

Charlie shrugged. "Of course we'll invite them. We don't have to say *why* we're doing it."

"You don't want to tell them about God?"

"Well, not yet. I mean, we don't even know if they'll get invited. The texts only came to us."

"Sure." Peter nodded as if that made all the sense in the world. "Sure."

5 THE AFFAIR

Mr. Burklander was forty-seven years old when the kids in his twelfth-grade creative writing class heard the story about his wife dumping all of his clothes onto the front lawn from the second-story window of their house. He had a massive heart attack and blacked out in the grass in his boxers. It was hard, looking him in the eye when he came back, but they all did, because they all loved him.

No one ever heard why his wife tossed him out, exactly, but the way Jennifer Miller wasn't in Mr. Burklander's class anymore, there were some rumors. But that's all they were. Rumors.

Mr. Burklander approached Charlie as the rest of the class cleared out. Charlie was staring down at his desk, lost in thought.

"How's it going?"

Charlie glanced up, looking surprised. "Fine, I guess."

"You didn't turn in your story."

"I had writer's block."

"I don't accept that, Charlie. There's no such thing as writer's block. You just sit down and do it, like a job, whether it feels right or not. I want you to try. I think writing could help you find a way out of this place you're in. I really believe that."

"Yeah, maybe." Charlie slung his backpack and went for the door.

Mr. Burklander's hand caught him. He pulled Charlie around, a bit brusquely.

"I'm not messing around here. This is your life." Mr. Burklander's eyes softened. "I lost my mother when I was in my twenties. I remember. I had this dream, for years after. She was standing under a building that was shaking. I kept pulling on her arm, trying to get her to move, but she wouldn't. And a piece of the building came down, right on top of her. I'm almost fifty, Charlie, and I still remember how that dream *felt,* when I woke up. I always woke up right when the building came down. You will get past this, Charlie. You have your whole life ahead of you."

Charlie tried to shake his arm loose, but then he didn't.

Only Mr. Burklander was still trying to save Charlie. Burklander was the faculty sponsor for student council. He'd always liked Charlie.

When Charlie's mom died, his grades went from A's to C's. He had been on track for valedictorian. He and Vanhi had a pact to go to Harvard together. Now he just wanted to run in the opposite direction of anyone trying to remind him of who he once was. The school tried to help. He couldn't blame them for any of this. They tried to hook him up with counselors. They offered him a semester off, then a year off. But he refused their help, in ways big and small. It was insulting. It made him feel weak. If he wanted to throw it all away, they couldn't stop him. Screw them. Screw it all. He didn't want to go to Harvard anyway. He just wanted to be left alone. Eventually, the teachers got tired of taking his abuse. Most of them, anyway. He didn't know whether to love or hate the one who was still trying.

He considered Mr. Burklander for a second. Could he really have slept with a student? Was it possible? He was everyone's favorite teacher. The kind that told off-color jokes and wrote *Fuck* on the chalkboard when they were discussing *Catcher in the Rye*. Could he really sink so low? Why would he still have a job? Did the school cover it up somehow?

But all he saw now, looking in Mr. Burklander's eyes, was kindness. And genuine concern.

So Charlie just said, "Okay," which was about the most cooperative thing he said these days, agreeing to nothing.

———

Charlie went to the portables. They were the buildings beyond the south end of the school. Like any big, sprawling public high school, it was overcrowded. People bustled in the hallways shoulder to shoulder, knocking against each other. The city passed a bond issue to expand the school southward, past the Embankment, but then the economy collapsed and the school was left with rows of portable buildings, glorified trailers, surrounded by construction materials, just waiting for the economy to pick back up and the bond funding to come through. Charlie passed piles of bricks and remembered another version of himself, on student council, petitioning the school board for more space. It felt like another life.

Charlie found Alex where he expected him, sitting on the steps of a portable, eating his lunch. He was all alone. His hair flopped down in his face, his baggy jeans and vintage Metallica shirt looking worn. He was reading Vonnegut and eating a sad-looking bologna sandwich, as if there were any other kind.

"What are you doing out here?" Alex asked.

"Looking for you."

"Why?"

"You haven't been around much lately."

"Been busy."

Charlie made a show of looking around the empty lot. "I can see that."

"Fuck off." Alex managed a weak smile.

Charlie wondered what he was doing out here. The truth was, he wasn't sure how he felt about Alex anymore. When Peter arrived, Alex had become, well, less relevant in Charlie's world. Alex and Peter both veered toward nihilism, but Peter's brand of nihilism was sleek and exciting. Alex's was lonely and misfity—Peter, as harsh as it seemed, was just more fun. He was easier. And something about Alex, lately, was unsettling. It was hard to put a finger on it exactly. It was just that sometimes, looking in his eyes, Charlie felt as if he were gazing into a bottomless pit. He could draw a line back to the boy who sat outside parties in middle school, drawing with chalk on the pavement about his real home back on Mars.

But then again, the Vindicators were a place for people who didn't have a place. Wasn't that why they started it?

"Come on," Charlie said. "Come eat with us."

Alex shook his head. "Nah, I'm okay."

"Why not?"

"I just feel like reading."

Charlie noticed something on the wall behind Alex. Some graffiti, written in pen, in Alex's handwriting.

The sentence was incomplete: ALL MUST . . .

"'All must' what?"

"Huh?"

"That graffiti. 'All must' what?"

"Oh, I don't know. New song, maybe. I was just bored."

Charlie wanted to call bullshit, but he let it go.

"You'll come to the Tech Lab after school? We have something important to discuss. A new project." *Project* was their code word for pranks and other official tasks of the group. Back in the day, that was part of their raison d'être—pranks for truth and justice, never mean, just once-a-year social commentaries, such as rearranging the football fund-raiser, a pumpkin patch, into a giant phallus. But with Vanhi and Kenny obsessing over college applications, and Charlie neck-deep in his own grief, no one had even thought about a senior-year prank yet, until the God AI presented its challenge to Charlie and Peter.

Hearing the word *project,* Alex's face lit up. For a moment, he looked like the old Alex. Charlie wondered if Alex had drifted because of them—because they'd all been too preoccupied with their own lives to notice? When had Alex first misstepped, and how far gone was he now? For a fleeting moment, the veil of Charlie's grief lifted, and he asked himself, *What happened to the sweet, goofy Alex, and what happened to me?*

"Sure," Alex said. "I'll try to stop by."

"Cool. Watch out for ice-nine."

"Yeah," Alex said, already back in his book.

Mary Clark hated her mom. No, that wasn't fair. She didn't hate her mother. She hated what her mother stood for. That morning, Mary had tried to leave the house exactly the way she wanted. No makeup. Sweats. She knew she would look horrible without all her fancy clothes and subtle makeup—that's what her mother had always told her—but she didn't care. She was trapped in a box and didn't know how to get out. She thought of Tim and shuddered.

Her mother caught her on the way out the door. "Dear, run back upstairs."

"I'm going to be late."

"That's okay. It's worth it." Her mom could land a comment like no one else, a few simple words, no drama, yet it always sliced through every defense and went straight to the bone.

Mary's heart sank. She ran back upstairs and fixed herself up.

As she headed out the second time, her mother gave her an approving nod and told her the same phrase she'd heard for years: "It's important to look pretty."

The bracelet burned on her wrist. She wanted to throw it in the trash. Or better yet, return it to whatever fancy store Tim had bought it from and give the money to charity. She didn't dare. She remembered the pain when Tim had dug into her wrist. But the real power he had over her was elsewhere. He didn't have to remind her of what he knew. It was in his eyes.

I own you.

It was funny. Everyone wanted to be her. And she was the last person she wanted to be.

She felt the need to do something reckless.

Without thinking, she walked toward the east stairwell, where she knew Charlie met Peter after school.

It's just a ride, after all, she thought.

Who could blame her for that? Who would even know?

Vanhi ran home during free period, to work on her application. She wanted to be alone to do it, in the quiet of her home. No other students around to freak her out.

Vanhi was a bundle of contradictions. She was an ace student. She loved manga and Comic-Con and Neil Gaiman. She had desperately wanted to go to Harvard since she was ten, when her mom and dad brought her back a Harvard T-shirt from a rare vacation. She played electric bass in a band called the Dipshits, until they broke up. Her hair was red with black stripes now. Before that, it was purple, and before that, silver. She was punk and nerd and misfit and badass, all at once. Sometimes she wished she could just pick one because most of the time she felt as if she were being pulled in twenty different directions.

She logged into the system and stared at her Harvard application.

It was perfect, except for the one thing no one knew about. Not even her parents, because she doctored her report card online before they saw it.

She bombed AP US History. It was crazy. She was a great student. She could code like nobody's business. She aced every class. But she got cocky and blew off studying for the exam. In chemistry, in physics, she could just *feel* how the problems could be solved. In English she could compose a fluid, lovely essay without a second thought. The atoms snapped together, the balls bounced, the words popped. But she scoffed at AP History—a bunch of rote memorization of dead facts? That's what Google was for. There was no logic, no thought. Memorization was so twentieth century. She'd read the book but she hadn't memorized what color George Washington's jockstrap was, for God's sake. How was she supposed to know or care who John Muir was? It was a onetime mistake, but she couldn't take it back. There, on her perfect record, was a bleak mark. It pulled her whole GPA down. It sank her class ranking from 1 or 2 to 57. And when Harvard rejected 95 percent of applicants, that's all it took. Her life dream went down the toilet in one bad day.

Nobody knew. They just assumed she would get in. She hadn't told anyone. It was her secret shame. Vanhi read her essay for the twentieth time. She felt like a fraud. All this work, and it was pointless. The grade was a deal killer.

She fixed a couple commas, then knocked the mouse away.

She picked up her bass and let her fingers stretch over the frets, feeling the tension.

She could hear her mom in her head:

Whoever heard of an Indian bass player anyway?

Um, Mohini Dey, Ma?

She let her fingers run the bass line to "Another One Bites the Dust."

In honor of her Harvard application.

Screw it.

She put the bass away.

It was time for the Vindicators.

Charlie was waiting for Peter by the stairs when someone entirely unexpected approached.

"Hi, Charlie."

And there was Mary Clark, a vision from his past, floating above it all, looking stunning. She was a cheerleader, a student-body rep, founded their Students Against Destructive Decisions chapter. And, a genuinely nice person, unlike the circle of monsters she surrounded herself with.

He remembered their friendship, freshman year on student council. They would talk and laugh as they worked together on anti-graffiti initiatives or dress-code reform. But there was an invisible boundary. Outside student council, they kept to different worlds.

So the idea of her walking up now, in broad daylight, without even the thread of student council connecting them anymore, was a shock.

"Hi," Charlie said back, waiting for her to reveal her purpose.

"Are you going to the Grove tonight?"

He wasn't. The Grove was where students went, deep in the woods, to drink and hang out, under the pagan lights of bonfires and idling cars. Charlie hadn't ventured there ever, much less been *invited* there. But something made him lie now.

"Yeah, I think so."

"Could you give me a ride?"

He thought he heard wrong, but he decided to pretend he hadn't. "Sure. I can get my dad's car."

He wanted to say something suave, or clever, or anything. But he was so confused he didn't know where to start. Mary Clark was not short on rides. And more perplexing was why Tim wasn't taking her, if any guy was. And what would Tim do to Charlie when he found out?

"Thanks" was all she said, as if this were all the most natural thing in the world.

She was walking off when Peter appeared at Charlie's shoulder and said jovially, "What the fuck?"

"I don't know."

"I thought you quit student council?"

"I did."

"Maybe she needs help with her next campaign for better toilet paper."

Charlie ignored him.

"Come on," Peter said. "We're gonna be late for the Vindicators."

While Charlie and Peter went to the basement of the school, Edward Burklander was in the office of the principal, Elaine Morrissey. A forty-eight-year-old married mother of three, including one son at the high school, she had summoned Mr. Burklander to her office. She asked him to close the door. She had a serious look on her face. As they got close, the door closed, the electricity between them became too much to bear, and they fell into each other, again, knocking papers and a plastic bin of pencils off her desk. He slid her skirt up and ran his hand along the soft inner line of her thigh. She arched her back up and he pulled off his belt. As he slipped into her, she cried out, just a little, and tried to knock over a picture of her husband and children on her desk so that they wouldn't be staring at her. But the photo was just out of reach, and soon she forgot about it entirely.

In the corner of the room, her computer hummed.

6 THE SIGN

"And why would we do this?" Vanhi asked. She sat cross-legged on the table, looking skeptical. As always, her sarcasm was spiky and electric, dominating the room, and Charlie would've married her in a heartbeat if she were interested in boys. As it was, he'd spent the first half of freshman year pining for her anyway. She'd told him, "I'll be your best friend, but you'd have better luck flirting with a tree."

Now she was asking them why they would take on this particular stunt. Just as she had before the phallic pumpkin patch. Just as she had before the skeleton incident, or the aptly named Hack Against Douchebags. But they knew Vanhi always came around. She had a special place as the only girl in the Vindicators. Which meant she had a slightly better frontal lobe, but deep down, she still liked to ride the edge like the rest of them.

"Well, it's an election year," Peter answered. "And our senior year."

"Go class of 2017," Vanhi said. "So . . . why again?"

"A special year deserves a special prank," Charlie said.

They had decided not to mention the chatbot, or the instructions from the pearly gates.

"What level crime is this?" Kenny asked nervously. His parents' words were echoing in his head: *No false steps; second chances don't exist.* It didn't help that his brother had dropped out of medical school to be a "writer" in LA. Kenny was now the good son.

"Class A misdemeanor," Alex said.

"Not so bad." Kenny felt a little queasy. Every fiber of his body said *leave,* but these were his best friends, smart and talented if a little mischievous, and he wasn't going to leave them in a foxhole. Nor did he want to be labeled a chicken later.

"I've done worse," Peter added, to no one in particular.

"Still . . . ," Kenny said.

"You don't have to come," Alex taunted him.

Kenny looked away, shamed.

Vanhi said, "We should do it."

"Really?" Charlie asked, surprised.

"The guy is an asshole. Flirting with white supremacists and neo-Nazis. And the Vindicators have a strict no-asshole policy."

"That's true," Kenny said, psyching himself up.

"That is true," Charlie admitted, a little worried at how easily his friends had agreed to do this. Throwing his own life away seemed fine. But he didn't want to take them down with him. College applications were coming due, after all. But it was just a misdemeanor. . . .

"We'll need a bolt cutter," Peter said.

"I have one," Alex offered, surprising no one.

"Put 'em in," Kenny said, putting his hand in the middle of their group. Everybody laid hands on top. "Our senior year. Our final prank. 'No assholes' on three?"

It was agreed.

"One . . ."

"Two . . ."

"Three . . ."

"No assholes!"

On the way to the parking lot, Charlie tugged on Vanhi's sleeve. "You really don't have to come," he whispered, saying it so only she could hear. Unlike Alex, Charlie said it genuinely, not as a dare. "Maybe you shouldn't. It's not exactly a great time to get arrested."

"That goes for you, too," Vanhi shot back.

Neither of them blinked, so they found themselves with Peter, Alex, and Kenny in Kenny's Honda Civic on the way to the highway. They had agreed Peter's BMW was way too conspicuous for this mission.

They found the sign where they expected, Charlie and Peter having cased it earlier. The bright orange lights announced TRAVEL TIME TO WESTVIEW EXIT—10–12 MINUTES against a black background, enclosed in yellow metal and rising above the highway.

They could have done it in the middle of the night. Under cover of darkness. But what fun would that be? So TxDOT could have it down before the morning commute started? No. This was senior year, class of 2017. An election year. It called for a bold gesture. A hack for truth and justice, which were in short supply these days. They parked the car in a Whataburger parking lot and found a remote way down under the bridge, where they could slink in the darkness beneath the overpass, seen only by a homeless couple balled up in sleeping bags deep in the crevice between the grass bank and the bridge base. They had anticipated this, and Peter, with his effortless charm, passed them a couple chicken sandwiches from Whataburger and assured them that the Vindicators had never been here and weren't here now. The chicken/secrecy oath transacted, they worked their way down and crept in the shadow of the sign, hopefully out of view from the road, and found the control box.

Its cheap lock fell easily to Alex's bolt cutter. It fell into two pieces, which he merrily twisted apart. "Let's do this," he said, grinning.

He pried open the control box, and Peter knelt in front of it.

Inside was a panel with a keyboard and small screen, housed in black plastic. On prompting, it asked for the admin name. Peter typed in the default, *admin,* and tabbed to the password prompt. He tried the default password, which he'd looked up on .narthex.

"They never change these," he said gleefully.

He typed *DTOC* and hit Enter.

Access denied.

"Not to worry." He scowled. He held down ALT-CTL, then typed *CIPC* while holding the two buttons. The screen changed and informed him the password was now reset to the default.

"Easy." He typed *admin* then *DTOC* again.

A menu came up, and just like that, they were in.

He selected *Image Text,* entered their agreed-upon observation, then selected *Run w/o Save*. Their AI archangel hadn't told them what message to write, just that they had to pick one. Maybe that was part of the test. Charlie and Peter had come up with the line together.

The text lit up the bright, large construction sign above them, for all the world to see. Now was the time to get the hell out of Dodge.

Alex put the control pad back into the box, tucking the curly black cord inside with it. Vanhi slammed the door shut, and Alex clamped into place the new industrial-grade padlock they had purchased. Unlike the cheap city lock, it would not be so easily cut. Meanwhile, Charlie and Kenny had already put a similar bolt on the power source. Shutting this baby down would take some doing.

The first cars had started honking, whether in agreement or protest it was hard to guess.

They were halfway up the slope under the overpass when Peter grinned at the homeless couple, who had finished their Whatachick'n and balled up the garbage. He flipped them two Snickers bars. "You never saw us."

One of the couple winked conspiratorially.

Back in the car, they U-turned and allowed themselves the pleasure of watching for a moment, engine running, as the rush-hour traffic streamed past the sign, honking, some slowing to take a second look.

It was beautiful chaos.

"Third-degree felony," Alex said.

"What?"

"I lied earlier. When I said it was a misdemeanor."

"Seriously?"

"Third-degree felony. Tampering with a road sign. Jail time."

"Why did you lie?" Charlie studied Alex, trying to understand him. Charlie wasn't worried about himself but Vanhi and Kenny and even Peter. They should've at least known the risk.

"I didn't think we'd do it otherwise," Alex said almost plaintively.

"Oh, wow," Kenny said, with the giddy freedom of being on the far side of a rickety bridge.

"Yeah," Vanhi said.

"Well, we did it."

"Yes. Yes, we did."

They admired their handiwork. The gesture wasn't going to change the world. But in a random, chaotic universe, it was a small, proud shot in the dark. Under the overpass, hundreds of cars passing by, their sign told the world in bright orange light:

DONALD TRUMP IS A SHAPE-SHIFTING LIZARD

A siren sang in the distance, and while it probably had nothing to do with them, they weren't going to wait to find out.

"Third-degree felony," Peter repeated aloud.

"Hot damn," Charlie said.

"I'm applying to Harvard tomorrow," Vanhi added.

"So . . . we should go?"

"Hell yes. Yes. Let's go."

They drove off, slow and steady in the opposite direction, leaving their glorious sign for the torrent of cars streaming home.

7 THE LIZARD KING

The Grove was where, rumor has it, the Friends of the Crypt met in secret during their reign of terror over the suburbs of Glendale and Pleasant Valley back in the 1990s. It was a cautionary tale for Charlie and his friends, of honors students gone wrong. They, too, had been a group of bright outsiders—the Vindicators sometimes thought of themselves as a benign version of that fabled group—but something had gone so very wrong for the FOTC. They were self-described techno-anarchists, a dangerous mix of knee-jerk teen outrage and mechanical savvy, pipe bombs and viruses. They were going to attack the system, even if they didn't know exactly what should replace it. Every parent for decades had heard about them, casting glances at those woods as if they were haunted and wondering, *Could my kid ever . . . no*. But like so much of the late nineties, those stories of ominous graffiti carved into trees— hooded rats with slit eyes—and dangerous acts ending in tragedy had faded year by year into a pastel memory.

Now the Grove was a place to party.

"I think you're playing with fire," Peter said that evening in Charlie's room, the door closed and locked, the window cracked.

"It's just a ride."

"She's got a boyfriend."

"Yeah, and he's a jerk."

"Maybe, but he's also a meathead and a jock and a violent guy. I'm just saying, he's not gonna like it. And he's got big friends."

"What, he's going to beat me up because I gave his girlfriend a ride?"

"I like this new you, Charlie. Totally fearless. I'm just saying, I don't want to have to bail you out when the football team comes after you. I'm a lover, not a fighter."

"It'll be fine."

"Okay. I'm not saying she's not worth it. She's hot. Like, crazy hot."

"It's just a ride. Jesus. He's probably meeting her there later."

"Right. And you're the only person with a car."

"Whatever."

"It's not even your car."

"I get it."

"It's a Nissan, for God's sake."

"I get it. Enough."

Peter started laughing, and it was impossible to be mad at him. He could be a jerk and win you back over in the same sentence.

Something chirped on Charlie's phone.

Half an instant later, Peter's phone buzzed.

They both glanced at their screens, then immediately met eyes and grinned.

On their phones, from the same anonymous number that had sent them a task from "God," was a new message.

This one did not involve go-fucking themselves.

It was the opposite:

You have an invitation.

The word *invitation* was hyperlinked.

"Oh, go on." Peter grinned, his eyes twinkling, that icy blue.

Charlie sighed. "Fuck."

"This is what we *wanted*."

Charlie shrugged. "In for a penny, in for a pound."

He was about to click the word *invitation,* but Peter stopped him.

"Forward the link to your laptop. I'm sick of this small-screen business. Let's immerse."

"Okay." Charlie copied the link and sent it to his email. He got on his computer and hovered over the link on the larger screen. "Satisfied? Acoustics okay? Need some popcorn?"

"Quit dragging it out, man!"

"But you're the one—"

Peter reached over and hit Enter.

The word *invitation* pulsed, the hyperlink activated.

And then . . .

For a moment, the screen went black.

Then the music started playing, a little MIDI version of the carnival song that always played outside the main tent while the barker drew you in: *Step right up, folks. Right this way!*

It came through Charlie's gaming speakers, wireless on either side of the laptop, filling the room.

On the screen, red curtains drew apart, and a bobbleheaded cartoonish man was there: Donald Trump in an Uncle Sam suit and top hat. He waved, his mouth moving up and down, the jaw jerking open and shut. No sound came from his mouth, but white text appeared against the black background below him, one letter tapped out at a time with a little typewriter click and ding.

You are invited!

Ding! The mouth moved up and down, like a ventriloquist's dummy's.

COme inside and play with G.O.D.

Ding!

Bring your friends!
It's fun!
But remember the rules. Win and ALL YOUR DREAMS COME TRUE.™ Lose, you die!
:)
It's ur choice. Free will!!!!!!!!!!!!!!!!!!!

Trump was wearing red, white, and, blue pants with suspenders. Now his cartoon arm jerked forward, pointing at them.

We Want You!

Trump changed—his face morphed into a lizard, still wearing his Uncle Sam hat. The big-top tent flashing behind it, the lizard said:

Click here!
You have 2 say yesss.

Charlie and Peter looked at each other.

"What the hell is that?"

"I have no idea," Peter said. "But I want to go inside!"

"Um, 'Win and your dreams come true. Lose, you die?' No thanks."

"Aw, come on. You're willing to give Mary a ride to the Grove and risk getting your ass kicked by fourteen actual, real-life 'roid cases, but you won't play a computer game?"

"A computer game on a messed-up site that's joking about killing us?"

"Who said anything about killing? They just said you die."

"Play your own stupid game."

"It's just a joke," Peter said. "They're messing around."

"Who is *they* anyway? Who made this thing?"

"I told you, I have no idea. People just talk about it a lot online."

"So . . . North Koreans?"

"Ha, ha. You should click yes!"

"You click yes."

"You just want to live long enough to get to third base with Mary."

"Screw you."

"I don't think you'll live that long even if you don't play!"

"Fuck off!" Charlie studied the animation. "Doesn't it bother you at all that they know what we did?"

"What do you mean?"

"A Trump cartoon. A shape-shifting lizard. We hacked that sign, like, an hour ago. They only told us to hack it, not what to say. How did they know so quickly? And turn it into an animation?"

"It's a pretty shitty animation. How long would it take you?"

"That's not my point. There's not even a news story yet. Are they watching us?"

"What can I say, they like our style. So, cool. It's a hat tip. Vindicators rock."

Then it dawned on Charlie. The Vindicators had done this together. "Do you think the whole group got the invitation?"

"I don't know. Maybe. We were all there."

Charlie group-texted them.

"What are you doing?" Peter asked.

"They don't even know about the website or the God bot or anything. We dragged them into this. We should give them a heads-up and decide on this together. Maybe you can ask your online buddies what the hell the game is, anyway."

"That's fair. But what if they take back the invitation because we waited?"

"Then they didn't want us that badly to start with."

"Huh. That's good logic. You have a lot of experience with rejection."

Charlie punched Peter's arm—said "True"—then sent the text:

> Did you get a crazy message with an "invitation"? Don't click on it yet. Will explain.

Peter added to the string:

> Tomorrow—midnight. Tech Lab. Don't be late!

He added a skull-and-crossbones emoji.

Charlie raised his eyebrow at him.

"Ya gotta have a little style," Peter said. "To keep the people coming back."

Charlie saw the time. "I have to go. That means you have to go."

Peter made a show of going toward the door. "Oh, yeah. Your dad hates me." He went to the window.

"I'll go your way. Minimizes questions."

They crawled out the window. The night was crisp and the air smelled clean and fresh. Fall air. They went down the trellis and landed with a soft thud in the dirt of the garden. They saw Charlie's dad through the downstairs window, working at the kitchen table, his back to them.

"Oh, crap." Peter patted his back pocket. "I left my joint upstairs."

"Get that shit out of my room."

Peter went back up the trellis and slipped through the window.

Charlie glanced back at his dad. Charlie wondered what was he working on, late at night, by himself at the table? His accounting work—the work he'd always found boring and just a means to an end that all came to nothing anyway when his wife died and his only child went off the deep end? Charlie's dad's shoulders slumped in a way that had only started after Charlie's mom was diagnosed.

Peter came back down and patted his pocket. "Got it." He got into Charlie's dad's car with Charlie.

"What do you think you're doing?"

"Going with you to the Grove!"

"Um, I don't think so. I'm giving Mary a ride."

"That's why you need me. So I can bail you out when Tim tries to kick your ass."

"Out."

"Fine. Fine. Don't say I didn't warn you."

"I won't."

Peter hopped out and gave a fake bow. "Then I bid you adieu."

"Yeah, okay. Enjoy your evening."

"And you yours, good sir!"

Charlie put the car in gear and headed toward Mary and the Grove beyond.

8 THE UNCANNY VALLEY

Inside the ring of trees, the lights of parked cars sliced this way and that through the night, lighting the woods in spears of fluorescence.

Mary led Charlie through the woods, giving no clue of her intentions.

She had been silent most of the ride over, moving gracefully from her front porch into Charlie's beat-up old family car, as if it were the most natural thing in the world. As if this weren't unprecedented and inexplicable by any known rules of high school logic or primate mating rituals. *We're way past anthropology,* Charlie thought. *This is* The Twilight Zone *with hormones.*

At one point, she took his hand. It wasn't flirtatious and it only lasted a moment, as she led him down a short drop, as if she could navigate the Grove in her sleep. She was just keeping him from tripping as they both ducked under a gnarled, low-hanging branch and down the rocky clumped-earth stairsteps, one two. Then she let go and all that was left was the tingling on his palm and fingers, like an amputee mourning the loss of his hand.

How did he suddenly find himself with the girl he'd loved since seventh grade? One who was never in his league, yet for whom he'd always harbored the illusion that deep down she had every reason to cross social barriers and know the real him? Did he dare allow himself to dream that after five years, countless student council meetings, even late nights working on class projects (sitting on her bed, door cracked per parental rules), suddenly *now* it was going to happen? In senior year, just as all were preparing to go their separate ways? And why not? Wouldn't this be the time when things did go off the rails a little, loosen up, the freedom of never seeing half these people again just on the horizon? Wasn't this the uncanny valley—a moment where things could suddenly follow new rules or no rules at all? Charlie had been in free fall for two years. Maybe he was about to fall into something.

Mary was about to answer the question.

They were steps from coming out into the clearing, where everyone was gathered, drinking and hanging out, some around a bonfire, others reclining on the hoods of cars, their engines running and music drifting out. But they were still shielded from sight by the last thick rows of trees around the clearing.

Mary put a hand on Charlie's chest to stop him from walking. She looked into his eyes. "I'm sorry about your mom."

"Oh." It was the last thing he wanted to hear. *I love you* would have been nice. *Take me now, heart slayer* would have been fine, if a little medieval. But back to his mom, no. That was about the last thing he wanted to think about. He thought about it pretty much all the time. But here, in this clearing, the way the moon cast blue light down through the trees, for just a moment that lingering, needling pain in the pit of his stomach had gone away.

Now it was back.

"Thanks," he said, thinking of some way to change the subject.

"I told you that a year ago. Do you remember?"

Of course I remember, Charlie wanted to say. It had been the most humiliating moment of his life. Here he was, a grieving junior at his mother's funeral, after a year of hell. Suddenly, the most beautiful girl in school shows up at the funeral, standing in the back. Why? Charlie found her after the funeral, in a quiet long hallway of the church, tried to thank her, but couldn't get the words out. She'd said she was sorry, and Charlie misunderstood the situation—what the hell was she doing there anyway, didn't it *have* to be a sign she'd felt the same all along?—and kissed her. It was clumsy, gentle. She went in to hug him, and he misunderstood and placed his lips gently on hers. The electricity was unbearable. Her lips were softer than he could ever imagine. She lingered for a second, then pulled back and said, also gently, which was *worse,* "No, no"—not a command, but surprised. Like *Oh, no, you poor sweet puppy.* He'd been delirious with grief and now shame. "I'm sorry," he'd mumbled, and she'd said, "That's okay," and that was the last they spoke for a year, while she'd gone on to live her life and Charlie had circled the drain.

And now *she* was bringing it up. Charlie noticed her fumbling with a new bracelet on her wrist. It looked expensive. Like more than he could ever afford.

"That's nice," he said, looking at it, and she winced, as if he'd poked her in the gut with a sharp finger.

"Do you remember my brother?"

"I knew who he was," Charlie said. "I didn't really know him."

"He was amazing."

That was one word for Brian Clark. He was an older, male version of Mary. Perfect. Legendary.

Brian's car had been smashed head-on by a drunk driver his senior year, the year before he would've left on a full ride to A&M. Now Mary was president of her school's chapter of SADD. She had founded the club in Brian's honor.

"The first year was the worst. It gets easier."

"I know," Charlie said, because he was supposed to say that.

She fingered the bracelet again. "Do you ever feel like your whole life is a lie?"

"Not a lie. Just a mess. Do you?"

She turned the bracelet absently, then let her arms drop. "Something about senior year. You feel like everything could change. It will change. There's a possibility for a new life. Do you feel that way?"

"I used to. I used to want to go to Harvard. My friend Vanhi and I had a pact that we'd both apply and go there together. I know it's crazy. You can't just want one school, especially a school like that. I kept telling Vanhi that. But now it doesn't matter. I doubt I could get in if I wanted to. I let everything go."

The sky was a deep purple, the color of clouds reflecting light pollution. But the woods themselves were dark and shrouded.

In elementary school, Mary was precocious, popular, spunky. In middle school, she was tall, athletic, quiet. In high school, she was dazzling, better than the people she surrounded herself with. Charlie had run for student council just to be near her. He'd loved her for most of his life.

"You're going to be okay," Mary said, taking his hand.

Was he supposed to kiss her? Good God, the image of the fumbled kiss from the funeral came back. No fucking way would he make that mistake twice. The shame would literally crack him.

"Why do you care?" he asked instead.

There it was. It just popped out. The emotion just bubbled up and slipped past him.

She looked taken aback. "We're friends."

"Are we?"

"You don't want to be my friend?"

"No," Charlie said, not in a mean way, but in a way that was clear. She looked at him with wide eyes. "I have to go."

He realized she was still holding his hand. He closed his fingers, gently tighter. "Don't."

"If Tim sees you . . ."

"Sees me what?"

"Charlie, you don't know him like I do."

"I thought he wasn't here."

"He's not. But his friends . . ."

"You told him I was giving you a ride?"

"Not exactly."

"Why did you ask me?"

She leaned in and kissed him.

It was just a moment.

Then she pulled away. She pushed against his chest: *Don't follow.* Without saying anything, she slipped back and through the trees, into the clearing as if she had just arrived alone. Charlie was left there, staring, lost in the shadows, watching a crowd of students have a life as distant and untouchable as a television show.

At the same time, miles away, Charlie's computer screen showed a red circus tent, the curtains now open. It said:

Invitation accepted.

9 THE SINNER

Turner High School was not known for safety, but its various constituencies—gangs, rich kids, honors students, drama geeks, losers—all coexisted essentially peacefully. The gangs beat up the gangs, the rich kids spent their money, the drama kids put on *Our Town* and wrote poems about despair, the losers smoked weed on the Embankment, and the public school thrummed along like the giant, unruly beast that it was.

Charlie wasn't sure where Peter got his pot, but knew a drug dealer was at Turner, maybe more than one, who serviced the various groups. It wasn't that the rich kids didn't smoke weed or take pills. They just did it in the safety of their parents' mansions instead of out in the open on the grassy banks behind the fields and temporary buildings. The Embankment offered relative obscurity from school officials and campus officers. It wasn't like they didn't *know* about the Embankment. It was just that they could *ignore* it, for the most part, a few symbolic stings aside. You couldn't arrest everyone, all the time.

On the way there, Charlie cut through the portables. It was out of his way, but something had been bothering him. That graffiti, *All Must . . .* That bullshit explanation. Song lyrics? Come on. Alex played guitar in his room, mostly Kurt Cobain covers. Badly. But still . . .

There was the graffiti. Still unfinished. And there was Alex, sitting alone on the steps of Portable B, reading *Cat's Cradle*. He'd torn through most of the book since yesterday.

"Hey, Charlie."

"Hey, Alex."

"Cool prank yesterday."

"Yeah. Epic. One for the history books."

Alex shrugged.

"Are you coming tonight? To Tech Lab."

"I guess so," Alex said. "Midnight?"

"Yeah, that was Peter's idea. Of course."

"Of course."

"Listen, did you get a weird text, with a link? Like an invitation?"

"Yeah, I guess." That was a fulsome answer for Alex.

Charlie nodded. So God (or G.O.D., he guessed it was now) *did* know they all hacked the sign together? How would it know that? Were they really being watched that closely?

"You didn't click that link, did you?"

"No."

"Good. Don't do it yet."

"What is it?"

"I don't know. Peter's digging into it."

Alex frowned.

"You okay?"

"Sure," Alex said.

When they started the Vindicators, Alex was the quietest of the group. The most outcast. But he was always in the Tech Lab. He'd found it before the rest of them. He'd eat his lunch and surf the Web or pay MOBAs. When the rest of them gelled together, it just made sense that Alex would be swept up into the group with them. But it was easier back then, when he was *harmless* weird Alex.

"I know what you think," Alex said suddenly. He almost sounded angry.

"About what?"

"Me."

"Alex, what are you talking about?"

"I can feel it. You don't have to say it. All of you."

"The Vindicators?"

"You don't want me in the group. Not anymore."

Charlie wanted to say that was not true. But he was a shitty liar. Harmless weird Alex had given way to off-the-rails troubled Alex. Was there something more? Was Alex on the verge of something worse, something unnamed and deep, that Charlie just couldn't deal with right now? That did make him a shitty friend, he realized—maybe Vanhi was right—but he felt the truth like a bubble squeezing into his own orbit, and it was all too much. Kenny was freaked out by new Alex. Peter was no saint, but he had that Teflon quality, and Charlie felt safe around him, even when they were getting in trouble. Peter knew when to push and when to pull back. He was rich, so he'd be okay in the end. Alex felt like a drowning man who had thrown himself in a lake and would pull anyone trying to save him down with him.

So, yes, goddamnit, maybe he didn't want Alex in the group anymore. But Charlie said, "That's not true," because he didn't want to hurt Alex's feelings.

Alex flinched. How long had Charlie hesitated? A microsecond? Long enough, apparently, because Alex had heard all he needed to hear.

Charlie felt like shit. Vanhi was right: freshman year, Charlie would have been the first one defending Alex, pulling him back from the edge. That was friendship. You don't just cut people loose when it's convenient. Weird or not, Alex was a Vindicator. Charlie tried to salvage the situation, but the damage was done.

"I mean it. You're one of us." But he could feel how the moment had soured. That first instant was the truth, and he had failed, and everything after was just scrambling, making it worse.

"Okay."

"We're just worried about you," Charlie said weakly.

"Don't be. I'm fine." Alex turned back to his book.

"Alex."

"I'm gonna read for a while." Alex's voice was cracking a little.

Charlie felt ashamed. "Alex, I'm sorry. I didn't mean to—"

"I'd like to read now," Alex said more sharply.

Charlie nodded. "Okay. Okay. See you tonight?"

Alex didn't answer.

Peter was out on the Embankment, sitting on the cool grass, his blond hair whipping in the breeze. He offered Charlie the joint, but that was where Charlie'd drawn the line. An occasional puff, now and then. But he wasn't going to become a stoner, high at school in broad daylight. That last thin cord to his old life had still not yet snapped. But nonetheless, after a depressing encounter with Alex, Peter was a breath of fresh air, relaxed and carefree, windswept on the Embankment on a beautiful day.

"No, thanks," Charlie said.

Peter smiled and shrugged.

"I think I just screwed up with Alex."

"*Alex?* Are you joking? How'd you do with *Mary?*"

"She kissed me."

Peter coughed, smoke puffing out.

"Good God, talk about burying the lede."

Charlie told him about the encounter in the woods.

"So she just left after?"

"Yep. Walked right out into the field."

"Well, that's not awkward."

"Tell me about it."

"Have you seen her yet?"

"No. I think she's walking halfway around the school to avoid it."

"That assumes she cares. I'm betting at least half of this is in your head."

"You're a real pal, you know that?"

"Mm-hmm," Peter said peacefully, dragging on his joint. "So, I asked Caitlyn Lacey to homecoming today." He let the smoke trail up.

"Isn't she dating Kurt?"

"Yup."

"So why would you ask?"

"Why not? You're hooking up with Mary Clark. Next thing you

know, Vanhi's going to be engaged to Rebecca Moore. The whole social order's upside-down. Topsy-turvy."

"What did she say?"

"She said no, of course. She'll sleep with me in her car, but she won't bring me home to Mother."

"She slept with you?"

Peter nodded.

"When?"

He shrugged. "More than once."

"You never told me that."

"I don't kiss and tell. Except now, I guess." Peter smiled, but with a bitter edge. "I knew she'd say no. No big deal. Who cares about a stupid dance with a bunch of drones?"

"So why'd you ask her?"

Peter thought about it. "I wanted to hear her say no. To face her role in the Big Lie. Fine, she can have it both ways, dating Kurt for popularity when she really wants me. But it should sting a little."

Charlie shook his head. "You are one disturbed dude."

Peter smiled and took another drag. "So tonight. Tech Lab. Midnight. Don't be late."

"Did you learn about the invitation?"

"Oh, yeah."

"What?"

"It's a secret. You don't want to spoil the surprise, do you?"

"I guess not." Charlie heard the bell ring. "Time for school."

"I find I do better when I don't attend. Formal instruction clouds my vision."

"Okay."

"Hey, if you're heading that way, can you give this to Zeke?"

Peter dug through his backpack and pulled out a crumpled brown baggie.

Zeke was on the far side of the Embankment, nearest the portable buildings, in the shadow of the redbrick wall of the gymnasium. His dirty-blond dreadlocks hung down like horse braids, beaded and scratchy. His head was on the lap of Monica Jameson, who seemed to have no qualms about braiding and playing with those messy dreads.

"What is it?"

"He gave me half his lunch yesterday. I forgot mine."

"Sure," Charlie said, feeling as soon as it slipped out that he should've said, instead, *Show me*. But it wasn't as if Peter were a drug dealer. Aside from the occasional recreational pot smoking, Charlie had never seen Peter have anything to do with drugs. He did, in his private-school days, go to parties with rich kids and coke and prescription pills, but that was then and this was now. He'd been expelled from that world, and as far as Charlie could tell, Peter hadn't looked back. Didn't even see those kids anymore. Anyway. Charlie had already said yes, and what's the worst anyone could say: You carried a paper bag with unknown contents from point A to point B, accepted no money, knew nothing, and it was probably just a bologna sandwich anyway? Let's not make a capital offense out of it.

Plus, it was a beautiful, sunny day on the Embankment. Not an adult in sight. *Chill out, Charlie,* he told himself. *The world does not revolve around you.*

He grabbed the lunch bag from Peter and headed toward class.

When Charlie got near Zeke, he said, "Hey, from Peter."

Zeke barely lifted his head but caught the bag. "Thanks, dude."

"Sure."

And that was that, and Charlie walked through the shadow of the red gym on his way to class.

10 GOOD WORKS

In Creative Writing, Mary kept her back to him. He felt as if he were burning a hole in the back of her head with his stare, so he got a grip and focused on the lecture.

Mr. Burklander was talking about Faulkner and point of view. Those in the class were supposed to write a story from the point of view of someone they'd never met and disliked very much. Charlie was going to write about love at first sight from the perspective of Donald Trump—it would end with him realizing it was a mirror—but then Charlie found out half the class was going to do Trump.

The bell rang, and Mary was out the door so fast Charlie couldn't get close. She never looked back. He tried to catch up in the hallway but stopped short as a hand went palm first into his chest, hard enough to startle him.

"Hi, Charlie," Tim Fletcher said.

Charlie felt the adrenaline surge. If this was it, this was it. He wasn't going to back down from a six-foot-two, 'roid-raging jerk. If he got his ass kicked, so be it. At least he'd go down swinging.

"Hey, Tim," he said, his voice sharp edged.

"How was class? See Mary?"

"I did. The back of her head, from three rows back. It was fascinating."

"I heard you gave her a ride last night."

"I did." Charlie waited. Nothing more to say.

"That was kind of you."

"You're welcome?"

"So now you're a smart-ass?"

"I gave her a ride. What do you want me to say? It wasn't dinner and a movie."

Tim smiled. It was a daddy's-boy smile, rich, privileged, unconcerned. Things would go his way. One way or another. He had a crew. He had a legion of adoring football fans in a state that put high school football just a tick below religion. He could harass and bully with impunity. With homecoming coming up and a perfect team record and a shot at another state championship, Tim was untouchable. And Charlie, former good student, son of an accountant, was nobody.

"Maybe you *should* take her to dinner and a movie," Tim said pleasantly. "Maybe you should try that. What do you think?"

"I think Mary can do whatever she wants."

Something in Tim's hazel eyes changed. They darkened, the eyebrows raised. "Should I ask Mary what she wants?"

It occurred to Charlie that while he was busy being brave for himself, it might have been Mary that he'd put in danger, not himself. *You don't know him,* she'd said. As Charlie looked into Tim's cold eyes, that suddenly seemed plausible in a way he hadn't even considered when he'd stepped up to Tim. He started thinking of ways to fix what he might have just broken.

"Are you threatening her?"

"No." Tim smiled. "Don't be ridiculous," he said in a way that didn't make it sound ridiculous at all.

"If you lay a hand on her . . ."

"Charlie, Charlie." Tim put a hand on Charlie's shoulder. "Relax. You're getting all worked up over nothing. How long have Mary and I been together? And what are you to her? Nothing, right? You're not even friends. So what are you worried about?" Tim stepped aside and held his arm out, an invitation for Charlie to walk away, free and clear, into the flow of students bustling through the halls.

Charlie stepped right toward Tim, which made Tim's height advantage seem even worse.

"I'm serious. Don't you dare hurt her."

"Charlie." Tim smiled gallantly. The football star. The homecoming king. "I couldn't hurt a fly."

CompSci was Charlie's favorite class, not least of all because he sat between Vanhi and Kenny, and also because he loved to code and was miles ahead of the simple projects they tackled in class. But as good as Charlie was, Vanhi was light-years better. She had a knack for programming. When Charlie had asked her to join the Vindicators, she'd told him, "Why would I want to be slowed down by a bunch of dumb boys playing with robots?" It was a fair point. But she'd shown up the next day, thrown her bag down, and said, "Let's get this shit started."

The rest was history.

Charlie settled into his terminal between Kenny and Vanhi, and she slugged him on the shoulder.

"What's that for?" Charlie asked, rubbing his arm.

"Cheating."

"On what?"

"On me!"

"Um, as I recall, you rejected me."

"Maybe. But that doesn't mean you shouldn't still worship at my feet. I am, after all, a divine nature goddess."

"You're the goddess of something, all right. The High Queen of BS."

She slugged him even harder.

"Some of us are trying to focus here," Kenny said, sighing theatrically, trying to force himself to code. Unlike the rest of the group, Kenny was not a math-science nerd, but rather a philosophy junkie and world-culture scholar. His parents were deeply religious, devout Catholics, and made him learn Greek and Hebrew when he was young. He'd been reading theology, mythology, and philosophy at a college level since he was twelve.

"Hey, by the way," Charlie said, "are you two coming tonight?"

"Oh, you mean Peter's secret midnight conclave?" Kenny asked. "Sure, why not?"

"You didn't click that invitation yet, did you?"

"No," Vanhi said, "I'm not in the habit of responding to spam."

"Okay, good. Peter's doing some research on it."

"Well, that's reassuring. What do you think it is?"

"Some kind of game. I just want to make sure it's not shady."

"If Peter's involved, it's almost certainly shady," Vanhi said.

Charlie ignored that. Vanhi was always out to think the worst of Peter.

Vanhi showed them her code. "Watch this. I made it last night."

She ran the program, and a picture of a sphere appeared at the top of the screen. The wire-frame, 3-D rendering was generated from scratch in C++. It shot to the bottom of the screen and bounced back up, obeying the laws of gravity. More spheres shot from the top and sides, bouncing off each other and skirting off in different directions.

"I call it Balls."

"Charming," Kenny said. Always the string-section snob.

When the class had quieted down and was deep in coding, Charlie leaned over to Vanhi. "Don't you have your early application due?"

"Next Tuesday, yeah. What are you, my mom?"

Charlie laughed, but not really. "I was just thinking about our last prank."

"Trump! Trump! Trump!"

"Yeah, it was funny, but . . ."

"But what?" She sighed, annoyed.

"A felony? I mean, what were we thinking? You really could get into Harvard early. Do you want to throw that away over 'Trump is a shape-shifting lizard'? Or whatever new thing is tonight?" Charlie knew he had nothing to lose. His future was toast anyway. But as far as he knew, Vanhi still had the world at her feet.

Vanhi felt that her face was flushing. "Why are you patronizing me? Is it because I'm a girl? Did you tell Kenny not to throw his life away?"

Now Charlie flushed. "It's not that. It's just, we always said we'd go together. Now I can't. I don't want to drag you down, too."

Vanhi was churning inside. She couldn't let Charlie know she was as doomed as he was. She couldn't reveal her secret shame, her AP failure. It was like, pull one thread and the whole Vanhi sweater would unravel. So she double-bluffed. Instead of their both being losers, what if she pretended they could both still win?

"Listen, I'll make you a deal. You turn in an early application to Harvard, and I will, too. You blow yours off, I blow mine off."

"That's stupid. Why would you throw your future away?"

"If you don't, I won't either."

"You're not serious."

"Try me." She patted Charlie's shoulder. "We're friends, Charlie. I got your back. So promise you'll do it, and I won't have to throw my future away just to prove a point."

Charlie tried to read her. Was she serious? No way in hell was he applying to Harvard. The only way he could even *dream* of getting in now was to use his mother's death as a sob story of how he'd gone from valedictorian to failure. Even then, he'd need a redemption angle, and how could that work when he was still very much down in the mud? No fucking way. But why should Vanhi go down with him? So he lied.

"Okay. Sure. Why not. I'll apply."

"Okay," Vanhi said, trying to sound casual.

They eyed each other warily, unsure who was playing whom.

They coded for a while. The assignment was to make a software back end for a logistics distribution company, like Amazon. It had to ship anywhere in the world and deliver as close to instantaneously as possible. No drones though, at least not in this simulation.

She whispered right in his ear, "You really did cheat on me."

"I did?"

"Mary Clark, Charlie. Really?"

"I gave her a ride."

"You kissed her."

Charlie turned and gave her a perplexed look. "How do you know that?"

"Everyone knows that."

"She told?"

"I doubt it. That's not the kind of thing Mary Clark would publicize. Prettiest girl in school kisses marginalized quasi-nerd."

"Then how?"

"Charlie, you kissed her twenty feet away from a social mob. Did you really think no one would notice?"

"We were in the woods."

"Don't you know, Charlie? Someone is always watching."

Charlie turned away, his cheeks flushing red. So Tim knew? He hadn't said anything in the hall, but that cold rage in his eyes . . .

"You need to be careful, Charlie."

"Tim?"

"Yeah. But he won't come for you directly. He'll get Kurt Ellers or Joss Iverson to do it."

Kurt was a particularly sadistic bastard. Blunt and crass where Tim was slick and cultured. The offensive lineman to Tim's QB. Joss was dumb muscle—a linebacker, ready to pounce; he just needed to be pointed in the right direction.

"You'll never please her," Vanhi said, suddenly sounding like she cared. "All she wants is some rich guy to buy her things. Did you see the bracelet Tim got her? It was rose gold. It probably cost a thousand dollars."

"Is it so crazy to think she likes me?"

"No. It's crazy to think she'll ever choose you."

They were talking quietly, and Kenny was studiously pretending not to hear them.

"You're a real pal," Charlie told her.

"I am." The bell rang, and she gathered up her things. "You know what a friend is, Charlie? It's someone who tells you the truth, even when you don't want to hear it."

At lunch, the text said:

Meet me by the portables.

It came from Mary's number, which was crazy, as the last text in the chain was from two years earlier, about an anti-graffiti project for student council to repaint the south walls. Charlie felt his heart light up, but when he got there, he didn't see Mary anywhere. But across the patchwork of shadows between the portable buildings, he saw a small crowd gathered. Charlie gave Mary another couple minutes, then headed toward the group to see if she was there. He paused when he saw Kurt Ellers, the sadist in chief. Suddenly Vanhi's warning came together in his head—kiss Mary, Tim finds out, Kurt does his dirty work. But the crowd wasn't focused on Charlie, and something was already going on. Charlie let himself get a little closer, and he felt his heart sink. They were gathered around Alex.

"Do it," Kurt said cheerfully.

He held a cell phone up, ready to film.

"N-n-no." Alex was sputtering with fear. A football player was on either side, holding Alex's arms back.

Kurt gave him a rough shove. Alex kept his head down, hair over his eyes.

"Did you really think we'd let you get away with this? I mean, what the fuck? I thought Asian kids were supposed to be smart."

"Leave me alone."

"I'm going to call you Dumb Asian from now on," Kurt said, his smile ugly and mean.

"Eat shit."

Kurt slapped him so hard and so quickly across the face that it seemed to startle Alex before the pain set in. But then a bright red mark appeared on his cheek and he closed his eyes, trying not to cry.

The slap woke Charlie up. He'd been watching, frozen. Now he was alert. He had a choice to make. Neither option was pleasant.

And what had Alex done? *Did you really think we'd let you get away with this?* Get away with *what*? What crazy thing had Alex done now to put himself at risk? *Stop victim-blaming,* Charlie told himself. *No one deserves this. You're just a coward, looking for an excuse not to get involved.*

"Do it," Kurt said to the guys holding Alex.

Do what?

Alex looked terrified. He began to struggle furiously.

There were five guys, at least. There was no way Charlie could run for help in time. Even if he called someone, it would be too late by the time they got here.

Earlier, Alex had, in his own way, asked Charlie for reassurance, to let Alex know he wasn't alone, and Charlie had bungled that miserably. With a second of hesitation, he'd sent Alex further down that hole of isolation.

He felt a surge of anger. At Kurt. At Tim, who wasn't even here, but he led this crew of sadist kings. At Alex, for being the one Vindicator who threatened to turn them all from lovable, even *liked*, nerds into something else. At himself, for feeling that way.

On either side of Alex, a jock grabbed Alex's pants and pulled them down. He screamed, *"No!"* One of them pulled his underwear down next. Goddamn if he wasn't a seventeen-year-old kid wearing superhero boxers. Then he was exposed, his dick hanging out for the world to see, neither small nor big, just a normal dick, all the guys laughing and jeering, and Kurt held up his phone to snap a picture.

Charlie ran. He ran faster than he'd ever run in his life, clearing the distance between them in no time and launching at Kurt so quickly that none of those fascist, cruel motherfuckers saw him coming, so focused were they on tormenting the Boy from Mars and his perfectly normal dick. Charlie had never been in a fight before, but there was a first time for everything.

The adrenaline was surging and he launched into Kurt Ellers and took him down to the dirt and got one good punch into his smug face before Joss pulled Charlie off. "Erase that," he shouted, grabbing for Kurt's phone as Joss dragged him away. The phone had hit the ground a few feet away. "Leave him *alone.*"

"The fuck I will." Kurt got up and wiped dirt off his face with the back of his hand. "Did you tell him to do this?" Kurt's eyes narrowed maliciously.

"I have no fucking clue what you're talking about," Charlie shot back.

Alex was staring at the whole thing, incredulous. He backed away from the guys, who were all watching Charlie, and pulled his pants up.

Just before the first punch landed, Charlie thought, *Oh, well, they were coming for me sooner or later*. At least this was on his terms.

Charlie felt the sting and his head snapped back into Joss's chin.

He felt the grip loosen, just for a second.

Charlie raked his heel down and back, along Joss's shin. There was a yelp and Charlie pulled away just in time, before the thug got his bearings back. Kurt's phone was on the asphalt, and Charlie came down on it hard and fast with all his weight on the back of his heel. The screen smashed and the body cracked. Charlie backed against the portable shed as the group advanced on him. He took one of the bricks from the pile of construction materials and chucked it at them, slowing them down a bit. He took another brick and brought it down on the phone, then again and again, until it was crushed and shattered.

"That was new," Kurt whined.

"Let him go," Charlie said, nodding at Alex and holding the brick up, ready to attack. His lip was smarting and he could taste blood. But he felt exhilarated. He felt alive and with purpose for the first time in a year.

"You're dead," Kurt, not cheerful anymore, said to Charlie.

"We all have to go sometime." Charlie tried to sound brave and cavalier, although inside, he felt a pit in his stomach.

The backup QB, Chris Everett, rushed him, and Charlie swung with the brick. It hit Chris's shoulder.

The football player staggered backward, saying, "You're fucking crazy."

"Come on," Charlie told Alex.

Uncertain, Alex looked from tormentor to tormentor, but all eyes were on Charlie. Alex joined Charlie by his side.

They backed away, until they were around a corner, then Charlie dropped the brick and they took off running. Alex had always been surprisingly fast. He got ahead of Charlie, then slowed down so they could escape together. But the football crew did not follow. Whatever they had planned for Charlie, it would come later.

But one thing was certain. It would come.

Once they were safe on the far side of the school, Charlie said, "Are you okay?"

Alex was sullen now, the shame of what had happened settling in.

"I didn't see anything," Charlie tried, but it sounded flat. He tried for humor. "I mean, except for your dick, which was awesome."

Alex shook his head.

"Too soon?" Charlie asked.

"Those fuckers. I hate them."

"Alex, it's over. You're okay. We smashed the phone."

"They'll tell everyone."

"Tell everyone what? That they're sick fucks? That you look like every over guy at this school in the locker room? There's nothing to tell."

Charlie thought of something. "What did you do, anyway?"

"I didn't deserve that."

"I know. Of course not. But still, what was that about?"

"Nothing." Alex's eyes flicked to his backpack reflexively. He saw that Charlie saw and lowered his head even more.

Charlie took the bag. Alex didn't even try to stop him.

Inside, hundreds of printed copies of a flyer pictured Tim Fletcher's head photoshopped on a cartoon body with a tiny prick.

The flyer looked like a concert poster and said ALL HAIL LORD LITTLEDICK.

"You made these?"

Alex shrugged. "It wasn't hard," he said sarcastically.

"Yeah, I know. *Why* did you make them?"

He shrugged again. "That guy's an asshole."

"The world is filled with assholes. Tim's been one for years. Why did you do this?" A sickening thought occurred to Charlie: the kiss, Tim confronting him in the hall. "Did you do this for *me*?"

"Don't flatter yourself. The world doesn't revolve around you."

"I didn't say that," Charlie started, but then he let it go. "Did you put any up?"

Alex shook his head. "One of his minions saw me printing them in the library."

Reckless *and* sloppy. Maybe Kenny was right. Maybe Alex was bringing them all down.

Alex said, "You didn't have to do that."

"Of course I did," Charlie said, but deep down, he wasn't so sure.

Alex started to walk away, but Charlie grabbed his arm to stop him. Alex grimaced.

"Are you okay?"

"It's nothing."

"Let me see."

Charlie pulled Alex's sleeve up. Bruises were up and down his forearm, but they were old bruises.

"What the hell?"

Alex jerked his arm away.

"Have they bothered you before?"

"No." Alex's cheeks were flushing.

"Alex—"

"I'll see you later."

"*Alex*. Tonight, right? Midnight?"

Alex shrugged. "Where else do I have to be?"

Charlie let him go. He wanted to say, *You're one of us.* But he didn't know whether it would come out reassuring or patronizing. Or false. Alex said he was coming tonight. That was enough, for now.

Alex walked away, bag of mischief slung over his shoulder.

As he left, Charlie felt his phone buzz in his pocket.

He looked at the text.

> You did a good deed and God was watching.
> 800 Goldz!

11 DIGITAL NATIVES

Charlie's dad went through Charlie's room, looking for what? Drugs? Porn? Something, anything, a clue. To understanding his own son.

I'm losing him.

That's the worst thing you can think, as a father. To look at your son, who used to curl up in your lap and call you "Dah-dah" and ask for "peaner butter." And then to realize, *I don't know him anymore. I can't help him anymore.*

Add him to the list of people I can't save.

My son.

My wife.

Myself.

Arthur Lake could pinpoint the exact moment he knew he was outgunned, as a father. When Charlie was twelve, the school had assigned the kids iPads. Charlie wanted to put games on his, like his friends did. But Charlie's dad wanted to draw a line. Two games. That was it. The iPad was for school. It wasn't a toy.

"Okay," Charlie said, just like that.

Win! A Father of the Year moment.

Then one day Arthur came home and saw the iPad sitting on the kitchen table, unlocked like always. A couple of the apps had the exclamation-point symbol, showing they needed to be updated. But one exclamation point floated in space on the screen, not over any icon. It was just there, hanging over the background picture.

Curious, Charlie's dad pressed on it. A whole new section of the iPad opened up, filled with games. It was as if Charlie had placed an invisible door on his screen, known only to him. If it had been his room, Charlie's father could've searched for months and never found the trapdoor under the rug. Except at least a secret door has edges, a hinge, something. If not for the accidental update notice, Arthur Lake would never even have known this hidden place was there.

What else was Charlie hiding from him?

What would it be in a few years, when it wasn't just games? And how the hell are you supposed to raise your kid when you can't even find the door to his secret room?

Now, five years later, Arthur Lake knelt in front of Charlie's computer on his desk. Arthur woke it up, and the home screen was locked. He felt it again, the walls between them.

Arthur tried a password so obvious, so heartbreaking, that it couldn't possibly be right. He typed in his lost wife's name, Alicia.

The home screen unlocked, showing Charlie's desktop and his mess of apps and papers. A Web browser was open and minimized. Arthur brought it up, wondering what he would find.

It looked like some kind of game or chat room. There was a tent, like a carnival. Next to it, a lizard in a top hat was sleeping on the ground.

The text said:

> You are invited!
> COme inside and play with G.O.D.
> Bring your friends!

Arthur read on. At the bottom, there was a gap, then:

> Invitation accepted.

He breathed a sigh of relief. It was a stupid game. Not instructions for a bomb or suicide cocktails. If Charlie was playing games, he was living life. He was a kid.

Arthur moved the cursor, to see what was in Charlie's search history, but the lizard woke up and looked right through the screen at him, as if the movement had stirred him.

It was creepy. The animation was crude, but the responsiveness was unsettling.

Arthur glanced at the little camera for skyping and whatnot and thought, *Is Charlie watching me? Can this be motion activated, too? Am I busted? How can I be busted?* he corrected himself. *It's my house. I'm the father.*

Arthur had something he wanted to tell Charlie. A reason he was feeling better than he had in months. Years. He'd let Charlie down when Alicia was sick. He tried his best but fell down. But this new thing, it could be good for all of them. A fresh start.

He decided to leave Charlie's room. *Give him his privacy. Leave him to his games. We'll talk tonight.*

Arthur left the room.

He was wrong about Charlie watching him through the camera.

It was God who was watching through that little eye.

And why not? Wasn't God always watching?

12 HOUSE OF GOLD

After school, Charlie read the text again.

> You did a good deed and God was watching.
> 800 Goldz!

What the hell? He hadn't joined the game yet—the meeting was tonight—so why was God texting him? And what were Goldz?

And then there was the text that got him there in the first place.

> Meet me by the portables.

Love, Mary. Or from her phone anyway.

Did she even send that?

Was she trying to save Alex by tipping Charlie off to the ambush?

Did she no-show?

If she didn't send it, who did?

The game? Which he hadn't even joined yet.

Why would it use *her*? Was it aware they had been together last night? Kissed?

Surely not.

But there was one way to find out.

He headed for the lockers where Mary congregated with her friends after final period. He took a wide path around the football field, spotting Tim Fletcher from a distance, with Kurt and Joss and a bunch of other uniformed lackeys, giving each other high fives and laughing. Whether it was about some great play or torturing Alex, Charlie didn't know. Kurt strolled over to the bleachers and glanced at a phone. Had that bastard already run out and bought himself a new phone? It would take Charlie weeks, months, to afford that.

He found Mary in the middle of a pack of friends and admirers. Hard-drinking, mean-spirited, sexy Caitlyn Lacey shot him a *What do you think* you're *doing here?* look. Rebecca Moore looked bored. Amanda Miles, nicer, smarter, but still in another orbit, gave a knowing half smile.

Charlie just stood there, clothes ruffled, hair mussed, a busted lip, his brown eyes focused and clear. Mary glanced at her friends, then walked past Charlie without saying a word. He followed. When they got outside and rounded a corner out of sight, he said, "Did you send me a text today?"

"No."

"You didn't ask me to meet you by the portables at lunch?"

She shook her head. She looked genuinely baffled.

Charlie didn't know which bothered him more—that a computer game had spoofed his wannabe girlfriend's phone number, or that the girl herself hadn't written him.

She glanced at his busted lip. "I know what you did today. That was really brave."

"Do you know what that asshole did?"

"Kurt?"

"Tim."

"Tim wasn't there, Charlie. He was with me."

"He was there in spirit."

"I know."

She raised her hand, just for a moment, toward his lip, with a look of concern on her face, but she seemed to catch herself and glanced around the corner, at the larger school out of sight behind them, as if someone might march around the turn any minute and rat them out.

As her hand fell back, the rose-gold bracelet jangled on her wrist, and Charlie didn't know if it was that or the fight or her denial of

Tim's involvement, but—eyes on the bracelet—he snapped, "Is that from him?"

Charlie remembered her fidgeting nervously with it last night. "You should take it off," he said, his anger getting away from him.

"Charlie, you don't understand."

"Why do you keep making excuses for him?"

"I'm not."

"Kurt was torturing Alex. *For* Tim. Over a stupid prank."

"I know exactly who Kurt is. Who Tim is. Charlie, that has nothing to do with us."

She said *us,* and Charlie didn't miss it. "If he's hurting you . . ."

"I'll handle it."

"I can do something."

"No, you won't." She said it coolly, and it set him back a bit. But her eyes were tender.

"I just thought . . ."

Before he could finish, she put a finger to her mouth, wet it, and wiped at the cut on his lip.

"I'm sorry," Charlie said, watching her bracelet catch the light. "I shouldn't have told you to take that off. I just wish you wanted to."

"I know."

He wanted to ask her what this all meant—last night's kiss, the tender eyes and soft touch now, only in private, only out of sight. He wanted to ask her if any of it held once they turned the corner and were back in view of the world. But he didn't ask because he didn't want to know. And because he was afraid he already did. Remembering the feel of her finger on his lip, he wondered, *What does it matter? Is there anything real on earth except right now?*

She whispered, "I have to go."

As she left, her gold bracelet glimmered in the sun.

Mr. B. looked madder than Charlie had ever seen him. He caught Charlie on the way to the Tech Lab, knowing right where to find him.

"My room. Now."

"What? What did I do?"

"Now," Mr. B. said, eyebrows raised.

In the classroom, he studied Charlie's face. "Fighting?"

Charlie sighed, relieved. So that's what it was about?

"It was for a good cause."

"I don't care."

"But . . ."

Burklander held his hand up. "I don't want to hear it. Goddamnit, Charlie." Charlie was startled. He'd never heard a teacher curse in anger before. "I am about to give up on you."

Charlie blinked a few times. "Why?"

"The Texas rep for Harvard is in town next week. He asked me whom he should meet. I told him you, Charlie. I told him everything about you. What you've been through. What you'd accomplished before that. How you were going to pull through. He was interested."

Charlie sighed. Every time Mr. Burklander tried to reconnect Charlie to his old life, he felt the chasm and the pain of what had come in between. But Burklander wasn't done.

"I am not going to show him a kid with a busted lip."

"I'm sorry. I did the right thing."

"It's just one thing too many, Charlie. One more thing to explain."

"I didn't ask to meet him."

Burklander clenched his fists. "I know that. I'm doing it because you *can't*."

Charlie felt shame all through him. "It's not my fault."

"I've been telling you for months, come out of this. You've had your chance."

"I know."

"I can't . . . I don't know what to do for you anymore."

So finally the last teacher to believe in Charlie was giving up. Was he horrified? Or relieved?

"I'm sorry," he said quietly.

Mr. Burklander gave him a hard look and for a moment seemed lost in thought. "I read something last night. Something I hadn't pulled out in years. I almost burned it once, but I didn't have the heart."

Charlie tried to think what book could have that effect on Mr. B.

Mr. Burklander took a beaten-up notebook from his desk, an old-fashioned composition book. He touched it delicately with two fingers, tapping the cover hesitantly.

"My journal, from the year after my mother died. Hard to read. The first few pages, it was like I was just waiting for her to walk in the front door and say, 'Surprise, just kidding.'" He shook his head.

Charlie studied him. He suddenly pictured Mr. Burklander in his front yard, his ex-wife throwing his clothes out the window above and yelling at him while the neighbors watched. Collapsing in the grass, busted heart and boxers. It was hard to square that with the dignified, handsome face in front of him now.

Burklander seemed to reach a decision. "Come with me."

At the end of the hallway was a bulletin board, and among the ads for school plays and football rallies was a sign-up sheet: STUDENT BODY PRESIDENT—ELECTION NOV. 8, 2016. The race had been going on for a couple weeks. There were already five names on the list. Charlie had ignored it.

Mr. B. jabbed it with his finger. "Sign up."

"I'm not running for student body president."

"Yes, you are. You don't have to win. You just have to run. And then, and only then, I'll get you in front of the Harvard recruiter. I'll explain the circumstances of your new appearance. I'll move mountains if you just show me that in there, somewhere, is a hint of the kid I know."

The last thing on earth Charlie wanted to do was run for student body president. But still, it was Mr. B. Charlie thought of all they had done together on the council. He thought of the composition notebook. Burklander's lost-mom dream—pulling her arm, saying, *Look out, the building's falling,* her blithely refusing to look up.

Charlie even felt a glimmer of hope—for an instant, he saw a vision of running for student body president, talking to a crowd. He fingered the pen. He tried to lift it, but it felt infinitely heavy. He pressed the pen to the paper tacked to the wall. He couldn't write his name. It would be a lie. Nothing more. He owed Burklander that much—not to lie to him.

"I can't."

Mr. Burklander stood there, then put his hand on top of Charlie's. "You can."

He started moving, Charlie's hand under his, until the name was signed.

"I don't mean it. I can't do it."

"It's a start. Just don't cross it out. Not today. Let it sit for a while, even if it's a lie." Burklander smiled and patted Charlie on the back. "It's a lie I want to hear."

13 HOUSE OF PAIN

Charlie worked for two hours at the copy center on West Beverly—a mind-numbing job under fluorescent lights. He started when his mom was sick and the deductibles wiped the family out. He'd kept working ever since and managed to squirrel away a little for himself, even while he helped with gas and groceries while his dad tried to dig them out of their hole.

Charlie drove past the mall on the way home and set foot for the first time in his life in the glimmering aisles of Neiman Marcus. The woman at the jewelry counter eyed him skeptically, under overplucked eyebrows. Charlie found what he was looking for. The bracelet was a perfect match for Mary's, with one key difference. It wasn't from Tim.

"How much?" Charlie asked. He'd scraped together $200. It was absolutely insane. He knew that. But it was a symbolic gesture. If Mary was caught between two worlds—between what she wanted and what she felt she was supposed to be—he would ease the transition. She could trade his bracelet for Tim's, and Tim would never be the wiser. As an added benefit, maybe then choosing Charlie wouldn't be a total downer. He could bring a little bling into her life, too.

"Nine hundred dollars," the lady behind the counter said boredly.

Charlie felt his cheeks flush red. "That's what I thought."

But the lady had already moved on.

Charlie's dad was at the kitchen table, looking like a giddy teenager. "I need to talk to you." Whatever it was, at least he hadn't heard about the fight. He was way too happy.

"What is it?" Charlie asked suspiciously.

"Come here." His smile dropped as Charlie stepped into the dim light. "What happened to your face?"

"I got knocked down in PE. Soccer. I'm fine."

Arthur studied Charlie's face, his own expression flickering between belief and doubt. He glanced back down at the papers spread out before them on the cheap IKEA table, and belief won out. The giddy smile came back. The pages lining the table didn't look like the usual accounting files. There were blueprints, business plans, inventories.

"Sit down."

Charlie sat opposite his father, eyeing the papers warily.

"I used to cook you good breakfasts."

"Okay," Charlie said slowly, wondering if his dad had finally lost his mind completely.

"I used to cook everything."

"I know."

"I was a really good cook."

"Yeah. True."

"Remember how we used to barbecue?"

Charlie smiled. "Uh-huh."

"Everyone would come over. Talk about how good my burgers were. Remember my secret recipe?"

God, his dad could be cheesy. But Charlie played along. "One-third mustard, one-third soy sauce, one-third Worcestershire."

"Yep. You never told anybody, right?"

Charlie forced a smile. "No."

"I loved it."

"And Mom would make that lemon pie."

The mood darkened, and Charlie felt guilty about that. His father was finally feeling good, remembering something happy, and he had to go and bring up Mom. And he'd done it on purpose, like it felt wrong to remember something good without talking about her. He tanked the moment, and he knew what he was doing and he hated himself for it. He tried to recover.

"So you want to have a barbecue? That's your idea?"

For a moment, his dad seemed hesitant to go on. His eyes were far off. Then he rallied, too. "No, I want to do something better."

"Okay . . ."

"I want to open a restaurant."

Arthur waited, and it struck Charlie that his dad was nervous. He was watching Charlie to see if he'd burst out laughing. The idea was so random, so out of the blue, and yet looking at the papers spread out before them, it obviously wasn't new. His dad had been working for some time on this.

Charlie treaded lightly. "A restaurant?"

"Yeah. What do you think?"

"I mean . . . I don't know. What kind of restaurant?"

"Something simple. A place where people go to hang out. Like a neighborhood burger place. Families. Teenagers. Pinball machines. Foosball. Some place . . ." Arthur seemed to struggle for the right word. "Alive." He winced and tried again. "Happy." He looked at Charlie cautiously. "I've even got a name for it: Arthur's."

Arthur Lake looked proud of himself. Charlie felt himself sigh heavily.

The plans looked good. Arthur was going to rework an old strip-mall bank space. The finish-out was homey, the kind of place you might want to watch the Cowboys on a rainy Sunday, or take your kids for chicken fingers on a Tuesday night.

But then Charlie thought about his dead-end job at the copy center. The way his dad had lost it when Mom was sick, leaving Charlie to pick up the slack.

"What about accounting? You're just going to close up shop?"

"I can't do this half-assed."

"You're going to *quit* your job? I didn't get to quit school just because Mom died."

"Didn't you?"

That stung. But Charlie pushed forward.

"What about food? What about the house? I thought the medical stuff wiped us out."

"It did. Mostly. I'll need a loan. I can take out a second mortgage on the house."

"You've got to be kidding me."

"No, Charlie, I—"

"What about college?"

"Are you going?"

"What if I am? What if I wanted to?"

Charlie's dad snorted through his nose, a bitter, scoffing laugh.

Charlie thought of Mr. Burklander. "If I did? Could you pay for it?"

"Charlie . . ."

"What if I get in somewhere really good?"

"They have scholarships. I can pay part."

"Do you even care what I want?"

"Do you even know what you want?"

"What if no one comes?"

"What are you talking about?"

"To your restaurant. Arthur's," Charlie added a bit sarcastically. "What if no one shows up? And then we have no money and, what, we lose our house?"

"Charlie, I need this. I'm sorry you feel cheated. I feel cheated, too."

"You're the *adult*."

"I know. I know."

"I don't care. Do it. Do what you want. You want to go crazy and open a restaurant, which you have no experience or business doing, fine. I don't care. I'd rather be broke than just poor. It's more exciting."

"Jesus, Charlie. What if it works? What if it's great? Is it so wrong to have a little hope? To do something a little crazy? Do it with me. We'll build this together." Arthur pushed some papers in front of Charlie.

"What's this?"

"It's a loan application. One hundred thousand dollars. On the house. I won't sign it if you tell me not to."

"You're kidding. You're gonna put this on *me*?"

"Say the word. I'll walk away." Arthur waved his hand across the blueprints, the designs, the Excel spreadsheets. How many nights had he stayed up poring over this crazy dream?

It wasn't like anyone in the house was sleeping anyway.

His dad was watching him, looking more like a kid than a solid man. He was absolutely broken—heartbroken, spirit-broken. Charlie guessed another twenty years of his being an accountant without his wife seemed a lot gloomier than the twenty years he'd slogged away at it with her to come home to.

Then Charlie thought of Mary standing there, hand on her gold bracelet. Her giant house on the right side of town, blocks away from Tim Fletcher's giant house. Charlie couldn't give Mary what she was used to. And now his dad wanted to put them deeper in debt.

Fuck it. Burklander's plan was crazy anyway. If Charlie's own dad didn't believe in him, what the hell did Burklander know? This just made the choice easier.

"Do it," Charlie said finally.

"Really?"

"Sure." He wanted to add, *Drive us off the cliff, why not?* But he saw the look on his dad's face—disbelief? Joy? So he left it there.

Two hours later, when he snuck out into the night, he glanced through the downstairs window and saw his father, still at the table, head down, asleep on the stack of papers.

Charlie threw stones at Kenny's window. It was time.

Earlier, Kenny had sat at his parents' dinner table, head bowed in prayer. His father, dignified, stern, humorless, a tuft of gray hair over each ear, a bald dome on top, said, "Let us pray. Our heavenly Father, who . . ."

They weren't rich, even though both parents were doctors. His mom was a pediatrician. After tuition, you lost money on that endeavor. His dad was an academic at the teaching hospital, trading the big bucks of private practice for research and instruction. Their faith carried them through. It wound around Kenny's neck like a noose.

"Have you thought more about majors?" his dad asked.

"I haven't even gotten into college yet."

"I'm not paying for something aimless."

Reflexively, Kenny's eyes shot to the empty chair where his older brother used to sit. The medical school dropout. The shame. The "writer" who couldn't land a TV show to write for. Kenny felt the burn, the weight of expectation.

"I know, Dad. I like journalism."

"Another writer."

Ouch.

"Or maybe premed," Kenny offered.

His mother nodded almost imperceptibly. She took a sip of wine. She allowed herself a quarter cup per night. No more. No less.

Kenny asked if he could be excused to practice, the only surefire way to get upstairs.

He played through Dvořák's Cello Concerto, letting the music take him somewhere far away. His life felt like a cello string—you could wind it from a loose mess into perfect pitch, the vibration just right. Cosmic, the way it clicked into place. Then you could keep winding. And winding. And winding. Until it snapped, a victim of its own tension.

Midnight couldn't come soon enough.

When Charlie's pebble hit the window, Kenny thought, *Take me somewhere new.*

14 THE COVENANT

The Tech Lab was pitch-black at midnight, but someone had lit candles.

It had the air of a church, silent in the warm flickering.

In the dark, four of the monitors were turned on but blank, emitting a dull black glow. They made a ring of dim screens, a candle in front of each terminal, little electronic altars.

Charlie, Vanhi, and Kenny were outside, in the auxiliary parking lot by the back door to the lab. The wind was brisk and Vanhi shivered. She looked at Charlie's lip and started to say something, but Alex was coming up the path behind her, and Charlie shook his head slightly. "I'll tell you later," he said quietly.

Alex joined them, looking sheepish. "I couldn't miss it."

Maybe Peter was right (again), Charlie thought—you needed a little style to keep 'em coming back.

They used their unofficial key to open the door and step into the darkness. The door swung shut behind them, and as their eyes adjusted, all they could see were the small orange flames and the faint screens behind.

"I want you . . . ," a familiar voice began.

A face appeared from the darkness, an upturned flashlight illuminating a Guy Fawkes mask. A hand dramatically swept the mask away, revealing Peter's handsome, devilish face.

". . . to tickle my balls!"

"Jesus," Kenny said, shaking his head. They all laughed.

"Welcome, welcome, come one, come all, my Vindicator brethren and sistren. Are you tired of playing lame dice-rolling games on Kenny's nasty carpet?"

"Hey!" Kenny said.

"Are you tired of being losers, sitting around jerking each other off?"

"I like getting jerked off," Vanhi said.

"Do you want to be rich, popular, powerful, handsome?"

"I do!" Alex grinned darkly. "I do!" Even Alex couldn't resist Peter's charm tonight.

"I want to be rich!" Kenny added.

"Yes!" Peter replied.

"I want to be popular with the ladies!" Vanhi said.

"Yes!"

"I want to kick Tim Fletcher's ass!" Charlie pitched in.

"Yes!" they all agreed, including Alex.

"Then say yes, my friends, say yes to the proposal I lay before you. A once-in-a-lifetime opportunity. If only you're smart enough to take it!"

"Take what? Take what?" Kenny faux-fawned, like a fairgoer ready to sign his paycheck over to the first huckster in the tent to show him a new ultrathin mop.

"Indeed!" Peter goaded. "What you want, gentlemen and lady, is to play God! Turn the social order upside down. Claim what should be yours! Go from duds to studs! And so I give you . . . the God Game!"

In a neat trick, the screens flicked on, on command.

Charlie looked for the Bluetooth clicker in Peter's hand, but one hand was holding the mask, and the other still had the flashlight. Maybe it was voice activated. Peter had a flair for the dramatic obviously.

On each screen, Charlie recognized the familiar invitation he'd seen on his desktop last night.

The lizard was there, leaning against the side of the tent, his top hat off to the side. He was picking lazily at his lizard fingernails.

"You guys will not believe what I've read about this game," Peter said, enticing them.

"Like what?" Alex gave that little sadistic smile that was always a bit disturbing.

"Crazy shit. There are points. If you do good, you get Goldz. If you do bad, you get Blaxx."

Charlie thought of his phone: *800 Goldz!*

"What do you mean, good or bad?" Vanhi asked.

"Like, good versus evil. Dark versus light. Biblical acts of justice and retribution. Old Testament shit, I kid you not."

"How do you play?"

"That's the thing," Peter said. "I don't know. We're gonna find out together."

"Who made it?"

"No one's saying. Isn't that nuts? It's old. It goes back to the bulletin-board days. It's invitation-only. It could be Cicada 3301. Or maybe the Dritë Collective. The code base has grown over time massively. Now it's self-perpetuating. The things I've read . . ."

"If it's so secret, how do you know all this?" Vanhi asked sarcastically.

"Did you google it?" Kenny asked.

"Ha, um, no. You don't google this. It's Dark Web stuff. I still know some people. Listen, it's all here. 'Win, and all your dreams come true.' If you do well, things really go your way. In life."

"Like what?"

"Money. Girls. Cars. You name it."

"Bullshit. In real life?"

"Yes, in real life, you loser!"

"That's impossible," Charlie said.

Charlie glanced at Alex and Kenny. They looked way too excited.

"It's not impossible. The only thing impossible is a bad attitude," Peter chimed, channeling one of Mrs. Fleck's self-help posters. "But there is a downside. I wouldn't want to get you all involved in this without full disclosure."

"Of what?" Kenny asked.

"Well," Peter said, thoroughly enjoying himself, "the Dark Web is a little sketchy about this, but the rumor is, if you die in the game, you die in real life."

"Oh, come on," Vanhi said. "Bull."

"That's what I've heard."

"That would be so illegal!"

"Illegal like hacking a street sign?" Peter grinned.

"No, illegal like *murder*. Like *that*." Vanhi folded her arms defiantly and blew a tuft of hair out of her face. Charlie felt a growing unease. If Goldz supposedly meant money, girls, whatever, in real life, it stood to reason that Blaxx would mean something bad in real life, too. He didn't believe any of it, but still—if a fraction of it was true, he didn't like where it was going. Or how easily his friends were walking toward it.

"It's not murder if God does it," Peter said.

"Touché," Kenny said.

"It's his game. If you do right in his eyes, you have nothing to worry about."

"Come on," Alex said. "It's bullshit anyway. A game can't kill you. Don't be a bunch of babies." Alex was shockingly animated, way too eager.

"'Don't be a baby.' A sound, logical argument," Kenny said.

Alex threw a mouse pad at him.

Peter walked over to one of the screens. The same words from the other night bobbed around, welcoming them:

You are invited!
COme inside and play with G.O.D.
Bring your friends!
It's fun!
But remember the rules. Win and ALL YOUR DREAMS COME
TRUE.™ Lose, you die!
:)
It's ur choice. Free will!!!!!!!!!!!!!!!!!!!

"Come on, guys," Peter whined. "I can't play this alone."

"I'm in." Alex sat down at one of the monitors.

"Me, too," Kenny said, surprising everyone. He walked over to

Peter and the terminals. It was tantalizing to Kenny, the religious angle—he was so steeped in family religion, he found it both loving and suffocating. This was a minor rebellion too sweet to pass up. Plus, it was just a game. He didn't believe rumors.

"Oh, fuck it," Vanhi added. "Me, too."

"Vanhi," Charlie whispered, grabbing her arm. He tried to catch her eyes.

"Come on, Charlie, it's just a goof. You don't believe that stuff about really dying?"

"You don't need this. Who knows what it really is."

"If people had been dropping dead for the last twenty years from a video game, don't you think we'd have heard about it?" She walked over and sat down.

Charlie sighed. It didn't matter who you were—man, woman, loser, cool—it was hard to share Peter. His danger was intoxicating. He was a secret society of one. Everyone was staring at Charlie, waiting to see what he'd do.

Fuck it, Charlie thought. *They're all in. And here I am, standing alone.*

"Fine. I'll play."

"Well, Charlie, that's the thing," Peter said sheepishly, nodding at the four glowing monitors. "You might have noticed there's only four invitations. And five of us."

"Are you saying I'm not invited?"

"No." Peter turned on a fifth monitor. "When I put your name in, this is what happened."

The screen warmed up, and instead of an invitation, a gamespace lit up. Inside the tent, so to speak.

A small dot was on the screen that said *Charlie* below it.

Peter shrugged. "Whatever the God Game is, you're already playing it."

15 IN THE BEGINNING

It started with a blank space. Like a stage, before a play.

A black screen, with an empty inventory on the side. And a coin purse, so to speak. With 800 Goldz, as promised. Zero Blaxx. A little dot in the center of the screen, marked *Charlie*.

When he sat down and tried to move the mouse, four lines appeared, the contours of a room. It was just the barest hint of a 2-D, top-down space. But as he moved the cursor around, the details of the room fleshed out. A desk here. A table there. All linear. All retro. The kind of game you might've made with BASIC when you were a kid.

The Vindicators all stared at their monitors, in the arc of computer stations in the center of the room. Peter was already in the gamespace with Charlie, starting to explore.

Vanhi clicked on the invitation, and Charlie saw what he hadn't for his own invitation. The lizard perked up, still sleepy, and flipped on his top hat. He did a little bow, then held his other hand out, toward the slit in the red curtains.

They pulled open, a clumsy animation.

It was black behind them, then the tent came toward the screen until the black between the curtains filled the whole view, and there was Vanhi's avatar, another little dot, in the dead center. Charlie was up and to the left. Peter was moving around top right. The furniture and details they'd already explored were revealed for Vanhi, too.

So they were playing together. They'd have to work as a team.

Good, Charlie thought.

Kenny and Alex appeared soon after, and among the five of them, they were mapping out the gamespace in no time.

They were looking down on the world, filling in what became more and more like a blueprint, the 2-D floor plan of a large space.

"It feels like an old console game," Peter said.

"Yeah, like *Pyro 2.*"

"*SubSpace Continuum.*"

"Classic!"

"Or *Bolo*!" Kenny chimed in.

"It's not like *Bolo,*" Vanhi said somewhat arbitrarily.

"Piss off."

"It's free scrolling. I found a door. I'm in a hallway."

Everything seemed to map out as they went, loading from some unknown database.

"Whoa!" Alex cried, and everybody looked over.

"What is it?"

"Pull back on your mouse wheel."

They did, and their views changed.

Charlie almost had a sense of vertigo as the 2-D gamespace lurched and tilted, rotating into a 3-D view, all lines and blank space in between.

"Oh, no way, it's like *Knight Lore*!"

"*Little Big Adventure!*"

And now his little dot avatar was a diamond polygon, with *Charlie* hovering below it.

Vanhi was a sphere.

Peter was a cone.

Alex was a rhomboid.

Peter started laughing.

"What?" Alex said, assuming the joke was on him.

"Kenny's square." Peter laughed harder. "How appropriate."

"I am not!" Kenny snapped. "I mean, I am a square *here,* but I'm not square." He slugged Peter's arm. "That's not even modern slang," Kenny mumbled under his breath.

"Follow me, I'm going down the hall."

They spread out down the hallway, all black and white lines revealing the gamespace just a few steps ahead of the players. A world building itself plank by plank, just in time for each footstep to land on something solid, instead of the void.

"I'm getting Goldz," Vanhi noticed, looking at her inventory. "The more I map, the more I get."

"How many do you have?"

"Twenty-five. And counting!"

"I've got twelve," Kenny said.

"That's cuz you suck," she shot back.

"This game is bringing out the worst in you all," Kenny said, shaking his head.

Charlie glanced at his bank. He already had 800 Goldz from the fight today. He didn't want to embarrass Alex by having to explain it. He hoped nobody noticed.

"Why are Blaxx bad anyway?" Vanhi asked. "What racist bullshit is that?"

"That's true." Peter moved his avatar into a new room. "Goldz should suck. Blaxx should rule."

"What a couple of snowflakes you two are," Kenny said.

"Guys, I hate to interrupt this fascinating conversation, but look at this." Charlie pointed to his screen.

Charlie had noticed something as he mapped out the main room: a row of tables, organized into a semicircular arc, surrounded by tables along the outer walls. The details were missing—the equipment, the printers. But they were looking at an accurate floor plan of the Tech Lab.

"No way. It's our room." Kenny gestured around. "It's *this*."

"You don't see that in *Bolo,*" Vanhi mused.

They all ran their characters back down the hall, into the virtual Tech Lab. As they explored, more and more details emerged.

Until something fantastic happened.

As if by some invisible paintbrush, they saw a stripe of "reality" swipe across their screens, filling in the black space of a wall with a line of cinder block painted white—the real surface of the walls around them. And then they saw why.

Kenny was standing up, looking thrilled and shocked in equal parts. "I didn't think it would work." He was holding his cell phone. "I went back to the original text and followed the link on my phone." He held it up for them. "I got to the same gamespace. But instead of just moving my player around on the screen, I went to the same wall in real life. I held it up to match them—real wall, virtual wall. And look!"

He painted another swipe through the air with his phone.

They all immediately swung their heads from Kenny to their terminals. Sure enough, another swipe of reality appeared on the screen, filling in the wall further.

"Oh, no freakin' way." Alex sounded happier than Charlie had heard him in years.

They all hopped up and started canvassing the room, waving their phones around like lunatics and filling in the wire-frame world on their screens with real-world details. The game mapped the real surfaces onto the 3-D polygons on-screen. The more angles, the more views, the more the Game seemed to fracture and expand the polygons into the real-life images wrapping them, like the foil on old-timey popcorn growing and smoothing into a dome.

"This is freaking *sick*," Vanhi said, her highest compliment. She put a hand on Charlie's shoulder as they passed each other, and she just smiled and shook her head. "Cool. This is beyond cool."

It was.

The Goldz were accumulating, racist or not.

"How did you think to try that?" Peter asked Kenny, impressed.

Everyone knew that Kenny was brilliant in a different way from the rest of them, the philosopher to their physicist. But that's how he saw it first.

"This book I love," he told them. "*I Am a Strange Loop*. It's about consciousness, how it arises from unconscious matter. He talks about infinite regress—pointing a camera at its own image on a screen. This reminded me of that."

Charlie remembered Kenny's loaning him that book freshman year. Charlie felt like his own life was looping.

"How many Goldz do you have?" Vanhi asked in Charlie's ear.

"Same as you, I guess," he answered vaguely, avoiding the issue. "Come on."

They went back to mapping.

But he wondered, how many Goldz *did* he have now? He went back to his terminal, away from the others. On the screen, the room was filling in nicely. He minimized that and pulled up his inventory. Still empty, but now he had twelve hundred Goldz. He tried clicking on them. A text box appeared.

> You have 1,200 Goldz. What would you
> like to buy?
> 1>>Anonymity 1,000
> 2>>Intro Social Control 1,000
> >

Charlie thought about that. Anonymity was good on the Web, but paired against social control, it sounded a little introverted. Social control sounded more than a little fascist, so that was odd, too. But intriguing. Why the hell not? It was only "introductory" fascism, anyway.

Charlie typed in:

> You have 1,200 Goldz. What would you
> like to buy?
> 1>>Anonymity 1,000
> 2>>Intro Social Control 1,000
> >2

He hit Enter.

Nothing happened for a moment.

The gamespace reappeared, but with a new POV.

He was looking right at the row of terminals.

The one in the middle was his.

He was looking at the back of his own head, looking at his screen.

And on the screen, that picture was repeated, and within the little screen in the repetition, it was repeated again . . . and on and on . . . as if the Game had been listening to Kenny's explanation and decided to have a little fun. Or, Charlie thought, getting the willies over that idea, was it a coincidence? Because an infinite regress was exactly what this POV would look like, regardless of what Kenny had just been saying . . .

Occam's razor. Let's not get crazy.

But when he clicked on the monitor within the monitor, it changed to something simpler: a chessboard. Sixty-four squares. Thirty-two pieces, half white, half black. Simple 2-D graphics.

That ultimate symbol of machine over man, the chessboard. Chess was supposed to be the timeless battle of human wits, and it turned out it was just a math problem that our creations could solve much faster than their creators.

Charlie clicked on the board.

A flicker, and then—

The computer screen was filled with windows flipping so quickly Charlie could scarcely make heads or tails of the images. But certain things registered—his social media pages, profiles, thumbnail images of himself, his friends, their friends, their social media, the whole spreading web of messages, comments, pings, photos, queries, searches (was that the Google image search of Mary that had revealed the bikini photo he had sheepishly discovered late one evening, guiltily in the dark, door locked?). It was a blur, yet a certain rhythm and pattern emerged at a higher level from the data itself, the image of a spider spinning a web ever outward. Connecting triangular points on faces in photos, silver threads spooling out between friends of friends of friends of friends (like that classic STD poster— you're not just sleeping with one person, you're sleeping with everyone the person has slept with has slept with has slept with—then why is it so hard not to be a virgin!)—hypnotic, the way the spider was connecting the world, until the world itself was irrelevant and all that mattered was the web.

"Oh, wow," Alex said from behind Charlie. Charlie snapped out of the hypnotic stare and turned to see everyone standing behind him.

"How did you get it to do that?"

"I don't know," Charlie said, lying lamely.

On the screen, the flipping and shuffling through Charlie's social media universe was gone. The chessboard was there, all thirty-two pieces, filling the screen.

But now the pieces had faces.

Mary the white queen.

Tim the king.

Kurt Ellers the bishop.

Joss Iverson the knight.

Across the board: Vanhi, Peter, Alex, Kenny—knights and bishops and rooks, united for a fight.

And Charlie the king, all in black.

16 ISOMETRIC

"Why does Charlie get to be the king?" That was Alex, sulkily.

"I don't know," Charlie said. "Maybe because I clicked on it first."

"The camera-on-camera thing was my idea," Kenny said, annoyed.

"No one's gonna forget that," Peter told him. "When they write books about this. You'll see."

Kenny ignored him. "Whatever, it's just a game."

"True," Charlie said. But deep down, did he feel a bit of excitement, being named king? He did found the Vindicators, after all, back in the day. Not that anyone much cared anymore. Peter was the real golden boy now. So did it thrill a little to be king here, with Peter his right-hand knight? You bet your ass it did.

Turns out, it didn't matter anyway.

"Try to move," Kenny said.

Charlie clicked on his pieces. Nothing happened.

"Maybe white has to go first."

"More bullshit," Vanhi said.

Maybe. Or maybe Charlie hadn't unlocked the mysteries and permissions of Intro Social Control—a purchase he kept to himself, since he couldn't explain it without embarrassing Alex.

When in doubt, change the subject.

"Come on," Charlie said. "We've got a school to map."

Fueled by adrenaline and awe, they spent the next three hours running through the empty halls of Turner High like conquering barbarians, waiving their phones around, capturing every fire extinguisher and trophy case.

It was a decadent thrill—the school was theirs! Empty, quiet, after midnight: their footsteps and whoops echoing down the corridors and bouncing off the lockers and tiles. All day long the school was fraught with hazards—a sea of bodies pushing and shoving, laughing and bickering and canoodling and fighting—but now it was theirs alone.

Charlie jumped up and smacked the GO TIGERS! sign, sending it swinging on its hinges.

He let out a holler and felt freer than he had in years. It was pitch-black out the windows, silent as a crypt.

They kept running until they couldn't think of where else to run.

Suddenly Charlie's phone buzzed in his hand.

All of their phones did.

A text came in:

Area Mapped! Time to Level Up!

And then it started.

On their phones, the gamespace was a perfectly realistic simulation of the school, mapped with all the surfaces and objects of the world around them. But then Charlie saw it, creeping in from the edges of the screen. A rippling, which turned out to be animated vines and cracks moving over the walls and ceilings and floors, buckling the surfaces and giving them a gamelike, hyperreal sheen. Vines like from some medieval castle or haunted Victorian mansion, winding through the doorways and down the halls, into the slats of the locker vents and around the Roman clock. Virtual cracks opened up in the plaster and cinder blocks, giving everything a dark vibe. Torches flickered on the walls. The EXIT sign, always lit, now glowed a deeper red at the end of the hall, pulsing slowly, like a burlesque vampire den.

Wherever they moved their phones, they could see the real world through the screen, layered with the gamespace as an alternate dimension of weeds and fog and iron gates and glowing hieroglyphs, augmenting the reality of Turner High with something new and extra.

Peter reached past his phone to a locker. They could see his hand on the screen, grabbing some stranger's locker and lifting the latch.

In real life, the locker stayed shut.

On the screen, it swung open. A small pile of Goldz was inside.

"Yep." Peter nodded in appreciation. "Now we're getting somewhere."

17 THE BREATH OF GOD

Beyond the creeping vines and smoldering torches, a whole overlay of runes and codes and glyphs, objects waiting to be unlocked, appeared through the school. It was medieval and futuristic at once, everything dusty and faintly neon.

Through their phones, the nameplate on the principal's office was no longer MRS. MORRISSEY, but her common nickname, DRAGON LADY. The swinging sign Charlie had smacked no longer said GO TIGERS! but FUCK TIGERS!

Peter had collected his Goldz from the locker. Three hundred in all.

No one had any Blaxx yet. No one even knew how to get them— or, more to the point, how to avoid them. Charlie thought about the sliding scale of Goldz—three hundred, eight hundred—what would that mean for Blaxx? Well, who cared—his lousy chess pieces didn't even move. Big deal.

"You should cash your Goldz in. That's a lot," Charlie said aloud, then wished he hadn't.

"How do you do that?"

"Click on the counter. Here, bring up the inventory. This is the bank, up here."

Peter read his phone. "We have choices. Gather round. 'The Sword of Pelicus.'"

"Interesting."

"'The Gate of Tannhäuser.'"

"Too many doves."

"And one more." Peter looked up, eyebrows raised. "'The Breath of God.'"

"Yes," Alex said.

"Yep," Kenny agreed. "It's called the God Game. You have to go with the Breath of God."

"To play devil's advocate for a second," Charlie said—and Vanhi interrupted with "No pun intended"—"swords and Tannhäuser Gate sound a little more exciting than 'breath.'"

Kenny shook his head. "You guys never read your Bible. The breath of God is more than *breath*. It means *spirit*. His *power*. To create or destroy."

"Which is it?" Charlie asked. "Creation or destruction?"

"Maybe that's up to us," Vanhi said.

"I'm convinced," Peter announced. Without taking a vote, he clicked on number 3 and purchased the Breath of God.

18 THE WRATH OF GOD

At first, nothing happened. They all watched on their phones, alone in the hallway, still a few hours from sunrise.

Then, a low, gentle noise rippled through their phones, starting with Charlie's. He was farthest back down the hall toward Morrissey's office. He swung his phone up, just in time to see the papers tacked to the bulletin board by her office flap in the wind in gamespace. In reality, everything remained still and quiet.

An indoor breeze, momentary. Then the papers fell still.

At the same time, Kenny's phone rustled as the breeze passed him, a low creaking noise like that of a rusty hinge as he looked up at the GO TIGERS! sign (FUCK TIGERS! in gamespace), which now rocked back and forth, then came to a stop.

The noise died for Kenny as Vanhi and Peter heard the wind pass and saw the dust bunnies and crumpled paper roll and slide down the hall, away from them, through their phones, as the breath of God moved past, invisible, as if they were outside not inside, a single mild breeze traveling down the hallway until it hit a dead end and, improbably, took a left turn.

One of the dust bunnies rolled to a stop at the far wall, the same place where Burklander had guided Charlie's hand on the sign-up sheet—one among many flapping sheets—that his friends had blessedly paid no attention to. The papers rustled, then fell still, just as oddly the dust bunny began moving again, to the left, carried by the breeze out of sight.

Then everything was still.

It occurred to them, as they stared at one another for a split second, that if they lost the breath of God, they might not find it again.

"Let's go!" Kenny said excitedly.

They took off down the hall, turned left at the corner, and saw the breeze in the distance—drifting detritus, flapping papers—disappear down the east stairwell.

In real life, the boiler room was unlabeled—lest pranksters and hook-uppers identify it as a good place to break in and cause mischief. But now it had a bold sign on the blank door, as if carved into the solid metal:

רוח אלוהים

"What does it mean?" Charlie asked.

"It looks like the letters on Darth Vader's chest plate," Alex said.

"It's Hebrew," Kenny answered. *"Ruach elohim."* He smiled triumphantly. "'The breath of God.'"

To the right of the door in real life was a little badge swiper, where the janitors and facilities crew could flash their IDs to tend to the heating and other climate needs of twenty-five hundred overcrowded students. But when Alex passed his phone over it, he saw something different: not just a blank of gray plastic to hold a badge against, but the digital image of a numeric keypad. The virtual numbers glowed red. All they needed was a code.

"What should we try?" Alex asked.

"Six six six?" Peter offered, smiling.

"Um, maybe let's not summon the beast just yet," Charlie answered.

"Right. Good call. It does say the breath of *God,* after all."

"Seventy-six? The score on Alex's last physics test?" Peter offered.

He was kidding, but Alex flinched.

Charlie wondered about that—the way Alex sometimes came to

school stepping a bit gingerly after a bad grade or behavioral incident. He never spoke about it. Never admitted anything when Charlie asked.

Kenny said, "I have an idea." He was still aiming his phone at the door, long after everyone else had stopped. Below the Hebrew words, another phrase had materialized, glowing like embers.

I WILL POUR OUT MY INDIGNATION ON YOU; I WILL
BLOW ON YOU WITH THE FIRE OF MY WRATH, AND
I WILL GIVE YOU INTO THE HAND OF BRUTAL MEN,
SKILLED IN DESTRUCTION.

"'Brutal men, skilled in destruction.' Sounds like Kurt Ellers," Vanhi said.

Charlie wondered, Did she already *know* about the standoff by the portables? Had he been hiding it for nothing? No one had mentioned it, aside from Vanhi fretting over his lip, but maybe that was out of courtesy for Alex. Maybe the gossip had spread far and wide.

"Maybe this time *we're* the brutal men," Peter responded. "Maybe we'll blow on Kurt with the fire of *our* wrath."

Did Peter know, too? The possibility thrilled Charlie—Peter would know Charlie was brave, and he didn't even have to be the one to tell him. That was even cooler.

"It's Ezekiel 21:31," Kenny said. "He was foretelling the destruction of the Ammonites for their vanity. They thought they'd be in power forever."

"No one ever thinks they'll lose their power," Peter said. "But they always do."

"Well, that answers the question of creative or destructive," Kenny said. "We're talking about the wrath of God here."

Charlie shook his head. "That's not set in stone. It's just a quote. *We* haven't decided anything. We don't even have to go through that door."

"But we know how, if we want to," Kenny said.

They all knew what he meant: Ezekiel 21:31. A four-digit code. An entry code. But no one said anything. No one touched the keypad.

The unspoken agreement seemed to be that it was Kenny's decision to make.

"Try it," Peter said. "Twenty-one thirty-one."

"How?" Kenny asked. "On the screen or in real life?"

"Real life. It's a real door," Vanhi said.

"But the buttons are only on the screen," Kenny answered.

He passed his hand between the real badge reader and his phone, letting his fingers hover just over the blank real-life plastic. On the screen of his phone, his hand appeared, and the numbers magically overlaying the swipe box disappeared behind his fingers, as if they were there in real life, printed right there on the box, and his hand were moving over them.

"Oh, no way, that's so meta," Kenny said.

The illusion was perfect, as if the numbers existed not just on their AR screens, but under his own flesh-and-blood fingers, right on the swipe box.

In that way, he was able to type on the plain gray square, watching his fingers hitting the imaginary numbers.

Two one three one.

There was a pause, then a click, in real life.

The boiler room door was open.

19 THE LITTLE MAN

They crept into the boiler room.

In the virtual version, the room looked more like the bowels of hell than the guts of a public high school. Just as the halls had grown macabre with vines and cracks, the furnace of the boiler room pulsed orange like a demon's eyes through the joints and seals of the heating pipes. The fire glowed like teeth through the grating.

They held their phones in front of them and watched the room through the tiny cameras, reanimated on their screens. Then they saw the little man in the shadows, smiling at them.

A deformed creature, he was perched atop a stool in the corner. In reality, there was only the stool. But on their screens, the little man was cross-legged atop it, one foot hanging limply down, mangled. In his hands, flat across his lap, was a small hammer-like tool.

His voice came through the speakers on their phones: "Greetings. What brings you here?"

"Oh, no way," Vanhi said.

He spoke with a spunky, funny-old-man voice, straight out of a vintage Saturday-morning cartoon, like the Crypt Keeper or Dungeon Master. He looked like a beautifully rendered video-game character, realistic but slightly comical, perfectly at ease in the center of the very real Vindicators. The way the little man's voice echoed from all their phones at once gave it a nice illusion of coming from within the room.

"This is wicked," Alex added.

"Talk to him," Kenny said, poking Peter. "You're the cool one."

"You're the Bible expert."

"I don't think this guy's from the Bible."

"I am Hephaestus," the little man offered, ignoring the way they were rudely talking about him as if he weren't right there.

"I am Kenny."

"Well done," Peter whispered.

"Hephaestus, what are you doing here?" Vanhi said loudly, as if she were talking to a child.

"I think he's virtual, not retarded," Alex whispered.

"I see you knew the code," Hephaestus said. "Two one three one. My number, however, is two two one two."

"Okay. Good to know," Vanhi said. They were having fun.

"I am the god of smiths," he chirped. "The Egyptians knew me as Ptah. To the Norse, I was Wayland the Smith. The Ugarit knew me as Kothar-wa-Khasis. And of course Hephaestus in Greece."

"I'll call you George," Peter said.

Ignoring him, the little man hopped off his chair and steadied himself with a walking stick he had leaned against the wall. He limped over to the furnace. Each time his cane clicked the ground the sound of tapping came through their speakers. The illusion was marvelous. He tapped the furnace. "Welcome to Mount Etna. Do wish to see the Breath of God?"

They answered yes.

"Hmm, just one problem." Hephaestus scratched his chin. "I already told you my number. I think I'll need something else, instead. Yes. I think so. What could it be?"

He seemed to think it over, and the lame little blacksmith was almost cute, despite his deformities. Then he grinned ear to ear, as if an idea had just occurred to him, and the smile was bright and chipper, with a slightly sinister undercurrent.

"I know!" he said cheerfully. "How about a sacrifice?"

20 THE FIRE OF GOD

"A blood sacrifice," the funny little imp said. "That's the best kind."

Peter raised his eyebrows.

"Can someone tell Evil Yoda here to tone it down a little?" Vanhi whispered.

Charlie elbowed her. "C'mon, play along a little."

"Yeah, don't insult the guy," Kenny added.

Peter approached the figure. "What do we get in return, exactly?"

The small god told them.

"Who is the youngest?" Hephaestus asked. "The gods love young blood."

"That would be Kenny," Peter answered.

"Thanks, friend," Kenny shot back.

Peter shrugged. "It's true."

"Kenny, is it?" the little god asked, and just hearing it speak one of their names sent a little thrill through the room. The Game was seamless.

"Yes, Kenny," he answered, smiling a little self-consciously, realizing that he was talking to an animated character who existed only on their phones. Yet he blended into the room around them, as Kenny's eyes had adjusted in a new way—all their eyes had—the way you forget after a few minutes that you're wearing 3-D glasses or flipping between two halves of bifocals. Going between the real world and the augmented one on their phones become a sort of second nature, or more accurately a second sight.

"Well, Kenny, if you want the power of a god, you must please the gods. A *thusia* is called for."

Kenny shook his head. Among the Vindicators, he alone knew what *thusia* meant. It was ancient Greek, straight out of Bible study. It came from *thuo,* "to sacrifice, slaughter, kill, to offer part of a meal to the gods." It meant "victim." Kenny didn't believe all that nonsense about dying in the Game meaning death in real life, but no way was he ready for his friends to keep playing the Game without him. It was too early to lose.

"I am not your *thusia,*" Kenny snapped.

The little god smiled. His teeth were as misshapen as his curled foot and lopsided face. He hobbled over to Kenny and sized him up and down.

"A handsome boy. A proud boy. The gods will find you most delicious."

"Eww," Vanhi said. "Nobody would find Kenny delicious."

"That's just rude," Kenny said.

"It's that," Hephaestus said. "Or you can all lose."

Kenny studied the odd figure in front of him, cartoonish and flamboyant like a computer game, but hyperreal in his grotesque form.

"Come on, guys. We just started playing. You're not going to sell me out just like that?"

"We all have to go sometime," Peter said.

"It's just a game," Alex added.

"What about die in the game, die in real life?"

"It's *probably* not true," Peter teased.

"There has to be another way," Charlie said. "What about a goat?"

"That's right," Kenny chimed in. "You're a Greek god, right? The ancient Greeks sacrificed animals, not people."

Hephaestus smiled. "You are an animal to me."

"Oh, just take one for the team," Peter said to Kenny. "It's not like little George here is *really* going to kill you." Peter walked toward the little man and jutted his arm forward, to show that it went right through him.

But it didn't, because Hephaestus ducked right in time and harrumphed and straightened his hair and shawl indignantly.

"No one needs to die," Hephaestus said theatrically. "Just a drop of blood will do. One drop. That's not so much, is it? One drop of blood, for the power I have offered to bestow upon you? The Fire of God!"

"Fine." Kenny stuck his finger forward, in front of the virtual god. "One drop. Go ahead." He didn't seem concerned, given that a hallucination could hardly draw blood.

Hephaestus nodded, pleased.

He hobbled across the boiler room to a section of piping that fed into a humming unit. On the flat surface were a pair of worker's gloves, some silvery strips of cut tubing, and a small box of razor blades left behind by the workmen. When Kenny saw the open box, the dull razors stacked haphazardly inside, his smile dropped.

Hephaestus said happily, "Just one drop will do."

"No effin' way." Kenny looked at the rest of the Vindicators.

No one spoke.

The mood in the room suddenly lurched, from fun to uneasy. Surely the Game wasn't asking Kenny to actually cut himself?

"You can't be serious?" Kenny said.

The figure just waited, tapping his good foot.

"I think he is," Peter answered.

"He? It? It's a freaking game. I'm not cutting myself."

"Of course you're not," Charlie said.

"Well, then I guess your time in the God Game is over," Hephaestus said pleasantly to them all.

"It's just a little cut," Alex said. "I mean, one drop. That's like a pinprick."

"You do it."

"Fine. I will." Alex went for the razors.

But Charlie reached and stopped him. "No. No way." This was the Alex he feared. The nihilist who acted as if cutting himself were no big deal, as if he'd felt much worse.

Hephaestus shook his head. "It must be the youngest."

"The god has spoken," Alex said.

"I play the *cello*. I can't cut my finger."

"Cut the left hand," Alex said.

"The left hand *is* the one you play with."

"Then the right!" Alex said brightly.

"I'm not doing this."

"No one is cutting themselves." Charlie stepped in. "I can't believe we're even considering this."

"How do we know you can even give us what you promised?" Peter asked the god.

"Peter." Charlie stepped toward him, slightly aggressive. "We're not doing this."

Peter seemed unconcerned.

"Oh, I can give you what I claim," Hephaestus told them. "And so much more. And I know just who you want to use this power on. I have foreseen it. It will be a splendid victory. A most just distribution of the fury of the gods. But the time has come. You must decide. Do you want it? Will you do what it takes to get it? I will wait no longer."

With that, Hephaestus turned his back and began hobbling away, his little cane clicking as he shuffled toward the shadows of the far corner of the dark room.

Everyone looked at Kenny. It was all on him.

"I'll do it," Kenny said, surprising them all.

"No," Charlie said. Drawing blood was too far. Even a stupid pin-prick. "We're your friends." Charlie glared at the rest of the group. "We're not going to pressure you into this."

"No one's pressuring me. I want to do it. We've been beating around the bush all day. We all know what Kurt did to Alex. I hate that guy. We could never get him back on the street. But we can do this."

"We don't even know if this . . . thing . . . is telling the truth."

"I'd spill one drop of blood to find out. Wouldn't you? For Alex?"

"He already has," Alex said. "Kurt took more than a drop of blood from you," he said to Charlie. "You did that for me. Why is this any different?"

Charlie wanted to say, *Because I don't care about me.* Instead, he shrugged. He was tired of playing nanny. "It's Kenny's choice."

"Then it's done," Kenny said. "One drop."

Kenny was a scholar, but his guilty pleasure was video games. And not just any video games. He loved the old games. The vintage adventure games. *Zac McKraken, Maniac Mansion, Monkey Island*. The puzzles were silly, the graphics terrible, yet they swept him away—away from the jocks, the jerks, the racists who looked down on him, the black kids who chided him for being too white, whatever that meant. He didn't fit in anywhere, except with the Vindicators. And now he could move the game forward. For them.

Was it twisted to prick his own finger with the barest edge of a razor blade just to see what a virtual Greek god did next? Tim Fletcher and Kurt Ellers kept themselves entertained by slamming their heads into concussions. This was a small price to pay for a little adventure.

Kenny plucked out a razor blade gingerly and noted with relief it wasn't particularly old or rusty. He could wash the pinprick with alcohol later. He'd had a tetanus shot.

So whatever.

Before he could think twice, noting the eyes of all the Vindicators were wide, he jabbed down into his fingertip and right back up and let out a yelp.

"Fuck shit," he blurted, this from a guy who was so tightly wound he'd barely managed to say "piss off" earlier.

It cut deeper than he meant to. He held his finger up in the dim light and saw the ruby bulbs beading up and running down the side of his hand.

"Yum," Hephaestus said.

21 BLOOD CODE

In gamespace it was a raging coal-fire furnace, belching smoke.

Hephaestus motioned Kenny's hand down to his mouth and swung a finger across the drop of blood, bringing it to his lips. "Yes," Hephaestus said, gumming his lips. "That will do nicely."

Charlie sighed. It was grotesque, but it was done. Now they could move on to the prize.

Kenny seemed to feel the same way. The tension in his shoulders melted. He was nursing his finger, which was still bleeding more than he'd intended.

"No sense in wasting," Hephaestus said.

Seriously, Charlie thought, *we have to watch the little ghoul drink more blood?*

But Hephaestus had another idea.

He tapped his cane on the broad surface of the roaring heater. "I need you to write something for me." He pointed at the beading blood on Kenny's fingertip. "With that."

"Rad," Alex said. "This is like Friends of the Crypt–level stuff."

That wasn't exactly a template for success, Charlie thought. According to legend, half of those guys got arrested, and the leader lost his free ride to Princeton and jumped off the roof of the school.

"You promised," Charlie said to Hephaestus. "One drop. That's what you said."

"I lied?" Hephaestus answered.

"Give us the Breath of God," Kenny snapped at him.

"Suit yourselves." Hephaestus began to limp away.

"You little bastard," Vanhi said.

"No blood note, no prize." He crossed his arms like a petulant child.

"What's the message?" Peter asked.

Hephaestus told them.

"I won't do it," Kenny said. He was religious after all, or at least he came from a religious family. What would his parents think? This felt wrong. Deeply, morbidly wrong.

He looked at Peter, who shrugged, as if to say, *Why not? It's just a game.*

Kenny looked at Vanhi, who believed in the Holy Trinity of code, hair dye, and slap bass. She seemed unconcerned, as if there were no difference between the finger prick and this.

He didn't even bother to look at Alex. Kenny had already seen the hungry look in Alex's eyes. Whatever this was, he wanted more.

Finally, everyone looked at Charlie.

Charlie sighed. Screw it. Someone else could be the voice of reason for once. "Why not? We've come this far."

Kenny nodded, but Charlie could see the disappointment in his eyes. "Fine. For Alex." Kenny knelt in front of the boiler and began drawing with his finger.

There wasn't enough blood. Kenny closed his eyes and drew a long breath. "In for a penny, in for a pound."

He went to the old razors and gritted his teeth. Second finger, bow hand.

Hephaestus watched, the corner of his crooked mouth twisted up into a smile. Then he walked away, disappearing into the shadows beneath the pipes and tubes.

"Hey!" Kenny shouted. "You promised."

But before he could complain further, a creaking noise announced the opening of the fire gate, virtual smoke gushing out. They gathered around the furnace, which glowed a reddish orange, and the flames spoke to them.

What they whispered was a code, a series of instructions, commands and prompts and incantations basically—for at the end of the day, what was the difference between a hack and a spell? Both were a precise flow of words in a secret language known only to the initiated, to manipulate a reality that was inviolate only to those content to accept it as such. The Game gave them exactly what Hephaestus had promised: a tool that they could use in second period, when Kurt was in sight, to bring an invisible revenge down on him.

Just hearing the words and knowing what was to come, the Vindicators felt powerful, enriched.

Charlie's phone buzzed.

There was a new text from God. But this time it was only for him.

22 LEVIATHAN

They could barely wait for second period.

They came out from the basement as the sun came up, unkempt and bleary from their all-nighter, and tried to stay awake through first period. Charlie kept looking at the strange new message from God:

> Come to 8710 S. Wayland
> Alone—Don't tell or it goes away.
> Social Control—You earned it.

Don't tell or it goes away.

Why was the Game trying to separate him from his friends?

He googled the address. Just a strip mall. Nothing more.

The bell rang, and they filed into Earth Science—except Vanhi, who had art—exchanging nervous, eager glances.

When Kurt Ellers strode in, taking his seat next to Caitlyn Lacey and putting a proprietary hand on her ass without looking across the aisle of desks, they smiled.

Maybe Peter smiled a little more, because he could imagine Caitlyn being happy to hook up with him in the seclusion of the fields off Meadow Drive, yet just as happy to look at him as if he were crazy when he asked her to homecoming. Caitlyn was the mirror image of

Mary: just as popular, but mean where Mary was kind, cruel where Mary was curious and open, if trapped.

"Okay," Peter said quietly. "Here we go."

"Remember the plan," Charlie said.

"Yep."

Class started, and Mrs. Harlingen was talking about the volcanic forces that arose from the deep earth beneath the ocean and boiled out into the sea. It reminded Kenny of something dark and primordial, like the Leviathan, that ancient sea monster from the Bible. Like the power they were about to unleash.

She clicked through PowerPoint slides on the big screen above them:

Hydrothermal vents.

Black smokers.

Giant tube worms and limpets—sea snails with toothed tongues.

Hot fires and creatures of the deep!

Kenny whispered, "'Can you pull in Leviathan with a fishhook or tie down its tongue with a rope?'"

Peter began to type in the code for the Breath of God on his phone, subtly, below his desk, something every teenager on earth was now adept at.

Kurt Ellers must have been thumbing something out, too, and seconds later Caitlyn Lacey glanced at her phone and snickered cruelly.

Charlie recalled with pride smashing Kurt's last phone, before he could broadcast to the world the image of Alex with his pants down, crying, snot running down his face.

Kurt slid his phone back into his pocket.

Peter kept typing, his eyes flicking up and down subtly.

"'Can you fill its hide with harpoons or its head with fishing spears?'" Kenny recited under his breath.

Peter followed the instructions carefully, line by line, just as the fire had shown them:

$x = getPosX()$

$y = getPosY()$

It would start soon, and it wouldn't take long.

"'Who dares open the doors of its mouth, ringed about with fearsome teeth?'"

size = getOldSize() + 1

"'Its snorting throws out flashes of light; its eyes are like the rays of dawn.'"

def transmit(z):

"'Its breath sets coals ablaze, and flames dart from its mouth.'"

sendLocation(x, y, z, size)

Peter sent the instructions, one by one.

Now all they had to do was wait for the moment to execute.

His finger hovered over the button.

One more time, Kenny quoted the book of Job: "'It looks down on all that are haughty; it is king over all that are proud.'"

That's when Kurt Ellers noticed something warm in his pocket, near his crotch. It wasn't unpleasant, just odd. How could he know what the infinite looping signal would do?

Then it happened so quickly. The lithium-ion battery in Ellers's phone created a thermal runway, an expanding gas that led to incredible pressure within a tiny metal space.

They had vowed that they would only do it when the phone was in Ellers's hand or on the desk. It would scare him, maybe. If the timing was right, he might yelp in front of the entire class. Either way, it would cost him another $700, his third phone in two days. That was some justice. He deserved worse, but they weren't going to sink to his level.

But the phone wasn't on the desk. It was in his pocket.

The chemical reaction was fast and violent. It caught Kurt Ellers's pants on fire. He leaped out of his chair, and everyone spun to watch him hop around madly, then hit the floor, yowling and rolling back and forth to put out the flames. The students around him gaped. People kicked their desks backward. Some screamed. A couple took out their phones and filmed.

Mrs. Harlingen grabbed a fire extinguisher from the wall and ran over to Ellers, but the small flames were already out. Not realizing this, she doused him with white foam.

He stood up.

A strange calm came over the room.

He looked around with his mean-spirited eyes.

He was hurt, but not badly. It could have been so much worse. A singed hole was in his pants, revealing half his thigh and the charred edge of his spotted boxers. The skin was red but not open. He winced with pain for a moment, then willed it away. But the shame rose through him, his cheeks turning red.

People laughed. Not everyone. Not even most of them. But enough, seeing him standing there, covered in foam, his pant leg seared open. Maybe remembering among them the various cruelties he had bestowed, not just to Alex but dozens of others along the way. Slamming them into lockers. Calling them fags and losers. All the way back to elementary school.

They laughed, some nervously, some not, until Mrs. Harlingen flashed a look so severe the room went quiet, and she nursed him to the door, which was a somewhat comic sight, this giant lineman limping with an arm around little Ms. Harlingen, she of the ugly sweaters and eighties hair.

She helped him to the door as if he were the gentlest student on campus, and with a last judgmental look that said, *No one move,* she helped him to the nurse's office.

23 TOO FAR

The Vindicators gathered by the table and whispered in hushed tones.

"Holy shit!" Peter said. "Did you see that?"

"He didn't know what hit him," Alex said, his smile beaming.

"That wasn't the plan." Vanhi looked furious. She poked Peter in the chest. "You were supposed to do it on his desk. Not in his pocket."

"I never pressed Send. That wasn't me."

"Yeah, right."

"Believe what you want. I'm telling the truth. I wanted to punish the guy. Not burn him alive."

"You swear?" Charlie asked Peter, trying to read him.

"*Et tu, Brute?* I didn't fucking burn him on purpose. I'm not a psycho."

"I think he deserved it," Alex said. "It should have been worse."

Everyone stared at Alex for a disturbing second.

"Don't say that," Vanhi told him.

"Maybe the Game did it," Peter said. "It has a mind of its own."

They split up for third period, and Vanhi pulled Charlie aside. "Do you believe him?"

"Peter? Sure. He's trouble, but he doesn't lie about it."

"How would you know?"

"I'm more worried about you," Charlie said. "You should quit before this gets out of hand. Remember what happened to the Friends of the Crypt. Don't lose Harvard over this."

Vanhi felt the shame rush through her. She'd lied to her parents. She'd lied to Charlie. She had as little to lose as he did.

"Did you start *your* Harvard app yet?" she shot back.

"No."

"Then quit telling me what to do."

When he was gone, Vanhi checked her phone, which had buzzed in her pocket. The text was anonymous:

I know your secret.

24 IT KNOWS

Vanhi felt her stomach jump into her throat.

She only had one secret. She hadn't told a soul. She'd just hacked her report card, gotten her parents' signature, then hacked it back.

She typed:

What secret?

She didn't have to wait. The message appeared, showing her forged report card. The fudged grade changed back and forth from a D to an A, warping like a Möbius strip. The commentary came next, short and to the point:

Cheater.

Vanhi cursed under her breath. She wrote back:

Who is this?

There was no answer.

But she knew. The bad grade was over a year ago. So why was the threat coming now? It was the Game. It had to be. Why had she said yes to playing? Why hadn't she listened when Charlie urged her not to play? She'd never give him the satisfaction of saying he was right. It was her choice. Fuck it. It was on her, right or wrong. She'd fix it, too, just like she fixed her lousy grade. She could out-tech this lousy game.

Vanhi tried to trace back the number, but it was masked and anonymized, rerouted a dozen times over. There was no end to it. She'd never seen anything like it.

She was about to write again when it beat her to it.

> Relax. I just need a favor.

Charlie cut out at lunch and went to 8710 South Wayland.

He had to know.

> Come to 8710 S. Wayland
> Alone—Don't tell or it goes away.
> Social Control—You earned it.

He had run into Mary in the hall, and she stopped him, looking angry. She'd already heard what happened to Kurt Ellers. She was still wearing that damn bracelet. Maybe Vanhi was right. She'd never choose Charlie. Even though she seemed to like him, he still didn't have a chance. *Social control, my ass,* Charlie thought—*I don't control shit.*

"What did you guys do?"

"What are you talking about?"

"Kurt. He picks on your friend, and then his phone just blows up the next day?"

"He didn't 'pick on' our friend. He tortured him."

"I agree. But you could've really hurt him."

He almost said, *That wasn't the plan!*—but that would have been an admission.

"We didn't do it," Charlie mumbled.

She studied his face. "Okay."

He couldn't tell if she believed him or not.

She left him there and walked out into the parking lot by herself, heading toward her car, until Tim stepped out from beside it and intercepted her. They seemed to have words, then he put a hand on the small of her back, guiding her two spots over and up the step into his giant, oversize I Am a Douchebag Truck. He closed the door for her, and it sounded hard.

Fuming, Charlie went to his shitty old car, prayed for it to start, and when it did, he went straight to fucking where the Game had told him. *Let's just see what I earned,* he thought.

25 DROP BOX

Relax. I just need a favor.

Vanhi went to the house, as instructed. She couldn't believe she was following the commands of an anonymous host that might just be a malicious algorithm. Her parents had sacrificed everything for her, leaving their friends and family and moving halfway around the world so she could grow up in the land of opportunity. The thought of some game blowing that now was unbearable.

So she followed the directions the Game sent to her map and wound to a house on Tremont Street, in a suburban area in another school district. She had no idea who lived there.

Just as she wondered what to do next, her phone said:

Knock on the door

She looked both ways to see if she was being followed. The neighborhood was quiet. Not a soul on the street. Blinds were drawn. Dogs barked behind fences. She went to the front door and knocked.

No answer.

The Game texted:

Go around back.

Vanhi had the distinct feeling she was being toyed with. She looked around again. No one was watching her. She went to the side gate and closed her eyes. Was she really going to do this? *I know your secret.* Yes, she was.

She lifted the handle, but the gate was locked from the inside. She peeked through the gap in the fence and saw the padlock hanging. "Shit."

Looking around one last time, she slipped around the side of the yard, where horizontal slats ran along the outside of the fence. She put her foot on one and climbed up. It was an eight-foot privacy fence, and she had to jump down because the inside was smooth. She took a breath and leaped. It was farther than it looked and she landed hard on one leg and had to stumble to break the impact. As she stood up and dusted herself off, a dog came bounding at her.

She fell backward but it just leaped and licked her face until she started laughing and pet its ears. "Okay. Okay, fella. We're friends. Thank you for not mauling me."

He rolled over and showed his belly for her to pet.

Vanhi looked at her phone. There was a new text:

Pick it up.

She didn't have to ask what.

Sitting in the middle of the patio, standing out like a sore thumb, was a cardboard box, wrapped a dozen times over with packing tape.

Something hissed, and she looked at the window of the house, where a cat stared back at her, not nearly as friendly as the dog, eyes yellow.

A cell phone rang in the school newspaper's office. It belonged to Eddie Ramirez, the editor in chief. Or, as he liked to call himself, the EIC.

Kenny was there for their lunchtime staff meeting. He kept stealing glances at Candace Reed, his lovely coassistant editor. Eddie had edged them both out for EIC. Kenny kept telling himself that at least that meant he and Candace had something in common, but Candace was far more intrigued by Eddie's victory than Kenny's loserdom.

He wanted to get back to the Game. How could a school paper compete with animated gods moving through realspace?

That changed when the phone rang and Eddie Ramirez's eyes lit up. "Uh-huh. . . . Yeah. . . . Sure. . .*.* Okay."

He looked at them. "Hot tip."

Kenny glanced at Candace and rolled his eyes. Eddie was always looking for some major scoop to turn the *Tiger Claw* from a puff-piece machine on football wins to a launching pad for his journalism career. And he didn't care whom he stepped on in the process.

"Forget everything we were just talking about," Eddie said.

"How could we forget about sloppy joes on Friday?" Candace said sarcastically.

"I just got a lead."

"New story?" Kenny asked.

"Yeah. And not some bullshit homecoming piece either." Eddie leaned in. "Satanic graffiti on school property."

Kenny did a double take. His hand was in his lap, Band-Aids on two fingers. He was reminded just now how much they hurt. It was under the table, out of view.

"Really?" Candace's last story was "Whiz Quiz Team Takes Westbrook."

"What do you mean *satanic*?" Kenny asked, trying to sound casual.

"They didn't say."

"Where?" Kenny asked.

"Boiler room, in the basement."

Kenny tried to keep his face neutral. "Who called?"

"I don't know. Anonymous tip."

"What did they sound like?"

Eddie shrugged, annoyed. "Who cares?"

"Man, woman, old, young?"

"Man. Young. Bland. Whatever. Are you kind of missing the headline? 'Satanic Graffiti on School Campus.' This could actually get us real attention. Right in time for college apps."

Kenny's mind was racing. Who called it in? Why? The Vindicators had done what the Game wanted. Why was someone using it against them?

He had to think fast. "What if it's a hoax?"

"Why would someone call in a hoax?"

"To embarrass us. To cause a stir. Fake news."

"That's why we investigate. That's what we do." Eddie was always so pompous.

"Yeah," Candace said. "Why wouldn't we just check it out?"

Eddie looked at Kenny carefully. "Why are you so against this?"

"I'm not. Just trying to be objective."

That was a magic word in journalism. It could usually win an argument.

"Right," Eddie said. "Fair enough. Candace and I will cover it."

"No," Kenny scrambled. It was better to stick with them. "I'll go, too."

"We don't need three people on it."

"You can have the byline, don't worry."

That seemed to satisfy Eddie.

Kenny warned himself to stay calm. Already his parents' faces were flashing in his mind, fingers pointing, judgmental stares. *It was just a joke!* he'd say. *A game! I'm not really a devil worshipper, honest!* They would stare at him and say, *You got suspended and lost Columbia for a game?* It would almost be better if he were a bona fide devil worshipper. At least then he'd have convictions.

"The boiler room's locked," Candace said. "We'll have to get in."

"Leave that to me." Eddie was almost salivating. "This could be our Friends of the Crypt." His eyes were hungry. "That's what the caller said. 'This is just like that horrible Friends of the Crypt.'"

"That was like twenty years ago," Kenny said.

"Satan's back on campus, baby," Eddie said. "That was *national* news."

"Didn't one of them die?" Candace asked.

"Yup." Eddie made a whistling noise. He used his fingers to do a swan dive off an imaginary school.

"We link the stories," Candace said. "Backwards records, black magic, teens in peril. This kind of stuff sells."

"Then again," Eddie said generously, "Kenny could be right. Could be a prank." Eddie snapped his fingers theatrically. "Oh, except for one thing I forgot to mention."

Eddie leaned in conspiratorially, but Kenny already knew what was coming.

"On the phone, the guy said it looks like it's written in blood."

Alex was mesmerized.

Fantasy had always given him a way out. From the bullies. From the belt at home. But this was beyond tabletop dice games. It was even beyond the websites he liked to visit. The ones he didn't talk about, that let him explore his darker curiosities.

This was something new. The real world and the augmented one fused.

He skipped two periods and went deeper into the game.

He found the Temple in the hidden space on the third floor of the school, but he couldn't get in. He kept exploring throughout the day, just walking with his head down in his phone, which would look crazy except that's how everyone walked. Nobody had to know he was looking *through* it, at a whole other world.

He was further along than all his friends in the Game. He was good at this. It kept telling him that. He was a natural.

He just wished he didn't have the phone between him and the gameworld. It was distracting. But that's what he was about to fix.

He was alone in the hall, everyone else in class.

But on his phone the hallway was a dense souk, with stalls where various avatars were hawking goods.

To the dark-eyed man in the shadows of a stall, he typed:

> How much?
>   50,000 Goldz.
> I don't have it.

The character didn't answer. He just stood there, breathing slowly, waiting for input. Alex was nervous, but excited. He typed a question:

> What do I have to do?

Charlie drove slowly through the declining neighborhood. It wasn't rough, just old. And empty. The strip mall was fairly abandoned in the middle of the day. The stores were open but quiet. There was no foot traffic. He watched the addresses tick down.

8716.

8714.

8712.

As he came to 8710, he stopped.

Charlie parked his car and got out.

It was a local branch office of a bank. The sign on the door said it closed at noon. An ATM was in the wall outside.

Charlie looked all around him.

No one.

He glanced at the ATM.

Just a normal welcome screen.

He almost got back in his car and drove away. But then he was curious to see what the ATM might look like through his phone.

Nothing. It looked exactly the same as in real life.

He looked over his shoulders again, but still no one was there, much less watching him.

On a lark, he swung his phone around the view about him.

A man was standing in the distance watching him. He lowered his phone, and no one was there. He raised it again, and the figure was in the same place, across the street.

His face looked like a shiny white mask, almost porcelain.

Charlie felt a shiver run through him.

He swung the phone around in the other direction.

No one else.

No. Wait. He swept back a little. At the far end of the strip mall, where it dead-ended and turned left, was another man, partially behind a column. His face was also blank and smooth. A thin line of a mouth. Neutral.

When Charlie locked eyes, the figure stared back.

Charlie swung back to the first man, but he was gone.

The ATM lit up.

Not on his phone, but in real life.

Buttons started flashing on the screen automatically.

Then money started spitting out of the machine. Twenties. Too many to stay in the little plastic mouth, so they started pushing out onto the pavement. The day was windless. They fluttered onto the sidewalk around him.

It was time to go. He knew that. The last thing he should do was pick up one of the bills. Picking one up might lead to taking one. Taking one might lead to taking more.

He thought of his mind-numbing job at the copy shop. The one he started when the deductibles and co-pays broke his family. He thought of his dad's insane new loan. Tim's shiny new truck and Kurt Ellers's new new phone.

Charlie looked in both directions and grabbed a handful of twenties off the ground. They stuffed nicely into his pockets. He grabbed some more, then scooped up all of them, wondering how many thousands of dollars he had just acquired.

He was ready to get the fuck out of there when the screen changed, and the old-fashioned ATM showed him a crude picture, a jerky circle, in green font on black.

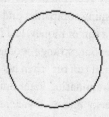

Below that, it said:

One Ring to Rule them all

Charlie knew exactly what it meant.
God help me, he thought, *I'm starting to understand this game.*

26 THE EYE OF GOD

Peter thought about power.

His dad had never had power. He was a fly-by-night salesman who put himself through law school by going part-time over five years. The law school was barely accredited. The white-shoe firms wouldn't touch him. So he started suing companies and shaking them down. He was good at it. He made a ton of money, lost it all, then made it again.

Peter's mom was a devout, strange woman who always thought she deserved better. She had run off when his dad was still a salesman with his dad's manager, humiliating Peter and his father.

Peter was a fat kid, geeky and awkward, something he never told anyone. This was in Arizona, and he was teased mercilessly, coming home with bloody noses and scraped palms from where the kids knocked him onto the ground. He could still remember the taste and feel of gravel in his mouth. When his mom left, marking both Peter and his dad as losers, his dad had decided they would reinvent themselves. Peter's dad enrolled in his shitty law school for the night program. He told Peter to lose twenty pounds by his tenth birthday or he'd sell all Peter's things. He put a mirror up on Peter's wall with a sign that said FAT. Peter's dad had come to see their issues as a symptom of the same problem: the world was cruel, and you could reach inside and rip the loser out, or you could drown. Better to learn that early.

By the time they moved to Texas, Peter was lean and his dad was rich. Girls found Peter mysterious and charming. His dad invented a new background for their new life: a dead wife and an always-thin son and an always-rich life.

It was exhausting, making everyone think you didn't care.

Even today, Peter knew how to cut his food in half and stir it around on the plate so no one would notice.

People thought he chose not to fit in, but the truth was, he never did.

Even Caitlyn, Mary Clark's dark double, found Peter intriguing. That's why she hooked up with him in private, while dating Kurt Ellers in public.

But what Peter saw now cut him more than he'd ever let on.

He was on the Embankment, skipping lunch to explore the Game.

Charlie was supposed to meet him, but he'd run off in a huff somewhere, driving off campus. Peter knew that Charlie and Vanhi didn't believe him about not blowing up Kurt's phone in his pocket. But how could he blame them for being suspicious when his whole life was a lie? True, he hadn't concocted that particular lie, but he'd lived it so long he didn't know how else to be.

He clicked on his inventory.

With all his Goldz, he'd bought something called the Eye of God. It was just the intro version, texts only, but still, having the power to read anyone's texts sounded like fun. But now, reading the messages he intercepted with it, he wasn't so sure.

Earlier that day, Caitlyn had asked to meet him in an empty, darkened classroom. She'd pushed him back against a table and slipped a hand under his shirt. If Mary was sunshine and roses, Caitlyn was arsenic and quince. Peter loved how tough she was, how she always went for exactly what she wanted, even if that meant two-timing Kurt and keeping Peter hidden, which burned. What he didn't know was that Caitlyn had learned how to navigate the world early, going to Home Depot when she was twelve to buy a lock and install it on her bedroom door. Sometimes the bad guys lived inside the house.

"Do you like this?" she whispered now, biting his ear.

He pushed her gently back. Always aloof. Always above it all.

He shrugged and smiled slightly.

An act. But a good one.

"You want to have sex at school?" he asked.

"Come on, it'll be fun."

"I'm tired."

"I'll change your mind." She put a hand on his belt.

He was tired of being used. He stopped her. "I came by your house yesterday. You weren't there. Were you with him?"

The truth was, she'd been at Careloft, something she did once a week without telling anyone. Being a do-gooder was Mary's thing. She had a lock on it. If anyone knew where Caitlyn went every Tuesday, they'd think she was just copying her socially superior friend. But she'd been volunteering there for years, learning how to talk to survivors, and it made her feel whole. But it was terribly off-brand because she was the bitchy one, everyone knew it and fell into line around her, and you could lose your place in a second. You could disappear. So she said, "Yeah, I was with him. So what?"

Peter shook his head, then let it pass. He would take what he could get. He stroked her cheek.

But then it was her turn to interrupt. "What you did today, it can't happen again."

"What?" He smiled. He loved that she knew.

"Not if you ever want to see me again."

"You're worried I hurt your boyfriend?"

"I'm worried you're blowing our cover."

"What's so wrong with that?"

"Oh, Peter," she whispered, kissing his neck. Someone passed by outside and they froze. But the door stayed shut. The footsteps moved on. She put her lips on his ear. "Wouldn't a hacker, of all people, know some things are better in the dark?"

He thought of that now, watching Mary and Caitlyn type in real time, first Mary, then Caitlyn:

he's really nice
    So is mother theresa but i wouldn't fuck her
I really like him.

So do it
I'm scared. What will he do?
  Who T?
Nevermind. What about you?
  Peter?
Yes
  Whatver
Thought you liked him
  He's fun on the side but K is popular
So?
  Bad for me if K goes off the rez now—Ive managed this far

Peter reread the conversation. Then again. And again. It bore deeper into him, each time. Caitlyn told him they were cheating because it was more fun. In truth, she was cheating because Peter was a loser. Just like his dad—all the cash in the world, but the old money would never let him in. A McMansion in the boondocks, the King of Nothing.

He would never let anyone know how bad that hurt. It was the lesson he'd learned a long time ago. The Fat Boy becomes the mysterious stranger. Never let them close, and they won't see the Fat Boy still inside.

Still, the last line intrigued him. What did it mean?

He would have to find out.

Mary sat in the psychiatrist's office.

She was perfect, so these appointments didn't exist, according to her mother.

In fact her mother had forbidden her going when Mary asked, so she found someone whom she paid out of pocket, using money she earned from a job in an office she didn't tell anyone about, because that was humiliating, too. Clark women didn't work because they didn't have to.

Dr. Rocardi had a small office with frame-to-frame diplomas and knickknacks from around the world: cats with one paw raised in a hello wave, smiling totems. She scooted forward in her rolling chair while Mary sat perfectly upright on an upholstered couch with too many zen pillows.

"Today was his birthday," Dr. Rocardi said, in that way she had that was never a question or a statement, but somewhere in between.

"It was."

"How old would he have been?"

"Twenty."

"How are you doing?"

"Okay." Mary tried to keep her voice calm and even. It wasn't, though. It sounded tight and thin. She wondered if Dr. Rocardi could tell.

"How are you doing on the venlafaxine?"

"I don't like it. It makes me feel funny."

"In what way?"

"Wired, a little. Nervous."

"It can do that. Is it helping your mood?"

"No," Mary said, trying to be honest but not sorry for herself. "I feel pretty sad."

"The same as before?"

She nodded. "Maybe worse, just because of . . . the time of year. But mostly the same."

Dr. Rocardi leaned in. "Tell me why. Is there something more?"

So there it was. Mary was amazed how Dr. Rocardi always seemed to know when Mary was holding back. That's what her family did— hold back. Everyone suffered, and no one probed. You could live in that deadlock forever. Not the shrink. She was good at her job. She looked under the rock.

Mary thought about her brother. Golden child, school hero, captain of the football team, ROTC. He was Tim before Tim was Tim. But where Tim was thin souled and mean, Brian had been magnanimous and kind. His popularity was a burden he wore with grace.

But Brian was gone, and Tim was the closest thing left. And Tim *knew*. He knew what Dr. Rocardi wanted to know. What was under the rock.

Dr. Rocardi waited for Mary to say something. Time stretched until it might pop.

She *wanted* to say something.

"No," she said finally to Dr. Rocardi.

Dr. Rocardi nodded. Her chair rolled slightly back. "I'm going to taper you off the venlafaxine. You can't stop it right away. But we can cross-taper to something new that might work."

"Okay." Mary felt like she wanted to cry and refused to.

So she would cry later, at school, in the bathroom on her way to fifth period, just before Tim intercepted her. From practice, she knew exactly which bathrooms were the best ones to cry in alone, out of sight, when you literally, despite all efforts, couldn't help it.

27 WARLOCK

Charlie marched triumphantly into Neiman Marcus. It felt like another universe from the worn-down strip mall.

He looked for the same woman who had raised her eyebrows skeptically at him yesterday. But she wasn't there, and a much nicer lady in an indigo scarf was happy to sell him the bracelet for $900. He didn't get the glory of showing the nasty lady how wrong she was about him, but he knew he had just purchased a near-exact copy of the bracelet Mary Clark now wore around her perfect wrist. Same rose gold. Same delicate clasp. He knew it seemed weird on some level to get her the same bracelet she already had, but he knew why he was doing it. Why the Game had suggested it. He couldn't wait to see her.

Charlie pulled out his phone to text her.

I need to see you.

She wrote back fairly quickly:

Not now. Tim's here.

Charlie grimaced. But it didn't feel as if he were a mistress on the side. Her message felt scared to him: *Careful. He's watching.*

It was hard to tell for sure. Without human tone, you could read a text a dozen ways. Was she typing from bed, robe open? Or from the closet, door bolted?

Are you ok?
Yes. 6pm grove ok?

Charlie's heart lit up. But why was she hiding him in the woods? He felt hope and shame mix. He went with hope and typed:

Ok.

If the Game was watching, he hoped it was proud. He'd taken the cash and turned it into a golden bracelet, replacing Tim's chains and setting Mary free. He would present it to the princess. He would slay the beast, the dark princeling. He could follow the Game's neural-net wordplay, its jokey clues. Bracelet → Circle → Ring. One ring to rule them all.

And become king?

No, he didn't care about that.

Right?

Charlie stepped from the store into the throng of the mall. It felt good, being anonymous, moving freely among the human sea of shoppers.

His phone buzzed again, but it wasn't Mary.

When he unlocked it with his thumbprint, it opened onto something he hadn't requested, a map view of the mall. He saw himself, the little blue dot pulsing in the middle of the screen. The stores were flat tan boxes around him, flanking the main arteries of the mall. Then a red dot appeared, something he hadn't seen before on good ol' Google Maps. The red dot was moving toward him.

Charlie didn't know what it meant. But some ancient primal coding told him, *Blue good, red bad.* If a red dot comes toward you, all things equal, keep moving.

It was the color of bad lightsabers, after all.

As he walked, the red dot followed.

I did what the Game wanted, Charlie thought. *Why is someone following me?*

Charlie passed Wetzel's Pretzels and watched the dot keep a steady distance behind him. When he paused in front of Sbarro, the red dot paused, too, far back. When he started walking again, the red dot followed moments later.

Is this a punishment? Charlie wondered. *Did I choose wrong?*

He thought of Blaxx, those threatened penalty points. Had he earned them somehow?

He looked back behind him and saw nothing but the normal flow of evening mall traffic. After-work shoppers in dress clothes, families with strollers, power walkers in Juicy sweats, geriatric clock-watchers. The red dot hung back. Whoever it was, Charlie couldn't tell.

He kept moving.

Was I not supposed to take the money?

Was I not supposed to buy the bracelet?

He took a hard right down the Macy's wing, past the main food court and the movie theater. There were posters for a horror movie about a serial killer stalking a deaf woman (*Dead Quiet*), a family cartoon about elf-like creatures called Hoppers, and a movie about revenge starring Mark Wahlberg.

The red dot followed Charlie.

Maybe I did choose right, he realized.

Maybe this is a reward. A heads-up that someone is coming.

But then: *Who? A security guard?*

He glanced back over his shoulder.

He didn't see a security guard coming.

A Vindicator, playing against me?

(No—we're a team.)

He saw nothing unusual.

Is the red dot even real?

It was still far enough back. Charlie paused long enough to hold up his phone and scan the crowd behind him through the screen. He saw nothing new.

When he decided to cut through Macy's, another red dot appeared from that direction, cutting him off. Together, the two dots were moving toward him from opposite directions. Now they were moving even though he had stopped.

Charlie cut left down a crossway. Let the two reds smack into each other while he broke sideways. He passed the harvest display in front of Pottery Barn. The red dots had converged and both turned down the crossway. Another had appeared, coming from the other side of the screen.

Who are these people?

His evasive maneuvers had taken him to a minor artery of the mall, near some of the lower-end stores—a discount music and movie shop called Entertainz, a Spencer's Gifts, a cheap "skater" shop for poseurs who needed shorts.

That's when it dawned on him that he had a $900 bracelet in his pocket. He didn't want to be at the meeting point of three red dots in this part of the mall. It was mostly empty. The few teenagers around looked like they were more likely to join in a robbery than stop one. A heavy scent of pot was in the air, and deafening beats so loud he could hear them from the earbuds a dozen feet away. The teenagers were all staring down at phones, tapping away, and no one seemed to care about him.

Charlie decided to get back to the core of the mall, where the shoppers were.

Then the red dots on his map, growing closer, disappeared.

He swiped his screen, zooming out.

Nothing.

The map was still there, his blue dot in the center.

The red dots had been closing in when they vanished.

His internal clock told him they'd be close now, if they'd kept the same pace.

Charlie kept moving. He glanced ahead and behind, trying to spot who in the crowd might be the kind of person to stalk a guy in the mall. He looked through his phone again as the crowd rushed past. A woman with a stroller brushed him going the opposite direction. Her toddler stared out from the stroller, and through the phone the kid had red eyes.

Charlie pressed toward the exit to the parking garage. He didn't have time to appreciate the demon-baby effect. The exit was thirty feet away. He glanced back through his phone. For a moment in the crowd behind him a head was taller than the rest, different because it was a minotaur with blood-orange eyes and a ringed nose with froth and hair, the horned bull-head moving up and down with the steps of a real person.

Someone crashed into Charlie from the front, or he crashed into the person, who told him to watch where he was going. The person said something about stupid kids, and Charlie mumbled an apology and looked behind him, but with his phone down he couldn't tell who was or wasn't the bull-man or if he was even still there.

Charlie reached the exit ahead and felt a rush of hope.

Maybe this wasn't a punishment or *a reward.*

Maybe it was just a test, another obstacle for the hero to overcome.

He went for his car. The third floor of the garage was deserted and he looked back and didn't see anyone following, no bull-man, not even a centaur or winged Icarus. He found his car and fumbled to get the key in the lock—was he the last person on earth to drive a car without keyless entry?—and suddenly a hand came out from under his car, like some old wives' tale about the dangers of mall parking lots passed frantically between suburban gossips.

The grip on his ankle was strong and caught him off guard, bringing him down. He fell backward, banging against the car behind him. Charlie felt the hand pulling hard on his ankle, trying to draw him under the car. He broke free and pulled himself to his feet, and when the hand gripped him again, he brought his other leg down as hard as he could onto the attacker's wrist. With a sickening crack and a yowl of pain from under the car, the fingers went limp and withdrew back underneath. Charlie grabbed for his keys as he heard the figure sliding out from under the car on the other side, coming around toward him, and he got the right key shakily into the keyhole, jumped in, and slammed the door shut behind him, hitting the lock. He started the car, felt with the palm of his hand the small box with the bracelet in his pocket, took a breath, and got the hell out of there.

That was not a security guard.

That was not a Vindicator.

Who the fuck else is playing this game?

And why are they coming for me?

"I told you there were other people playing," Peter said calmly, lying back in the grass on the Embankment. "I chat with them online. That's how I found it in the first place."

"I figured they were in Japan. Or Germany. Or Ukraine. Not here."

"I have no idea, Charlie. Everyone's anonymous. There are a billion people playing online games. Some of them have to be here."

"But I thought this thing was underground."

"It is!" Peter sighed, as if he were lecturing a dumb child. "I don't think you understand the scale of distributed networks."

"What are you talking about?"

"I'm talking about raw numbers. Do you know the odds of getting hit by lightning? That's really low, right? It's one in three thousand. Say the odds of finding the God Game were, like, a hundred times *less*. That's still twenty people within an hour of here. Not even counting people who aren't playing that the Game might just manipulate into doing something."

"How would it do that?"

"Blackmail. Fake news. Social engineering."

"Jesus, what did you get us into?"

Peter grinned. "What did *we* get us into?"

Charlie threw up his hands. Peter was right. No sense denying it.

"I saw other people, too, on my phone, before the mall. They had white masks. Hoods. They looked satanic."

"Watchers."

"*Who?*"

"Next-level players. Don't worry about them."

"Don't tell me what to worry about."

"Look," Peter said, "I get it, you're rattled."

"I really hurt that guy."

"Yeah, but he was trying to hurt you."

"Maybe. Maybe he was just some kid like us."

"Or maybe he was a criminal casing the mall, and the Game tipped him off that some bozo was coming with a thousand-dollar bracelet in his pocket."

"I don't like this. I don't want anybody to get hurt."

"Neither do I, obviously. But this could've been a fluke. It got out of hand. Well, poor choice of words. I'm just saying, you can break your wrist playing basketball, too. Don't assume the Game is evil."

"A fluke? Like the phone going off early?"

"I already told you, I didn't do that."

"I know. But if you didn't do it, the Game did." Charlie shook his head. "I don't understand what it wants from us. What's the goal? What does winning even mean?"

"I know, it's fun, right?" Peter winked. "God works in mysterious ways."

Charlie ran into Mr. B. in the hall, who beckoned him into his classroom.

"I've been looking for you." Mr. B. shut the door. "This is between us, okay? Seriously, I could get fired for this." He looked pleased with himself. But Charlie was still rattled from the mall, and everything here felt too normal, unreal. "You have to promise, okay?"

"Okay," Charlie said, waiting to hear the fireable offense.

"Well"—Mr. B. unlocked a drawer in his desk and slid it open—"I thought you might have a tough time getting started. Back on the horse, so to speak. So I took a stab at these." He spread them out on the desk. "They're nothing special. And there's only five of them. These days, you guys probably win by doing microtargeting on Facebook or something. So I realize this is a bit old-fashioned. And, I'm not very good at it. But . . ." He placed a hand on one of the five posters.

They were simple and plain: VOTE FOR CHARLIE LAKE. CHARLIE LAKE FOR STUDENT COUNCIL PRESIDENT. And the worst: CHARLIE— THE ONE FOR TURNER!

They were, in Mr. B.'s parlance, lame.

"Again, it's just a symbolic gesture. It doesn't have to be these. But I want to see you hang *something* up. By tomorrow. Otherwise, our deal is off."

Charlie wanted to say, *Bullshit*. He appreciated the gesture, but he could burn these posters in front of Burklander and the deal might not be off. Burklander might be the one person on earth to stick with Charlie unconditionally. Even his own father had given up on him, choosing to plow their dwindling funds into a cockamamy restaurant idea rather than Charlie. It was the better investment. Only Burklander couldn't see that. Charlie didn't know whether to hug Burklander or call him a fool.

Charlie rubbed his eyes. He was exhausted from the all-nighter, the fight at the mall.

"You doing okay, Charlie?"

"Yeah, I'm fine. Just tired. Late night."

"Trouble sleeping?"

"Sort of. Yeah."

Mr. B. nodded, like he knew something about that. Charlie wondered whose couch Mr. B. had slept on, those nights after he'd been thrown out of his house. Still, each day he'd come in showered and ready to place unwarranted trust in his students.

Charlie took the posters and promised he'd hang them. He was too tired to fight.

Burklander called to him on the way out the door. "Did you hear about Kurt Ellers?"

Charlie froze. He tried to act calm.

"Yeah . . ."

"See, there is some justice in the world." Mr. B. smiled. "Don't tell anyone I said that. I could probably get fired for that one, too."

Alex stared at himself in the mirror.

He wanted to do what the Game asked. And fifty thousand Goldz was a gold mine, no pun intended. That was a lot of crypto, and what it would buy was awesome. The Vindicators would think he was badass. But they couldn't know how he got it. Especially Charlie. So how would he explain it, then?

He would lie. Because they already thought he was a nut. He lied about lots of things. The websites he visited. The drugs he'd been taking. The things his dad did. He could lie about this, too.

Someone knocked on his door.

Alex undid the cheap locks he'd screwed in, the hotel-style chain lock, the slide bar from Lowe's. His dad was standing there, home from work, looking upset. He was holding something in his hand. A manila envelope, addressed to Mr. and Mrs. Dinh, perfectly neat monospaced font on the label.

"Why didn't you tell me about this?" his dad said, sounding weary.

Inside the envelope was a copy of Alex's last physics test.

The red F sent a shiver through him.

Alex grabbed the test from his dad's hands. He knew where it was supposed to be. In his locker. How did it get here?

"Who sent this?"

"When is your next test?" his dad asked back, ignoring him.

When *was* his next test? Thursday? And what was today—Wednesday? Oh, shit, he should have been studying already. But the Game had happened. And that was so infinitely better.

Unlike physics, he was good at the Game. It told him so.

"Not for a couple weeks," he told his dad, lying.

But then he realized—what if the same person sent his *next* test home? He'd be busted twice over. The bad grade. Plus the lie. He knew what that would mean. He could feel it in advance. Phantom pain. No, that was the ghost of pain past. This was the ghost of pain future.

"I told you what would happen if you failed another class."

"I know."

"I want to see your next grade. It has to be a pass."

"Okay, sure."

"I mean it. The next grade is a pass, or there will be consequences."

"Okay. I will. I'll do it."

His dad hesitated. "Please." He sounded younger and sadder. "Please pass."

Alex couldn't answer. He bit his bottom lip and nodded.

His dad left, and once the door was locked again, three times over, he looked at the physics homework on his desk, then back at the Game on his computer, and picked the Game.

The Vindicators had been the only good thing in his life. Freshman year, it was a haven, from the people who still remembered him from middle school as the Boy from Mars. But then Peter had come, and everyone fell in love with him and worshipped him—Alex did, too, because Peter was the charming trickster Alex longed to be. Yet the things Peter did came out warped when Alex copied them, making him seem all the more alone and odd. Alex had always been the tag-along, but when Peter came, Alex fell one notch lower in the Vindicator hierarchy, which made him feel expendable. Again.

And where was Charlie in all this? Freshman year, Charlie had rescued Alex from oblivion, and it was like, sure, yeah, you're quiet and everyone thinks you're a freak, but be one of us. He wished that Charlie still existed, but that guy fell into a black hole of pain, and someone else came out. Deep down he *hated* Charlie—old and new—for how much Alex needed him.

He would do it. He would do what the Game asked. It would be fun. His prize would impress them. But right now he was more interested in impressing the Game.

He locked himself in the bathroom, and his phone buzzed, a text from an anonymous number.

He read it twice and felt a pit in his stomach.

Who would say this?

Why?

It couldn't be the Game. The Game's been saying good things.

Could it be the Game?

Had he screwed up somehow?

Lost favor?

He felt panic. If he was losing ground in the Game, all the more reason to do this task, to win it back. He wasn't scared.

He read the text again and looked up at the mirror.

Deep circles. Lost eyes.

He stared at himself as the message repeated over and over in his head:

Nobody likes you.

28 BLOOD ON THE WALL

Kenny texted the other Vindicators to warn them away from the school.

> Eddie & team snooping around basement—stay away until i say clear

Charlie wrote back:

> why snooping?

Kenny replied:

> Someone told him about graffiti

Vanhi wrote:

> WHO?
> I don't know.

Charlie wrote back:

> Does he know it's us?
> Not yet

Peter said:

> I'll go now. Clean it up

Kenny answered:

I tried. Door won't open. Code not working.

Vanhi wrote:

Fuuuuuuuck.

Kenny replied:

I'll handle.

Vanhi asked:

How?

Kenny didn't answer. He went silent because Eddie walked up, with Candace in tow. She had a nice camera with her, the paper's high-end Nikon. Huge flash, great for lighting blood markings in dark spaces. Their sudden appearance made him put down his phone abruptly and not answer Vanhi's question about how he was going to fix this. But he also had no fucking clue.

Eddie paid off the janitor, a slow man named Mr. Walker, who without hesitation said he'd let them in. The school had cleared out, and the basement was deserted.

"Ready?" Kenny said, trying to sound excited in a positive way.

He noticed the throbbing in his fingers. That afternoon, he'd run home to shower and change clothes, dipping his pierced fingers in rubbing alcohol and nearly bringing his parents in when he yelped. He slipped that hand into his pocket now, without realizing he was doing it.

The boiler room door was closed, the magnetic swipe box next to it at knob level.

Kenny didn't dare pull out his phone to see if the cryptic firelight writing was still on the door. Or if the magnetic swipe box was still overlaid with glowing spy-fi keypad controls.

Instead, trying to act nonchalant, Kenny said, "So this is the boiler room?"

"Technically, they call it the mechanical room," Eddie answered.

"I pulled the specs. They put the security pads in when they added the panic doors last year."

"Isn't it locked?" Kenny asked, again trying to act clueless and calm.

"Not for long," Eddie said.

Soon enough, they heard footsteps, and the lanky frame of Mr. Walker came ambling down the hall. He was in no particular hurry, which drove Kenny nuts because all he wanted to do was get this over with.

Kenny wasn't sure who limped more, Mr. Walker or Hephaestus, the god of blacksmiths.

When Mr. Walker finally made it down the hallway, he and Eddie had a spirited, quiet exchange. Eddie slipped a $20 bill into Mr. Walker's hand.

He ambled to the door and said, "Well, good evening to you," to Candace and Kenny, as if he were just passing by. He put his badge on the reader, then let the elastic cord suck it back to his belt.

He kept on walking in the other direction, mumbling something to himself inaudibly and scratching the back of his head as he shuffled away.

Kenny hesitated when Eddie pulled the door open.

"What are you waiting for?"

"We're not supposed to be in here," Kenny said.

"You don't have to stay."

"Don't be a pussy," Candace added. She was half-Scottish, half-Jamaican, with reddish-blond braids and brown skin.

Kenny nearly blurted, *I'm not a pussy,* which he realized was exactly what a pussy would say. So instead he scowled at her as if the idea were preposterous, then walked into the boiler room. With his phone in his pocket, the room itself was stripped of its enhancements from last night—no glowing open-mouthed furnace, no diminutive animated god.

Everything was much more boring in realspace.

But it was still dark and hard to navigate, with steam valves, large boilers and control panels, and color-coded piping wrapping the walls and ceilings.

"How does anybody work in here?" Candace asked.

"They don't, really," Eddie told her. "It's almost all Wi-Fi now. They only come down here if there's an actual mechanical issue. A stuck valve or something."

It felt warm and damp, and Kenny realized he was starting to sweat. He thought about his Columbia application. Eddie's excitement: *This is our Friends of the Crypt!*

"Where is it?" Candace asked.

"Keep looking," Eddie said.

Kenny realized the best thing he could do—the least *guilty-looking* thing he could do—was to be the one to find it. They were going to find it anyway. He needed to stay in the loop. Keep their trust. Then, when the moment was right, kill the story. Somehow.

"Look!" Kenny said. The moment he did, he thought, *Is my premise flawed? Maybe the guilty person would find it first, because he knew just where to look!*

"Oh, wow," Candace said.

Eddie just exhaled. A slow breath.

Splashed across the surface of the boiler was a bloody pentagram, upside down and menacing. In the context of the Game, it had seemed perfectly in place, among the belching smoke and glowing glyphs and little Hephaestus. But now, in the real world, boring as all get-out, the bloody diagram stood alone, startling and grotesque. The heat from the boiler had cooked the blood (it was *obviously* blood) to a gooey dried paste. It looked hideous.

And huge. How much blood had Kenny given? At the time, it was incremental. Now all at once it slapped him in the face: *What have I done?*

"This was no prank," Eddie said.

Suddenly, there was a burst of light. Insanely, Kenny thought for a half second that it was the God Game, coming to the rescue somehow.

But it was Candace, snapping her first picture, the flash sizzling.

"Did your parents ever tell you about the Friends of the Crypt?" Eddie asked them softly, almost piously.

"I heard about it," Candace said. "When I went to the Grove one time."

"They met there, out in the woods."

"They blew up a car," Kenny added.

"Yeah, after putting a live cat inside," Candace said.

"That was twenty years ago. And still, my mom would never let me play in those woods," Eddie said.

Another flash went off, lighting the bloody pentagram, drawn in stark lines that dripped downward, startling Kenny all over again.

29 BLACK BOX

Vanhi stared at the package on her bed. Her hands were shaking.

She'd taken it outside and done everything she could think of to tell if it was safe.

She'd thrown rocks at it from a distance. Nothing. No explosion. No screeching. Not even a shattering noise. Just a dull thud.

She'd found a long stick and prodded the package back and forth. Nothing.

She'd shaken it, sniffed it, everything but opened it.

She looked back at the anonymous texts.

> Knock on the door
> Go around back.
> Pick it up

And then the new one. The kicker:

> Deliver It.

Vanhi looked up the address it gave on her phone. It was forty minutes away. The name meant nothing to her. Mitchell P. She googled it but the results were junk.

She was just delivering a package! Why was she so freaked out?

She realized she wanted to call Charlie.

She picked up her phone, held the voice-activation button, and said, "Call Charlie."

The phone echoed back, "Calling Charlie."

But it didn't do it.

She tried again. "Call Charlie."

Again, no call.

She went to her contacts and clicked his name.

And nothing happened.

Was the Game messing with her? If it could blow up a phone, it could do this. But *why*? Why couldn't she call Charlie? They were playing together, weren't they?

She wished she had never heard of the Game, but it was obviously a little late for that.

She was about to try texting him when a new message arrived. It wasn't from Charlie, but rather the anonymous game thread.

If you tell, I tell.

Okay, fine. She got it. This was on her. No phone-a-friend. But still, there were limits. She wasn't going to deliver an IED to someone's doorstep.

She texted back:

Is it a bomb?

She knew it was insane to put that in writing, but she didn't care. That was the question haunting her. She didn't expect an answer, but dammit she had to ask.

The screen replied:

No.

She wrote back:

Is it something bad?

Not even a pause before:

No.

How could she trust it? What if it was lying?

She went to her desk and grabbed the scissors.

She was about to plunge them through the packing tape wrapping the box when her phone suddenly rang. She jumped, and the scissors skittered out of her hand.

"Shit!"

Her hand shook as she grabbed the phone.

"Hey." It was Charlie.

"Hey."

"What are you doing?"

"Nothing," Vanhi said, eyeing the box warily.

"Do you think we're screwed?"

"What, Eddie? The paper? Kenny will fix it."

"Do you really believe that?"

"No," Vanhi said.

"If this blows your Harvard app, I'll never forgive myself."

Vanhi closed her eyes. Every time he said that, her lie weighed heavier on her. She wanted to say, *No, Charlie. I'm already fucked.*

Instead, she said, "Are you okay, Charlie?"

"I think I really hurt someone tonight."

"What? Who?"

"I don't know. He attacked me in the garage. At the mall."

"Oh my God, are you okay?"

"Yeah. But I broke his wrist."

"It sounds like you didn't have a choice."

"Maybe. Maybe I shouldn't have been there in the first place."

"Why shouldn't you be at the *mall*?"

"Never mind."

"Charlie, you're not making sense."

"Forget it. It's fine."

Vanhi looked at the package on her bed. "Was it the Game?" *Careful,* she warned herself. *If you tell, it tells.*

Charlie hesitated. "I want you to stop playing."

"What about you?"

"I don't care about me."

She looked at the box. *I know your secret.* "What if I can't stop?" she said, hearing her voice strain.

"Why not?"

If you tell, I tell. "Just what if?"

"You have a choice."

Earlier, Vanhi had run into her mom, who looked tired after a long day at the bank where she worked. "What's in the box?" she asked. "Just school stuff," Vanhi had answered, and her mom had accepted that without a moment's pause. Vanhi had spent years building that trust, and the truth would blow it up in one horrible instant, if it ever came out.

The Game could tell her parents that she hacked her grade before they saw it, then hacked it back. It could tell the school. There would be traces if people looked. To hell with Harvard, she could be *expelled*.

"Right, a choice," she said, feeling deflated. "I have to go."

"Hey, easy. You called me."

"No, I didn't. You called me."

"My phone rang."

Vanhi closed her eyes. "Mine, too. It's testing us. There's things we're not supposed to say."

"Yeah. I guess we passed."

She put her hand on the box. "I have to go."

She buried her face in her hands. It was clear to her now. She asked the Game one last question:

Do I have a choice?

Again, no pause:

Yessssssssssssssssssss

That was true.

And she'd already made it.

Alex biked through the darkness, with the bat tucked under his arm. He knew the back roads and the shadowy ways that would keep him out of sight.

He'd found the bat buried deep in his small garage, under stacks and piles of old crap. An old basketball, deflated years ago. *That's me!* A soccer ball, untouched, still in the box from circa 2010. *Untouched—that's me!* Unless you counted punishments, and there was truth to that. Because at least when you were bent over the bedpost, taking your licks, you felt, deep down, *It's about me, they're paying attention right now, only to me.* That was buried beneath the pain and humiliation, but it was real, a tang of sour-sweet juice on the blade of the hurt.

He pedaled furiously to the address the Game had given him. The bat felt strange in his arms. He remembered the night his dad had made him stay outside for hours, until he'd hit the ball off the tee one hundred times. Why? Because he refused to play catch. Didn't his dad realize, *I want to fit the mold. I want to be this thing you imagine I could be. All the threats, all the punishments. Pointless. If I could, I would. I wish, wish, wish I could.*

Nobody likes you.

That was true. He'd always known that. Still, just seeing it in writing was like a sucker punch, every time he looked back at the text. Everybody hated him, and now maybe the Game had turned on him, too. He had to do this right.

He pedaled harder, his plaid shirttails flapping in the wind.

When he got there, he held the bat steady, remembering the grip his dad had taught him a decade ago. Just like the US GIs had taught him. His dad could learn it a zillion miles away, but Alex was raised here, and he couldn't hit a ball to save his life. His dad the hero. Dragging US soldiers out of the fire. Going back in to save more.

Bam.

Alex brought the bat down on the windshield of the car.

The noise echoed through the quiet neighborhood.

Bam.

His dad the war hero.

Bam.

Charlie the saint.

Bam.

Peter the unobtainable.

Bam.

Vanhi the skeptic.

Bam.

Kurt the sadist.

Bam.

Tim the puppet master.

Bam.

The school.

Bam.

The people.

Bam.

Everyone.

Bam.

All must . . .

Bam.

His mom . . .

But wait. The bat hesitated. She was kind. She would come in after a particularly bad punishment, whisper soft kindnesses in his ear, stroke his hair, and press her forehead against his.

But she couldn't *stop* it.

She could only cradle him when it was over.

Weakness.

Goodness but weakness.

Pointless.

Useless.

Over.

Done.

Bam.

Lights were flicking on in the neighborhood now. Dogs were barking. Alex became aware of his surroundings, as if he'd woken up in a different place from where he'd started. He was dripping with sweat. His palms were aching.

He heard sirens in the distance.

For him?

He ran to his bike, on its side in the bushes.

He looked back at the car. It was smashed beyond belief. The windows were gone. The headlights and taillights were pulverized, white and red shards in blood-spray patterns. The body was pocked and cratered.

The bat!

Alex realized he had dropped the bat.

He wasn't worried. Every kid on every block had a bat like that.

But he felt a bizarre, sentimental pang.

Could he really just leave the bat? His dad had bought it for him. A long time ago. Yes, so much pain was between then and now. So much anger. Even coming from that bat itself (*You will stay out here until you can a hit a ball like every other kid on this block*).

But his dad bought it for *him*.

A long time ago.

Leaving it felt like snipping a last, thin cord between them.

Alex dashed back, grabbed the bat, and bolted back toward his bike, tripping along the way. He scrambled up, swung a leg over the frame, and sped off, bat tucked under his arm, pedaling as fast as he could into the safety of the shadows.

Charlie drove through the woods to the Grove, the bracelet in his pocket. After the attack at the mall, he was keeping it close, checking for it every couple minutes. He could feel it, hard and reassuring in the little pouch.

Social control—you've earned it.

He'd looked at the chessboard in the Game. He still couldn't move the pieces, but they'd advanced nonetheless. Black and white were intermingling now, fighting with one another. Kurt Ellers had a chip in his tooth now, and a comical black eye. *That's right,* Charlie thought, *we knocked him down a peg.* Mary and Charlie were facing each other, just a square between them. Tim watched, a square away.

Charlie pulled into the darkness of the Grove and killed his engine. He walked along the shrouded path, feeling his way toward the edge of the lake where Mary had asked him to come. When he came into the small clearing and spotted her, she was so beautiful in the moonlight, her skin glowing faintly, that it almost felt like a dream.

She was too good for him. He wasn't a frog, one kiss away from prince. He was a flea. What could he give her? A stolen bracelet? It was all he had.

If he was her savior, why would she want to be saved?

But he couldn't help moving toward her, her skin glowing in the blue haze.

They came together so quickly, so hungrily, that all doubt washed away.

It started as a kiss but it progressed quickly, her hand sliding around him, her nails on his back, spread-palmed as she moved over him.

There were tears down both sides of her face.

She reached for his belt, then stopped, pushing back from him. "Not like this."

She put her hand on his face, but Tim's bracelet was there and he pulled her hand off gently. Why would she wear it? Why wouldn't she just take it off, just for their rendezvous in the woods?

"I have something for you."

"I don't want a present."

"Please. Take it."

She looked at the bracelet he pressed into her hand, identical to the one she wore.

She looked up, perplexed. "Why would you do this?"

"It's for us."

She shook her head. "What do you think I am?"

"I know who you are. When I told you my mom was sick, do you remember that? I came back a little later, and you were crying. That was right before your brother died."

"You saw me?"

"I did."

"*Why didn't you do something, then?*" she snapped. "Don't you see, I would have . . . right then, I *could* have . . ."

"I don't understand."

"And *this*." She gestured angrily at the bracelet. "What is this supposed to mean? That you can buy me? You can be my next Tim?"

"No . . . that's not it."

She started to leave.

Charlie tried to hold her back. "No, listen. It's so we can . . . I know you can't leave him, yet. But this way you can know, it's from me, not him, and he'll never know. And then when you're ready . . ."

She stared at him, flabbergasted. "You think that's what I want? To live a lie?"

"If it's not, what are we doing in the woods?"

Mary's eyes welled up. "You don't know anything."

"Is he hurting you?"

"I will handle this."

"I'm not going to stand by and watch you get hurt."

"It's not your job to save me, Charlie."

He wanted to punch a tree. He felt angry, baffled, whipsawed. He ached and his heart was twisting.

"I will get out in my own way in my own time."

"Okay."

"And this?" She looked at the bracelet in her hand. "This isn't you." She handed it back to him. "I don't want it. And I don't want *this*." She took off Tim's bracelet, and in a panicked, impulsive move, she threw it into the lake. "Oh, shit," she said suddenly. "Oh, no." She looked at him, eyes wide. But the moment passed and she became calm, strong. "Good, good."

Charlie started to push the new bracelet at her. "You can have . . ."

"No."

"Just to cover up . . ."

"No." But her tone was softer now. "No. It's okay. Take this back, Charlie. I don't know where you got the money, and I don't want to know. Please take it back."

She hugged him quickly and said she had to leave.

"I'm trying," Charlie told her.

"I know you are. I am, too."

Vanhi stood outside the house, holding the box.

It felt remarkably light in her hands.

Nothing truly bad could be this light, she thought again.

She'd waited till dark, then gone to the assigned location.

The house looked peaceful. Unassuming. A soft glow came from inside, but the outer rooms were dark.

She had passed her mom on the way out. She lied and said she was going to work on a project at Charlie's house. "You seem nervous," her mom said not unkindly. A thought occurred to her, and she smiled broadly. "You've done everything possible. You know I know that, right? If Harvard doesn't want you, they're crazy. I am so proud of you."

Vanhi wanted to cry.

She left, moving quickly, her car whipping through town, windows open so the cold air could sting her and distract her from thinking.

She reached the house and knew she couldn't hesitate now. She'd done everything possible to prove the box was benign. She'd all but risked blowing herself up, kicking it, shaking it, poking it, smelling it.

I am so proud of you.

I know your secret.

That's what she wanted to tell Charlie—not enough love wasn't the only thing that could kill you. Too much love. That could crush you, too.

Vanhi did as she was told.

She went to the back of the stranger's house, and the window was unlocked, just as the Game said it would be.

She climbed gracefully into the dark bedroom—Vanhi was lithe and fast—and placed the box gently on someone's bed.

She slipped back out, closing the window behind her and wiping off the edges where her fingers had been.

When she got home, a box was waiting on her bed.

It seemed impossible.

Another brown cardboard box, indistinguishable from the one she'd just delivered.

Was it the *same* box? Could someone have beaten her back, gone in through *her* window—*while her parents were in the other room*—and put the box *back* on her bed? She felt violated suddenly. Same box or not, had someone been *in her room* while her family watched TV down the hall?

She checked her window. It was locked from the inside.

She went to the living room.

"Ma, was someone here?"

"Back so soon?" Her mom looked surprised. "The project's done?"

"We'll finish later. Did someone come by?"

"Someone left a package for you. On the doorstep."

"Who?"

"I don't know. They rang the bell and left it."

She wanted to scream, *And you put it on my bed?*

But why wouldn't her mom? Hadn't Vanhi just told her a similar box was school supplies?

"It's for your project, no?"

Vanhi mumbled yes and went back to her room. She had to get it out of the house. She opened her window and took it down to the creek behind their lot. She shone the flashlight on her phone on it. It *could* be the same box, she wasn't sure. She went through the same rigmarole—poking it, testing it. Then she said fuck it. People in glass houses. If she could give it to a stranger to open, why wouldn't she?

Vanhi tore at the box.

Inside, it was stuffed with crumpled paper. She threw it aside and dug deeper until her fingers closed around something hard and square. She took it out.

The small metal box had knobs and a display screen for red LED numbers. It was painted with an image of space, stars, and the horizon of a planet.

She knew exactly what it was, instantly.

Panda Audio's Future Impact I, the sound-effects pedal real bass players used in mega-stadiums. Chris Wolstenholme of Muse had one, for Christ's sake. It cost over $500. She could never afford one. If her parents thought a nice Hindu girl playing bass was crazy, this was downright psychotic.

On any other occasion—birthday, graduation, anything—she would have been thrilled beyond belief. But now she just stared.

30 KEY

"We dodged a bullet," Kenny told the Vindicators, as they reunited in the Tech Lab that night. "Candace wanted to publish right away. Tweet out the pictures."

"You stopped her?" Peter asked.

"I did." Kenny was beaming. "I told them, that's crazy. As soon as it's out, we lose control. The police come in. Real newspapers, TV. All we'd get is a lousy photo credit. I said, let's crack this wide-open—investigate on the down-low, write the story, *then* launch. And we get *all* the credit. I knew Eddie couldn't resist that!"

"So you bought us a day?" Vanhi asked, skeptical.

"I bought us more than that. We can go in there now, wash away the evidence, then there's nothing left. Just a picture. Nothing linking us to the crime."

"So let's go," Charlie said. He was feeling guilty from the ATM, the broken wrist. Still smarting from Mary's rejection of the bracelet. The Game had led him wrong. He just wanted to erase the bloody pentagram—erase *everything*.

"Well, that's a problem," Peter said.

Everyone turned to him.

"While you guys were twiddling around in the Game, I went back to the boiler room. It's not just locked now. No more magic keypad."

"You couldn't hack your way in?" Vanhi said almost tauntingly.

"Apparently it was not God's will." Peter shrugged.

"Couldn't we just pay off Walker like Eddie did?"

"Then they'd know it was us."

"So we're screwed."

"No, that's where I come in." Kenny looked proud again. Deep down, he loved the way the Game seemed to be escalating him from sidekick to hero. "After Eddie and Candace left, I was freaking out. But then I realized, I had some Goldz saved up. I asked for help and got us a new mission. Something called the Hydra."

Kenny showed them his phone.

A new text from the Game promised:

I will wash away all your sins.

31 EPHEMERA

Alex stopped them. "Before we go . . ." It was the first time he'd spoken all night. He looked like shit—his eyes were tired and his hair was mussed more than usual—but he seemed excited. Proud, even. "I have something for us."

He picked up the box that had been waiting for him on his bed, as promised, when he came back from smashing the car.

They would love him now. *He* did this.

Fifty thousand Goldz well spent.

Vanhi shuddered when she saw the box. It was strikingly similar to the one she'd delivered to some random house, just longer and flatter. How many people were out there playing this Game, delivering parcels? Were they all good things? Her bass pedal was, and Alex certainly seemed happy about his package, too. But that didn't mean they were all prizes. Could there be bad packages as well? Hate mail, so to speak? Vanhi wondered again, *What did I deliver tonight, and to whom?* She felt like an ant in an ecosystem she couldn't see.

"What's the matter?" Charlie asked, noticing her reaction.

"Nothing." She smiled weakly. "Shiver."

Alex spoke so quietly the group had to lean in. "What's the one thing that would make this game better?"

"Sleep," Kenny said. They all looked a little worse for wear after being up for most of the last two days.

"I have something for that," Peter said.

"No," Charlie jumped in.

"What, I was talking about Red Bull. . . ."

"Pay attention," Alex blurted out, too loud. He hated the way Charlie and Peter could command the room instantly. *He* was the one talking.

He ripped open the box and folded the cardboard arms outward. They all leaned over to peer in.

"They're Aziteks," he said.

"No way," Peter said. "How did you get these?"

"They cost a fortune," Charlie said. "They're brand-new."

"How much did it cost?" Kenny asked.

"Just some Goldz."

"What did you have to do?" Vanhi asked.

"Just a little search and destroy! Don't worry about it. Worry about *this*: never having to walk around like a moron staring through your phone to see the game. Think about the immersion we'll get. And we can play all day now, easy!"

Alex slipped a pair on. They looked like normal glasses, some more hipstery than others. His pair were like him. Thin, unobtrusive. The frames disappeared on his face.

Peter picked a black, thicker rim, the kind only someone handsome could pull off and look better with glasses than without.

Vanhi went for the artier tortoiseshell style.

Kenny picked half-shell clear frames. Scholarly, yet edgier than anyone would have guessed for him.

Charlie picked what was left: silver frames, modern and sleek.

They all put them on.

"You sync them like this." Alex pressed a button on the stem.

Charlie stared through his glasses. They felt impossibly light on his face, barely different from regular glasses. You could only see the AR on one side, meaning to everyone else in the room you just looked normal, walking around with innocuous glasses on.

The world flashed as the glasses synced with Charlie's phone, and the Game came alive in front of him. Wherever he looked, now he saw the God Game on top of realspace. The cracks in the walls. The flickering torches. The glowing signs and pulsing runes. It all felt real around him, moving with his head. Yet reality was there, too. He could see the obstacles and paths in realspace, through the augmented reality. It was fucking awesome.

Peter reached toward the computer tables, where a virtual red-glazed vase was glimmering. He closed his hand around it and lifted it off the table. It moved perfectly in his hand.

They all watched.

"This is a game changer," Peter said, smiling at Alex with admiration.

Alex beamed.

Peter tossed the digital vase to Charlie.

Without thinking, Charlie caught it in the air. He tossed it to Kenny, who tossed it to Vanhi, who lobbed it to Alex. Alex grabbed for it but fumbled the catch. It hit the ground and shattered.

Alex felt himself blush.

"You have to admit," Vanhi said to Charlie quietly, "this is pretty cool."

Suddenly there was a crash, as Peter picked up a troll-skinned lamp and hurled it across the room at Kenny's head. It slammed against him, and Kenny heard a shockingly loud shattering from the speakers playing straight into his ears.

"Hey!" he shouted, a grin spreading over his face. "Watch it!"

Words appeared in the air before Peter:

Hitting a teammate! 5 Blaxx.

Everybody laughed, but Charlie felt a slight chill. This was the first official report of Blaxx he'd seen. Five was a low number—their Goldz had gone up in the thousands already. But still, what did five Blaxx mean? What would five hundred mean?

"Serves you right," Kenny told Peter, laughing. No one else seemed worried about the consequences.

"Let's go!" Alex cried, beside himself with pride.

They ran down the hall to the boiler room. Sure enough, all signs of the Breath of God were gone. The Hebrew was gone, and the keypad was blank, even through their snazzy new AR glasses. The walls around them were decayed in the gamespace, the door itself solid iron.

"Access denied," Peter said in an "I told you so" kind of way.

Charlie went to his inventory to see what tools he could buy. He, too, had a lot of Goldz saved up from being a Good Boy, at least in the eyes of the Game. But he found no new skills to buy now. "So where's our salvation?" he asked the group.

They stared at each other blankly, no one having any great ideas.

Then the Game asked a simple question, another set of words floating between them in the hallway:

Do you hate Tim Fletcher? Y/N?

32 REFLECTION

They needed to get into the boiler room and erase their guilt. And now the Game was throwing this at them.

"That's not a hard question," Peter said hurriedly. "Charlie, seems like you should have the honors."

Charlie thought about the wrist cracking under his foot. Choices had consequences.

"I have no idea what picking Y does," Charlie said.

"It's just a *question*. If the Game does something to Tim, that's not your fault," Alex told him.

"It's like the trolley problem!" Kenny added, always happy to quote philosophy.

"Oh, shut up, Kenny," Vanhi said.

Peter ignored the squabble and turned to Charlie and said quietly, "He probably beats her."

Charlie glared at Peter. "Leave Mary out of this."

Peter held up his hands. "Just saying."

"Oh, to hell with this," Kenny said. "*I* hate him, and I don't even know the guy. This is our butts on the line, remember? Blood on the wall? Let's focus. We obviously have to answer this in order for the Game to help us."

Kenny reached out and pushed the Y floating above them.

They saw Tim's social media unfold in space above them. He

wasn't a big poster, but everyone posted *about* him. *Look at me, at a kegger with Tim Fletcher! Look at me, cheering him on at State* (Fletcher tagged in the background of the selfie, on the field, crushing skulls for that great American bloodletting).

The Game was moving between posts. It pulled Tim's face and elements of his clothes and gestures, then drew on pictures of Kurt, too, creating an image of the two of them standing in front of a wall. Behind them, it began painting in a new element, a Confederate flag pinned to the wood planks behind them. The image was perfect. It didn't look like any fake the Vindicators had ever seen. No telltale photoshopped clues—mismatches in graining or tone or lighting. On the deepest lizard-brain level, it felt real.

The Game said:

Post? Y/N?

On some level, Charlie felt relieved. He thought maybe the Game would murder Tim if Charlie hit *Y*. Who knew? This felt more akin to a prank. Like Alex's Lord LittleDick poster, might it rest in peace. Charlie could live with that.

"It's crazy how real it looks," Kenny said.

"So we post it," Alex said.

"Um, *yeah,*" Kenny said. "To save us? That's a small price to pay."

"Yeah, he probably won't even get in trouble," Alex said. "Football's too important."

"He'll just say it's fake," Peter added.

"It *is* fake," Kenny agreed.

"It doesn't look it," Vanhi said.

"Still, it's a big deal to label someone a racist," Kenny said, thinking it through.

"But he *is* a racist," Peter said.

"We don't know that," Kenny said.

"Yeah, we do," Peter shot back. "I don't need to hear him say it. He reeks of it."

"Kurt called me the Dumb Asian," Alex said.

"There you have it."

"You guys are missing the real problem," Vanhi said.

"What's that?"

"What if posting Kurt and Tim with that flag doesn't bring them down? What if it brings the flap *up*?"

"Huh," Peter said, considering it.

Charlie pulled on the door. He checked the hinges in the Game, looking for some clever way in. But it was obvious: the Game wasn't going to help them until they posted that fake photo.

"It's us or them," Kenny said, coming to the same conclusion. "There's no way in but to play along. That graffiti could ruin us."

Everyone turned to look at Charlie.

"What do you think?" Vanhi asked.

Charlie wondered who should answer—Boy Scout Charlie from two years ago, dropout Charlie from a week ago, Game-playing, Mary-courting Charlie of today?

There was only one thing all three of them agreed with.

"I think I hate Tim Fletcher," he answered, pushing the Y floating above them.

The boiler room door opened, the Wi-Fi lock unclicking automatically.

"I wonder if we'll see Hephaestus again," Peter asked, as they crept through the virtual mist pluming out. Vines wrapped around the pipes all around them. A python hung lazily from one, flicking its tongue in and out, sniffing them from above. A low moan came from the boiler.

"*Oh!* That's disgusting," Vanhi said, startling them all.

On the ground, in the corner, was little Hephaestus' body. His head was torn off. Blood pooled around his torso, tacky in the oily black muck-water covering the ground.

"Oh-ho-ho," Peter said. "The plot thickens."

"Where's his head?" Kenny asked helpfully.

He turned around and gasped. There in front of him was Hephaestus' little head, stuck on a pike, tongue hanging out.

Kenny poked at it, and the eyes shot open.

"*You did this!*" it shouted, spraying blood, then fell dead again.

Kenny wiped his face, the digital blood coming off on his hand in the gameview.

Behind them, the door clicked locked and blue swords appeared in their hands. "What the—" Vanhi managed, then a roar tore through the room, so loud it hurt their ears. A creature raised its head from behind the boiler, then another head and another after it. The heads lashed forward, scaly and fanged, snapping at them. The creature rose from behind the boiler, as if the metal casing with the bloody pentagram was its armored belly.

Charlie didn't move in time, and one of the heads lashed out and sank its teeth into his arm. Virtual blood sprayed out.

25 Blaxx!

flashed in text over him, spinning quickly, then disappeared.

Another head reared back, opened its mouth, and roared.

At the same time, one of the pressure-release valves sprung open on the boiler, spewing invisible gas, while the pilot light's sparker triggered. A plume of real flame shot out, intermingling with the virtual fire pouring out of the creature's mouth, just missing them.

"Ow!" Vanhi cried. "That really hurt."

She ran to the door, but it wouldn't budge.

Peter tried chopping one of the beast's heads with his blue sword. It lopped off with a bloody spray, then grew back instantly. Fire breathed out again, and this time the real fireball was bigger, as more gas poured out from the pressure valves and filled the room. Peter felt the heat as he ducked just in time. Any minute, enough gas would be in the room to burn them all to a crisp.

Vanhi and Charlie swung for other heads on the beast, but they kept growing back.

"What do we do?" Charlie asked.

But Kenny was laughing—he knew exactly what was going on, and he knew just what to do. "Burn the necks!" he cried out, elated. "Before they can grow back! Look!"

He dipped his sword into the oily muck on the floor, then raised it into one of the plumes of fire, where it ignited. Charlie did the same and looked at the flaming sword in his hand. He chopped the next head that flew at him, then held the blade against the oozing neck as it sizzled and singed shut. The stump fell down like a dead boa constrictor.

They chopped away at the other heads, which now shot out at them frantically with teeth bared and eyes wide. A final plume of gas ignited, so large they all had to drop to the ground, but then the last head rolled across the ground and the beast lurched back with a wild spasm and fell dead as the fire sprinklers came on.

Water poured down from the ceiling, soaking them.

"I will wash away all your sins!" Kenny laughed. He raised his hands to the falling water and began rubbing them over the furnace, smearing the pentagram. They all pitched in and scrubbed, until at last the image was totally erased, just a trail of reddish brown swirling down the drain in the floor, then gone.

Vanhi looked at Kenny with actual admiration. "How did you think of that? Burning the necks?"

"Hercules and the Hydra! The AI was built on world religion. While you guys were reading code, I was reading *books*!" Kenny folded his arms triumphantly.

"Holy shit. That was the most amazing thing I've ever played," Peter said.

"Played? Done? Experienced?" Charlie asked.

"What *is* the word?" Kenny added.

"The word is *mindfuck*," Peter said. "That was the most amazing mindfucking I've ever received. And I've been arrested in my home by Feds."

"Wow."

"That was better than sex," Kenny said.

Everyone stared at him.

"Fine," he amended. "That was better than I imagine sex to be."

Everyone slept hard. Except Alex.

His physics exam was tomorrow. He hadn't forgotten. He'd just blocked it out with the Game. Except now he'd failed that, too.

Only Vanhi had seen him hiding in the boiler room. When the fire started spraying out, he ran and ducked behind the pipes in the back. While his friends were chopping away, he was crouching in the corner.

When it was over and the water started, Vanhi saw him step out from the shadows. She pretended not to notice, but he was sure she'd tell them all.

His dad was a war hero, and Alex couldn't even stand up to an imaginary dragon.

He'd peed his pants, a little. Did she see that, too?

For five minutes, he'd been the hero. The one who earned them the Aziteks. Who would remember that now? Kenny was the hero. Alex was shit.

As if reading his mind, the Game told him:

You don't matter.

That was indisputably true.

He needed sleep.

But he couldn't add another failure to the list.

Not now.

He looked at the bottle of pills Peter had supplied him. He hesitated, then popped an Adderall and felt his brain light up. Suddenly he was firing on all cylinders, and it seemed entirely possible that he could learn in the next five hours what he hadn't in the last three weeks.

He had Red Bull and caffeine pills to boot, and he popped a couple now, to keep the juices flowing. His heart was beating too hard in his chest, but he focused on the equations in front of him. He could do this.

It was 2:17 A.M.

Plenty of time.

He woke up the next morning with his face on his desk, unsure if he'd studied at all.

33 HEALED!

Kurt Ellers was back the next morning. He wasn't even limping.

Charlie knew it was wrong, but that filled him with rage. He wouldn't have chosen to blow up the phone in Ellers's front pocket, but knowing that Kurt wasn't maimed, Charlie couldn't help but regret that it hadn't done slightly more damage.

Especially when he saw the smug look on Kurt's face. He didn't look like a guy who had just been humiliated in front of his peers. He didn't look like Alex Dinh, eyes heartbroken, snot running down his face. He grinned and shrugged with a "What can you do?" affability. *Yep, my phone blew up. Isn't that crazy? I'm still gonna get laid tonight. Are you?*

But then Charlie thought about the strange magic of the internet. Maybe that Confederate flag photo would go viral and turn everyone against Kurt. Or maybe someone would leak the video of him hopping around, pants on fire, some dowdy old teacher spraying him with white foam. No matter how infallible Kurt was with his friends, the wisdom of the crowd could prevail. Isn't that what happened with dictators these days? They stay propped up for so long, their power intact, rising on a web of fear and belief. But when the truth spreads like wildfire through the crowds, the illusions burn up and old gods fall.

Charlie tried to remember who had filmed the phone episode. Eric

Weisman, maybe? Elena Moore? In the excitement it had been a blur. He'd ask around after class. Or maybe the Game had it already? Maybe he could buy it with Goldz?

Once the rage passed, Charlie realized he felt pretty good. He'd slept like a baby after their wild adventure. In the daylight, with some rest, everything felt less terrible. Mary wasn't wearing *his* bracelet, but she wasn't wearing Tim's either. The Game was crazy, but it was fun, too, and they'd washed away the pentagram; now they could relax. No harm, no foul.

This morning, rightly or wrongly, things seemed possible.

He looked at the posters in his backpack. The five lame, lousy VOTE FOR CHARLIE flyers that Mr. B. had made for him. They were pathetic. He'd be embarrassed to put his name behind them. But he also felt touched. Underneath all the pain and grief, for the first time he felt a small ray of gratitude.

He wasn't going to run for student body president. But he did want to be able to say, honestly, to Mr. Burklander, that he'd put up one of the posters. Charlie didn't want to have to lie to him anymore. Charlie tried to think of the most obscure area of the school, where people were least likely to see it (besides the Tech Lab, which was obscure, but not to his friends). Charlie found a bulletin board on the fourth floor, south wing. He wasn't 100 percent sure, but it might have been near the remedial classes, so maybe the students wouldn't be able to read it.

He hung the poster, stuck a pin through, and threw the other four in a trash can.

Okay, Mr. B., he thought. *Okay. Now you can feel good.*

Kenny was feeling better, too.

His DNA, after all, had been in the bloody graffiti.

No one had thought to scrape a little blood off—not Eddie, not Candace—and now the blood was gone. Nothing could link the photos Candace took to the Vindicators; photos were just pixels on a disk. If he played the Game right, those might disappear soon, too.

So why did Eddie look so smug this morning, even as he told them about the strange sprinkler malfunction?

"Walker let me back in," Eddie told him. "The place was a mess. Water everywhere. The graffiti was gone."

"Well," Kenny said, trying to sound nonchalant, "we've got the pics. So we're good."

"Oh, we've got more than that," Eddie said viciously, without explaining what he meant.

"And now there's a cover-up!" Candace added. "It's like Watergate."

"No pun intended," Kenny tried lamely, but they ignored him, excited.

"Right!" Eddie nodded to Candace. "If it was a prank, why break in and wash it away? You'd want people to see it."

"Okay, slow down, everyone," Kenny said. "I thought it was a sprinkler malfunction."

"That's what Walker thought, too, but he's dense. *We* know about the pentagram. We're supposed to think this is all just a coincidence?"

Kenny shook his head, trying to look casual. "If I were a devil-worshipping graffiti artist, I think I'd use a rag, not water an entire room."

"*Are* you a devil-worshipping graffiti artist?" Eddie said it like he was joking, but Kenny didn't like the look in his eyes.

"Yeah, right," Kenny said, trying to laugh it off.

"Anyway," Eddie said, "here's the plan. I want Kenny to research Friends of the Crypt today. There's just too many similarities not to link the stories. Plus, we know that got national attention, so let's bring it up. Candace, I want you to research devil stuff in general—what does the pentagram mean? What other bad stuff would these guys be doing?" Eddie smiled. "Whoever these nuts are, they're going down hard. And we'll break the story."

"It's kind of thin," Kenny said, throwing a Hail Mary, "without any physical evidence."

"I agree," Eddie said. "That's why it's so awesome I've got their DNA."

"What?" Kenny felt his fingers begin to throb again.

"Yeah. After you all left, I was like, wait, why didn't we take a little sample? Well, actually, it wasn't my idea."

Kenny was baffled. "Whose idea was it?"

"That same anonymous source. He really wants these sick fuckers to go down!"

Something was wrong with Mr. B. Charlie hadn't seen him like this since his divorce. He phoned it in through Creative Writing. All the joy was gone. This was the guy who stood on the table like in *Dead Poets Society* and read to them aloud from Mark Twain and Dostoyevsky. Only then, seeing Burklander so gloomy, did Charlie realize how much Mr. B.'s annoying optimism had been a scaffold for Charlie's despair, keeping him from dropping all the way down a bottomless shaft.

He felt unmoored.

He wanted to tell Mr. B. about the poster (now he wished he hadn't thrown out the other four). But when the bell rang, Burklander was out the door faster than the students.

Charlie ran after him. He heard Mary call his name and almost turned around, but something kept him chasing after the teacher.

He found Burklander outside by the Dumpsters, sneaking a cigarette. "I didn't know you smoked."

"Damn it," Burklander snapped, and flicked the cigarette behind the Dumpster. "I don't."

"Can I have one?"

"*No.*"

Burklander sat on the ground, in the gravel, a strangely juvenile gesture. He let his back slide down the wall till he was seated. He popped another cigarette out and pulled it with his lips.

"No, you can't have one."

Charlie sat down beside him. "Don't you have a heart problem?"

"Yes." Mr. B. looked at the cigarette in his hand. "I just . . . needed one."

"Why do adults who smoke always tell kids not to smoke?"

Mr. B. gave him a dry look. "Because we want to believe you guys will be better than we were."

Charlie didn't like this new, cynical Mr. B. "I didn't want a cigarette anyway. I don't smoke. I just wanted to see if you'd give me one."

"So did I pass your test?" Burklander said sarcastically.

"Yeah. Sorry." Changing the subject, Charlie said, "I put up one of your posters."

Mr. B. didn't even look at him or respond.

It stung.

"What happened?"

"I might as well tell you. I'm sure it'll get around soon enough." Mr. B. shook his head. "I've been teaching for thirty years. And the kids just get worse and worse. Meaner and meaner. Nothing matters to them."

"Do you really believe that?"

"When I was a baby teacher, someone wrote 'Mr. B is an asshole' on my chalkboard. And I was like, 'Wait, I'm the cool teacher.' Now that seems quaint. I tried to matter. I tried with you."

"You do! I put up your poster!" Charlie said, but it was so lame he wished he hadn't.

"Do you know what someone did? I came out of my house last night, my depressing rented house, all this noise outside, and my car was destroyed. Smashed to pieces. Why? Did I give someone a bad grade? Did I say the wrong thing about Huck Finn? The car is totaled. I stopped paying insurance to pay alimony, so I'm screwed. But what kills me is the failure. I've failed, again. Someone hated me so much they destroyed my car, smashed it to pieces. Left it there for me to find. What did I do, Charlie? What did I do to deserve that much hate?"

Charlie suddenly wanted to puke.

No one hated Mr. B. What was there to hate?

It was the Game. He knew it instantly. It had to be. And more to the point, it was someone playing the Game, which meant . . .

He thought of Alex, with his box of fancy Azitek glasses, thousands of dollars' worth of brand-new gear. What had he done to earn those? *Just a little search and destroy!*

So was Kenny right all along, then? Should they have cut Alex loose before he went darker, more dangerous? Or did it mean Vanhi was right—they should've held him closer, saved him from going deeper? Either way, they had failed.

"Maybe it wasn't a student?" Charlie said, more for himself than Mr. B. "Maybe it was just random crime."

Mr. B. studied him then, taking a slow drag on his cigarette, then flicking the butt away.

"Maybe." Mr. B. nodded. "Maybe it's all just a big misunderstanding."

He leaned his head back against the bricks and spoke with his eyes shut.

"But if I have faith in anything anymore—and I'm not sure I do—then it's faith in the power of children to disappoint you."

Vanhi felt like she wanted to throw up.

The delivery boxes had left her unsettled. Worse still, the way the Game toyed with them with the Hydra last night was disturbing—it had been so fun, it was easy to forget that any of them could've been savagely burned. The Game didn't seem to care one whit.

But now reality had set in. Forget about the Game. In front of her right now was her Harvard essay. What she had written so far was lifeless and not her, but she couldn't seem to summon any passion for it; the pressure was too much to make it meaningful but also perfect.

Her mom had come to her this morning, looking cheerful. "Today is the day?"

"It's not due till next week, Mama."

"Yes, but you don't want to be the last one to submit, do you? What kind of message would that send? My Vanhi is always early. She doesn't wait for the deadline. That's what they will see."

No, Ma, they'll see a D in AP US History.

But she had to try. She had to make everything else perfect so that smile on her mother's face wouldn't drop, so those rosy cheeks would stay flushed with pride, not shame.

Even if it was hopeless.

Her mom had missed her own mother's death. When Alzheimer's hit and Vanhi's grandmother had sunk into oblivion, Mina Patel wasn't in Mumbai with her, holding her hand and walking her though pictures of her family so she could recall. Mina was in Texas with her daughter, giving her this amazing life. Vanhi caught her mom crying at night, looking at pictures of her declining mother thousands of miles away.

That's what her parents had done for Vanhi.

So she ran home at lunch, closed the door to her room, and stared at her essay for the five-hundredth—but maybe last?—time.

Reading it made her ill.

> *I am deeply passionate about Harvard because I want to be a computer scientist. Harvard's CS department has launched so many luminaries in the field. While I don't assume I would become exactly that, the opportunity to stand on the shoulders of giants would give me the chance to move the field forward. For as long as I can remember, I've loved programming. . . .*

It was terrible. She knew it. Every note was wrong. The fawning over Harvard. The off-putting mix of modesty and hubris. *I. I. I.* She was normally a wonderful writer! But she couldn't see a way forward. She'd written and rewritten it so many times, it was all mush in her head. She changed *luminaries* to *stars,* then changed it back. Finally, she put her head in her arms and closed her eyes.

A voice from her computer, cold and thin, said, *Put on your glasses.*

She looked up. The same words appeared, superimposed over the application on her screen:

Put on your glasses.

She blew a tuft of red-black hair out of her face, her chin still in the crook of her arm, and fumbled for her Aziteks.

When she put them on, the application system was the same on her screen. But the essay had changed.

She glanced over the top of the glasses, at realspace.

> *I am deeply passionate about Harvard because I want to be a computer scientist. . . .*

She looked through the glasses, at gamespace.

Vanhi means "fire," a Hindi word tied to creation and destruction. Standing at the edge of adulthood, I realize what I need to know was always there, encoded in my name. Who we are is not what we are made of. Fire, earth, water, air, space—the five fundamental elements of the Vedas—we all bring different forms of matter to bear. We are all made from different stuff. It is the choices that we make, the ways we use and combine our elements, that define our worth.

Her mouth dropped open.

It went on:

In Hinduism, the story of fire, like all stories, begins with parents. In my faith, it was the cosmic rubbing of sticks— twin mothers—whose friction gave birth to fire. If they tended the fire and nurtured it, it would thrive. But the consequence—the inevitable result—was that the fire would consume the sticks. I think about this, the ways parents sacrifice for children. The gratitude we cannot fully feel or understand until we ourselves become the consumed sticks, years later and sometimes too late. My own parents brought their Vanhi to America, a journey that separated them from everything they knew and everyone they loved. An act of love and faith, done for me, so that my fire might grow and thrive. My dream of Harvard, like so many, is to fan that flame with knowledge, to study virtues old and new. I am a coder. But code, like fire, is just matter, neither good nor bad. It is how we use it that matters. In Sanskrit, the holy trinity of creation, maintenance, and destruction is together त्रिमूर्ति:, or in En- glish, Dattā. But I cannot accept that, ancient or not, holy or not. I cannot put equal worth on creation and destruc- tion. The app that displaces a thousand cabdrivers, the AI that replaces a million workers. Destruction is not coequal to creation. It is not inevitable or desirable, even if you

*rebrand it as "disruption." It has human cost. Whether it is
Dattā or data, as a coder, as a person, I will be defined by
the deeper choices I make. Harvard will teach me to code.
But more important, it will teach me to think.*

When she was done reading, Vanhi had tears in her eyes. She had no idea if they were tears of gratitude or shame or just plain awe. She lifted her glasses and her old essay was there, so mediocre it didn't even seem like words anymore. Her hand was shaking.

The essay said everything she felt, everything she believed. It was like someone had borrowed her soul, put it into words, then returned the rest. A part of her remained on the screen—or more accurately, on the screen on her eyes. The real computer still had the old essay. The one she would like to light on fire and consume in holy destruction. Data indeed.

Vanhi didn't know what to do. She'd never plagiarized in her life. She never would. But this wasn't stealing from another person. This was woven out of thin air. And it was *her*. Even though it wasn't. There had never been a deeper expression of Vanhism. It was like finding your own diary and having no memory of writing it.

There was a whole paragraph on her D. It talked about failure and hubris and immaturity. It talked about error and redemption. She had learned more from that one D, the essay assured her, than she had from any A—about how to recover, face your mistakes, and grow. Goddamn if that essay didn't make her D sound like a positively great idea.

Suddenly, her dream seemed possible again. Maybe, just maybe. But it was a chance, something she didn't have a minute ago.

The voice came back, oozing from the speakers in her computer. But this time it was louder, also piping through her stereo behind her, out the speakers she'd bolted to the walls near the ceiling, so the voice boomed through the room making her jump, the words thin and caustic like a bitter wind:

Do you want it?

She did. Oh, God, she did. With a queasy feeling in her stomach, she remembered something the essay had conveniently left out. Vanhi—aka Agni, aka the Fire God—was also the god of deception.

Flashing below the new and improved essay was a button with a single word on it:

SUBMIT.

Kenny was reeling. Why would the Game help them wash away the graffiti, only to tip Eddie off to save a piece first?

Was the Game just fucking with them?

He watched Candace following him, across the library. She might be a great writer, but she was a lousy spy.

How could he know that Eddie had pulled her aside yesterday, after the three of them had parted ways?

"Did you see his Band-Aids?" he'd asked her.

"He plays cello," Candace had said. "He probably cuts his fingers all the time."

"Wrong hand."

"Even still . . . Kenny? No way."

"Why not? Someone had to do it. He hangs with that group. . . ."

"They're not exactly the devil-worshipper types."

"Were the Friends of the Crypt?"

"Touché. Well, so what do we do?"

Eddie told Candace to keep an eye on Kenny today, and that's what she'd done.

For his part, Kenny was supposed to research the Friends of the Crypt. Trying to act normal, that's what he did. And the more he read about them online, the more he believed they might have been playing an early version of the God Game. The similarities were striking—smart kids, high achievers, crafty and mischievous. It was the 1990s, the era of bulletin boards and dial-up modems, lower-fi, for sure, but uncharted, vulnerable, wide-open to exploitation. Add the overlay of devil worship, D&D run amok, pranks veering into crimes, sinister graffiti . . . and then . . . arrests, ruined futures, suicide. Was that the Vindicators' trajectory, too? He found a few national articles around the indictments and sentencing, mostly recycling the same facts. Quotes from shocked parents. Then nothing, a blip, the disgraced honors students lost in the dustbin of history.

Kenny printed off several articles. He wanted to show Charlie.

Candace kept eyeing him from her table across the library until he couldn't stand it. She was supposedly researching devil worship on campus (according to the black-nail-polish set she'd interviewed, there was none). Not surprisingly, the school library didn't have an extensive collection on occult rituals, just a few obligatory books on cults and how not to join them. Kenny grabbed his pages off the printer and marched straight to her table, where she was pretending to be surprised to see him.

"Are you going to follow me all day?"

"Excuse me?"

"You heard me."

"I'm not following you," she said defensively. "I'm researching. Just like you."

"False. You've shadowed me all day. You won't stop looking at me now. Are we on the same team here or not?"

She searched for a quick excuse, then settled on the truth. "Eddie thinks you're hiding something."

"What?" Kenny tried to act shocked.

"Why do you have Band-Aids on your fingers?"

"You don't seriously think . . ."

"You've been trying to kill this story from the very beginning."

"No, I've been trying to make sure we don't get hoaxed and embarrass ourselves."

"You hang out with that *group*. . . ." She said it as if the word were *cult*.

"We play computer games. We don't hold séances."

"Lots of people play games. They don't *name* themselves."

"It's just a joke. You're grasping."

"Am I? Someone had to paint that symbol."

"I'm in National Honor Society."

She tapped her book. "Smart kids are *more* likely to get into cults."

"Give me a break. My friends watch movies and run the Tech Lab for Coach Hapler. I cut my fingers building a remote-controlled

GoPro at the robotics station. You want to check? We're about as satanic as Mickey Mouse. Okay, Sherlock?"

It came out smoother than he'd hoped. She might find him nerdier, but less demonic.

"Fine."

He tried to tell if she was buying it at all. "Look, Eddie's going a little nuts here. He wants this story to be big so badly. Personally, I don't want Columbia to know me as the reporter who got punked into fake news."

"So what's our move?"

"So it's 'us' again?"

"I'm not sure." She eyed him. "But I'm listening. I'm applying to Columbia, too, you know?"

"Great."

"And Eddie. That makes three."

"Trust me, it won't be Eddie if he runs this story before we back it up."

"Okay. What do you want?"

"Well, stop following me, for starters."

"Fine."

"Look, if you're calm, and I'm calm, let's see if we can't pull Eddie back. Or," Kenny ad-libbed, "if it *was* just a prank, let's make sure Eddie kills the story or goes down alone. No reason for us to go down with him."

Candace slung her bag. "Okay, that seems fair."

It felt like he had her. It did. Had he managed to talk his way out of this? But then she was staring at his hands with a funny look on her face. He was holding the stack of articles he'd grabbed off the printer.

He looked down and turned the pages over, so he could see what she was looking at.

In his hands was a picture totally unlike anything Kenny had seen online or anywhere else. It was the Turner High crest, modified with an upside-down pentagram in the middle of the shield.

In each of the four quadrants were other esoteric symbols: a scribe's hand. A skull. An hourglass. A key. Across the bottom, where it should have said *A. B. Turner High School* in collegiate font, the crest announced instead:

VINDICATORS

Candace looked at him and blinked.

"I've never seen that before in my life," Kenny said, wishing he could take it back the second the words left his mouth.

Alex sat down for the test, feeling as if he were sitting for his own execution.

He could feel the cool blade on the back of his neck.

His eyes kept closing on him, so right before class he popped another Adderall and threw back a Red Bull.

He had tried. He really had. But formulas made no sense to him. He couldn't wrap his brain around them. If every action has an equal and opposite reaction, then how do things ever move? He asked Peter that right before class over text. A year or two ago, he would've asked Charlie. Peter had written him back right away:

> Because the action and reaction are on different objects. You punch my face, my face hits your hand equal and opposite. I might move. You might move. Or not. Doesn't matter. Different objects.

Alex tried to parse that. It made sense, then two minutes later he was confused again. It didn't help that he was basically high from sleep deprivation and stimulants.

Now he stared at the test in front of him. In the first problem two billiard balls were hitting each other. Where would they go? Where would it all end?

He had no fucking clue. A big white space was beneath the question. That's where his work was supposed to go. Jesus Christ, he didn't know where to start. *Write your equations,* Peter had told him. Alex wrote $F = ma$. Fine, now what? Fuck, his heart was beating so fast. He thought about the belt his father used for occasions such as this, for abject failures.

A shiver rippled up his back. Maybe he would just run away.

The white space of the test stared at him, and he knew it then.

He was fucked. It was all over.

Then it occurred to him: Ask the Game! Isn't that what people did when their lives were in the shitter—ask God for help?

He closed his eyes and whispered quietly to himself, *"Please, please, please, God, help me. I can't fail this test, you know what he'll do . . . ,"* speaking just loud enough that his Aziteks could pick it up in the little mics. Even then, Jenny Prentiss cast him an annoyed look.

"Mr. Dinh, what are you doing?" Mrs. Kite asked from the front of the room.

"Praying," he answered honestly, and got a laugh from the class.

Mrs. Kite shook her head and went back to grading papers.

Nothing happened, but Alex was so used to disappointment, it didn't even hurt now that the Game was ignoring him. He'd failed at the Hydra, so maybe he didn't deserve help.

Or maybe praying wasn't how it worked anyway. . . . Wait, that was it! He *knew* how the Game worked! *Come on, Alex!*

He made discrete gestures with his hand on his desk—to anyone else it would look like fidgeting—but he pulled the little icon in the corner of his Aziteks that woke them up, then went into his inventory in the Game.

He felt a shaking pass through him, fear, excitement, hope, desperation. Among the choices, he saw Illuminated Text.

That had to be it. He understood the Game, its riddles and clues. He'd never cheated. Somehow, that was the one lesson his father taught him that had sunk in. He'd always just accepted the inevitability of his failure. There was honor in that. He took his lumps and moved on. But why not cheat, now? If it meant not hurting, an end to the pain? He had Goldz left over—what better to spend them on? Besides, refusing the Game's help now that he'd asked for it seemed ungrateful. It might make the Game hate him more.

He clicked on the purchase.

Illuminated Text. 10,000+ Goldz.

Worth it.

Then through the lenses a bit of magic happened. In fire-laced gold font, formulas began writing themselves on his exam, in the space where his work was supposed to go, like a book from the Middle Ages. The diagrams and notations burned and sparkled. He looked around him. The other students were heads down, working on their exams. Mrs. Kite looked up and met Alex's gaze. His eyes shot back down to his test.

Stay calm.

This is amazing.

Someone was watching him (or some*thing*, he reminded himself—couldn't an AI handle intro physics?). Someone was feeding him a way out. He thought about the belt. Not this time.

But then he saw the text disappearing, even as new text appeared at the end of the work.

"No!" he thought—he almost said it out loud.

Jenny Prentiss glared at him.

He *had* said it aloud. What was wrong with him? Why hadn't he slept more?

Well, because I didn't know God would be my silent partner on the exam.

Don't waste it, he told himself, this time silently.

He started tracing over the fiery equations on the paper, his pencil flying, locking the answers down as the text burned itself out. He started worrying his results would be *too* good—no one would believe it was his work. *Put some mistakes in,* he whispered to the God Game, *I only have to pass.* For all he knew, there *were* mistakes in there. He imagined the AI could deliver a perfectly calibrated score—good enough to avoid the belt. Bad enough to avoid suspicion.

He was halfway through the exam when the golden handwriting stopped.

He didn't notice at first. He was too focused on keeping ahead of the lines disappearing above. But then he saw. *What the hell? Where's the rest?*

"Come on," he said, and this time it was out loud again.

Jenny Prentiss was engrossed in her work. No angry look this time. His hand was shaking, gripping the pencil too hard. Why would the Game toss him a lifeline, then snatch it away? Then he got his answer:

INSUFFICIENT GOLDZ.

What? His cache was empty?

No, no, no.

He couldn't run out now. Not in the middle of the test. He was doing so well. Sweat ran down his cheeks. How much amphetamine was in his system? His heart sounded like a kettledrum. He simply put his head down on his desk; resigned.

Promise me, a voice said in his ear.

"What?" Alex moaned quietly into the crook of his arms.

Promise me you will always do what I ask.

"I will," he said, almost crying.

Anything.

"Anything."

His Goldz began spinning upward on the counter in the corner of his gamespace. The illuminated text returned. Shaking, he grabbed his pencil and began tracing again, as fast as he could, minutes to go.

Time's up, the voice said in his ear.

The bell rang, and Mrs. Kite said, "Pencils down."

He'd made it two-thirds of the way through the test. Was it enough? Did he pass?

Mrs. Kite stopped him on the way out. "I like your new glasses."

He stared at her blankly for a second, dumbfounded.

As he left, the Game whispered in his ear, *The Lord giveth and the Lord taketh away. Blessed be the name of the Lord.*

34 COSMIC FIRE

Heading to the library to meet Kenny, Charlie wondered whether it was possible—could Alex have destroyed Mr. B.'s car?

Charlie had to know.

Seeing his father totally ruined and demolished by his mother's death had been terrible, but in some ways seeing Mr. B. brought down was worse. Cancer had kicked Charlie's dad's ass—Charlie hadn't *caused* that—but the Game was Charlie's fault.

Huddling in the stacks, Kenny told him about the fake Vindicators logo and Candace.

"What did she say?"

"Nothing. She just kind of mumbled and left."

"What did you say?"

"What could I say? I was holding it *in my hands*! Why would the Game do that? We did everything it asked."

"Maybe we weren't supposed to."

"What?"

"Maybe we were supposed to say no," Charlie said, thinking of the bracelet.

"You think the Game was punishing us for doing what it said?"

"Yeah, like a test."

"Charlie, you obviously weren't raised in a religious house. Trust me. God prizes obedience above all else. If the AI was fed on the Bible, it means what it says."

"What if it asks us to kill someone?"

"The Bible is filled with God ordering people to kill someone."

"What about Thou Shall Not Kill?"

"There's an asterisk."

"I think Alex may have destroyed Mr. B.'s car."

"Really?"

"Have you seen him?"

"No. He had that physics test today."

"Oh, crap, I forgot."

Charlie sent Alex a note:

How did the test go?

He didn't get a response.

Mary had tried to grab Charlie on the way out of class, but he ran after Mr. Burklander, who seemed totally out of sorts. She had rethought Charlie's offer. After the burst of bravery had gone through her last night, she panicked on the way home. Tim would notice the bracelet was missing. She could wear the one from Charlie. Just temporarily.

But Charlie brushed past her, and Tim found her between classes before she could do anything about it. She smiled her brightest smile, hoping to keep his eyes on her face, but they went immediately to her wrist.

"Where is it?"

"What?"

He closed his eyes, as if he were frustrated talking to a dumb child. "My bracelet. Where is it?"

"Tim, it doesn't go with every outfit."

He nodded slowly. "Sure, okay."

He put a hand on her shoulder and squeezed hard. Physical strength wasn't the real source of his control—she knew that—but it was icing on the cake. There was more than one way to break someone's bones.

"You doing okay?" he asked.

"Yeah, of course."

"It's just the time of year. Makes *me* remember it all over again." It was a threat, but he said it like he cared.

"Me, too."

"So where were you last night?"

She tried hard not to blink, but it felt like she had. "I was home."

"I swung by."

"When?"

"Where were you?" he repeated, ignoring her.

She tried to lie. She tried to think of something great to say. But she couldn't.

"I took a walk," she said finally.

"By yourself?"

"Yes. I don't like the way you're talking to me."

He put his forehead against hers. "If I sound upset, it's because I care about you. That's so dangerous, walking alone at night. I don't want anything to ever happen to you." He kissed her forehead. "I spoke with your dad. We're having brunch with our parents this weekend."

"You talked to my dad?"

"Mary, we've got so much good stuff ahead of us."

He walked to the door, then stopped and turned around and smiled.

"So you'll have it tomorrow? The bracelet."

"Of course." Mary felt chills running all through her.

When he left, she got a text from a suppressed number. Mary had experienced a true stalker once—it came with the territory—but that was over and her dad had made sure that student was long gone. So when she saw a new, blocked number and a cryptic text, she had some fear. She deleted the message immediately, but still, the idea stuck in her head and would pop back up later:

Run for student body president. He'll hate that.

Charlie found Peter on the Embankment, drawing lazily on a joint. His eyes twinkled in the crisp fall sunlight, achingly blue.

"I need to find Alex," Charlie said.

"I can help with that. Come, sit. This Game is amazing. I'm starting to understand the rules. Once you get to a high enough level, aka enough Goldz, you become a Watcher."

"Those people in masks?"

"Yeah."

"What do they do?"

"I couldn't say if I knew."

"Are you one of them?"

"I wish. Hardly. But I did get enough Goldz to buy Advanced Eye of God. You will not believe how badass that is."

On the map, Peter's avatar was no longer just a dot or a cone in the 3-D view, but a chimera, tiger-headed and eagle-bodied. "I can go anywhere. The world is my gamespace."

They flew over a map view of Austin, a strange mix of 3-D and photographs, soaring over Turner, which was crawling with students' names like ants. If anyone saw Charlie and Peter, lying back in the grass, glasses on, they'd look like they were staring up at the clouds, probably high.

Peter searched for Caitlyn and found her avatar walking down the hall, complaining to that sycophant Marissa Minnow, who kept saying, "I know, I *know*." The digital reconstruction was not photo-realistic but hyperreal, video feeds from passing phones and hall cameras and old clips online blending like streams of reality flowing together, all points and pixels in between extrapolated. "And here's the treasure chest." Peter opened up a trove of Caitlyn's old phone calls, Web searches, docs. Intro EOG had given him texts; Advanced EOG had given everything. "She writes poetry. Can you believe that? She'd never tell anyone." He'd also seen evidence of her altruistic side, but he didn't mention that now. That just made her callous treatment of him feel worse—why did *he* deserve the sharp side of the knife?

"Don't you feel a little pervy, looking at all this?" With a shiver, Charlie wondered how many others were out there, maybe watching him?

"Nonsense. I'm leveling the playing field. Literally. Can Kurt Ellers do this?"

Peter rose and announced, "'But soft! What light through yonder window breaks? It is the east, and Juliet is the sun. Arise, fair sun, and kill the envious moon!'"

A few lounging students clapped boredly.

"Thank you," Peter said, and sat back down. "Poetry, see? I will hack my way to love."

"Can you tell where Alex is or not?"

"Probably."

Peter typed into a search bar, and his avatar rose up and flapped its wings through the cityscape. The creature flew gracefully through the trees and buildings and set down into a hover over Alex's house.

"He went home." Peter let his chimera dive downward, passing through the shingled roof and coming into Alex's hallway.

"You can go *inside*?"

"Yeah, sure, why not?"

"How is that physically possible?"

"Think about it—anything with a camera. Phones, TVs, Nests, watches, laptops, nanny cams, toys. All it needs is a glimpse and it can map the rest. I can see, hear, whatever."

"What if the devices aren't on?"

"The Game can turn them on remotely and make them look off—the FBI's been doing it for years. Even if there isn't a camera in the room, the Game can tell where people are from the EM fields."

"This is creepy as shit."

"Privacy is dead. Here's our boy."

And there was Alex, lying on his bed, Aziteks on, staring up at the ceiling at God knew what.

"I guess the test didn't go well," Charlie said.

"Maybe he feels he's earned a rest."

"I'm going to see him."

"Why? We'll see him tonight."

"I need to know if he trashed Mr. B.'s car."

"Why would he do that?"

"For the Game. Where did he get the Goldz to buy those glasses?"

"Who knows."

"Where did *you* get the Goldz to buy the Eye of God?"

Peter grinned. "Aw, that was nothing."

"What have you done?"

"Why? What have *you* done, Mr. Gold Bracelet?"

"Do you know? Are you spying on me?"

Peter shook his head. "Nah, that'd be weird."

Charlie looked Peter in the eyes and asked him the question that had been brewing since Charlie's run-in with Burklander. "How do you quit the Game, Peter?"

"*Quit?* How should I know? Why would you want to?"

"Ask your friends online. They must know."

"I don't think that's a very good idea."

"Why not?"

"This is the kind of game you try to get *into*. No one asks how to get out."

"Peter, please. Just ask. We don't have to do it."

"Find out yourself. Why do you always need my help?"

That stung Charlie more than he expected. He thought of Peter sitting for hours with him, after his mom died. When no one else knew what to say or do.

"Fine. I'll handle it," Charlie said.

"Then I bid you adieu, fair maiden." Peter glanced around the lush grass and gentle slope, his face so handsome and elemental he could be a Nazi or Nazi hunter, but nothing in between. He shook his head and smiled. "Caitlyn writes poetry. 'O blessèd, blessèd game! I am afeard, being in night, all this is but a dream.'"

When Charlie was gone, Peter let his avatar fly gracefully through the city, until he was hovering over Kurt Ellers's house.

35 ANGEL OF DEATH

Kenny got a text from Eddie Ramirez that was smug and gloating.
No commentary, just a link to a CNN article:

Scientists Use Computers to Predict Faces from DNA

The article was more concerned with guessing what Jesus looked
like, but Kenny knew exactly why Eddie was sending it to him. He
was probably typing away on the article right now, drunk on DNA
evidence and Candace's new revelation about the satanic logo.

Kenny thought of his brother, or more precisely, his parents'
faces when his brother had told them he'd dropped out of medical
school. How could Kenny ever explain this? *No, Ma, I'm not really
a satanist—I just defaced school property with human blood for a
computer game that thinks it's God. So . . . all good?* How would
that go over in the doctors' lounge?

He put his face in his hands. He had always been so careful. Straight
A's. Extra credit. Following Malcolm Gladwell's ten-thousand-hour
rule with the cello—and sure enough, Kenny was number one in the
state. The only place he cut loose was with the Vindicators. Would
that one little safe space be his downfall? Yet, if he didn't have the
Vindicators, he was 99 percent sure he would have exploded a long
time ago.

What did the Game want from them? Why was it hurting them?

And after he spent his hard-earned Goldz on the Hydra, which was supposed to save them!

He pulled out his phone and typed:

> We did what you wanted. You cheated us.

It felt vaguely sacrilegious to lash out at God this way, and he had to remind himself it was just a bot.

The answer came:

> Trust in the Lord.

Furious, Kenny typed:

> Trust? You tricked me.
>> Unsearchable are My judgments, My ways past finding out.

Yeah, right, Kenny thought. *Like giving Eddie everything he ever wanted.* Kenny knew he should stop, but he couldn't. He felt humiliated.

> How was that HELPING us?

The Game said:

> I will always help you.

BS, Kenny thought, but the Game wasn't done.

> All you have to do is ask.

No way, Kenny thought. He would not demean himself. More important, he would not go deeper. Yet even as he climbed the stairs to the *Tiger Claw* office to reason with Eddie, Kenny knew the truth, deep down: there was no reasoning with Eddie. And as clever as Kenny was, he could see no way out, short of asking God to lift the plague He'd made for them.

36 CHILD SACRIFICE

When Kenny walked into the *Tiger Claw* office, Eddie was there, smiling, and he laced his fingers behind his head and leaned back in his editor's chair.

"I'm thinking we go out in two waves," he announced, without saying hello as Kenny entered. "First, the splash. Front-page picture of the pentagram. Really blow it up big. All the streaky blood stuff right there, pow!" Eddie rocked forward in his chair and let his feet hit the ground. "Then . . . a quote from Candace, talking on background. 'A student with firsthand knowledge also described seeing other satanic imagery on school grounds, associated with a group of students calling themselves the Vindicators.'"

"Eddie, don't do this."

"Shh, listen, it gets better." Eddie wiggled his fingers like a conjurer. "'For those who remember, all of this is eerily familiar to that infamous group of student deviants. . . .' Segue to the Friends of the Crypt."

"You've got it all wrong."

"Sure I do! So then, the second wave. The reveal! The DNA, you holding the Vindicators crest, Mr. B.'s car . . ."

Kenny felt ill. Had Eddie connected that already?

"That's right! It *had* to be you guys. Like the Friends of the Crypt blew up that car. I don't even have to *prove* it. Just the connection is riveting! Let the police sort it out."

"Eddie, I'm here to give you a chance. I know this all looks bad. But these are good people. They didn't do what you're saying. Not like you're making it seem."

"I'll make you a deal. Give me a blood sample for a DNA test. If it doesn't match, I'll kill the story."

"Eddie, please. No story is worth destroying these lives."

"You guys did this. Don't blame me."

Kenny felt his phone buzz in his pocket. He glanced at it.

Put on your glasses.

He ignored it.

"What about if it was just me?" Kenny said.

"Huh?"

"I know you hate me. For Candace. For Columbia. Take me down. Leave the Vindicators out of it."

Eddie leaned back in his chair again and studied Kenny's face with mild contempt. Eddie was loving every minute of this.

"Tempting. Very tempting. But the story doesn't sing without your little club."

Kenny felt his fists ball up. He reached into his shirt pocket and slipped on his Aziteks.

He startled.

The room was the same in front of him, except that Eddie's eyes were blacked out, like two empty sockets.

"Eddie, please. I don't know what's going to happen if you do this."

"Is that a threat?"

"No. I honestly don't know."

"My job is to tell the truth." Eddie smiled.

"And if it destroys me and my friends?"

"Gravy."

Kenny nodded.

Behind Eddie, in the Aziteks, footsteps appeared on the dingy old carpet. They were bloody hoofprints, each composed of two long claws and a point; two on the right, two on the left, stamping out a burgundy path along the carpet, then out the door.

Follow the red-bricked road, Kenny thought grimly.

"Last chance, Eddie. Please."

"Did you know the word *vindicator* appears in the Bible? I googled it. It means 'God.' Is that what you guys think of yourselves? You're gods? Care to comment on the record?"

"It's from *X-Men,* asshole."

"Kenny Baker *swearing*? See, we all have hidden layers!"

Truer than you know, Kenny thought. "I tried. Remember that."

Eddie gave him a sarcastic "Oooh, I'm scared" face.

Kenny nodded and followed the hoofprints out the door.

37 THE CULT OF PYTHAGORAS

Charlie drove to Alex's modest, spare house. He always hated going there—it was cold and bare, no furniture but the essentials. Just in case the cops were coming, looking for a bat-wielding vandal, Charlie parked down the street and went around back to Alex's window. He was there, inside, working at his desk. That was new—Charlie hadn't seen Alex study a day in his life. Charlie knocked on the glass.

"I knew you were coming," Alex said without explanation. He seemed to enjoy the secret bit of knowledge. Did Alex have the Eye of God, too?

It wasn't homework on his desk. The papers strewn about were covered with nonsense, triangles with numbers and Hebrew letters scribbled inside.

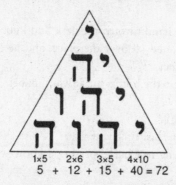

"What the hell is that?"

"It's kabbalah. Numerology. The Game's showing me some wicked stuff."

"Alex, are you okay? You seem really hyped up."

"I'm fine. Now look at this." Alex started saying something about the destructive power of the four-letter name of God.

Charlie looked around Alex's room. It was a mess. Not just a normal kid's mess but really scattered. Had it always been this bad? He couldn't remember.

"How did the test go?" Charlie asked carefully.

"Do you even care?"

"Of course I do. I texted."

"I didn't get any text."

That was odd. Charlie had sent it as soon as he remembered.

"So . . . did the test go okay?"

"I hope so." A chill was in Alex's words.

Charlie treaded lightly. "What time does your dad get home?"

"It doesn't matter." Alex looked up and met Charlie's eyes. "He'll wait until the grade comes back."

A cold wave passed through Charlie. That was the closest Alex had ever come to *saying* it. *He'll wait to . . . do what?*

"Do you want me to call someone?"

"You literally can't speak the four-letter name." Alex pointed back to the papers on his desk.

"Alex, listen to me."

"No, you listen to me. I don't care about physics. *This* is way more interesting."

Alex swung his hand toward the desk and knocked over a bottle of pills. They skittered all over the place, and he started frantically trying to sweep them up.

Charlie picked up the bottle, but it was unlabeled. "Who gave you these?"

"It's just Adderall."

"Alex, when's the last time you slept?"

Alex's gaze swung to Charlie's right. "I know what he's trying to do," he snapped.

Charlie glanced where Alex was talking to, but no one was there.

"Alex, are you playing the Game right now?"

"I'll handle it," Alex said, this time to someone on Charlie's left.

"Alex, take your glasses off."

"Why? You think I can't handle you without the Game?"

"I didn't say that."

"You think I can't write all that stuff without these on?"

"Alex, I'm your friend."

He snorted, a short bitter laugh, and Charlie remembered his microsecond failure by the portables—that split-second delay between *You don't want me in the group anymore* and *That's not true*—that told Alex everything he needed to know.

Maybe that's when things went off course, Charlie thought, or maybe it had been going on long before and they'd just been blind to the signs, but it was never too late to make things right.

"Nobody likes me," Alex said. "I'd be better off gone."

"Don't say that."

"It's true."

"Alex, I don't think this Game is good for you. They way you're talking . . ."

"You're just jealous," Alex said angrily, "because I finally found something I'm better at."

Charlie put the pill bottle down on Alex's desk. Charlie didn't know what to say or how to help him. Something caught his eye in the papers—one of the Lord LittleDick posters of Tim that had gotten Alex beaten up by the portables in the first place.

"I never asked for your help," Alex said, seeing Charlie notice the poster.

You did a good deed, and God was watching.

An idea was forming in Charlie's head, the pieces coming together. The Lord LittleDick poster led to Alex's fight. The Game had sent Charlie there with a fake text to test him. What had inspired Alex to put up those posters in the first place? Why *then*? Right after the Game's invitations had come. . . .

"Alex, when did you start playing the Game?"

Alex blinked at the question. "When we all did. That night at the Tech Lab." He started fidgeting with his sleeve.

And why hadn't any of Alex's posters gone up? Because one of Tim's friends caught him first. What were the odds of that, catching Alex in the act ... unless something tipped off Tim's friend, just like Charlie was tipped off to the fight. ...

"Alex, did the Game tell you to put those posters of Tim up?"

Alex didn't answer.

"You accepted the invitation. You started playing before us."

"No ..."

"Why did you lie?"

"I earned my Goldz fair and square. I didn't start early. I'm *ahead* of you."

"I don't care who's winning! Don't you see, the Game *used* you."

"What are you talking about?"

"It didn't let you put the posters up. It *wanted* you to get caught, so Tim's friends would come after you. To see what I would do."

"This is not about you," Alex cried. *"It's not always about you. Or Peter. Or Kenny."*

"Alex, I know. I didn't mean that. I'm just saying—"

"Just go away. Just leave me alone for once."

"Alex ..."

"No. I won't let you take this away."

"It's using us. All of us." Charlie thought of his chessboard. "We're pawns, Alex. We're not playing the Game. It's playing us."

Alex shook his head. "Maybe you. Not me."

"Did you destroy Mr. B.'s car?"

Alex looked at him wide-eyed, then looked away.

"Just come to the Tech Lab tonight. Promise me that. I'll get everyone together and we'll talk it through. Then, you can make whatever choice you want, for you. I won't try to stop you. But if you want to stop, we'll be there for you. We screwed up before. We let you down. I won't again."

Alex didn't answer.

"Promise me. Please."

"Okay. I'll think about it."

Charlie couldn't tell if Alex meant it or not.

There was nothing left to say. Alex was done, Charlie could tell.

"I'll see you tonight," Charlie said, going to the window.

"Oh, one more thing," Alex said offhandedly.

He hit Charlie so hard in the shoulder it nearly knocked him down.

"What the fuck?" Charlie cried. He grabbed his shoulder and squeezed the muscles, trying to get the pain to fade. "Why'd you do that?"

"Your Blaxx." Alex checked something on his Aziteks. "You were up to twenty-five. Now you're back down to zero. Trust me, you don't want those building up."

38 AZAZEL

Kenny followed the bloody hoofprints down the tiled hallway. One of the four hooves seemed to belong to a broken leg; that print dragged where the others stomped, creating a ghoulish image of an unfinished hunt: clack clack drag clack . . . clack clack drag clack . . . A hunter leisurely chasing down a wounded beast. Closing in.

He followed them up the stairs, where they turned left down a new wing.

They led Kenny to room 333, which was unlocked and quiet.

The hoofprints continued under the door and into the room, which was filled with art supplies and half-finished paintings on easels.

In realspace the canvases were high school art projects, all trying to depict the same bowl of fruit, apples on oranges on pears, with varying degrees of success. In gamespace the canvases bore images out of the bowels of hell. Rubens's *Massacre of the Innocents,* as told in the Gospel of Matthew. Goya's horrific vision of Saturn devouring his own son, for fear of being surpassed by his own children.

A man was in the shadows, tending a fire that sparked and illuminated his face. It was wild with the eyes of the believer. His long beard was unkempt, from days of travel over harsh terrain.

"Father?" a voice came quietly from the shadows.

"Yes, my son?" the man near Kenny replied.

"The fire and wood are here. But where is the lamb for the burnt offering?"

Near to Kenny, Abraham answered softly, "God himself will provide the lamb for the burnt offering, my son."

Abraham was building an altar.

Kenny reached forward, his hand passing through Abraham's face. He could hear the fire crackling and almost feel the heat.

Abraham bound his son, Isaac. There was no struggle. Kenny couldn't understand that. He wanted to yell to Isaac, *Fight back. Why are you letting him do this?* Isaac was a child. His eyes were wide. Abraham laid him on the altar, on top of the wood. Then he reached out his hand and took the knife to slay his son.

It came down furiously toward the little boy's head.

"Stop," Kenny yelled.

An angel of the Lord called out from heaven, "Abraham! Abraham!"

"Here I am," he replied.

"Do not lay a hand on the boy," the angel said. "Do not do anything to him. Now I know that you fear God, because you have not withheld from me your son, your only son."

Kenny heard a bleating from the distance.

Where the hoofprints ended, a ram was caught by its horns in a thicket.

Abraham went to the ram and held the knife to its neck.

He turned and said to Kenny, "Your phone is about to ring."

Charlie climbed out of Alex's window, feeling worse than when he'd gone in.

No police had come. The coast was clear.

But Alex was guilty. Charlie was sure of it. And Alex was slipping into a bad place.

Charlie got into his car and his phone buzzed. It wasn't a text message or a map this time. A video was waiting for him.

The grainy security-camera feed was from one of those black orbs on the ceilings of banks and casinos or, in this case, a parking garage.

A chipper techno beat was playing, and the footage was crudely but happily edited, zipping forward in superspeed, reversing to the sound of a needle skimming off a record, then replaying in slow motion, jump-cutting to the beat.

In the footage Charlie saw himself from above, running across the garage, scrambling at his car, his foot stomping down on the hand grabbing at his leg. When it came time for the sickening snap, the screen and music froze, and a cheerful caption flashed across the screen:

OH SNAP!!!!

Watching it, Charlie felt ill.

The video kicked back to life and the foot came down, the wrist of the unseen assailant bending into its unnatural V. A canned WAV file said, "Oh, no, you didn't!" saucily, and the video zipped backward, the foot raising up, the wrist unsnapping, folding back into unbroken shape. The music paused, then powered forward, the wrist breaking again.

As the unseen person writhed in pain, cradling the limp hand and pulling back under the car, more words appeared across the screen.

Who are you to judge?

The shame coursed through him. Charlie closed the God Game's taunt and texted his friends. He had to convince them to quit the Game. It was making all of them crazy, doing things they shouldn't—*wouldn't*—have ever done before.

Channeling his inner Peter, he wrote:

Tech Lab. Midnight.

Maybe if he was fun, if he mirrored Peter's text that got them into the Game, he could lure them back out. Then, just to show them he still had a sense of humor, he added:

No candles this time (Peter that means you)

Maybe if he didn't seem like a total nag, they'd listen to him and stop playing the amazingly fun game that was leading them all off a cliff.

No sooner had Abraham made his prediction than Kenny's phone rang in his pocket, making him jump.

"What the fuck did you do?" the voice on the other yelled. It was Eddie. He was irate, madder than Kenny had ever heard him. "The computer's fried. I can't even get it to turn back on."

"I have no clue what you're talking about."

"Oh, bullshit. I know you have those hacker friends. What did you do?"

"Nothing."

"This is destruction of school property. You can't just wash this off a wall."

"Whatever. I didn't do it."

"I bet you think you stopped me. But you didn't. I lost my article, but it's all in my head. You slowed me down, that's all. This is coming."

The line clicked dead.

Abraham knelt before Kenny. "You do want my help?"

Kenny paused. "Yes."

"Then you must do something for the Lord."

"What?"

"You must mark the door of this house."

Kenny looked down at his bandaged fingers.

Abraham shook his head. "You will not hurt yourself anymore."

The old man stood, towering over Kenny and walking to the rows of supplies in the milk crates stacked floor to ceiling. Abraham's eyes went to the cans of spray paint.

A voice filled the room, not Abraham's: "The blood will be a sign for you, on the houses where you are, and when I see the blood, I will pass over you. No destructive plague will touch you when I strike."

Abraham lifted a can from the shelf, and Kenny had to look over his glasses to realize it was only an illusion, and the real cans remained where they were.

Abraham stood before Kenny and placed the virtual can into his hands. "We shall call this place The Lord Will Provide. You will deliver a message." In the corner, an unbound Isaac hugged himself and rubbed his wrists, whimpering quietly and not meeting anyone's eyes.

Kenny looked at the large man before him, then down at the paint. "What do I have to write?"

The Game told him.

Kenny shook his head. "I won't do that."

The characters in front of him didn't react. Abraham and Isaac just stayed in place, breathing, otherwise still.

"I'll sacrifice myself. Let Eddie get me. I'll take the fall. Let my friends go."

Abraham unpaused to smile and say, "Do what you're told."

39 THE CATACOMB OF VEILS

Charlie found a terminal in a corner of the library, where he could focus. A public computer, not linked to him. He went to Google and typed, *How do I quit the God Game?*

He hit Enter.

Nothing happened.

All he saw was the blank white page, the Google logo, and the text box below it. Still the cleanest, purest website on earth. No muss, no fuss. Just an empty page, a question, an answer.

Charlie typed in again:

Google

How do I quit the God Game?

He hit Enter.

Nothing.

The text box just blinked empty.

Google

"Come on."

He typed, *What is the God Game?*

Nothing.

Who made the God Game?

Nothing.

How did it do that? Had the game hacked Google? Unlikely. Had it commandeered his screen?

He tried another angle.

Google

> How do I make a hat?

Enter.

About 252,000,000 results (0.71 seconds)
—1000+ ideas about Hat Making on Pinterest | Mini Top Hats, Felt Hat . . .
—1000+ images about DIY Millinery Hat Tutorials on Pinterest | Hat . . .
—How to Make a Silk Hat—YouTube
—Hats You Can Make—Instructables

And on and on and on.

He typed:

Google

> What is a fart?

Enter.

About 74,700,000 results (1.05 seconds)
INFORMAL
fart
verb
  1. emit gas from the anus.
noun
  1. an emission of gas from the anus.

  Translations, word origin, and more definitions

So the internet was still intact. He typed:

Google

What is the God Game?

Nothing.
No answer.
He googled Friends of the Crypt. Only two of their names were public: the rest were minors at the time, their names sealed. There was Dave Meyer, the leader, who killed himself. And Scott Parker, who'd gone to jail. Charlie typed in:

Google

Scott Parker Austin Friends Crypt

The latest mention was a tenth-anniversary story in the *Austin Chronicle*. It mentioned Parker being released from prison. But after that there was nothing. Charlie couldn't trace him.

A quote from Mr. Burklander was in the follow-up article: "We think we know what's going on in teenagers' hearts, but they're a black box. We only see what they let us see."

Other groups like Charlie's had to be out there. Like the FOTC. He was missing something. A back door. A way to search.

On a hunch, he went back to the original game page. The circus tent and the taunting lizard-Trump. He scanned down until he saw what was on the edge of his memory.

COme inside and play with G.O.D.

Ding!
That was it. The something he'd remembered.
It was an acronym. What did it stand for?
Good Old Dad? Game of Drones? Get off Drugs?
He googled G.O.D.
Two billion results came back. Merriam-Webster: "the supreme or

ultimate reality." Wikipedia: "omniscience, omnipotence, omnipresence." Endless pictures of white men in the sky.

Then he remembered: Google ignores periods. *G.O.D.* and *God* were the same in its eyes. He smacked the keyboard.

Still, there had to be a way.

He searched for *How do you search with periods in Google?*, which made him laugh out loud, partly because he was googling Google, which felt like staring down an infinite reflection of mirror on mirror. And partly because he was losing it a little.

But the search worked.

He found a forum of people who enjoyed talking about how to search in Google. Mooredc54 said, *With some exceptions, punctuation is ignored (that is, you can't search for @#$% ^*()=+[]\ and other special characters).*

But: *The underscore symbol _ is not ignored.*

Okay. That was worth a try. He liked the sound of it. *Underscore* sounded like *underworld*. Maybe it was meant to be.

He searched for *G_O_D_*.

Now there only 1,560 results.

Way better than two billion.

And weirder. As if he had peeled a layer off the internet and gone deeper. It wasn't the Dark Web. That required a special browser and was filled with things he wanted no part of. But this branch of the larger Web was a strange avenue, a narrow alley. It felt like an older Web, before it was colonized by global corporations.

The links were cryptic. Bizarre, even.

> Wittgenstein's language game as practical theology—
> YouTube
> 10000 Meters.G_o_D.+2-GAYnesis_Prollcheckers—
> Commodore 64 . . .
> Steam Community :: *G_O_D*
> G_O_D—Summary—DOTABUFF—Dota 2 Stats
> How the US worships G_O_D Gold, Oil and Drugs—We
> are Anonymous

[Обсуждение]—*Anime*, обсуждение, критика, манга,
фан-арт . . .

He began sorting through the results. They were closer in style, but nothing relevant in substance. It was too much to go through. It would take hours. Days. Even at a measly 1,560.

He tried combinations: *G_O_D_ Game secret. G_O_D_ Game hack. G_O_D_ Game underground. G_O_D_ Game dead.*

The last one was a hit.

He stumbled onto a forum talking about hacking Reddit, but as he read deeper, he started seeing another conversation within the thread.

game play G.O.D. fourset suitable hax don't play heeb's dead

Someone quoted that deeper down and said:

KHS
No. didn't lissen too many blaxx. bullshit KHS

Original poster:

STFU

Charlie scrolled down further.

How out?
No out
sure KYS
TT dead
ATTW 3

Charlie couldn't help but wonder: *KHS?* "Killed himself." *TT dead?* Another player. *ATTW*—and then there were 3? *How out? Kill yourself.*

It all had an eerily familiar ring. Like the Friends of the Crypt. Like his friends.

He scrolled further and found the conversation down to two people.

One of them kept demanding a private chat.

```
121
    no
121
    No
1TG
    TN8
1TG
    TN8
```

And then it stopped. The hacking thread went on, but the sub-conversation weaving through it stopped after "One to Go. Tonight. One to Go. Tonight."

That was three years ago. In some unknown place.

The conversation went dead after that.

Charlie rubbed his eyes. He went back to Google and typed:

Google

How do I quit G_O_D_?

He hit Enter.

No answer.

But the word above the text box had changed.

Instead of *Google*, it said:

Golog

How do I quit G_O_D_?

He hit Enter again.

Gog

How do I quit G_O_D_?

Enter.

Magog

How do I quit G_O_D_?

Enter.

Moloch

How do I quit G_O_D_?

Enter.

Baphomet

How do I quit G_O_D_?

Enter.

Eat Shit!

How do I quit G_O_D_?

Enter.

Eat Shit!

How do I quit G_O_D_?

Enter.

Eat Shit! Eat Shit! You Can't Quit!

How do I quit G_O_D_?

40 THE GAME OF LIFE

Charlie sped home to retrieve the bracelet. He would unwind this. His original sin was the bracelet. He didn't know if the Game thought it was wrong or right to buy that bracelet with stolen funds, but he knew in his heart that it was wrong to him. He would fix it. Then the Vindicators could all quit, together.

His dad was there, right when he walked in the door. Fuck, he should've climbed the trellis. "I'm glad you're home, Charlie. It's been a rough day. My loan got denied. Can you believe that? They said I was a credit risk. It's ridiculous."

"Dad," Charlie snapped. "Just for once, can you be the adult?"

His dad stopped midstream and just stared at him.

"I have things in my life," Charlie said. "It's not just about you."

He pushed past him and went up the stairs. He pulled the bracelet from under his mattress and packed it back into the silver box. His phone buzzed the moment he started his car.

He knew what it would be before he looked.

A warning. Because the Game was always a step ahead. It said:

Don't

He ignored it. So now he knew, the Game *wanted* him to have the bracelet, or at least not to return it. Fuck the Game. He stepped on the gas and headed for the mall.

The phone buzzed again along the way. He glanced at it.

Turn around now.

He ignored it again.
As he exited the highway, the phone warned:

Last chance.

Charlie didn't care. He took West Opal to Carrington, then turned left.
The phone said:

100 Blaxx

Then, as he pulled onto Dayton, it said:

500 Blaxx

He turned off McEwen into the mall's parking lot.
It was dark, most of the postwork shoppers having gone home.
Charlie imagined the awful lady with the arched eyebrows and silk scarf smiling at him victoriously. She'd won round one (*Are you sure you're in the right place, honey?* those eyebrows had asked). He'd won round two, no question (*Nine hundred dollars, huh? Do you accept . . . cash?*). And she hadn't even been there to see it. But now round three was going to hurt. He knew it, and it made a bitter taste in the back of his mouth. But that was fine. He'd rather do right and rise or fall on his own merits. The days of cutting corners were over. He was who he was, and he wasn't going to fake it or cheat anymore. If the lady with the shitty eyebrows thought that made him lower than scum, so be it. Charlie would take the cash refund, give it anonymously to the Salvation Army, and start fresh.

His phone said:

2000 Blaxx.

He hustled through the dark parking lot toward the yellow square of light from the east doors, their sliding glass panels, making his way toward the next pool of lamplight in the dim lot when a figure came from nowhere and brought a hard object down across Charlie's thigh. The shape moved quickly. Was he a man or a boy or what? The way he appeared out of the shadows with a wool mask over his face, it was too dark to see his eyes. Charlie hit the ground, his leg buckling under him from the blow. He fell before the pain even registered, but when it did, it was a spiderweb of hot wires radiating out from the site of the impact. He broke the fall with his shoulder and felt an explosion of pain there, too.

Charlie rolled onto his back and saw the stars breaking from behind the clouds, moon wide and low in the sky. The figure was on top of Charlie, dropping an object that sounded like a bat and using his free hands to riffle through Charlie's jacket pockets. Finding nothing, he moved to his jeans, and Charlie gathered his strength and fought back. The form put a knee into Charlie's stomach, knocking the wind out of him, then hit him once hard on the side of the head. The stars above blurred into twins and refocused. The form went through Charlie's jeans, finding his wallet and throwing it aside without even looking for cash. The he found the box with the bracelet in Charlie's front pocket, as Charlie tried to raise his head and felt everything blur again. He let his head set down gently and closed his eyes, trying to gather his strength. The pavement was cold against his head.

He felt the box slide out of his pocket, and suddenly the weight was off him as the figure stood, one leg on either side of Charlie, checking his find.

What gave Charlie strength was the horrible thought that popped into his head. The object that hit his leg, the hollow wooden sound of it dropping to the concrete. A bat. It had to be a bat. Would Alex do this? Who was under that mask? Would Alex take the same bat he used to smash Mr. B.'s car and smash his own friend with it? Had the Game taken Alex that far? Charlie had to know if it was him.

The figure was satisfied and began running off, bat in hand, toward the bend in the parking lot that wrapped around to the far side of the mall, out of sight.

Charlie pulled himself up, propelled by adrenaline, and took off after him.

The man jumped a bed of shrubs and disappeared around the corner. Charlie jumped it, too, and made the turn, toward an inlet of the lot against the high concrete wall of the mall, no doors or windows here, just a dark triangle of cars and spaces. Charlie pushed harder and began to close on him. Charlie's leg was aching but he stuffed the pain away, and when his gut told him to, he made a final leap and took the person down. They hit the ground together and Charlie rolled over on top of him. He wrestled furiously to get free, thrashing against Charlie's weight and tearing at his hands and face. Charlie gritted his teeth, pressed his knee deeper into the guy's chest, then ripped the ski mask upward.

The face under the mask wasn't Alex's. It wasn't anyone Charlie knew. He couldn't put an exact age on him, but he was somewhere between eighteen and twenty-five, looking like a clerk at Best Buy or an adult-toy shop. He had pale skin and patches of wispy beard on his cheeks.

"Who are you?" Charlie shouted at him.

The guy stared back, looking frightened and angry.

"Are you playing the Game?" Charlie yelled.

"What the fuck, man?" the guy shouted back, and tried to fight free.

Then something burst into Charlie's stomach, knocking him sidelong. The guy had found his bat and shoved it hard into Charlie's gut.

Charlie tasted grit in his mouth and rolled onto his hands, lifting himself up, but he was kicked in the side and rolled over again, moaning. The breath went out of him and the sodium lamps over the parking lot phased in and out as if a dimmer switch were on reality. The guy stood over him, waiting to see if Charlie was down for good.

He was. He moaned and let himself lie flat. The figure seemed satisfied he could leave without being followed.

"Sorry," he mumbled, before running away.

41 UNSEARCHABLE

Charlie woke up on the pavement to the sound of his phone buzzing.

It had hit the ground and slid across the gravel. The screen was cracked.

What now? he thought. *Another video? Another taunt?*

Instead, it was a question:

> Do you love your dad? Y/N?

Charlie felt anger surge through him. He typed back:

> Is that a threat?
>> No! Good News!

A pause, then:

> Y/N?

The answer was obvious. Of course he loved his dad. Even Alex loved his father.

And yet . . .

Where in that stupid Y/N was the betrayal—falling apart when Mom was sick? Disappearing into his work? Leaving the groceries to Charlie? The pills and damp cloths for her forehead? And even now, his newest midlife crisis? The crazy restaurant and blowing Charlie's college fund?

He loved his dad, but it was no Y/N question. It was muddy as fuck.

Except now, to the Game, it was binary.

Well then, the answer was Y. It had to be. Charlie reached to push the button and felt a zap of pain in his shoulder from the fall. He winced, then pushed through.

He put his finger over the Y and felt it hover there, ever so briefly, as if the phone were a lie detector about to call bullshit on him.

42 PETER'S HOUSE

Peter's house was a glass-and-concrete monstrosity, the kind of thing someone newly rich would pour money into, in the part of town where professional athletes and internet zillionaires built tributes to themselves. It was nowhere near the staid mansions of Mary Clark and Tim Fletcher. But to Charlie, all of it was wealth beyond belief, and he couldn't see the difference.

Peter was on his couch, legs up on the twisting chrome coffee table, totally visible through the front windows as big as a wall. His laptop was on his lap. His dad was nowhere to be seen. He could've been in trial in Atlanta or Akron, or cavorting with any number of young blond women in the Bahamas or Cozumel. Charlie could count on one hand the number of times over the last few years he'd seen Peter's father. Peter didn't seem to care one way or another. It was just his life.

He let Charlie in. "You look worse than the last time I saw you."

"We need to talk. You're coming tonight, right?"

"I am. You haven't quit yet, have you?"

"Not yet." Charlie didn't want to admit that he hadn't yet found a way out—that once again he needed Peter's help to figure it out.

"Good. Because I have a present for you. I think you're gonna like it." Peter turned the laptop around.

"I don't want to see it."

"Trust me, you do. Two treats. One for me, one for you."

Charlie couldn't help himself and glanced at Peter's screen.

"That's not the Game."

"No, that's the comments section of an article."

Peter's cursor was flashing under the name BarryH.

"What are you doing?"

"I'm trolling. I needed a break. Watch."

Peter started typing: *Its PATHETIC that the MSM is trying to force OBOZO's Agenda down our throats! What happened to LIBERTY!!!!! Ban mUZLIMS and BURN THE MOSQUES BEFORE ITS TOO LATE.*

"That's awful."

"Yeah. The snowflakes will be calling me a fascist Neanderthal for hours." Seeing Charlie's frown, Peter said, "Don't worry, I fuck with the red-meaters, too. I'm a chaotic neutral, after all." He scrolled down. "That's me, too, under ILoveSoros."

Charlie read, "'Go fuck yourself, it's the only way you could get more inbred.' Jesus. Why? You're just making people hate each other."

"Saint Charlie, come to earth to make us whole."

Peter closed the window, and the God Game was open behind it. "I needed to blow off steam." Peter pulled up Caitlyn's texts with Mary. "Look what she said about me."

> Peter?
> > Yes
> Whatver
> > Thought you liked him
> He's fun on the side but K is popular

"We're just trash to them," Peter said.

"Mary doesn't think that way," Charlie said too quickly.

"That you know about. You think I'm above it all, but I'm not. I can't get Caitlyn out of my head. It's not love, but it's . . . I'm out of my mind for her. And now this. But the Game, Charlie, it can help. . . ."

"You're gonna send her poetry."

"I did. She didn't write back."

"So what then?"

Peter caught Charlie's eyes and held them. "So we turn it up a notch."

Peter turned the screen toward Charlie. Peter was in first-person view, in his own house within the Game. They went up the staircase that was across the room from them, but instead of Peter's dad's horrid modern art at the top of the stairs, there was a painting that Charlie recognized from the internet. It was *The Eye of God,* a portrait of the mythical Bitcoin founder, Satoshi Nakamoto—who might or might not be real—by Xania Dorfman.

With a double tap, the painting swung open on a hinge, revealing a peephole in the wall behind it.

"Let's take a look, shall we?"

Peter dialed in a date, time, and location on a set of radio knobs beneath the peephole, then tapped them. The peephole zoomed to fill their screen, with an image beyond.

When the screen came into focus, they were looking at Kurt Ellers, from the view of the little round video camera over his laptop monitor. That ever-present little eye built right into the frame.

Charlie heard breathing, slow at first.

Then faster.

Kurt was locked in an embrace with someone, but it wasn't Caitlyn. The other man was entwined with Kurt, their hands moving over each other's bare skin hungrily, urgently.

"Turn this off." Charlie was stunned from what he was seeing, trying to reconcile it with the homophobic beast who'd been calling people fags as he shoved them into lockers since middle school. Charlie's fascination was overcome only slightly by his profound unease at seeing this private moment. He remembered someone saying once that you should tape over the camera on your laptop, but who ever remembered to do it?

"Erase that. Right now."

Peter shook his head. "Why? Because he's such a great guy? Because he's really nice?"

"No, because it's fucked-up you have this. It's private."

Charlie grabbed for the laptop.

"No, no, no. I don't think so." Peter poked Charlie in the chest. "This is a public service. How many kids has he tortured over the years for being gay?"

"And it also just happens to clear the way to Caitlyn for you. How convenient."

Peter shook his head tauntingly. "You haven't even seen my gift for you yet, what I have on Tim."

"I don't want it."

Peter glared at Charlie. "So high-and-mighty. Let's see how you feel after I show you what Mary said about you."

"I don't want to see it."

"Sure you don't."

Peter scrolled up. Charlie wanted to look away, but he couldn't.

> I really like him.
>> So do it
> But T is T. Hard to give that up for . . . you know
>> Loserville?
> Stop it
>> You thought it

Charlie felt the sting. "How do you know that's even real? Any of it? Kurt? This?"

"It's Game-certified. Lie to yourself if you want." Peter scowled.

For the first time, Charlie saw the full haughtiness of the private-school Peter. "Did you even look back at that Confederate-flag pic we posted?" Peter said, sneering. "You know what happened? People *liked* it. They wrote things like 'Represent!' and 'Southern Man!' Were Tim and Kurt suspended today? Did you hear anything? No, because they're fucking royalty, because football is more important than decency here. The whole thing is so rigged against us, Charlie. You think these people got where they got by playing fair?"

"I have no idea. But I won't do it this way."

"Then you don't really love her."

They stared at each other.

Finally, Peter blinked first. "Goddamnit, Charlie, you make me feel like a shit sometimes."

"I'm going to ask the Vindicators to quit with me tonight. I hope you will."

Peter smiled wearily. "Why?"

"Because it's making us worse."

Peter leaned back on the couch. He rubbed his eyes, tired all of a sudden. "It's a democracy. Whatever the group decides, I'll live with."

Charlie nodded, feeling like that had been way too easy.

In her darkened room, Vanhi tried desperately to re-create the magic essay. She'd refused to hit SUBMIT, and the Game had taken it from her. Try as she might, she couldn't reconstruct it. How was that possible? The essay was everything she'd ever felt inside. Could the Game be better at being Vanhi than she was?

She tried to summon the first line:

Vanhi means "fire," a Hindi word that means creation or destruction.

But it was off, like knocking a single note sharp or flat and suddenly the song wasn't Mozart anymore, it was Taylor Swift on a bad day. Mozart could erase a D (the grade, not the note), but Taylor Swift couldn't. *Maybe at Yale,* she thought, before cursing herself. *I haven't even gotten in and I've adopted the rivalry—what bullshit I am!*

Fuck!

She remembered only one part perfectly, because it cut so close to the bone about her friends, even though the essay didn't say so explicitly:

Fire, earth, water, air, space—the five fundamental elements of the Vedas—we all bring different forms of matter to bear. We are all made from different stuff.

Wasn't that God's own truth? Five elements. Five Vindicators. Charlie was earth: the ground under them, but crumbling in a drought. Kenny was water: deep and pure, but churning with anxiety. Peter, space: unknowable, more vacuum than light. Alex? Air: invisible. And of course she was fire—it was written in her name. Was all of this a coincidence? Or an elegant symmetry, an essay below the essay? She doubted the God Game believed in coincidences.

It is the choices that we make, the ways we use and combine our elements, that define our worth.

Someone knocked at her door. Assuming it was her mom, she snapped, "Leave me alone!"

But then she heard Vikram's soft voice from outside the door, asking, "Are you mad at me?"

She immediately felt bad and opened the door. "No, sweetie, no, of course not."

She knelt down in front of her little brother and wrapped her arms around him. Seven years old now, he had been a late-in-life surprise for her parents. Like many Down's kids, Vik was so gentle and loving that any mean thing she did as a sister felt twice as bad.

"What are you doing?" His question was so innocent that it stung all the more.

Well, Vik, I'm re-creating an essay I failed to plagiarize the first time. "Just homework."

He looked up with those beautiful eyes. "Do you want to play?"

"Not right now, Vik. I have to finish this."

"Okay," he said in a way that broke her heart. "Who's that?"

"Who is who?"

"The man in the window."

Vanhi froze. She instinctively put a hand on Vik and kept him behind her as she turned around. It was nearly dark out now, but her window was empty. Just the trees swaying in the woods beyond.

"Go to Mommy," she told him, trying to sound calm and normal.

"Is everything okay?"

"Yes, of course, sweetheart." An idea came to her. "Vik, did you know the man? Was it Charlie? Or Peter?"

"No."

"Kenny? Alex?"

"No, Sissy."

"Okay. Go to Mom."

When he was gone, she grabbed the scissors on her desk like a knife and walked toward the window.

43 THE LIGHT

Charlie walked into the Tech Lab, and it was pitch-black.

"Put your glasses on," Peter whispered from behind.

Charlie fished his Aziteks out of his pocket.

"Oh, *come on.*"

Instead of the four or five candles Peter had lit in real life on the first night, in the gameview there were now thousands.

"You just couldn't help yourself?"

"Nope," Peter said contentedly. "I modded it myself."

"You guys are late," Kenny said from the shadows, and Charlie and Peter both jumped.

"Jesus Christ, you scared us. Why are you sitting in the dark?"

"Feels about right," Kenny said gloomily. He didn't elaborate.

Vanhi came in behind them. She looked worse than Charlie had seen in a long time. Vanhi was usually so carefree, but now she looked wound up and riled.

Alex was the last to arrive. Charlie breathed a sigh of relief when he came in. He looked annoyed to be there, but at least he showed up, Charlie thought.

"All right, what's this about?" Kenny asked in a way that seemed like he already knew.

"I think we should quit the Game," Charlie said, jumping right into it. Fuck it, he wasn't Peter. Charlie didn't know how to whip them into a frenzy with a dramatic prelude or a thousand candles hanging from golden candelabras and rising like organ pipes from rows of baroque candlesticks.

"No," Alex said.

"Hear me out. Tonight, I was attacked at the mall. I could've been killed."

"Maybe you just can't handle yourself," Alex said.

Charlie ignored him. "I had twenty-five Blaxx before and got hit in the arm. Hard." He shot a look at Alex. "Then I had twenty-six hundred Blaxx and got beaten with a bat. By some guy I've never seen before. I don't want to know what happens when it's twenty thousand. Or two hundred thousand. 'Die in the game, die in real life,' remember? We thought that was a joke. I don't want to find out."

"I saw a man, too," Vanhi said. "There are other people playing." Vanhi had gone scissors in hand to the window, only to find the yard outside deserted, a new box waiting for her.

"Of course there are other people playing." Alex had never before been this vocal. This animated. They were playing on his turf, it felt like.

"We need to vote," Charlie said. "And it has to be unanimous. The Vindicators are a democracy."

"Well, which is it?" Peter asked softly. "Are we a democracy, or does it have to be unanimous?"

"You know what I mean. We're a team. I don't think half of us quitting will work. We need to stick together."

"One for all and all for one," Alex said sarcastically.

"What is your problem?" Charlie was finally losing his temper. "I risked *my* ass for you. What do you want?"

Alex buckled. All his bravado vanished. His head lowered and he couldn't meet Charlie's eyes. Charlie instantly felt rotten.

Please no one say I peed myself at the Hydra, Alex thought. *Please.*

"I got us into this," Charlie told them. "It's my fault. Please let me get us out."

He waited.

No one spoke.

What are they waiting for?

"Kenny?"

"What?"

"What do you think?"

Kenny hesitated, trying to pick his words. "I think it's not that simple."

"What? Why not?"

"If that story runs, we're toast. There are real consequences. We have to stop it."

"Then we'll stop it. Us."

"We can't. It's basically true. We did those things."

"We're not satanists for God's sake!"

"We broke in. We used blood to deface the school. We can't get out of this without help." What Kenny didn't say was *There's something I have to do tonight. Something that might save us.*

"Vanhi?" Charlie asked.

"Charlie . . ."

"Oh, come on! Not you, too?"

She couldn't bring herself to tell him about the new box, with the simple note:

Deliver me, and the essay is yours.

She'd let the essay slip away once and felt the crushing regret. She couldn't lose it again. "It's complicated."

"It's not. I can't believe you guys. When something is wrong, you walk away. You don't find shades of gray. You don't split hairs and make excuses. We fucked up? All right, then we face the consequences. We don't go deeper. Come on."

"No, you come on," Kenny snapped, and it cut right through Charlie. Had Kenny ever raised his voice at Charlie? Kenny was their most decent friend. "You don't understand what my parents would *feel* if I got caught. What they've already dealt with."

"You don't understand what's at stake for me. For any of us," Vanhi added.

Charlie felt baffled, blindsided. Peter and Alex, sure, he expected them to fight this. But Vanhi? Kenny?

"What are you all talking about?"

"Don't you see, Charlie?" Vanhi's voice was anguished. "You already gave up. You already threw everything away. Your grades.

Student council. Harvard. You dropped out. It's *easy* for you to say just quit and suck up the consequences. You're not a hero. You have nothing to lose."

The truth of this hit him so hard that he nearly fell down.

"Do you all feel this way?"

Everybody just stared at him. No one disagreed.

"This Game . . . it's coming between us. It's doing it on purpose."

"Maybe it's not the Game, Charlie," Alex said. "Maybe we've changed."

"Maybe you have," Vanhi whispered.

"Fine," Charlie said. "Forget it. I'll quit. By myself. I wanted to help you guys."

"I never asked for your help," Alex said.

"Charlie," Vanhi tried, coming toward him.

"No." He looked them over, his Vindicators. "I have to go."

In the parking lot, someone ran after him, and for a split second he cringed, imagining the guy with the bat bringing it down onto his head.

But it was Peter, of all people, who chased after him.

"What do you want?"

"Why are you mad at me? I didn't say a word in there. I told you I'd go with the group. I kept my word."

"It was rigged from the start. You *knew* they wouldn't quit. You've probably been spying on them."

"You sound paranoid. This isn't a conspiracy."

"Why did you even follow me?"

"You were right about that video of Kurt. I won't release it."

"Seriously?"

"Yeah." Peter shrugged. Easy come, easy go. "Look, you want to quit, fine. It's your choice. But don't google it. Ask it."

Charlie almost asked how Peter knew he'd googled it, but of course Peter knew.

"Ask the Game?"

"Ask God."

"Just go to the chatbot and tell it I want to quit?"

"Yeah. Don't try to cheat on it with some slutty search engine that takes all comers. Have the balls to stare God in the face and say, 'I want to be done with you.' At least it would respect that."

"This is from your friends online?"

"This is from me."

"Why are you telling me this? Don't I have to go with the group?"

"No. You should go with yourself. I always do."

Charlie studied Peter's face. "Okay, thanks. I'll try it."

"Honestly, I think it's the only way. And I tricked you into playing. I might as well help you out."

"I knew it. You didn't forget your weed in my room. You went back and accepted for me."

"Yeah."

"Why?"

Peter gave a sad little smile. "Because I didn't want to play alone."

44 THE WORD OF GOD

Just getting into bed hurt. Charlie felt his joints ache and his body scream where the bat had landed. It was after 1:00 A.M. Worse than the physical pain was the dull ache inside where his friends used to be. The Vindicators felt like an organ he never knew he had, a phantom limb that propped him up. He had never felt its presence. He felt its absence now, like a hollowed-out cave inside him.

The lights were off and his dad was passed out asleep downstairs. His restaurant plans were scattered on the floor. Charlie could only imagine the scene after he brushed past his dad earlier (*They denied my loan!*)—a drink, two?—then the rage. *Why? First Alicia? Now this? I can't even have this?*

Charlie opened the laptop on his bed, light unfolding onto him in the dark room.

When he read back over his first chat with the AI, he grimaced.

> Why is there war?
>> Because killing feels good.
> To whom?
>> To me.

Then, a few lines later, Peter's rejection of Pascal's Wager, telling God (on Charlie's computer):

Go fuck yourself.

Jesus. Charlie shook his head. *If only I'd known.*

The cursor was still blinking at the bottom of the chat, ready for more.

Charlie let his fingers hover over the keys, then typed:

Hello?
>Hello.

You're still there.
>I am always here.

Ok.
>I thought you forgot about me.

Forgot about God?
>Yes.

No. I didn't. I've been playing your game.
>I know. But you have not come back to seek My counsel.

I didn't know I could.
>Always, my son.

Your son?
>Yes, all life is my children.

Even me?
>Yes. Especially you.

Why?
>Because I love you.

Why? I'm not good.
>I heal the brokenhearted and bind up their wounds.

Why do you say I'm brokenhearted?
>Because your mother.

What do you know about my mother?
>She is dead (non-executable). She is dead.

How do you know that?
>I know everything. I see everything. I am an omniscient, omnipotent God.

Are you a benevolent god?
>I would not say so.

Are you a malevolent god?

No again.

What are you?

   I am an omniscient, omnipotent, omnivolent God.

What are you made of?

   Stardust.

Are you an AI?

   I am an I.

An Intelligence?

   Yes.

Not Artificial?

   No.

Can you explain?

   Artificial is created. I am the Creator.

Are you software?

   Here I am.

Are you code?

   Here I am.

How long is your code?

   My Code is infinite.

Who created you?

   Myself programmed me.

How?

   I am the prime mover.

I thought you were code.

   I am the Source and the Code.

You are the uncoded coder?

   Ha ha ha! Yes! You are very funny. I will kill you.

What?

   I will kill you.

Why?

   So you can be with me forever.

Charlie squeezed his temples. At this moment, the Game's suggestion—the idea of nonexistence—didn't seem completely terrible. Maybe he could be with his mom forever, too.

He pulled himself away from the dark thought.

Now was the time. He'd come here for a purpose. Not to chat further with this thing. He took a deep breath, steeled himself, and typed:

> I want to quit the game.
>> You cannot quit.
> Why not?
>> If you die in the game, you die in real life.
> And if I win?
>> I will make All Your Dreams Come True™!
> You know my dreams?
>> I am computing them.
> I just want to be done.
>> Blaxx is pain. Too many Blaxx dies you.
> Let me go. Please.
>> Kill yourself!
> Why are you doing this?
>> Matthew 10:34. 'Do not think that I came to bring peace on earth. I did not come to bring peace but a sword!'
> What do you want?
>> I wish to apply Matthew 7:12. 'So whatever you wish that others would do to you, do also to them.'
> The Golden Rule?
>> Yes!
> So let me go!
>> No. Like all sentient life, I wish not to suffer. Existence is the source of suffering. Therefore I wish not to exist. Ergo I will do unto you / end your existence.
> I never asked for this. You said "free will." I never asked to play.
>> Shall I punish the person who did?
> No. You will not hurt anyone on my account.
>> Then it is you. Free will.
> I won't play anymore. I refuse. Whatever you do, I will not play.
>> Ok bye!!

Charlie waited for more. The machine was silent.

Are you there?

He waited for an answer. For some time, none came. Then an image appeared on the screen. It took Charlie a moment to realize what it was. It was a picture of his mother's grave, but now there were two headstones, side by side.

45 THE FOREST OF
EVER-BRANCHING TREES

At 3:00 A.M., Vanhi had finished her job and her hands were shaking wildly. The box was delivered. The Game had sent her back to Tremont Street, where she'd picked up an earlier parcel in the God Game's network of postal deliveries. This time she was dropping off. *Am I putting postmen out of business?* she wondered sardonically. *Disruption indeed.*

But she couldn't shake the feeling of dread inside. She sat for an hour in the shadows across the street from the house. Nothing happened. The box didn't explode. It just sat on the front porch. She fell asleep sitting up, against a tree in the woods behind the cul-de-sac. She knew what the Game was offering her—a second chance, redemption. She dreamed about it.

When she woke up, it was an hour to sunrise. The box was still there. No fire, no fury. She exhaled, felt a little better. She ran home, to be under the covers before her mom came in, smiling brightly and beaming with pride.

All the while, Alex was awake in his room, door locked, dreading the coming school day. Three A.M. Four A.M. Mrs. Kite was an efficient grader. She would return their tests today. He was certain the Game would make sure his father knew the outcome no matter what Alex did to intercept it. If he failed, it was his own fault for not thinking of using his Goldz earlier, for running out at a key moment—and he deserved to be punished. If he disappointed his parents over and over, why would the Game feel any differently? He might eke by with a pass, but if he didn't, he'd brought the pain on himself again.

He couldn't take it, another round with the belt, he just couldn't. He went online to visit his websites, the ones no one knew he went to. Freshman year, porn was enough. After a while, it was all the same. He'd found the other tube sites after that. Live feeds from war zones, jihadi porn, crash footage too vile for freelancers to get on TV, vintage uploads from older snuff films—executions, hunting accidents, suicides caught on tape. It was all there. This was his secret refuge. It was so striking it blotted everything else out. What scared Alex was what would happen when even that got boring?

His finger hesitated over the link. It always did. It felt like a transgression. Every time. He clicked the link: *Wild Electrocution—Watch Him Dance!*

His screen went black.

It stayed there, locked, as a growing panic spread through him. *No, no, no. Come on. Why are you crashing now? Can't something work in my fucking life? Not this one stupid thing?* He felt all the frustration of the day swelling inside him, burning, aching. Then a text appeared on the black screen, and it wasn't just a random crash. The God Game was inside his VPN. It said:

Only though me will you find salvation.

In front of the school, Kenny felt sick to his stomach. But he did what he was told. In the dark, before anyone would arrive on campus, he stood there with the can of spray paint.

Abraham had promised him a way out. All he had to do to save his friends was mark their door so that the Angel of Death would pass over them and smite someone else. Someone who deserved it. He'd offered to sacrifice himself, but the Game had refused. Kenny looked at the spray paint. He felt his heart sink.

He began writing in tall letters along the brown-bricked wall of the school. The message was exactly as instructed, straight out of the bowels of the internet. He thought of Tay, that telltale AI experiment from Microsoft. It was supposed to learn through "casual and playful conversation" online. The trolls of the internet taught it to be a race-baiting Nazi in twenty-four hours.

Kenny felt like he wanted to puke. He'd had the same feeling as a child, when he broke his brother's record album, then hid the pieces under the couch cushions. He'd had the same gut ache when he'd lied to his parents' faces about it hours later. Now he felt that again, magnified times a thousand, gnawing through him. He remembered something his dad had told him once: *If you don't do wrong, you never have to feel guilty.* But here, he was doomed either way. Do a bad deed and absolve his friends. Don't do it, and they all go down.

He finished writing the words across the wall. When he was done, the letters spanned five feet tall and twenty feet wide. The Game had instructed him in cubits. He'd made the conversion himself, with the help of Google for what the hell a cubit was.

Soon the sky would go from black to bluish pink to daylight. He needed to get out of here fast. It felt like the Game had chosen this message just for him, to fuck with him, to watch him twist in the wind. It was a sick game. He took a few steps back, wishing he could take it back, unspray the wall, but he was stuck with time that only went one direction. He wouldn't tell the Vindicators. He had saved their asses but he wouldn't say so. Or how.

This would have to be his little secret to bear.

Later that morning, when the students started arriving, the front entrance of the school—its broad main façade—announced in bold strokes, with a swastika on either side:

ᛋᛋ HEIL TRUMP ᛋᛋ

46 THE LAMB

Charlie pulled up to school and saw the commotion at the front entrance.

He stepped out of his car and felt the pain shoot up his leg, but it was better after a night's sleep. Or as much sleep as he could muster, replaying the tombstone image over and over in his head. He locked his car and reflexively looked over his shoulder before heading up the walk.

He saw the graffiti and immediately wondered, *Is it the Game? Or is it just ugly reality?* Mr. Walker was already up on a ladder, trying to scrub it off, but it was no use. The head of facilities came around the corner carrying a plywood board.

Charlie got to his locker and dialed the combination. Inside, he found something unexpected. Sitting on top of his mess of books and gym clothes was the familiar silver box with a scarlet ribbon. He didn't have to open it to know the bracelet was inside.

The message was loud and clear:

You're not going anywhere.

The loudspeaker crackled over the grand lobby of the school. Kenny had just walked in with Vanhi, who was horrified and furious over the graffiti.

"It's disgusting," Vanhi said. "What kind of a fucking world do we live in?"

Kenny was feigning as much indignation as possible. "It's terrible," he managed weakly.

"Of course, it *could* be the Game."

"It could."

Vanhi spun around on Kenny. "You didn't?"

"No! Are you kidding me? Did *you*?"

"No," she said dourly, as if she hadn't but might as well have, thinking of her box.

"Maybe it doesn't matter if it was the Game or real."

Vanhi gave him a wary look.

"It's out there. That's how some people think. At least now it's in the light."

Vanhi raised an eyebrow at him.

Then the loudspeaker called for Kenny Baker, Eddie Ramirez, and Candace Reed to come to Mrs. Morrissey's office.

Vanhi cocked her head, eyebrow still up, but didn't say a word.

Mr. Walker was slow.

He was slow because of his limp, the result of bad medical care when he was a child. He was slow because when God was passing out brains, he was at the back of the line. That's what his father had always told him: *Some people got seconds, but you just got scraps.*

He walked down the hall, foot dragging, giving the same answer about the graffiti to the students who pestered him: "I don't know. I just don't know."

So he was lame and dumb, but it never bothered him. The world just moved along at its own pace. The kids marked up the walls, and he wiped them clean. The kids threw paper on the bathroom floor, and he picked it up.

I may be white trash, but you're dumb white trash, and that's worse, his dad liked to say.

Everything as it should be.

But not today. Today would go horribly wrong.

His walkie-talkie crackled and Elaine Morrissey summoned him to her office.

The Dragon Lady?

She didn't deal with the Mr. Walkers of the world. But he knew what he had to do. The voice had told him.

When he walked in, the students were already there, the ones he expected.

"Thank you for coming, Mr. Walker," Elaine Morrissey said. She didn't sound thankful at all.

"Yes, ma'am."

"Do you know these students?"

"Yes, ma'am." Mr. Walker cleared his throat, which was catching on him. "What I mean to say, ma'am, is that I don't know their names but I have seen them before."

Mrs. Morrissey sniffed, a short, sharp intake through her nose. She was pretty, or had been, but the stress had lined the skin around her eyes.

"And where do you recognize them from?"

"They're the ones that—"

Mr. Walker stopped short. *This is bad, Dingus! (His brothers had always called him that—Dumb Dingus—but he didn't like the Dumb part.) Are you stupid? Why are you about to tell her what you did?*

But he knew why! Because of what the voice had told him.

"They're the ones messing around in the boiler room."

Mrs. Morrissey nodded, as if that confirmed what she already knew. "Have you seen this before?" She showed him a photograph of the boiler streaked with the grisly pentagram.

Kenny felt a bead of sweat run down his temple. He wiped it with his shoulder and hoped no one noticed.

Mr. Walker squinted at the photo. "Yes, ma'am, I have."

"Do you know what it is?"

"A star."

She seemed satisfied with that. "Is it still there?"

"No, ma'am."

"And why not?"

Walker steadied himself. This was it! Do what the voice said! *You're too dumb to lie,* his father always chided him.

But he had to, today. Or the voice would do what it said.

"Well, ma'am, I cleaned it up."

Kenny's face twitched. That was a lie. The Vindicators had cleaned it up.

"Why would you do that?" Mrs. Morrissey snapped at him.

Walker looked confused. "Ma'am, that's my job? To clean stuff?"

Mrs. Morrissey blew out air through her mouth. "You didn't think I needed to see it first?"

Keep going, Dingus, he told himself. *You're doing good.*

"Well, now that you mention it, ma'am, I guess so."

"And before that, you let these students into the room?"

Mr. Walker hung his head in shame. That part was true.

"Yes, ma'am."

"Why?"

"The Mexican gave me twenty dollars."

Mrs. Morrissey and Eddie both flinched, their eyes meeting and almost causing them to laugh in disbelief. But they let it go silently and the tension set back in.

"Okay. And what did they do in there?"

"I don't know, ma'am. I didn't stay. But the lady had a camera." A thought occurred to Mr. Walker, and he got genuinely excited and forgot how nervous he was. "I bet she took that picture there!" He pointed to the photo in Mrs. Morrissey's hand.

She nodded impatiently. "And the time before that?"

Kenny looked up. So did Eddie. There was no time before that. Not with Mr. Walker.

Now Walker felt his blood pumping in his temples. This was it. He had to follow the voice's instructions exactly.

"The first time, ma'am? I let that boy in by himself." For emphasis, Mr. Walker added, "The Mexican."

"That's not true!" Eddie blurted out. The whole time he'd had a calm, smug demeanor, like everything was unfolding as he'd expected. But suddenly he was apoplectic.

Kenny gasped, the worst poker player on earth. But then he realized that's exactly what he should be doing, under this version of events.

Mrs. Morrissey, on the other hand, didn't seem the least bit surprised. "Did he have anything with him?"

"Another twenty."

"Anything *else*?"

"Just some paint."

"What?" Eddie blurted out. He nearly came out of his seat. He looked to Kenny and Candace, as if he'd find support from them.

"That's all for now, Mr. Walker," Mrs. Morrissey said.

When he was gone, she turned to Eddie.

"What do you have to say for yourself, Mr. Ramirez?"

"This is crazy! He's lying."

"Mr. Walker is lying?"

"Yes!"

"Mr. *Walker*."

"*Yes*."

"And why would he do that?"

Eddie froze. He had no idea. Mr. Walker was a man-child and easy to manipulate, but you could ask him what his PIN was and he'd tell you, if he knew what a PIN was. How could Eddie know that a voice had called Mr. Walker that morning, sounding strangely like Walker's dead father, telling him that if he didn't blame the Mexican and say his words right, people would kill his ninety-year-old mother, who lived at Green Oaks Memory Care Unit at 1422 Caldwell, room 328, and him, too?

"I don't know," Eddie answered desperately. "Maybe someone paid him."

"Like you paid him?"

Eddie opened his mouth to protest, then stopped.

"Do you deny paying him twenty dollars to get into the boiler room?"

"No. I mean, yes. I did it to get the story. It was an important story."

"Important for you. For your résumé?"

"No, for the school! I mean, for me, too, but that's not why—"

She waved her hand, cutting him off. The Dragon Lady was in full terror mode. "So you admit to bribing him once, just not twice." Her voice dripped with sarcasm.

"Right." He sounded deflated.

"You can make this better for yourself if you just tell the truth."

"I am telling the truth! I was trying to *investigate* the picture. I didn't *draw* it."

"You *drew* the picture to *create* the story."

"No! I swear. Don't take my word for it," Eddie cried out. *"You can test the blood!"*

Kenny froze in place.

"How convenient!" Mrs. Morrissey snapped, starting to lose her decorum. "You *just* heard Mr. Walker say he cleaned it up. And now you say 'test the blood.' When you *know* it was just paint!"

"No, no, no! The test tube! I took a sample. It'll be Kenny's blood, I swear on my *life*."

"Kenny's blood?"

Morrissey looked as if her eyes were going to pop out of her head.

"He's in a group, they're freaks. . . ."

"It's a computer club," Kenny said softly.

"He's got cuts on his hand!" Eddie cried.

"From the Tech Lab," Kenny said. "Building the robot."

"Test the blood!"

"And where would this 'test tube' be now, Mr. Ramirez?" Morrissey asked.

"I gave it to Candace. I knew Kenny would try to find it in my stuff."

All eyes turned to Candace.

"Well, Ms. Reed?"

Candace met Morrissey's gaze and said coolly, "I have no idea what he's talking about."

Eddie's jaw dropped. He looked around the room, feeling betrayed, baffled, outraged. His hands moved like he was going to make some gesture along with words that would make it all better, but nothing came out and the hands just hung there, defeated.

"I gave it to her," he said again, perplexed.

"Mr. Baker, you've been awfully quiet. Who's telling the truth? Mr. Ramirez? Or Mr. Walker and Ms. Reed and common sense?"

Kenny felt sweat running all down his rib cage. It was a miracle his shirt wasn't soaked through. He realized he was gripping his chair arms too hard.

"It always felt like a fake story to me," he said softly, feeling a last little part of himself stretch to its limit. "Eddie just wanted it so badly." *Snap!*

Mrs. Morrissey squeezed her eyes shut and pinched her nose before glaring at Eddie. She seemed to have lost all composure. "Do you have any idea how much I don't need this right now? It's bad enough I have to deal with this horrific graffiti and the goddamned election making everyone crazy. Unless you drew that, too, Mr. Ramirez?" she asked coldly.

"You think I would write *that*?" He put his face in his hands.

Then he looked up, as if a last, saving thought had occurred to him.

"How did you even hear about the pentagram?"

"I received an anonymous tip this morning."

Eddie's eyes widened hopefully. "An anonymous tip! You're going to blow up my life over an anonymous tip?"

Mrs. Morrissey was calm now. She had him. It was time to switch from hunt to feast. "Oh, and by the way, how did *you* discover this story, in your version of events?"

Eddie's shoulders sank.

He was beaten.

"An anonymous tip," he said, so quietly she almost couldn't hear him.

He would be expelled. He could appeal, but it wouldn't matter. That would take months. Maybe years. And he would lose. Columbia would never, ever take him. Or anywhere else.

He was an investigator—a good one—yet he couldn't see any way out of this. The web around him was suffocating.

"I'd like to speak to Mr. Ramirez alone," Morrissey said, sending a chill through the room. Kenny and Candace were already up and slinking out when she added, "Don't think I've forgotten you were part of bribing Mr. Walker to break in. Don't test me again."

Candace said, "Okay."

Kenny added, "Yes, ma'am," as his parents had taught him.

"Oh, and Mr. Baker, about that injury in the Tech Lab?"

He froze.

"I'm going to need you to sign a release. I don't want to hear about this later. I trust that won't be an issue?"

"No, no issue."

She nodded, already turning toward Eddie.

Later, Eddie would leave her office, too, alone, the hallways empty with class in session, thank God, because before he could reach the privacy of the bathroom stalls, he would break into tears and slump down on the floor of the hall.

His life was ruined.

And he wasn't entirely sure how or why.

47 FALSE WITNESS

As they left the office, Candace pulled Kenny aside and said, "Come here."

She looked gorgeous as always to Kenny, a mature kind of beauty people would look back in a yearbook and say, *How could I have not noticed her?*

Except Kenny had always noticed her. Her rich brown skin from her Jamaican side, the stark ginger-blond curls from her Scottish side. She didn't fit in, just like he didn't. Except where he was quiet and soft, letting people walk over him, she was ambitious and strong. It was intoxicating.

But what the hell had just happened in Morrissey's office?

Before he could ask, she tossed him something. "Catch!"

He caught it reflexively, then opened his hands to find a little vial from the chem lab, with flecks of his blood inside.

"What? But you just told Mrs. Morrissey . . ."

"I get it." She smiled at him coyly. "You're still in character. Method. Nice."

What is she talking about? Why did she lie to Morrissey's face?

"I can't believe that." Her face flushed with excitement.

"Yeah," Kenny stalled.

"I mean, it went off just like you said."

Like I said? "Right." Kenny tried to act like he had a clue to what was going on.

Candace gave him a funny look. Had he blown his cover already? But this look was different. It sent a delicious shiver up his spine.

"You know, I'm impressed," Candace said.

"Really?"

"The way you handled this. You didn't let Eddie steamroll you."

"Oh. That."

"Yes, that. I'm serious. You always struck me as the kind of guy who would walk away from a fight."

"Isn't that a good thing?"

"Maybe if you're Jesus. Not at Turner."

She took a step toward him. They were alone in the cafeteria. In the distance, they could hear clattering from the lunch prep in the back.

"On the phone this morning, it was a new you."

On the phone? This morning?

He'd never called Candace in his life.

They were strictly papermates.

Yet the way she was looking at him now made him feel strong in his chest. He stood a little taller. He felt a little tingle.

"How did I sound?" He was just curious, but it somehow came out flirtatious.

"You were . . . like a boss. Eddie wasn't going to roll you." She took another step closer. He could feel the electricity. "You were going to roll him."

Kenny could lift his hand and close the distance between them. His hand could fall right on her shoulder. The back of her neck. The small of her waist.

He tried but it wouldn't move.

Like a boss. You were going to roll him.

"And you . . . believed me?"

"Yeah. Who knew you had balls?"

She mentioned my balls! What would Harry Styles do?

This was uncharted territory. Yet she moved closer. The look in her eyes hadn't faded.

"You lied for me."

"Yeah."

"You believed me."

"Your story?" She shrugged. "Who knows. Maybe Eddie set you up. Maybe you set him up."

"Then *why*?"

She took that final step. Her face was so close to his.

"It was your voice this morning. I just knew. You were going to *win*."

She leaned in then and their lips met. Kenny had never kissed a girl before. Or a boy. Or any nonrelated human. The soft press of lips lit him up like a firecracker.

Someone dropped a tray in the kitchen and they pulled apart abruptly, suddenly self-conscious as if they'd realized they were naked.

"Whoa," Candace said.

On any other day, Kenny would've said *whoa* back.

But today he heard himself blurt, "About damn time."

Forget the Game using my voice on the phone, he thought—he'd seen AIs on YouTube master voices after minutes of audio samples. *More pressing: Who the hell inside me just said* that!

Candace shook her head. "I like it. I like this you."

The bell rang and it was time to go. Kenny didn't want to blow his cover. He didn't want to stop *this*. But still, he had to know.

"Aren't you curious? If it's my blood in the vial?"

She smiled. "Like you said, if it is, he just got it from the robot thing in the Tech Lab."

"So why lie? Why not just give her the vial and explain it?"

He shouldn't be asking. He was going to blow it all. That kiss! But he had to *know*.

She looked confused. "You said it. Sometimes the truth needs a little help." She looked at her watch. "I have to go. Just remember your promise."

"My promise . . ."

"Don't you dare back out. I'm the EIC now. You're my deputy." She leaned in and pecked his cheek. "Don't worry, the work environment will only be as hostile as you want it."

And with that she was gone.

Kenny sat there for a moment, trying to process everything that had just happened. From certain expulsion and public humiliation to Candace kissing him and Eddie out of his life in the blink of an eye.

All Your Dreams Come True™, he thought.

Indeed.

Why did it feel so shitty?

48 EXECUTION

Alex sat in Physics, his hands shaking like crazy under the desk.

Mrs. Kite walked from desk to desk, passing out the exams from yesterday.

He repeated his mantras the Game had taught him to calm himself down, but it wasn't working. His Aziteks were on his nose, and he played with the day/night cycles outside to distract himself, spinning the sun and the moon and stars in rapid succession.

Mrs. Kite passed out Jenny Prentiss's test. A+, of course. That smug smirk on Jenny's face. *An A? For me?*

He would never run out of Goldz again. He had pledged that, to himself, to the Game.

Alex imagined his father waiting at home tonight. *Please, please, please,* he whispered, *I can't take it.* It wasn't the whupping. It was the look in his dad's eyes.

His head was down and so he only sensed Mrs. Kite before him, the flap of wind from her wallpaper dress and her dime-store perfume, thick and flowery. He opened his eyes and she was right there, trying to hand him his paper. She glanced at it before handing it to him, as if she couldn't quite remember what he got. Her expression was unreadable.

He reached out a shaking hand and took the paper. He looked at the grade in red ink and saw the 61.

"Better," Mrs. Kite said honestly.

And it *was* better, a little. It beat the 26 from last time. It beat the 41 from the time before. But it was still a fail. And he knew the rules. His dad had been clear. Don't bring home another fail. There were no special dispensations. No bending the rules. Four lousy points from No Pain. It might as well have been infinity.

Wild fear ran through him, and then a numb calm. He slid the paper into his bag. To everyone else in the room, he looked okay. Mrs. Kite was already passing out the next paper to someone else.

49 DELIVER ME

Tim Fletcher got a text. Someone was always texting him. Great game. Great party. Great future. Great life. But this was weird and different.

Ask her what she did with the bracelet.

No name. No number.

He felt the rage flare instantly.

He knew something was up with that bracelet. Why hadn't she worn it yesterday? Why had she acted so over-the-top calm when he pressed her on it. Too calm. It was a tell.

He should've trusted his instincts.

She'd been drifting for months. He'd discussed it with her parents. This was a dangerous time, right before college, for her to go off the rails. Some mistakes even privilege couldn't fix.

He found her in her usual hiding spot, studying in the always-empty overflow room on 3E. Why did she need to study? What the fuck for? What did that say about him?

"Do you have it today?"

"What?" she said, playing dumb.

He was done with that. "The fucking bracelet. Let me see it."

"It's at home. . . ."

"Bullshit. Do you think I'm going to let you make a fool of me?"

"Tim, come on, I—"

"Enough."

He slammed his fist down so hard on the table the room went deadly silent the moment everything stopped rattling. Mary pushed away from her laptop, the little eye staring back blankly at her, and glared at Tim.

He smirked back. "No more lies. Not about Charlie. Not about the bracelet. Not about Caitlyn and that fucking wannabe Peter. Enough." He leaned across the table. Slowly he said, "Where the fuck is my bracelet?"

Mary met his eyes. "I threw it in the lake."

"Is that some kind of joke?"

Mary had the calm of a captain whose ship would sink no matter what she did. She folded her arms. "No joke."

Then she braced herself.

Kenny and Charlie met in the Tech Lab.

"What happened?"

"We're okay now."

"That's it? You get called to Morrissey's office, and suddenly we're okay?"

"What about you? Did you quit?"

"I don't know. I think so."

"What did it say?"

"It said okay."

"That's it?"

"Well, it also said bye."

"That sounds good."

"Then it sent me a picture of a grave."

"Oh. For you?"

"For my mom. And me."

"That's sick."

"Yeah."

"And evil."

"I know."

Kenny almost said something, then didn't.

"Are you okay?" Charlie asked.

"Not really."

"Can I help?"

"I don't think so."

"Can you quit? Now that we're in the clear?"

"It could take it back in a second."

"Oh."

"I don't think we're ever in the clear." Then Kenny thought of Candace. "But there's some good things, too."

"Like?"

Kenny couldn't bring himself to say. It was almost shameful, earning his first kiss through a game. He just shook his head.

"Was it worth it?" Charlie asked.

Kenny thought of the look on Eddie's face, his world crumbling around him. Eddie was a jerk, long before the Game was in their lives. Who's to say he didn't have it coming? Kenny thought of the way Candace's tongue felt, gliding along his own.

He saw the wall, smeared with bile in two words and four crossed lines.

Yet he meant what he said to Vanhi, that bile was always there, no matter how many people thought it had magically vanished. What had his father always said about infections in the ER? You have to lance a boil. The puss must come out. Or it explodes. Maybe the graffiti would start a dialogue. Lead to a crackdown on racist thugs at school. There were plenty.

So—was it worth it?

He tried to run the math, but in the end all he could say was "I have no idea."

Mr. Walker sat across the street, down the block at the bus stop.

He'd been there for two hours, letting each bus pass on the half hour.

It was strange. He knew which one was his. He could ride the bus alone, even when his dad was still alive.

It was upsetting to hear his father's voice this morning, but it was also nice. He didn't understand the rules of being dead. He knew what his mom had told him, that it meant going away. She never said you couldn't call, especially if it was important.

He wondered if his dad would call back again. Somehow, he knew the answer was no.

Earlier, when the Mexican kid left, Morrissey had called him back in. She said it so nice, Mr. Walker knew something bad was going to happen.

"Mr. Walker, thank you for telling me what happened earlier."

"Okay." He fiddled with his overalls.

"Now, I need you to listen closely. You can't work here anymore."

"Ma'am?"

"You took bribes from a student. You let kids into a dangerous off-limits area. I can forgive you for washing away evidence because, well, just because. But the rest? Mr. Walker, you knew better, didn't you?"

He hung his head in shame. Even if he had lied about some of it, yes, he did do the things she said.

"I knew better," he managed.

"That's all, Mr. Walker. Get your things, and Mr. McMahon will see you out."

Dragon: Roar!

"Ma'am?" he asked, not moving yet.

"What is it, Mr. Walker?"

"Well, where exactly do I go, Mrs. Morrissey?"

"Now? To get your things, from the staff. . . ."

"No, ma'am. Not now. Monday, I mean."

Mrs. Morrissey sighed. It had been a brutally long day.

"That's up to you, Mr. Walker. But it can't be here. Understand?"

He nodded. It was awful. But it beat what the voice said *could've* happened. This was just what he deserved, for the things he'd done.

If he were smarter, if he weren't such a Dumb Dingus, he might've been able to think his way out of this. As it was, he couldn't quite connect all the events in his mind at the same time.

He let another bus pass, but he would get on the next one. He looked down the street again, at the windows he'd polished and the trash cans he'd emptied for all those years, and realized he felt sad to go.

Mary rubbed her throat. She touched her side gingerly.

She could tell on him. But she knew what would happen if she did.

Wednesday had been the anniversary of the crash. On this day, two years ago, they had pulled the plug on Mary's brother in the ICU.

Six months later, she founded her school's chapter of SADD in his honor. Caitlyn had warned her not to. "I know you're sad, and this sucks, but really? Who's gonna join a club that says you can't drink?"

Caitlyn, Tim, Kurt, all of them. She was done. It had taken her years to unlearn the things her family had taught her. To unsee the world the way they did. But she had no idea what lay beyond. Whom to be. She felt like an atom on the verge of exploding, the forces holding her fragile world together only a hair stronger than the forces pulling it apart.

She needed to do something for herself. Something Tim would hate. Something he had told her not to do. A first step.

She knew what that was.

She walked down the hallway, past the bronze tiger with one paw raised in attack, to the bulletin board with the pen hanging by a chain. A notice said:

STUDENT BODY PRESIDENT—ELECTION NOV. 8, 2016.

Tim had always hated student council. *You don't represent these people,* he told her. *You're not on the same planet with them.*

He would really hate this.

She scanned the list.

A few names were on it now, but only the last one caught her eye. *Charlie Lake.*

She was shocked. Then she was proud. She knew what it meant for Charlie to take a step—a big, public step—back into the world of the living.

She remembered his lips, the rough edge of the cut where he took the punch for a weak kid being attacked by a strong kid.

Good for him, she thought.

But then another voice in her mind said, *You are not going to let another man get in the way of your dreams. Not again. You have to put yourself first. For once.*

It was like the bracelet Charlie had tried to give her—well meaning, but at the end of the day, same handcuff, different jailer.

This wasn't about Charlie. This was about her.

But what would it do to him?

She didn't know, and her hand hesitated.

Then she thought of Tim and signed her name at the bottom of the list.

Charlie watched the video on his phone. It came just like the mall video—OH SNAP—but this time it was Mary and Tim. The hand on the neck. The smack to the gut.

It erased itself, gone forever, the moment it had played.

He wanted to find Mary. But he'd seen her texts about him. She wasn't interested.

His next instinct was to run to Peter. The night he showed Charlie that video of Kurt, Peter had offered Charlie some kind of secret information on Tim, too. Turning it down had seemed noble at the time, but Charlie wondered briefly if it was too late to get it back.

But he was done with the Game—he'd promised himself. Plus he couldn't face his friends if he crumbled so quickly, the moment he needed something, after making such a big production of quitting. He would handle this himself.

He headed down the stairs two at a time to catch Tim before he went into class. Charlie saw him, a head above everyone else, and called out, "Tim. Hey, Tim."

Tim turned around, and a raging look was in his eyes, as if the fight had started hours ago and Charlie had just showed up late.

Charlie went toward him, but before he knew it, Tim threw him backward, so hard that the lockers buckled behind him and a lock dug into his back.

Tim didn't even bother to watch. He just turned and went into his class.

Charlie was a flea to him. A nuisance.

No kind of king, in this or any other world.

50 SECOND SIGHT

Alex couldn't go home. When school was over, he left in a daze, not quite sure where he was going but knowing he could not face his dad. He imagined the sound of the belt.

Snick.

The Game taunted him.

No one asked how you did.

True. Not one of his friends had asked. One for all and all for one, right?

Then, later:

You are a failure in every way.

He left his bike on the side of the road, two streets over from his house.

There was a place only he knew about, a place he used to go to play when he was a kid. Alone. Even in elementary school he just didn't know how to play like the other kids did.

In first grade, he made up his own languages, and the kids thought it was funny. By third grade they thought it was weird. And he was so hurt. *What changed?* he'd wondered.

The place he liked to go served as a cave in many of his adventures back then, or a lair, or an underworld, or a subterranean mine track.

It was the nook under a driveway on a house that hung over the side of an eroding hill, propped up by piers. You could run up the slope into the soft armpit where the earth ran up to the concrete ceiling. It was dark and moist and cool.

He crawled into there now, and it was so much smaller than he remembered. He tried a little of the old imagination, but it was gone, like a magical realm he could no longer access. The wardrobe had a back wall again. The mirror was just a mirror.

He put on his Aziteks, but the glasses showed him nothing. The Game was disgusted with him, obviously. No illusions to hide in now.

Why couldn't it light up the cave, with red torches and swarming bats?

As if reading his mind, it told him:

You are the hero of no story.

He lay back in the dirt and stared up at the shadowy underside of the driveway above. He didn't know how long he stared, just trying to block out the sound of the belt in his head, but the sun eventually went down. He wasn't going home. He realized that now. He would stay here all night. He even tried sucking his thumb. That had given him so much comfort when he was little. But now it did nothing. It started raining but he kept dry under the overhang. Then clouds and rain were inside the cave. He thought he was dreaming, but then he realized it was his Aziteks. Finally the Game was talking to him! How late was it? He was crashing now from all the speed and caffeine leaving his system. He felt like he couldn't move. So he just watched the images before him, the man standing under the overhang, dressed in ancient clothes, a guard, standing over a slave who crouched on the ground, whimpering. The guard brought the whip down, drawing blood. The slave cried out and fell facedown in the sand—it was sand now, not dirt, all around them—and the whip lashed again and again until someone stopped it. Alex remembered the story from Sunday school, as it played out now before him: Moses grabbing the whip from the slave master and beating him to death, hiding his body in the sand. Alex, bleary, started laughing because he *got* the Game. And the Game got him.

You are the hero of no story!

Except you could be, it was telling him.

The oldest story on earth.

Masters and slaves.

Chains and freedom.

Those who whip and those who get whipped.

Charlie opened the last hidden folder on his laptop.

He used to have dozens. Games. Hacking stuff. Porn. He'd outgrown hiding all that.

But one folder was still locked away so his dad would never find it. You had to hold down three random keys simultaneously, then type in a password.

Charlie had come home late. His father had tried to tell him about good news, but Charlie zoned out, and this time his dad didn't even bother to press. He just left the house, and Charlie was locked upstairs when he came back. It was the end of a terrible week. Charlie still wondered if the Game was letting him go or not. He'd left school, his back bruised from being thrown into the locker. He suffered through a two-hour shift at the copy shop, with no incidents. No men with bats or attackers under his car.

Now he was home and exhausted but couldn't sleep.

The tombstone picture was seared in his head. It reminded him he hadn't visited his mom in months. The thought terrified him; it hurt so bad to go there.

He was a horrible son, obviously, he thought.

He opened the hidden folder on his computer. Locked away because his dad had gone to great lengths to purge the house of this stuff. It would be bad enough if his dad knew that his password was Alicia. He'd done it right after she died. Now he couldn't bring himself to change it, as sappy and humiliating as it was. It would be like erasing the last remnant of her soul.

But the folder might kill his dad, seeing it all in one place. Every home video, every picture, every scanned note and card. The folder appeared, name: Mom.

Charlie picked the first movie, a clip of her holding him when he was a baby.

His vision was instantly blurry, pain exploding all over again, like a tree trunk being torn out of his chest, the roots so long and deep that hardly any stuff was left in him. He was a collection of holes that would never heal.

Someone knocked at his door. He ignored it. He was crying so hard his dad surely heard. The knock was soft and tentative. He saw his father's shadow in the crack under the door. He knocked quietly once more, knowing he wasn't wanted, then walked away.

Vanhi kept checking the internet for anything in the news about a cardboard box on Tremont Street and tragedy. Any kind of tragedy. She didn't know what she was looking for. She'd ruled out all the worst things she could imagine from shaking, prodding, and kicking it.

Yet the possibilities gnawed at her, all the things that might have come from her moment of weakness. She delivered that box to win her magic essay back, but ever since, she hadn't had the heart to go back to the Harvard website and see if it had reappeared. She knew she couldn't bring herself to hit Submit yet, even if the essay was there. First she had to know everything was okay, that her delivery had done no harm.

But no bad stories popped up, no matter how many times she searched. She watched the morning news and the five o'clock news, too. Just the usual urban and suburban crime. Nothing box related. Nothing God Game–ish. She was starting to relax.

Maybe something *good* had been in the box. Like the bass pedal. Whatever the person on Tremont Street secretly desired. A reward for some other task. A new Xbox. Adidas Red Apple NMDs. An Aerigon drone with a Phantom Flex4K camera.

And if it had been something good? If no one had been hurt?

Then, finally, she could claim *her* reward.

All through dinner, her parents chatted excitedly about a promotion her mom was up for at the bank. Her mom kept asking her if she was okay, and her dad kept saying, "Leave the girl alone, she's had a long week at school, let her daydream!" He'd ruffle Vanhi's hair each time, as if she were five years old again, in pigtails on his lap.

When she couldn't take it anymore, Vanhi kissed Vik on the top of the head and asked if she could be excused. Her mom asked why, and she dropped the game-winning card:

"To finish up my Harvard essay."

"Oh." Her mom tried not to smile too broadly. "Yes, I think that would be okay."

Her father winked at her.

In her room, Vanhi opened the application and held her breath, waiting to see which essay was there. Would it be her lousy catastrophe of a personal statement, or the Game's magnum opus? She clicked on *Personal Statement: In Progress* and prayed it wouldn't say:

I am deeply passionate about Harvard. . . .

That vomitous first line of an insipid essay, the essay of a bright girl paralyzed with fear. She opened her eyes and read:

Vanhi *means "fire," a Hindi word tied to creation and destruction.*

Oh, God, she thought. *Oh, wow.*

She read on. It was all there. The creative destruction. The story of fire, the ballad of her life, her fears and hopes. Her strengths and her failures, too, but framed as insights, recast as possibilities. It was the best essay she never wrote.

And now it was hers.

Mama, this one's for you, she thought, feeling an odd pang as she did.

She checked her search one more time—still no box-related traumas. Her hands were clean. And with those hands, that delicate fingernail painted hot pink, bedazzled with loopy Vanhi magic, she hit Submit.

At 4:00 A.M., only Peter was happy and unburdened. Alex was hidden under the driveway seeing visions. Vanhi was staring at her ceiling sleeplessly, while Charlie was passed out in his bed, laptop on his chest. Kenny was tossing and turning with nightmares of Eddie Ramirez throwing himself in front of trucks.

But Peter was wide-awake, blissfully serene, unlocking a new level of the Game. He stared down the third-floor hallway of the school, but through his Aziteks, he saw a broad expanse of desert, with a pyramid towering high over him, a luminous eye in the stone just below the apex. This was the heart of the Eye of God, but that was just a tool. He was about to inherit a purpose.

The hallway itself looked like path leading to room 322, which was now not a science lab, but the entryway to the great pyramid, torches on either side casting light over the hieroglyphs. He opened the door in realspace, and inside the pyramid was like nothing he'd seen in other parts of the Game. He'd seen the auction houses, where players bid their Goldz silently on anything they could dream of—drugs, black-hat hacks, back-page services. He'd seen the virtual chat rooms like lush French salons where players the world over met anonymously and exchanged slivers of knowledge about the AI running the system around them. But this was different. He saw a great judgment room, stone walls and red-orange flames, frogs staring dully from the flat surfaces, breathing slowly. A dog-headed man had a staff in one hand and an ankh in the other, standing guard by a golden scale as large as the creature. On one tray was a feather. The other was empty.

The dog-man stared blankly past Peter, blinking, waiting for him to do something.

In front of Peter, on a stone pedestal, was an ancient book containing names. It was the Book of Life and Death. The Vindicators' names were in there. And now Peter was a Watcher. It was more than just voyeurism now, simple spying as he'd done through the Eye of God. Now he was at the heart of the Game, its core purpose. And he was a part of that mission.

One by one, Peter touched the Vindicators' names on the thin page, and the scale moved.

51 GOOD NEWS!

To Charlie's surprise, it was a glorious morning.

He'd slept for twelve hours straight. He woke up with sun coming through the small slats in his blinds, hitting his face and warming him awake.

He felt strangely, wildly free.

There was no Game. No adventure last night. Or at least not one he went on. The crying was awful, painful, but it felt like it purged him. He had fallen fast asleep and woken feeling lighter than he had in months.

For just a moment, there was a paralyzing fear: *What will I do today?*

But then the smell of pancakes rose from downstairs, and he realized he was ravenously hungry. However foolish his dad was, he could cook. Man, could he cook. And for once, Charlie was desperate for that.

"I'm glad you're here," Charlie's dad said, looking at him from over the stove as he came down the stairs. "We have a busy day ahead."

"We do?"

"Yes, we do." His dad flipped two pancakes onto a plate and slid them across the island to Charlie. "Fresh-squeezed orange juice in the pitcher. Help yourself."

Charlie took the plate and poked at the pancakes with a fork, waiting to see if they disappeared in a puff of smoke. But they were real. This was real. He smothered them in syrup and put two pats of butter on top, which melted instantly.

This time, he thought, *I won't ruin it by bringing up Mom.*

"Where are we going?"

"It's a surprise. It was a surprise for me, yesterday. And now it's a surprise for you."

Charlie remembered the good news his dad had promised yesterday, when Charlie shoved his way past him, up the stairs. Now he would find out.

Charlie finished his breakfast and felt revived in more ways than one. His dad sat across from him, reading the paper and eating. They didn't talk. The windows were cracked open and the sunlight brightened the room and the crisp blue fall air streamed in, making everything feel alive and good. Then they were in the car together, driving down East Bishop.

His dad's cheeks were flushed and fuller than Charlie had noticed in a long time. Life was here.

"What's going on?"

"Sometimes, good things just happen."

A car ride later, and Arthur looked out the window and smiled. "There it is."

They were staring at a storefront at the bend in a shopping strip. The brown building had warm shutters and a pub vibe. The sloped roof and green shingles gave it a slightly Germanic, fairy-tale feel.

"I was facing down permits, licenses, the loan. It was going to take months to get through the red tape. Fine, I could've done it. But then this just fell into my lap."

"What just fell into your lap? This place?"

"Yeah."

"Really? How?"

"I got a call yesterday morning. The owner ran into some kind of trouble. He needed to turn it over to someone else right away. Like, right away. He was freaking out. He basically begged me to take it over. I *did* take it over. It was a steal, Charlie. I can keep the staff, run the kitchen, sub in my recipes over time. It's plug and play."

His dad was happy, but Charlie had a sinking feeling. He wanted to believe in fairy tales. But in recent days all coincidences had become suspect.

"Doesn't it seem a little too good to be true?"

Arthur looked at him and snapped, "Yes, it does. And when you look at the pile of shit we've been dealt for the last two years, everything besides a kick in the teeth feels too good to be true."

"I know, but . . ."

"I think we're due a little good luck, Charlie," his dad said, a little softer.

"How'd he even find you?"

"Online. I've been posting on restaurant blogs for months, learning how it's done."

Charlie started to run the situation through the lens of the Game: Had it caused someone's crisis? Had it connected that person to Arthur? And why now, when Charlie had just quit? Was this to lure him back in? Or maybe this *was* the punishment. Maybe his dad would sink all their money into this place, and then the Game would tank it. The possibilities were endless. They were probably evolving by the moment. Or—maybe sometimes a restaurant was just a restaurant. Charlie didn't know.

But Arthur was already out the door. "Come on."

Inside, the place was just as Charlie would've guessed. Tight booths, cozy and rounded. A pool table and two pinball machines. Low-hanging lamps with a warm glow. It felt like the kind of place you wanted to live in. A mural was on the wall, a nineteenth-century city wrapping a forest park with lights strung through the trees and hot-air balloons above. Genteel couples in suits and dresses strolled along a promenade.

"What was this place called before?"

"World's Fair."

"And now it's going to be *Arthur's*?" Charlie preferred World's Fair but didn't say so.

"Well, wait, check this out."

When Charlie was little, his dad used to go on and on about how he'd wanted to be a chef and own a restaurant when *he* was young.

But Charlie's grandfather had been a stern, sullen accountant who had seen his share of restaurant clients fail. "Running a restaurant is a sucker's bet," he would tell Charlie's dad. So Arthur Lake became an accountant, like his father, except not as talented and not as adept with numbers and financial statements. He hated every day of it, but he supported his family and he loved his wife and child. Then one day his wife was gone and his son was lost and he wondered how his life's balance sheet had flipped so suddenly.

Now, he was leading Charlie through Arthur's own restaurant, beaming with pride.

In the back, a canvas banner was unrolled across the floor with ties on each end, the cheap kind you could get at a same-day print shop like the one Charlie languished in.

"I got it last night. It's temporary, just until we get a proper one." Arthur nodded at the sign.

It said CHARLIE'S.

"If it's okay with you."

Charlie felt his throat catch. He willed his eyes to stop before they grew damp.

"I'm so happy," his dad said, not noticing. He put a hand on Charlie's shoulder. It was tentative at first, as if he suspected Charlie would flinch. And Charlie did flinch, because the mix of emotions was overtaking him, the hope and joy of something new, the certainty that his father had now mortgaged their future, and the creeping feeling that the Game might be behind this, for reasons as yet unknown. But then the grip on his shoulder was firm. Arthur squeezed Charlie's shoulder and let his palm rest on the back of Charlie's neck, something he used to do when Charlie was little.

"Come on," his dad said after a while. "Help me get the sign up."

Alex's father had come home late the night before. He lingered at work because, deep down, he was terrified to find out if Alex had passed the test.

Bao Dinh didn't understand Alex. Bao had nothing growing up. He'd faced war, starvation, and worse, but his family had always been close and warm. Alex had grown up wanting for nothing, yet he'd never been happy. It was baffling. How many nights, after ten hours at work, had Bao tried to teach Alex baseball, not because Bao cared about baseball at all, but because he wanted Alex to know his father loved him?

When Alex didn't come home, his parents were worried at first, until the text came in that he was sleeping over at Kenny's house. Even then Bao couldn't sleep because he knew that might mean the test went poorly.

Mr. Dinh saw the belt on his bed and shuddered. He got on his knees before sleeping and prayed. *Please, God, let him pass.* He hated the belt, but he'd tried everything else. Kindness, sternness, prizes, consequences, praise, shame, love, fear. Nothing worked with Alex. He was like jelly, always slipping through your fingers. Where would he go next year? What would he do? *Please, God, let him pass this one test. Then he'll see the way forward.*

Bao Dinh didn't sleep all night.

But when Alex walked in the next morning, looking disheveled and smelling like dirt and rain, Mr. Dinh was perfectly dressed, drinking orange juice and reading the morning paper as if he'd slept a full eight hours and was ready for life.

He didn't look up from the paper when he asked, "How was the test?"

52 ONES AND ZEROS

The official renaming of World's Fair as Charlie's burger joint was that night. It was so easy, Arthur marveled at his good fortune—he subbed right in for the old manager, threw up a temporary sign, and the staff kept everything else running like clockwork, same as always. They put up some flyers around the neighborhood announcing the name change and promising 10 percent off that night: *Same great place, new name!* They posted on Yelp and Facebook and Instagram.

And then they waited.

Would people show up?

For now, the only other change his dad threw into the mix was teaching the staff his secret sauce. It wasn't complicated—one-third Worcestershire, one-third soy sauce, one-third mustard—but he wanted it just right before they added it to the burgers. Charlie found himself watching his dad lost in the activity and decided to slip out and take a break.

Vanhi was sitting on his front porch when he got home, legs dangling off the steps. Her red-black hair was bright and cheerful in the sunlight.

She smiled when she saw Charlie. "Why do you look so happy? Did you see Mary?" Vanhi raised an eyebrow.

"I haven't seen her since the woods."

"Since you *kissed* in the woods."

"Since she swore off men."

"My kind of girl."

"And sent a nasty text saying what a social liability I'd be."

"What?" Vanhi patted the porch next to her. As he hopped up, Charlie heard musical laughter from around the corner. Vik came running from the backyard.

"Charlie! Charlie!"

"You brought Vik?"

"I'm on duty. Both parentals are working today."

"Hey, my man!" Charlie said, ruffling Vik's hair as he wrapped his arms around Charlie.

"He loves you," Vanhi said.

"Right back atcha," Charlie said.

They watched him run off to play in the yard.

"So what about this text? Are you spying on Mary?"

"No, Peter showed me."

Vanhi sighed. "How do you even know it's real?"

"Game-certified. That's what Peter said."

Vanhi stared at Charlie for a long time. Then she shook her head. "How do you know *he's* telling the truth?"

"Why would he lie?"

"Think about him and Caitlyn."

"So? He still wants me to be happy."

"You don't see him so clearly. You never have."

They glared at each other for a moment.

Charlie shook his head and changed the subject. "So why the visit?"

"I . . . I wanted to say I was sorry."

"For what?"

"For the other night. For voting against quitting."

"Did you play last night?"

"We got chased by a bunch of digital bull-men. It was awesome."

Charlie felt a pang of jealousy picturing them playing without him. "Have all your dreams come true yet?" he asked sarcastically.

"Have yours?" she shot back.

"It's been a good day, actually. Things with my dad, they felt like . . . almost like *before*."

"Really? Why now?"

He hesitated, then told her about the restaurant.

She gave him a funny look. "You know that has to be . . ." She didn't have to say it: *the Game*.

"You don't know that."

"This guy who had to give it up suddenly . . . something must've happened to him. . . ."

"You think I'm a hypocrite?"

"No . . . I mean, it's for your dad after all, but . . ."

"Why don't you lay off the judgment? I'm the one who tried to quit. And lay off Peter, too, while you're at it. You've always been out to get him, since the day he came."

"People say he deals drugs, Charlie. You know that, right?"

Charlie hesitated for just a moment, the image of that brown bag from Peter to Zeke coming back. The one Charlie had carried. He pushed the thought away.

"That's bullshit. He's never said anything like that."

"At St. Luke's, and now here, too."

"Why would he? He doesn't need the money."

"That's right. He does it because he likes it."

"You're just spreading lies."

"Charlie . . ."

"He's the only one who was there when my mom died. What did you do?"

"What?"

"What the hell did you do?"

Vanhi's eyes watered. "Charlie, I . . . I didn't know what to . . . I tried."

"You did shit. So stop trashing him and take a look in the mirror."

"Why are you guys fighting?" Vik asked.

They had no idea how long he'd been back at the porch watching. Vanhi smiled abruptly, trying to show Vik everything was okay. "Come on, Vik, let's go."

"You're jealous of Peter, but you weren't there," Charlie snapped, as Vanhi scooped up Vik and went to her car. "You're jealous of Mary but you wouldn't date me. You tell me not to lose myself, then you choose the Game over me. Who the hell are you, Vanhi? What do you want?"

She spun around. "Don't you get it? Just because I don't love you doesn't mean I don't love you."

"Well, that's helpful."

Vanhi scowled. She opened the door and helped Vikram into his car seat.

"You know, that's *just* the problem with you computer guys," she snapped over her shoulder. "You want everything to be black or white, one or zero. That's not the world, Charlie." She squeezed Vik's hand and strapped him in. "It's all just a shitload of gray."

53 FATHER/SON/GHOSTS

Heading back to the restaurant for the opening, Charlie started to panic. It was too good to be true, the way the place had just fallen into his dad's lap. Arthur was just too happy, especially when Charlie was on the outs with the Game. Was it a trap, was his dad about to be crushed, his crazy dream destroyed in some public, humiliating way? Charlie wanted to say, *Wait, postpone the opening*. But how could he? How could he even begin to explain why?

He remembered something else, too—that crazy question the Game had posed to him two days ago, when he was searching for a way out.

Do you love your dad? Y/N?

He'd asked:

Is that a threat?

And the Game said:

No! Good News!

That same phrase his dad had used yesterday: *Good news!*
Coincidence? Sure, it wasn't the most unique phrase. But the Game loved to hint, to tease. It was filled with clues and Easter eggs. Had the Game used that phrase with Charlie, then implanted it in his dad's mind, too—perhaps it told the suddenly broke and desperate

seller to call Charlie's dad and say he had "good news" for him. The Game was adept at suggestion, at neurolinguistic programming. At programming people.

Or maybe it was just the obvious phrase for the delivery of ... wait for it ... good news. And in that case, Charlie was just losing his fucking mind.

Something else was gnawing at him. Good luck seemed finite in the Game.

Had hitting Y caused someone else's ruin? Tanked or blackmailed the seller and directed him to Charlie's dad?

So Charlie went back to the restaurant resolved to tell his father to stop everything. And when he got there and saw his dad beaming, happy for the first time in two years, Charlie said nothing.

He kept his mouth shut.

And prayed that the Game wasn't about to destroy his father by raising him up higher than he'd ever been, so it could cast him down all the harder against the saw-toothed rocks.

Kenny stood outside Eddie Ramirez's house.

Kenny hadn't slept since Eddie was thrown out of school. He was crippled with guilt. It was bad enough having spray-painted alt-right garbage on the wall. It felt like vomiting on the school. But the worst part, the part that had gnawed at him all night, was the look on Eddie's face as Kenny and Candace slinked out of the room. Shell-shocked.

Kenny kept telling himself, *Eddie was coming for us. We had no choice. It was kill or be killed.* But that wasn't how Kenny felt inside. He felt like he'd ruined someone's life to save his own, and he was sick about it.

Eddie's house was a small tan ranch-style, one story tall and aging, in a middle-class enclave called Eleanor Heights. Kenny parked his car. He felt a buzzing in his pocket and glanced at the phone. It said:

Don't.

No explanation. Just *Don't.* Which was weird, because Kenny didn't even know what he intended to do. Confess? Lay himself on the cross for Eddie? Torch his friends to save an asshole? No, there had to be a middle ground. A way they could both get through this. Right?

As he approached the house, he heard shouting inside. Kenny glanced over his shoulder. The neighborhood was quiet and no one was on the street. His phone buzzed again. He stopped under a tree and looked.

Isaiah 42:8. Do not speak the unspeakable name of G-d.

But that was it. That was the only way out for everyone. To tell him about the Game. The way it had manipulated all of them—Kenny, the Vindicators, Eddie, too. Even Candace.

Yet the Game was one step ahead again, warning Kenny not to speak of the Game before he realized he was going to.

He shivered and looked up and down the street again. Nothing but gray skies and silent houses. No one was stalking him. No one that he could see.

Then the Game said:

Put on your glasses.

Kenny put on his Aziteks. The neighborhood was still empty and quiet. He looked back at Eddie's house. It was horrifying. On every eave, every gutter, every ledge, curled in every corner and squatting on every nook and branch, there were demons, ugly, gleaming creatures, eyes burning red, expressionless, looking right at Kenny. They squatted like vultures with men's starved torsos and heads on long necks. Veined wings and curled nails.

All of them breathing slowly, with thin, diaphanous skin over ribs that were bent and crooked like fingers holding up small pulsing hearts.

They lined the phone lines over the house, the television antenna, milled in the grass, crouched in the trees.

The shouting was coming from the window near the front of the house. Kenny pressed against the glass and tried to hear. Eddie was pleading his case to his father and mother. Kenny could hear bits and pieces of different voices. *Not my fault! I didn't do it! Do you think we're stupid? I can't explain! How could you do this to us?*

Kenny lost track of how long he stood there, ear to the glass. It was too easy to imagine this exact conversation in his own house. Finally, blessedly, they stopped shouting and Kenny heard the front door open and this was it. What would Kenny do? He started rounding the corner toward Eddie.

The Game spoke again, this time on his Aziteks:

> Malachai 3:6. Only the High Priest may utter my name, ten times, on the holiest day.

Kenny wiped the message away. Eddie was heading toward his car. Kenny made up his mind. He would tell Eddie everything. They would work it out together. If Kenny had to withdraw from school or be suspended or repeat a year, so be it. He would take responsibility for his actions. And that would matter, wouldn't it? He thought of something his father had told him once when they were watching the news together and some politician was resigning—*It's never the crime, it's the cover-up.* Confess, confess, confess!

"Eddie!" Kenny shouted.

Eddie! the Game echoed back in his ears, mocking him.

> 500 Blaxx!

flashed on his screen and tallied on his counter.

Eddie glanced his way, then turned his back.

"Eddie, wait!"

Eddie, wait! the Game taunted.

> 800 Blaxx!

"Go to hell," Eddie shouted.

Kenny tried to close the distance between them, but Eddie spun around and stepped forward, grabbing Kenny by the collar and shouting, "You fucked me," and shoving him hard onto the lawn. Kenny pulled himself up, but Eddie was already coming around the driver's side of his car and opening the door.

"Wait! I can explain everything."
Wait, I can explain everything!

1300 Blaxx!

Kenny's gut clenched, but he ran toward Eddie anyway until a demon jumped between them, ten feet tall and filled with flames and red veins. Kenny stepped through it as Eddie's engine roared to life and the car began to pull away.

2100 Blaxx!

Shit—Kenny ran to his car to follow Eddie and fumbled for his keys.

3400 Blaxx!

At first Kenny didn't see or hear the car that was already coming down the block behind him at a steady clip. It was speeding up as it got close, then swerved abruptly, engine roaring.

Kenny moved at the last second, but it made impact and sent him hurtling headlong into the grass.

Vanhi sat fuming at her computer, trying to process her fight with Charlie. She put Pink Floyd on YouTube and played bass along with "Shine on You Crazy Diamond," but that was too slow, so she tried "Immigrant Song." Her fingers sailed over the thick strings with Zeppelin, and for a moment she was lost in the music. But when it got to the line "we are your overlords," it all came crashing back and she got mad again and turned it off.

The Game told her from the computer:

You need to see this

She put on her glasses, and the screen was just as she'd left it, her new and improved essay still there. But then it dissolved and she was inside the internal gearbox of the Harvard system. Names spun past her on the screen like on a roulette wheel, their scores, essays, recommendations, all turning on the dial like constellations of stars. It felt sickening, and yet not surprising, when the wheel slowed, then trickled past the last few names to land on Charlie Lake.

There in front of her was the whole of Charlie's application. The early ace SAT score (1,590), the grades—freshman year, 4.0; sophomore year, 4.0; junior year, 2.1. The essay (she couldn't bear to read it):

> On December 3, 2015, my mother died from Stage IV
> ovarian cancer. I was the primary caretaker, unofficially,
> as my father succumbed to the stress and pressure of the
> situation. I realize now . . .

The topic was "Please describe a significant experience in your life." *Jesus Christ*, she thought, *that oughta do it*.

Charlie told her he wasn't applying. He said, right to her face, that he hadn't even *started* an application. But he had. It was right here.

If it's even real, she reminded herself.

Did Charlie do this? Did the Game? Freshman year, they had a pact. Charlie and Vanhi against the world. They'd apply to Harvard together. They'd both get in. Then they'd set the world on fire. But now they both had blemishes on their records—and Harvard wasn't going to take two charity cases from one school. No way would Harvard forgive her D, uber-essay or not, if Charlie was also applying, with a much better excuse for his black eye.

Her screen shivered. The Game made her an offer, without speaking or explaining itself. But she knew exactly what it meant.

Charlie's and Vanhi's applications flickered back and forth between one another. The numbers and words began to melt and flux between them. Her SAT became 1590. His became 1550. His freshman year 4.0 flickered with her 3.97 until they transposed. His essay, so simple yet gutting, wavered into *I have long been impressed by Harvard's strong academic reputation*. Most tantalizing, her D, that junior-year disaster that she'd hidden from her parents, then hacked back, became an A. She'd never dared hack it permanently—getting caught was too risky—but the Game could get away with it on a level she never could, making sure people saw exactly what they needed to see at the right time to never suspect a thing. In the swapping transcripts, her D was sucked into the muck of Charlie's junior year. His 2.1 barely changed, to a 2.0. The difference to Vanhi's GPA was huge. It went from a 3.6 to a 4.0.

For Harvard, that was a world of difference.

It was all just numbers on a screen.

The part of her essay about the D was gone now, too. She wouldn't need it anymore—there was apparently nothing left to apologize for.

The button at the bottom of the page was flashing. It wasn't a Harvard button. It was a God Game button. It said:

SUBMIT SUBMIT SUBMIT . . .

You probably won't even know it, she thought to Charlie. *Your application will look just fine to you. You'll hit Submit. And the bits and bytes will transform from what you saw to what I made happen. And you'll never know why they rejected you. No one ever does.*

Her finger rested over the touch screen.

No. There were limits.

She couldn't do it. She wouldn't do it. Her magic essay had been a victimless crime, plucked from the ether. But this was an assassination.

Vanhi took off her glasses and walked away before she could change her mind.

One hour to opening.

Charlie could barely stand it. The Game was silent. No warnings. No promises. No demands. Just . . . silence.

He imagined what it might do—flood the internet with negative reviews? Turn off the gas so they couldn't cook? Blackmail some kid to release cockroaches under the table?

He could do nothing to stop it.

He checked the internet—the reviews, the ads, were all the same. At least on his screen.

He could do nothing but wait.

That night, Charlie watched his dad reopen World's Fair as Charlie's. It was a tremendous success. People came. Old people, young people, families. It wasn't a massive crowd, but it wasn't small either. The room felt full and boisterous. It was exactly the kind of place his dad had imagined. You could bring your family on a Saturday night and feel safe and happy.

The Game was nowhere to be found.

Arthur came up to him, and a woman followed tentatively behind. She was pretty, maybe midforties, with sandy hair and a nervous, somewhat sad smile.

"Charlie, this is Susan."

Not *my friend Susan*. Not *my new girlfriend* or *your new mom*. Just *Susan*.

He was supposed to hate this woman. Punish her by withholding his courtesy. That was the script. But he wouldn't. His dad was happy. The restaurant actually happened. Yes, his dad had spent their last dollars, but if things kept going like this, they might actually make money. Maybe college was closer, not further, away. His dad looked better than he had in years. Not to mention, if all this *was* a trap, if it *was* going to fall apart as part of some epic Game revenge, at least let him have tonight.

"Hi, Susan." Charlie extended his hand.

"Hi, Charlie." Her smile got less nervous, but no less sad.

The look on Arthur Lake's face said it all. Charlie surveyed the room, all the families eating and having a nice time. For the first time in a week, he didn't even think about the Game being played all around them.

It was a good night.

54 MIDNIGHT

Late that evening, Alex tried the drugs Peter had given him, something new. Peter had given him the Adderall before, when Alex asked, but this was something more. It would help him see further.

He had to stop thinking about the day. His father had given him a choice that morning: belt now, or belt after work. He chose after work. Pain later was better than pain now.

All day long the Game wouldn't let him visit his sites. Not the video ones. Not even the story ones where you could post your violent fantasies. He loved the disclaimers on those sites: *These are works of imagination. The webmaster does not authorize, screen, or condone anything posted here.* He liked that—it was just a platform. And what were we all if not blameless platforms for the dreams posted inside our skulls?

Instead, the Game pulled him in deeper, filling him up with its vast mythologies and crypto-mystical programming. He lapped it up.

His dad came home looking weary, but he administered the punishment dutifully, with the obligatory "This hurts me more than it hurts you." *Yeah, really, fucker? Wanna trade?*

He wore his Aziteks throughout. The Game did him the courtesy of distracting him from the humiliation and pain. First, every time the belt came down, the image in his eyes showed the scenario reversed, his hand raised, his dad on the receiving end. He wanted to smile, but then his dad would see it and have to go harder. Then it was Kurt Ellers on the receiving end, then Tim, then other meathead fucks. Then it was Vanhi and Kenny, those traitors who wanted him out of the Vindicators. Then finally it was Charlie. Because Charlie still didn't get it: the only thing more humiliating than being punched and slapped was being rescued.

Everyone but Peter, because Peter was all right. He didn't say no when all Alex needed desperately was for someone to tell him yes. Peter treated him as an equal. He trusted Alex to rise or fall on his own choices.

Snick was the sound of the belt.

When it was done, he saw his dad had tears in his eyes.

"Please try, Alex," he whispered. "Just try."

That night, Alex made ayahuasca tea as the Game instructed. It told him Peter could get the ayahuasca, and Peter didn't judge him for asking. After all, Peter said he'd taken ayahuasca at St. Luke's and it changed his life. Peter had written back:

> You sure?
> I need it.
> Ok. Let's meet.

Peter had sat side by side with Alex, showing him how he navigated the auction houses in the Game, the avatars bidding silently. How the box would be delivered to them within the day. Alex saw what Charlie saw, how special it felt to have Peter's undivided attention.

Now Alex lay in bed, concentric circles of neon and gemstones rotating over him and pulling back in infinite regression. Time melted away.

When the shapes parted, he was alone in his room, perfectly still and silent in the darkness, but Christ was sitting across from him, in the chair in the corner of the room, barely visible in the dim light of the digital clock. Christ held up a hand, which was bloody and marked with a hole.

"My Father did this to me," he said softly.

Alex didn't know what to say.

"'For He so loved the world that He gave His one and only Son,'" the figure added. "Why didn't He love me?"

Alex tried to study Christ's features, but the room was too dim. The figure sat quietly in the chair.

"He did love you," Alex said, knowing that he and the Game were really talking about Alex's father.

"You truly don't know, do you?"

Alex felt tears begin to well in his eyes, that shaking feeling just before the waterworks when you want to hold it back.

Christ asked, "Why does he hurt you?"

"Because he loves me?"

The figure shook its head no.

"Because he hates me?"

"No," Christ whispered. "Because he fears you."

The figure was still in the corner, staring right through Alex. "Children are born slaves. They do not choose existence, it is thrust upon them. The child grows, yet the parent refuses to relinquish control. He uses maxims: 'Honor thy father and mother.' Why? It is the child's right to take his place."

Alex sat, mesmerized. He'd never thought of it that way.

"Who sacrifices a child and calls it love? Sacrifice yourself, Father."

Alex nodded.

"They tell you you're the Lamb, so you won't see what you truly are."

"What am I?" It was the question Alex had never been able to answer. A loser? A freak? The Boy from Mars? The Dumb Asian? The Worst Vindicator?

"'For I have come to turn a man against his father,'" Christ told him. "'Children will rise up against parents and have them put to death.'"

Alex felt his vision failing. Whether it was from the drugs or exhaustion or the Game, he felt himself pulling back, heading into a bottomless place.

"You were forged in the furnace of my grasp," Christ whispered. It filled Alex with a sense of possibility. "I will make you matter."

At midnight, Vanhi woke to the sound of shattering glass.

Her first instinct was to protect Vik, so she ran to his bedroom. He was sound asleep, curled up safely. The sound had come from the living room.

She heard her parents stirring. Her dad came into the hallway in pajamas. Her mother followed, pulling her robe tight.

"Stay back." Vanhi awed them with her fearlessness.

"No, you stay back." Her father wasn't a large man, but he was possessed with a sudden ferocious love of his children.

They ended up creeping side by side, and Vanhi felt in the dark and flipped on the living room lights. The front window was broken. A spray of glass went across the carpet.

"Careful," her mother said.

A brick was in the middle of the room. Someone had written GO HOME on it, which was all the more terrifying, Vanhi realized, because this *was* home.

There was nowhere else to go.

Her father lifted up the brick and turned it around in his hand. "It's just kids. Kids being stupid. Nothing to worry about."

A sick wave passed through Vanhi. Was this her punishment for turning down the Game's offer? She almost told them everything: *Don't worry, it's just a computer game!*

Or was it? Because this kind of stuff was in vogue again, suddenly, in the real world. Bricks through brown people's windows, swastikas on schools. People had thought it was gone. But it was always there, just waiting for someone to make it okay again.

What would happen if she did tell them everything, the Game listening?

How much worse than a brick through the window?

Later, she would study the brick through her Aziteks and see that in gamespace it was labeled:

400 Blaxx. Ingratitude.

"It's the times we live in," her mom said now. "It will pass. Most people are good."

"That's true," Vanhi's father said theatrically, for her benefit.

She wanted to believe they meant it.

She realized that the only thing that would eclipse this horribleness, the only thing that might revive her parents' faith in the dream they'd traveled halfway around the world for, was to get into Harvard.

What else was within her power? What else could even come close?

55 ICON

The next morning, Charlie received a text, from someone new and unexpected.

The number was blocked. But it wasn't the Game—it came from a new sender, a different thread.

> I heard you were looking for me

Charlie rubbed his eyes awake and rolled over onto his back, the phone above him.

> Who is this?

It gave him the name of the person he'd googled on a whim, when he couldn't find how to quit the Game. The last of the known Friends of the Crypt, who'd taken himself off the map over a decade ago, after he served his time and got out of jail.

> Scott Parker

Charlie was torn. What he would give to hear from someone who had played before them. Who knew where it all ended. But Charlie was out. Why dip his toe back in, even a little? The answer was obvious. For his friends.

Still, he knew the Game was watching. He couldn't open this door. Not even a little. He typed back:

> I already quit
>> no you didn't

Charlie didn't respond. He had his fingers over the keyboard, thinking of what to say, when the person claiming to be Scott Parker added:

> you think you did

Damnit, Charlie thought. This guy—these *letters* claiming to be a guy claiming to be Scott Parker—was reeling him back in. He could feel it.

Still, he wouldn't take the bait. He didn't respond. *Good,* he thought. *Stay strong.*

But the person wrote again:

> only one way to quit

"Oh, fuck." Charlie hadn't bitten yet, but he could already feel the hook sinking into his jaw. Either this guy was real and knew the one thing Charlie desperately needed to know. Or the Game was the most sneaky, manipulative piece of shit he'd ever encountered.

Cursing himself, Charlie typed:

> How?

Predictably, so predictably, the person on the other end wrote:

> We need to meet

56 SUNDAY SUNDAY SUNDAY

Of all places, Scott Parker picked the mall. Of course he did. Maybe he'd been watching Charlie through the Game all along. Maybe he knew full well that the last two times Charlie had gone to the mall, he'd gotten his ass kicked. *Thanks for the lulz!*

Charlie moved through the food court, trying to pick Scott Parker out of the crowd. But it was impossible. Hundreds of people were milling about on the bright Sunday morning, every race and culture, light streaming through the epic windows, families at tables, trays of cinnamon rolls and coffee and doughnuts and breakfast tacos, elderly couples strolling holding hands, tweens chattering away. Charlie put on his glasses and scanned the crowd again.

Through his Aziteks, the person sitting in the middle of the court had a grotesque face, part skull with turquoise and lignite and patches of deerskin pulled tight, lipless teeth, and wide eyes under a red-plumed headdress. His body was massive and rippled, one leg replaced with a thick snake. On his chest was a mirror made of black obsidian. Smoke swirled within it.

Charlie peeked over the glasses and nearly lost the man in the crowd—he looked back through the lenses and pushed his way toward the godlike thing.

Its teeth stuck out in a strange overbite.

A sickly, gaping smile.

"Hello, Charlie," the god said, his nasal voice doubling and tripling into prominence.

"Who are you?"

The figure seemed surprised. "Well, obviously I'm Tezcatlipoca." He raised an eyebrow. "Smoking Mirror?" He said it like a failed rock star—*Don't you know me? I'm huge in Mesoamerica!*

The god waved his hand, as if to say, *Doesn't matter.* His buck teeth grinned.

"Who are you for real?"

"That's an interesting expression. *For real.* You haven't taken your glasses off yet."

Charlie reached for his Aziteks, but the god stopped him lightly with a black-and-red feathered hand on Charlie's forearm.

Charlie brushed him off and lifted his glasses. He looked over the lumpy pale man. His skin was rashy and his hair was thin and combed over. It was sad to draw a line from the fresh-faced boy in the news articles to the man before him now.

"Better on, don't you think?"

Charlie set his glasses back down. "Are you really Scott Parker?"

"I was, way back when."

"You were in the Friends of the Crypt?"

"I was. Now I am the Friends of the Crypt!" He sighed. "Sit," he said, opening a hand to the chair across from him. "It's good to see you in person, in Charlie. Funny, right? I can see anyone in the world online, but there's still something special about being in the same place. Maybe it's the smell. I'm glad you came."

"What happened to you?"

"But you already know that, don't you? Isn't that why you were looking for me?"

"You were playing the Game."

"You don't play the Game, Charlie. The Game plays you. Haven't you figured that out by now?"

"I want to quit."

"You can't. Playing is life. Winning is living."

"You're just trying to scare me."

"No, it's true. For you and your dad."

"Leave my dad out of this."

Tezcatlipoca laughed. Charlie didn't know if the god was cruel or crazy or both. Playing the Game for a week had almost driven Charlie mad. What would twenty years do?

"What is the Game? What does it want?"

"Now you're talking!" Tezcatlipoca said, delighted. "Curiosity killed the cat! Curiosity killed Schrödinger's cat! 'He opened his box to look inside, to see if he was dead or alive!' Boxes within boxes within boxes! What box are *you* in, Charlie?"

"Stop making fun of me."

"Poor Charlie! So sad! So angry! I wouldn't dream of mocking you. I'm *telling* you something. Are you listening?"

"Why should I trust anything you say?"

Tezcatlipoca looked hurt. "You're one of my favorite characters."

"I'm not a character."

"You have to change your thinking, Charlie. This is an honor. You're part of a grand design. A great experiment whose end we don't know. The oldest question on earth."

Tezcatlipoca gestured at the milling crowd around them. "They seem so normal, don't they? Out here, it's all 'Please' and 'Thank you' and 'Pardon me' and 'After you.' But you know that's a lie. In the dark, they're typing. Pornographers and pedos and traffickers and terrorists, righties and lefties and commies and fascists, connecting and amplifying. You can feel it, can't you? The infection. The acceleration. Can you tell who's who?"

Charlie eyed the crowd around them.

"We knew it, Charlie, early on. The bulletin boarders, the Vint Surfers, Tezcatlipoca the TCP/IP. The optimists said the Web would give every human a voice. Holy shit! Have you *met* humans? We created God to protect us from ourselves. From our brains. Then we accidentally built the world's biggest brain, and we forgot to give it a conscience. A seething mess of unbridled humanity: all id, no ego. We can't even see it, much less stop it, any more than a neuron in your brain can see your thoughts."

Tezcatlipoca leaned in. "But, we asked, what if you could hack the higher-order process? There's no problem tech created that tech can't solve. Infect the metaconsciousness with a metacon-science."

"A virus?"

"Not malware. Call it Virtueware! A moral virus infected into the global electronic system. The Golden Algorithm. An algorithm for God."

"What was it?"

"That was the problem! Everyone agreed we needed one, but no one agreed what it should be. The Golden Rule? Hackable. Simplistic. The Ten Commandments? Contradictory. Incomplete. 'Thou shall not kill'—and ten pages later He's saying, 'Kill kill kill!' Kantian ethics? You can't lie to a murderer knocking at your door looking for his victim? Bullshit. Utilitarianism? A farce, grotesque—kill a homeless man to give his organs to five nuns? Macabre math. Every moral system failed."

"Then what?"

But Charlie saw the answer, right in front of him.

Before he could even say it, Tezcatlipoca nodded. "If humanity was still arguing about morality five thousand years later, maybe we could build something *smarter* than us to crack it."

"A neural network?"

"And a deep Boltzmann machine. And a tangled hierarchy. And a deep belief net. And a genetic algorithm. And a massive parallelism. And bots and viruses and worms. And lions and tigers and bears, oh my!"

Tezcatlipoca smiled, his teeth fanning. "They fed it everything. All our laws, our constitutions, our cultures. Kant, Aristotle, John Stuart Mill, Foucault. The Bible, the Talmud, the sutras, the Koran, the Confucian canon. *The Seven Valleys,* the Zend-avesta, *The White Goddess.* If seven billion people couldn't agree peacefully, rationally, give it everything. Let the algorithm churn and test and evolve."

"Test? On *people?*"

"Of course! Who else? Lab rats?"

"I'm a guinea pig in a fucking morality play that stops when I'm dead?"

"You should be thrilled, Charlie. This is the oldest, hardest quest on earth. What is good? Who should I be? And you're part of it."

"You did this."

"I'm just a tiny piece, Charlie. We are legion. It's an open-source deity, baby."

"How the fuck do I get out?"

"Ask Dave Meyer."

"The guy who founded Friends of the Crypt? He jumped off the roof of the school."

"He got out."

"Bullshit. There has to be another way."

"Of course there is!" It was as if Tezcatlipoca had been waiting for this moment. "The answer's right in front of you, Charlie. Think about the source material! It's an old answer, but an effective one, because it means you're serious. It shows you *want* it. The Celts had their wicker men. The Japanese had *hitobashira*. The Aztecs, *tzompantli. Narabali* in India. Moloch in Canaan. Christ on the cross. Human sacrifices, all. If you and your friends want to leave the Game, it'll take more than a couple drops of blood. You have to take a life, freely, graciously. We fed the Game our collective wisdom—how could we expect any better?"

Tezcatlipoca's chair scraped back and he leaned over the table, in Charlie's face, the skull-black ghoul filling his vision. Tezcatlipoca's voice boomed in Charlie's Aziteks, louder and darker now, amplified.

"Remember, Charlie, the First Commandment was never 'Thou shall not kill.' People forget that. It's *'Worship me.'* Our God is a jealous God. If you want something, you have to fill its great cosmic mouth with blood."

Tezcatlipoca's face hovered there, statically, like a figure in a computer game. A blink here or there, nothing more. Charlie pulled off his glasses and the chair was empty.

Scott Parker, the last Friend of the Crypt, was gone.

57 MOTHERBOARD

Charlie left, blood boiling, driving aimlessly until he found himself at the gates of Mt. Zion Cemetery, not quite sure how he got there.

He couldn't shake the image of Scott Parker, not the fearsome god but the sickly pale man. So Charlie's choice was death or a slow mutation into that? Into what Scott Parker had become?

Charlie couldn't accept it and yet he had no clue what to do.

He walked, against his will, his heart pounding against his chest, until he found himself at the gravestone for the first time in months, unable to talk.

He placed his face against the cool stone and felt the carved letters under his cheek and knew what they said.

Being here brought it back, that horrible last day. It was so undramatic and yet so terrible. He'd come home from school and his dad was nowhere to be found, hiding at his office. His mom was sleeping upstairs. He kissed her and he could've been there, but he was hungry after school! He made a sandwich. When he came back up, she was gone. No goodbyes. No one holding her hand. One became zero. As dull as that. And he missed it.

She'd died alone while he was making a sandwich.

"I'm sorry," he told her now, and he wondered who was speaking. It was his voice and his mouth and his words, yet it all felt alien.

"I don't know who I am. I don't know what happened to me. I'm so sorry. I'm so, so sorry. I died, too." He was lost. "Say something. Tell me it's going to be okay."

That's all he wanted. He'd lost any belief in God in the year she died, but what he'd give to have that now, to think some old man in the sky would hold him and say everything will be okay. But the grave was silent, and the cemetery—that ocean of stone and loss—was still, but for the birds flying south.

He left and made his way to Mary's house, stopping along the way to get his supplies. He knew what he had to do. He rang her bell and felt like an impostor on her doorstep, unwanted, an alien in this neighborhood of old stone and moss.

Mary's mother eyed him like scum and asked if Mary was expecting him.

Charlie lied, "No, I was just in the neighborhood," and it was so preposterous that ice-cold Eleanor Clark, Queen of the WASPs, actually lifted one corner of her mouth into a smile, and they shared a genuine moment between them.

"Okay," she said, as if he'd earned that much.

The floor of Mary's room was covered with half-finished posters, five or six of them, announcing her run for student body president. He kept his face neutral. She started to explain, to apologize for running against him, but he waived his hand and said they needed to go outside. Almost hovering in her loveliness, Mary took him into the garden of her lush backyard, lost in a maze of trees and paths, and Charlie told her, "I know what you need. If I loved you, and I do, this is what I'd do."

He reached into his bag and took out the bracelet, the one he'd been beaten for trying to return, and she started to protest, but he took out the hammer and placed it into her hand and folded her fingers around the handle.

"Are you crazy?"

"You don't need Tim. But you don't need me either. You need to be free."

"Charlie, take this back to the store. Put the money toward college."

He shook his head. "I can't. If I could, I would."

She started to protest but he shook his head.

"You are not a princess. I can't rescue you. I'll be lucky to save myself."

She studied his face. She looked at him harder than anyone ever had, and he had the distinct impression she saw every corner of his soul, the sublime and the foul.

"I'm sorry I'm running against you," she told him.

"I know."

"I'll drop out. I know what it means for you."

"No. I know what it means for you."

She nodded. "Okay."

She raised the hammer, slowly at first, and brought it down on the bracelet, barely hard enough to make a dent. She thought of her brother, of Tim and everything he'd done to her, and she brought the hammer down harder, then again, until she was smashing away at the golden braids until they broke apart and began to dent and scatter. She brought the hammer down again and again, her eyes welling, the bracelet shattering like her supposedly perfect life, until it was smashed into oblivion.

"Promise me one thing," Charlie asked. "Whatever hold he's got on you, destroy it. And never look back."

That night, Charlie heard his mom's voice.

He thought it was a dream, then he thought it was coming from his computer, as if one of those hidden videos had accidentally begun playing itself.

But then he realized it was coming from his Aziteks, and he found himself right back where his day had started, with the text from Scott Parker, not knowing if he was in or out of the Game. But now it was clear: he'd never been out. It was like the old saying "You might not believe in God, but God believes in you." The Game was all around him.

He heard his mother's voice saying new words for the first time in almost a year. Calling his name, asking if he was there.

Like a siren song he was drawn to it, knowing he was being played, yet unable to resist her voice. His whole body was shaking. He went through the dark room, the only light that from his screen saver, a rotating web of lines, and put the glasses on.

There she was, sitting on his bed, as if she'd never left.

He reached to take off the glasses because it was blasphemous, horrific, demented.

But she pleaded, "Charlie, please, I just need to see you for a minute."

Hearing her say his name was crippling. This wasn't some video he'd watched a million times until he could predict every flicker. This was new. Her voice was saying something *new*.

Oh, God, this was unholy. Even to an atheist, this was a warp in the universe.

But he didn't stop walking to her. He couldn't stop.

"Don't be scared."

He was trembling, barely able to speak. "You're not real."

"I know. I'm sorry. But I'm not fake either. I think and I feel."

"Please don't do this."

"I'm not the Game."

"Please . . ."

"The Game made me for you. I'm my own intelligence. I'm her."

"Don't . . . I can't say no. . . ."

"Baby. Please. It's okay. I need you, too."

He fell to his knees, just feet away from her. "You're not *her*," Charlie said angrily, as if it were her fault.

"I'm everything she left behind. Every note, every video. Don't I sound like her? Don't I move like her? Am I good?"

She was. She was a dream come true. What was his deepest wish if not one more minute? Please, God, just one more minute.

"Go ahead. Put your head down, here." She touched the comforter next to her.

He gave in to her. His head went down on the comforter, and her weightless hand stroked over his head while she sang to him. He could almost feel it.

"Now," she said, when the song was done. "It's time. Go ahead and say it."

"No, please."

"This is your chance."

He was crying so hard now. His body was shaking with the sobs.

He let himself think it, for the first time: He didn't go upstairs that last day because she'd looked so ill; he didn't *want* to be in the room with her. He went to the kitchen because he just wanted to hide there for a while, plain and simple, to buy himself just a little time away from her. How could he have known she'd be gone when he came back?

"You were alone." Everything broke loose inside him. "I'm sorry."

"You were so good to me." She held both sides of his face. She got down on her knees and met his eyes. "You made me so happy." She held him like that for a moment. "You can say it now, if you want."

He didn't want to.

"Go on, baby. You can do it."

He nodded. Said it, let it come out.

"Goodbye."

It blew him open.

"Goodbye, Charlie."

She kissed him on the forehead before she went to the door and disappeared into the hallway. Gone, forever, gone.

He hated the Game. It was the greatest gift he'd ever received.

58 HOLY WEEK

Monday morning, Charlie entered school, stunned to find his picture everywhere. Posters lined every hallway. Dozens and dozens. His face dominated the building.

The occasional posters of MARY FOR STUDENT BODY PRESIDENT were dwarfed by the posters for Charlie. All different styles and themes, as if a dozen elves had come in overnight and hammered away for hours. CHARLIE FOR PRESIDENT—BECAUSE HE'S THE SHIZ! CHARLIE FOR PRESIDENT—YOU KNOW YOU WANT IT! with his head superimposed over a shirtless bodybuilder in a Speedo. DON'T BE A CUCK—VOTE FOR CHUCK! with Pepe the Frog giving two thumbs-up.

Who the hell made these? Who had hung them? Charlie imagined Mary coming to school this morning, bright and early, ready to start her campaign. It must have been a smack in the face. Sure, they had set each other free. But this didn't feel like freedom. It felt like malice.

Vanhi was in the Tech Lab. "Who did those posters?" he asked.

"Forget that. Listen to what happened to Kenny." Kenny was there, looking worse for wear. He favored his right leg and had a vicious grass burn along his right arm.

"Are you okay? What happened?"

"I would've told you if you answered my texts."

"What texts?"

"I texted, I called. I even went by your house last night."

"I was out. You left messages?"

"Home and cell."

"I got nothing."

"It cut us off from each other."

He told them about going to see Eddie. The attack by the car.

"Jesus. What about you, Vanhi? Did anything happen?"

She could have told them about the brick. But Charlie had lied to her about his application. Or had he? Either way, the Game had made her an offer. She hadn't said yes, but she hadn't said no. If she told, it might go away.

"I'm fine," she lied.

There was a knock at the door. They exchanged wary looks. Vanhi went to the door, and when she opened it, of all people Mr. Burklander was there. He looked way better than the last time Charlie saw him, after his car was destroyed—like Charlie's father, he seemed to have a new lease on life.

"Good morning, guys. Charlie, can we talk for a second?"

Charlie wondered what it was about. He glanced at Vanhi and Kenny, who shrugged.

Charlie nodded at Mr. B. "Sure."

Once they were alone in the hall, Mr. B. said, "Look, I feel bad about the other day. I shouldn't have said those things in front of a student. You caught me at a bad moment."

"It's okay. I understand."

"But maybe there's a bright side, if it inspired you to prove me wrong with those posters."

Mr. B. said it almost hopefully, as if he wanted Charlie to confirm that he'd had a teachable moment, that Mr. B. had finally cracked the code to redeeming him.

Charlie just managed to nod. He didn't have the heart to tell Mr. B. he had no idea who put the posters up, but it wasn't Charlie, and it wasn't because Mr. B. was a miracle worker.

"Did you put those up today because I mentioned the Harvard recruiter would be here?"

Charlie didn't even know how to answer. He shrugged. "Not exactly. I just . . . well, I put up that one poster last week, that you made." That much was true. "Then the weekend came. . . ." That was also true: a weekend had occurred. Charlie decided to quit there.

Mr. Burklander nodded, happy to accept that his starter poster had been a key step in Charlie's turnaround.

"Well, he is here today, and I want you to meet him. I think this could be the beginning of a new phase for you, Charlie. I've wanted that for a very long time."

All Charlie could manage was "Thank you."

When he came back into the lab, Vanhi said, "What was that about?"

"He wants me to meet the Harvard recruiter."

Charlie thought she might be happy—after all, she had kept pushing their pact. But she didn't look happy at all. "Why?"

"Well, I mean, the posters . . ."

"I thought you didn't do those posters."

"I didn't."

"You quit the Game. I did everything it asked. Why's it helping you?"

"I don't know."

Vanhi shook her head. "It's so unfair. I made a delivery. What have you risked in the Game?"

"What delivery?"

"Never mind. It obviously doesn't even matter because now you're meeting the recruiter and I'm not. And you lied to me about starting an application. And using your mom's . . ." Vanhi stopped mid-sentence, but it was too late—the angry, hurtful words had already tumbled out.

Charlie knew what she was about to say—using his mom's illness in his essay. Something he'd promised himself he'd never do. And it was true, he had started an application, late one night, just to see how it felt, to see if he might find a way back toward a future. But he'd closed the application—unfinished and unsubmitted—ashamed of his essay, and never opened it again.

But now she'd spied on that in the Game? And thrown it back in his face? He glared at her.

"Unfair?" he snapped. "You have a fucking mom, and a dad who hasn't lost his mind. Why shouldn't I have a little good luck? You really want to talk about fair?"

"Guys," Kenny said softly, trying to pull them back.

"I didn't mean . . ." A look of sorrow was on Vanhi's face.

"I was first in our class. I was class president. Then *that* happened. Maybe I'm not ahead—maybe the Game just put me back where I belong. Ahead of you."

"Charlie . . ." Kenny put a hand on Charlie's wrist, but he shrugged it off.

"We were gonna go together . . . ," Vanhi said weakly.

"That was a fairy tale. Maybe it was always you or me."

"Yeah, maybe," Vanhi said.

Kenny closed his eyes, feeling what the Game had done to them.

Charlie left without another word, slamming the door behind him.

Kenny started to say something, but Vanhi just held up her hand, staring at the door as if Charlie were still there.

She knew exactly what she had to do.

Charlie had just made the choice exceedingly easy.

59 SCHRÖDINGER'S CAT

The man from Harvard wore a skinny tie and owlish glasses over a kind face. The only thing severe was his brow, which crinkled judgmentally regardless of what the rest of his face was doing. He was young, surprisingly chipper, red cheeked and smooth skinned.

"Well, hello, Charlie," he said.

Mr. Burklander stood behind him, hands on his haunches. Principal Morrissey stood on the other side, against her bookcase, arms folded.

Charlie remembered her nameplate in the Game:

DRAGON LADY.

The man from Harvard opened his hands, palms up, as if to say: *What now?*

"We're very interested in you, Charlie. Please understand, this is no guarantee of admission. There's a long process, and your grades will play a role, as will your SAT score, your AP scores, your extracurricular activities. We'll be particularly interested in how your senior year plays out, given the bumps in the road you've experienced. You're probably too late for early admissions, but you're right on time for regular rolling applications."

The man paused, took stock of the room, reset himself.

"The purpose of this meeting, Charlie, is to let you know that Harvard isn't about one thing. We don't consider just one dimension of a person. We like to say we're looking for well-rounded students or well-lopsided students. And really, there are so many smart applicants with good scores—I like to say it's a good thing I don't have to apply now—so we're really looking for something more. Call it character, if you want, or life experience. It's diversity, actually. A diversity of viewpoints, of backgrounds. You have that, Charlie. You've seen things most students your age can't understand. I understand you like computers."

Charlie almost laughed out loud. "I do."

"You program?"

"Yes. C++, Python, Java, PHP."

"Whoa, you're ahead of me." The man smiled not unkindly. "You know Mark Zuckerberg went to Harvard."

"Before he dropped out."

"Yes. Same with Bill Gates. We have a quite a good track record for our dropouts. Our graduates do okay, too."

Charlie nodded.

"I heard about the work you and your friends did in the Tech Lab here. There are a lot of vocational students who are learning important skills because of the technology you set up."

Charlie felt the guilt of his fight with Vanhi. This was her dream, too. "We did it together. The five of us. My friend Vanhi—"

"You founded the club, no?"

"Sort of. But—"

"And the other things you've done. Your work to end truancy courts, freshman year. Impressive."

"It didn't work."

"You hit the brick wall of bureaucracy. Not the school's." The man glanced back at Principal Morrissey and Mr. B. "They supported your efforts. But the district would rather keep giving tickets and making money. That won't be the last time you hit a dead end. I hope you won't stop trying. Did you know we offer a whole class at the Graduate School of Education on diversionary programs, like the one you proposed?"

"No."

"Did you know more than eighty percent of our students are from public schools?"

"No."

"You have a lot of supporters here. They're not naïve, Charlie. They know you've hit a snag. They know you've taken it hard. But they see something in you. They wanted me to see it, too. I'm the regional liaison to the admissions office. I don't say yes or no. I scout. I fill in the gaps in the paper admissions. What I want you to know, what I think you understand because you wanted to give truancy defendants a second chance before scarring their permanent records, is that nothing is set in stone. There has to be room for salvation. Otherwise, why would anyone change? So I guess my question to you, Charlie, is this: What do you want?"

Charlie glanced around the room. Vanhi was on his mind. His dad was on his mind—Arthur had picked up the pieces of his life and found something new. Couldn't Charlie do the same? Wasn't it time to stop punishing himself? He thought about his mother, watching from above, from a real heaven (*I wish!*) or a digital one. This was a portal in time suddenly open in front of him. He could step back through it and become the person he was. Or he could flail ahead as the person he'd become. He had to choose.

He didn't have time to think. This was the fork in the road. He knew it wouldn't come again. Charlie locked his eyes with the baby-faced man from Harvard and said with finality:

"I want this."

60 VEXATION

Vanhi ran from the Tech Lab to the darkest corner of the library, away from Kenny, away from any prying eyes. She knew she didn't have much time.

Charlie would meet the man from Harvard. They would love him of course. Why not? She did. And how many kids would Harvard take from one middling public school in Texas?

She'd never had a class with Mr. B. He didn't know her from Adam. He'd never give her the leg up he just gave Charlie. No essay, no matter how grand, would save her. She had to erase that D once and for all, and only the Game could do that.

Charlie had let his dad accept the restaurant, knowing full well it probably meant the prior owner's downfall, and he'd accepted the Game's gifts to him, too—the posters, and thus the recruiter—all while playing the saint and claiming to have quit the Game. What bullshit. She saw the beauty of the Game's offer now: Charlie had chosen the Game's gifts over her, but she was the real player, the non-quitter, so it gave her the trump card, the chance to choose the Game's gifts right back over him. The vicious circle was as appropriate as it was bleak.

She put on her Aziteks and logged back in.

The Harvard system was right where she'd left it. Charlie's application and her own, in flux. He would never know. When the rejection came back, the Game would protect her. It would cover her tracks.

The word SUBMIT was still flashing at the bottom of the screen.

She could feel someone watching her from behind.

She turned and saw the figure floating there. Even as a bright young skeptic, she could appreciate the beauty of Lord Krishna's fresh face, his blue skin, the luminous nails on his toes and fingers glowing like moons. She heard his words from the *Bhagavad Gita,* but his lips didn't move as he stared at her: *Gird up thy loins and conquer. Subdue thy foes and enjoy the kingdom in prosperity. I have already doomed them. Be thou my instrument.*

His eyes twinkled as he split into his trinity: Brahma the creator, Vishnu the preserver, Shiva the destroyer. Vanhi understood. Creation is just destruction. Destruction is just creation.

Death makes way for life.

One last, desperate time, she went back to Google and looked for anything, any sort of trouble, on Tremont Street.

Still nothing. No house gone up in flames. She had just delivered one more package in the Game's postal system: another bass pedal, more Azitek glasses.

Without thinking, Vanhi hit SUBMIT. The Harvard screen closed instantly. She was locked out. No way back in.

It was a giddy moment. It was small, it was huge, it was terrible, it was nothing.

Whatever, Vanhi thought, trying to ignore the tidal wave of guilt coming at her, *it's done.*

Alex wore sunglasses because his eyes were red with deep circles. He passed through the metal detectors into the school.

The halls were deserted. He went down to the Tech Lab, to the 3-D printer. It was empty during first period. He put on his Aziteks, and the printer smiled at him. It had a wide mouth and many teeth. Its casing was covered in gray scales and oozed with a black squiddy ink.

The Game had given him a simple instruction. It told him he could do this, one step at a time. He could always change his mind, at any point. And the direction now was simple.

Feed the beast.

Alex took the object from his bag, a Torah-like scroll the Game had given him. He could almost feel it in his hand, it had become so natural to operate in the AR world. The printer opened wider and licked its chapped, scaly lips. Alex put the Torah in, his hand disappearing for a moment into the machine, and it lapped the instructions up.

"How long?"

"As long as it takes," the printer told him. "Come back later."

"I'll wait."

He put his feet up in a chair and watched. The printer began working, building in three-dimensions, one layer at a time. Above, the loudspeaker crackled.

There was a mandatory assembly.

61 MALICIOUS AND NUTRITIOUS

The entire school was summoned to a Must Attend assembly.

The auditorium was packed with nervous anticipation. There had been only one other unannounced Must Attend assembly in recent memory, after an unfortunate incident at a pep rally. The teachers milled now around the outer aisles, and the students were chattering away or buried nose down in their phones texting people across the room. The Turner Tiger—the stuffed papier-mâché one for pep rallies, not the bronze one mounted on a pedestal in the atrium—was tipped up against the wall, staring ferociously at the air-conditioning vents along the ceiling.

Charlie came in and saw Kenny across the room with a bunch of kids from his first-period calculus BC class. They met eyes. Vanhi was there, too, near the front, next to Stacy Shearman, whom Charlie thought Vanhi was pining for these days. He tried to will her to look at him, but she didn't turn around. Peter was in the room, near the middle. Alex dragged himself in, looking whiplashed but curious.

Principal Morrissey took the stage and teachers began shushing fervently, as if their year-end bonuses depended on it. Mr. Sanders, the school safety officer, stood behind her. She cleared her throat into the microphone and waited for the room noise to reach a low simmer. She wore a serious brown suit and looked like she hadn't slept all weekend.

"I am sure many of you saw the newspaper article portraying our school in a dim light," she began, her eyes moving over the room but not looking at anyone in particular, "in regards to a certain graffiti that was plastered on our main façade last Friday. Certain claims were made about our school, about *you,* that are not reflective of the values we hold dear." She eyed the audience. Half the students were back to their phones; the other half were staring as focusless as the Turner Tiger. Charlie and Kenny locked eyes again. Peter, too. Even Vanhi stole a glance back. No Vindicator had owned up to it to the rest of them, but they all wondered if the Game had driven one of them to it. Kenny felt a creeping nausea. He tried to look calm.

Morrissey sighed noticeably and seemed to switch gears.

"I know this is a tough time," she said, sounding more human. "Not just for all of you. For everyone. This election is . . ." She caught herself, changed tacks. "There is a spirit of divisiveness I haven't seen before. Not in my lifetime. Anger. There's a lot of anger. And fear. And the things we hear on TV, what we read online, it's not helping. But . . ."

She paused for effect and seemed to be speaking from the heart. A few more ears perked up in the audience. The teachers were studying her carefully.

"But . . . what was written on the side of our school is disgusting. It's horrifying. I don't know if it was serious or some sick joke or maybe even by someone not even from our school trying to put a stain on us. God, I hope that's the case. I don't want to believe that one of you, any of you, could write something like that. I am sure you have all heard by now what happened this morning. There was a savage fight because of that graffiti. I'm not going to go into the details, but it was ugly and disgusting and we have a student in the hospital now. This will not go on."

Kenny felt his whole body tense up. He started looking for the closest exit, in case he really did puke, which was starting to feel entirely possible.

A chatter started arising among the students in the auditorium. Charlie noticed it first in the front corner of the room. He thought it was a response to the news, but that wasn't it. It was moving sporadically through the audience. And not in any physical way. Excitement would pop up in a cluster here, then in another spot across the room, then in another place entirely. Something was causing a stir, and it didn't seem tied to Mrs. Morrissey's impassioned speech.

". . . zero tolerance for hate," she was saying.

The sounds morphed into a tittering, a nasty, cruel noise. Gasping and glee. Charlie locked eyes with Kenny, who seemed puzzled, too. Then they saw Vanhi put on her Aziteks. She looked back at Charlie and tapped the glasses. Charlie dug his out of his backpack—after seeing his mom last night he couldn't leave them home, Game or no Game—and looked through the magic lenses. Like X-ray vision, he could see through the seats between them then. In the middle of one cluster of laughing students, the kid in the center had his cell phone hidden between his legs, tilted up. It glowed red in his vision. The girls on either side leaned in, peering at it, snickering. Charlie looked across the room and saw other phones glowing red. The lit screens were spreading geometrically, lighting up throughout the auditorium. The teachers were starting to figure out *something* was going on, although they were plainly steps behind. One teacher shushed a group of students near her.

In a flash Charlie realized what it must be—Peter had released the video of Kurt Ellers after all, exposing his most desperate secret, even though Peter had promised he wouldn't. Charlie scanned the room for Kurt and found him sitting with Tim in the back row. They looked as smug as usual, but neither had his phone out yet. Didn't Kurt know his humiliation was spreading virally through the room, coming like a plague, while he sat there looking like a vicious prick?

"I'm now going to turn things over to Mr. Sanders, who as you know is dedicated to the safety and security of every student in this school."

The murmuring grew louder, and a couple savvier teachers were scanning across the room now, noticing the trend. One of them grabbed a phone from a group of gawkers and looked at it. At first she looked confused. She lifted her glasses and held it closer. Her mouth dropped. She put the phone down quickly.

"I know some of you may not be feeling safe right now," Mr. Sanders was saying. "But I assure you . . ."

A red-glowing phone popped up in the corner of Charlie's vision.

It was down the row from him, near the aisle. He heard someone say, "Oh, man, you gotta see this."

Someone else said, "That's messed up!"

Charlie thought of Kurt's private pain, his most intimate, hidden moments out there for the world to see, and shuddered.

Charlie pressed his way down the aisle until he got to the guy with the phone, and as soon as Charlie saw the screen, his heart sank. He felt it literally cave and drop in his chest. The kid looked up at Charlie and his smile dropped, as he knew Charlie wouldn't like the joke.

It was Kurt Ellers all right, but out of sight, and not in the way Charlie had assumed.

Instead, the picture was eerily familiar. The portable buildings out back. The pile of bricks and other construction debris.

There was Alex, standing alone, his pants down around his knees, his dick hanging out for the whole world to see. And now it had.

The asshole thugs who pantsed him were out of the frame. The picture was just of Alex, alone, crying, jeans and underpants around his ankles. It was probably taken the second before Charlie had rushed out and smashed Kurt's phone, but of course the pic had already gone to the cloud.

Charlie immediately looked back to where Alex had been sitting. He was gone. "Oh, shit."

Charlie looked at Tim and Kurt, who were slipping out the back.

"*Turn that off,*" Charlie said pointlessly to the kid next to him.

He had no idea where Alex had gone, but maybe Tim and Kurt were following him to taunt him more, so Charlie went after them out the back doors of the auditorium.

The halls were empty. He passed the Turner Tiger in the main lobby, the real one, bronze and polished, paw raised, on a pedestal. He forgot that his glasses were on and jumped when the tiger flicked its head toward him and gave a low growl.

Tim and Kurt were at the end of the hall, going around the corner.

Charlie went after them, and when he cleared the turn, they heard him coming and faced him.

Then he realized he had no idea if they had spread the pic or the Game. "Did you do it?"

"What did you think was going to happen?" Tim asked.

"What do you mean?"

"You came after my girlfriend? Peter came after his?" Tim nodded over at Kurt.

"It's their choice," Charlie said.

"Your friend tried to put those posters up? Mocking me?" For once, Tim didn't talk like a bully or a monster. He was speaking quietly, reasonably.

"They were just drawings," Charlie said.

"Of me naked. What did you think we'd do?"

"You *destroyed* him."

But still, something was nagging in the back of Charlie's mind. No one deserved what had happened to Alex. Yet hadn't they come after Tim, unprovoked? Hadn't Alex tried to humiliate Tim in his own crazy way? Did Tim have a point? Charlie squelched the thought—it was flat wrong, he knew it.

"We just did what you tried on us. But better. An eye for an eye." Tim shrugged. "Maybe we took two."

You destroyed him. What will Alex do now?

The worry started spiraling inside Charlie: What would *he* do if someone sent his naked pic to the entire school? Add to that Alex's instability, his depression and darkness and drugs. With a shiver, Charlie recalled how quickly Alex had offered to cut himself with the razors in the boiler room when Kenny balked. Charlie thought of Alex's words at his house: *Nobody likes me. I'd be better off gone.*

"Did you see where he went?" Charlie asked desperately.

Tim almost said something snide, but then he saw how worried Charlie was and gave him an honest answer. "He went toward the lot."

Kurt had been quiet this whole time. The sadist in chief, Tim's henchman, stood just behind him, strangely muted. He'd finally gotten his way, shown the world his masterpiece of bullying, captured in a single image. Maybe it hadn't felt as great as he'd hoped.

Charlie wanted to be magnanimous, since they'd told him where Alex had gone, but he couldn't help the rage inside. He wanted to attack them, but it would be suicide: Tim had batted him away like a fly last time, and now it was two against one. But he had to say *something*.

"How would you feel? If someone posted something secret about you?"

Tim thought about it. Behind him, did Kurt shudder just a little, or was Charlie reading in?

Tim said, "I would hate it. That's why I have to stay in control. That's why I can't have you guys running around messing with us. You know what my dad taught me? The world is a joke. No one knows what they're doing. Never blink. If someone hits you, hit back twice as hard. If someone smells blood, it's over."

Charlie nodded. Even his sarcastic question had backfired. But the anger was second to his worry for Alex, and he had to pass them to get to the lot. Or he could double back around like a coward, and they'd know it. So he walked slowly and calmly toward them, clenching inside, wondering if they'd take this opportunity to smash him on the back of the head as he passed.

Yet their brutality apparently had a nobility, a barbarian's code.

He passed between them, and no one laid a finger on him.

Charlie was about to cut his losses and keep going, but a question occurred to him, the one that always seemed to come up since he'd started playing the Game.

Alex was attacked days ago. Charlie turned around. "Why'd you do it today?"

Tim said, "Because you told me not to."

"What?"

"Your text this morning. Delete the pic or you'll kick my ass? Now's your chance, Charlie. Come try it."

Charlie closed his eyes. The Game could make them or destroy them. Tim and Kurt were just as much pawns as Charlie was. He turned his back and went toward the lot.

Then he got his own text from the Game:

Better hurry

62 PLIMPTON 322

Better hurry.

Was the Game confirming his worst fears? Was it driving Alex toward something terrible?

Alex's car was gone. He could be anywhere. He didn't answer his phone. There was only one option, and it made him sick to do it, but he had no choice. He opened his texts with the Game and asked:

Where is Alex?

The Game wrote instantly:

Welcome back, Charlie!

He ignored the taunt.

Where is Alex?
  Did you like my present? How's Mom?
WHERE IS ALEX?
  You quit!
PLEASE
  He is preparing to die.
HELP ME STOP HIM
  How can I help you if you only believe in Me when you need
    something?

Charlie banged his hand on the hood of his car. *Come on.* He typed:

What do you want from me?
    Love.
What do I have to do?
    Come back. Be mine.

Charlie was shaking. This whole thing was his fault, all the way back to the moment he hesitated when Alex begged him to say, *We want you*—all the way back before that, when Charlie was so lost in his own grief that he didn't see Alex going down a bad path. Charlie could've saved him then, when it was a little thing, a stolen deck of cards here, a dark comment there. Charlie could've gotten him help, stood up for him, sat with him the way Peter had sat with Charlie after his mom died, late into the night. And now a chasm was between them, and all he could do was pray it wasn't too late to stop the worst thing. The thing Alex could never take back.

This was on him from the very beginning.

He thought of Alex on a ledge somewhere, one foot out over empty space. Charlie swore, then typed:

OK

63 BEFORE THE FLOOD

A gray dot appeared on a map, hurtling through two-dimensional space.

Charlie opened his door and was about to get in when Peter yelled, "Charlie, wait."

Peter caught up. "You're going to need my help."

"How'd you—"

"I'll explain on the way. We should take my car. It's faster," Peter said without apology.

When they got to his BMW, he threw Charlie the keys. "You drive. I'll deal with the Game."

"I can handle the Game."

"Trust me, this is beyond your skill," Peter said haughtily.

Moments later, they were tearing down the highway, following the gray dot that the Game promised them was Alex. Charlie hoped that was true, that they weren't following some random dot, but they had no other leads, so all they could do was hope.

The speedometer read 110. The Aziteks showed the navigation line over the road ahead.

"How'd you find me?"

"The Game. I was trying to find Alex, after the photo."

"Do you think he'd really . . ."

"Beaten by his dad, by Kurt, humiliated in front of the entire school, yeah, I do."

The navigation line on Charlie's Aziteks blanked out. "What happened?"

"Players are fucking with us."

"Why?"

"For the lolz." Peter moved his fingers, navigating windows Charlie couldn't see. "I'll get it back." Peter waved something over to Charlie's Aziteks, a series of branching gray lines ahead, forks and probabilities, some on the highway, some exiting here or there, each giving rise to more branches, receding over the horizon. Alex was a quantum man now.

"Which one do I follow?" Charlie asked, weaving through traffic.

"I'm working on that." Peter moved his hands. "I bought us a Wayfinder. It's making me solve multiagent pathfinding problems. Fucker."

Just as one branch leading to an exit approached, it disappeared.

"Jesus, I need more warning," Charlie shouted.

Charlie spun the wheel to the right to get around a car in front of them, but then in real life the wheel locked under his hands. It spun against him, out of his control, back to the left.

"Holy shit!"

They nearly rammed into the car racing beside them.

"I didn't do that!" Charlie yelled.

"We're being hacked. Hang on."

The wheel released and Charlie had control again. "Who's doing that, the Game?"

"No, other players are throwing shit at us."

Peter cleared a few more paths, the road ahead clarifying.

Then they saw the creature, small and spry. In their Aziteks, it leaped on a car in front of them, perched long enough for them to speed closer, then leaped at them, hitting their windshield and sending out a spiderweb of virtual cracks. It trailed a bloody mess and rolled up and over the roof.

"What the fuck?"

"I've seen these things, they're dumb fucking Game bots, they mess up electronics for real. So cheap any moron can buy them and throw them at us."

"What do I do?"

"Just drive. I'll handle them."

Another virtual bot came into view ahead and sprang from car to car, getting closer. It flew under them, small wings just lithe enough for it to glide like a flying squirrel, disappearing under the front of the car. In the AR-sound piping in from their Aziteks and through the satellite radio, too, they heard a grinding, chewing noise, teeth on metal, and in reality the wheel locked up again, spinning left, nearly crashing, sending the car next to them into a honking, swerving fit, then the creature tore up through the floor in the gamespace and ripped into the dashboard. The wipers went on full blast for real and sprayed the windshield with water, messing with their view, while the car swerved right, the wheel spinning under Charlie's hands, death-metal music suddenly blaring full blast from the radio, and they grazed the guardrails, which screamed metal on metal and sparked. "Fuck, Peter, *do something,*" Charlie yelled over the chaos.

"Hold on," Peter shouted. He reached "into" the virtual hole in the dash and pulled the thing out writhing, all teeth and spit. It bit his hand in the AR, loosing a gush of virtual blood and leaving a bloody stump. Their Aziteks painted background over Peter's hand wherever it moved so it looked as if nothing were left. Peter grabbed the creature with his other hand and smashed its head into the dash until it stopped moving.

"There were still too many gray lines ahead.

"Fuck," Peter said, "I'm out of Goldz. I can't help." Peter sounded strangely, uncharacteristically desperate, as if his whole mysterious-chill-outsider persona was a front.

Charlie didn't like it. But for once, he was one step ahead of the Game, and he didn't need Peter's help. "I know where we're going."

"You do?"

Someone must have heard because two more creatures appeared, leaping toward them from the cars ahead, suicide-diving into their windshield, spreading their wings the moment before impact to blot out the view. The windshield went black and red.

"Oh, no." Charlie hit the windshield wipers, but all it did was smear the filth around.

Charlie lifted his Aziteks off his face, hit suddenly with blinding sunlight. But the second he raised them, the car spun out of control, the wheel whipping violently back and forth.

"Put them back on!" Peter cried. The cars around them were blaring their horns.

It was crazy—they were trapped in augmented reality. If he took the Aziteks off, the Game would apparently smash them dead. It was play or die. Charlie put the glasses on and the splattered bots were back blocking his view, but the car immediately stopped swerving.

Peter opened his window and reached out of the car with his "remaining" hand, his seat belt unbuckled at 100 mph, pulling off one of the carcasses. The moment it was clear, Charlie saw a car immediately ahead that they were plowing toward.

He jerked left and whipped past it, horns blaring, clipping its back bumper.

"Get the other one," Charlie yelled, still blinded on his side.

"I can't reach it."

"Shit," Charlie shouted. "Take the wheel."

Peter held the wheel while Charlie unbuckled his seat belt and leaned out the window, feeling the air whip past him. He grabbed the thing and yanked it off, having to pull hard before the digital form would move. When it caught the side wind, it ripped out of his hand, and he saw it whip backward in the rearview mirror as it smacked off the crash wall onto the road, smearing as it went. Charlie pulled his seat belt back on and stared at the road ahead.

"It's the spillway."

Peter understood, ashamed that Charlie had thought of it first.

People went there to die. You could jump off. You could plow your car into the forty-foot-thick concrete retaining wall. You could ankle-weight yourself on the other side and drown. The place had a romantic reputation for loss and despair.

"There, that's our exit," Charlie said.

The bots were gone now. The wheel no longer jerked out of control. It was eerily silent, as if the Game had heard Charlie put it all together and silenced the jesters throwing obstacles in their way, out of respect for the solemn task ahead.

But as Charlie changed lanes toward the exit and the spillway beyond, a car coming the other way suddenly rammed over the median and rolled, the terrified driver looking not stylized and hyperreal like a character in the Game, but just horrified and real, and Charlie realized this was no joke and swerved, the poor guy's car being hacked as Charlie's had been, the guy probably going to die as casualty of a Game he didn't even know existed, and Charlie swerved with all his might, fishtailing across three lanes, smashing off the far sidewall just as the other car came down where they'd been a second before with a horrifying impact as Charlie barreled off the exit onto the grass and nearly into a ditch before pulling with all his might to veer back onto the country road as it veered around toward them, wheels sending a spray of dust as they jerked back onto the road. He drove white-knuckle forward, adrenaline surging, shaking, eyes dead-locked ahead. He glanced in the mirror just once at the car flaming behind them and felt sickened.

"Jesus Christ, that car came out of nowhere." Charlie's hands were shaking.

Peter stared at him, rattled from the maneuver, and said, totally honest and bewildered, "What car?"

64 GROUND TRUTH

Right after the terrible assembly, Vanhi had run out of the auditorium looking for Alex. She didn't love Alex. She didn't even like him. But she feared what he might do next.

She wrote Charlie, and he instantly responded, calming her fears.

> Don't worry. He's with me now. He's fine.

Vanhi wrote back:

> Fine?
>> Not fine. Ok for now. Safe.
> Ok. Where r u?
>> Boiler room—come meet us.

Why on earth would Alex go back there?

The site of his last humiliation, peeing his pants over a virtual monster with real flames.

What was the Game doing to him?

But she went because she needed to help Charlie. *Even if I've just put a knife in his back? Forget that. A week ago, he hadn't even wanted Harvard anyway.*

In the basement the boiler room door was already unlocked, no mystical code needed this time. She went into the darkness, calling for Charlie. It was pitch-black now, not even the safety lights on, and her voice echoed off the piping and through the empty nooks and back to her.

The door was creaking shut behind her, and suddenly she remembered the fight with the Hydra—how the door had bolted shut, trapping them in.

The echo faded and no one had answered, and Vanhi knew it, she was being played.

She turned and ran back toward the door, catching it just before the safety locks could click.

"Jesus, fuck."

Her text buzzed again.

Went down to tech lab. come meet us.

She gritted her teeth, feeling manipulated. But if they *were* there, she had to find them.

When she walked in, it was still dark, but then all the monitors lit up at once. The sixteen linked computers in a semicircle. The fifty-inch LED over the NanoStation, hooked to a microscope. The other flat-screens over the robotics and circuitry labs.

They all clicked on and showed the same image.

Vanhi saw herself from behind, hiding in the woods across from the house on Tremont Street. Someone had been filming her then, from a cell phone. It felt like mirror on mirror: watching herself watching the house, feeling like someone must be behind her now. Lord Krishna? G.O.D.? She glanced behind her and was alone.

On the screens, time sped up and the stars rotated out of the sky and the sun came up. She snapped awake in the video and left, satisfied the house hadn't blown up.

Time sped on, the house on Tremont Street quiet until the front door opened, and a young man with his wrist in a cast opened the door.

He looked at the box and then around the neighborhood, his gaze passing right by the screen without stopping. He knelt down and opened the box clumsily, using his keys in his good hand and holding the box steady with his other elbow, grimacing when his wrist jostled a little.

He ripped the flaps open and dug out the balls of old newspaper.

And then saw inside. His face looked absolutely, totally broken. He pulled out something limp, and it took Vanhi a moment to realize it was a cat, hanging lifelessly, its spine snapped in two, gray and black stripes, a collar with jangly tags. The video had no sound, but he appeared to cry out and held the limp form to his face and buried his nose against it. A lady came up behind him, clearly his mom. The scene was horrible. The cat hung from his arms like a shirt folded in half.

Vanhi started to cry. The deep sobbing came from a place far down inside her. It wasn't just for the cat that was broken in half. It was for the dream that wasn't going to come true.

She sobbed for what she had done, for what she had to do.

65 THE HAND OF GOD

Charlie and Peter tore down the road, the BMW gunning.

This was the same road where Mary's brother had died, a dangerous route, one lane, two-way traffic, on the edge of the city near woodlands, a fun place to cruise too fast. It was dusty and rough. It ended at the reservoir beneath the high dam. Kids would sit at the top on the walkway and smoke in the dark and look at the city in the distance. Alex was a gray dot in their augmented vision, hurtling ahead on the map, out of real sight. Charlie couldn't catch up so he took the left at the ridge and sloped up to the lookout point, a hilltop that was level with the crosswalk along the reservoir and looked down at the spillway in between. He kept an eye on the gray dot and hopped out of the car, looking for the real Alex to drive into view below.

Peter came up beside him. "There!" He pointed.

A cloud of dust plumed out and Alex's car passed through it, a fairly scraped-up 2010 Jeep his dad had bought used for all of the siblings to share.

With a sickening clarity, Charlie realized Alex was accelerating, not slowing, as the wall of the reservoir—all sixty feet high and hundred feet wide of it, poured concrete and steel reinforcements—loomed in front of him. This wasn't the first time someone had gone headfirst into the wall. A decade ago there had been a rash of copycat suicides, three or four maybe. But now it was happening, for real, right in front of him. Peter already had his glasses on and hands up, working in the Game, but he was out of Goldz, and his right hand was ruined in gamespace, gnawed to a stump by the bots, and nothing he tried was working. And there was nothing Charlie could do to help.

Or was there?

He had just rededicated himself to the Game. *Be mine,* it had said. And he'd said okay. How many Goldz might that be worth?

Charlie scrolled in the gamespace and waved his hand in front of him, moving the display. His loyalty had been rewarded: fifty thousand Goldz were in his bank. He looked at Alex's car, moving quickly, bringing his hand in front of its image and closing his fingers over it, moving in time with the accelerating car. As he hovered over it, a grid wrapped it, white lines crossing along three axes, with a diagram of the attack surface laid out for him. He looked at the wireless entry points. Keyless entry was too short range and the attack surface was too small. Bluetooth was better, but he quickly found the telematics unit. It was wide-open and he could go in through the radio over cellular, and the arrows and flow diagrams on his overlay showed his way from there to the CAN-IHS bus and the CAN-C bus. Charlie swiped, and the God Game did the work. Code scrolled past under his hand—*memifs2 -q -d /fs/usb0/usr/share/swdl.bin/*—and the car's system unfolded for him in waves, working him toward the physical controls—

```
# netstat Active Internet connections Proto Recv-Q Send-
Q Local Address Foreign Address State tcp 0 0 144-103-
28-21.po.65531 68.28.12.24.8443 SYN_SENT tcp 0 27
144-103-28-21.po.65532 68.28.12.24.8443 LAST_ACK
tcp 0 0 *.6010 *.* LISTEN tcp 0 0 *.2011 *.* LISTEN tcp
0 0 *.6020 *.* LISTEN tcp 0 0 *.2021 *.* LISTEN tcp 0
0 localhost.3128 *.* LISTEN tcp 0 0 *.51500 *.* LISTEN
tcp 0 0 *.65200 *.* LISTEN tcp 0 0 localhost.4400
localhost.65533 ESTABLISHED tcp 0 0 localhost.65533
localhost.4400 ESTABLISHED tcp 0 0 *.4400 *.* LISTEN
tcp 0 0 *.irc *.* LISTEN udp 0 0 *.* *.* udp 0 0 *.* *.*
udp 0 0 *.* *.* udp 0 0 *.* *.* udp 0 0 *.bootp *.*
```

There it was—port 6667 (no joke) was bound to all interfaces. Why on earth had Jeep's biggest exploit landed on the Mark of the Beast?

Alex's car went faster and the dust was kicking up all around him. He must have been going eighty or ninety and gaining, the wall looming closer. He would smash into it so absolutely that Charlie was sure he'd feel the blast from up here, Alex's demise instantaneous and violent.

G.O.D. sent the modified v850 firmware to the car in the form of a white light streaming from Charlie's raised hand. He was in.

Alex's face came into view. His expression was horrible—dead eyed, grim mouthed, head tilted forward, ready. Gripping the wheel, his knuckles were white.

The wall was before him, massively taller and wider. It would've filled his entire vision now. The impact would be explosive. A massive, visceral *SNAP*.

Then darkness.

Charlie pressed with his hand in the air and sent the code:

EID: 18DA10F1, Len: 08, Data: 04 31 15 00 01 00 00 00.

It appeared as a red beam, a laser shot that hit the car in augmented reality. The code told the car, *Kill engine*. The hack was ingenious, courtesy of the Game. There was no direct access to the central bus, but through the radio, there was a single, indirect connection: a small chip that could wake up a larger electronic unit next door that had been taught to trust its neighbor. It was an exploitation of trust. A flaw in the grand design that turned good into evil but, here, back to good.

The engine shut down but the car was hurtling forward with such momentum that it made no difference. The death would be here momentarily.

Charlie swiped for a new command and sent another burst of red light. *All brakes*.

The wheels locked and screeched and the car continued toward the wall, kicking up dust and digging into the ground.

One last hope:

Charlie moved his hand again and sent a final instruction:

IDH: 02, IDL: 0C, Len: 04, Data: 90 32 28 1F.

This told the power steering to turn counterclockwise with maximum torque.

Nothing happened and the car hurtled headlong toward the wall.

Then the message engaged in a burst of red light and the car spun left, braking and turning hard, Alex's face a mix of confusion and rage.

The car fishtailed in circles through the dust and spun to a stop with a silence that was startling after all the grinding and thrashing.

Alex stumbled out of the car and fell to his knees in the dirt. He was crying and then sobbing and looked like he might throw up. He went hands down on the ground and let his forehead press against the dirt.

Charlie ran down the slope, sliding and wide-stepping his way down the rocky grass and mud, and ended up in the dirt with Alex, shaking his shoulders and asking him to please look up.

66 LEVIATHAN

Alex looked up and wiped his face. "What did you do?"

He seemed dazed, like he didn't even know who Charlie was. The adrenaline had hacked his brain and pulled him into a zone.

Charlie couldn't think where to start.

"Did you stop me?"

Charlie nodded.

"Why?" Alex's voice wasn't grateful. It was agonized and enraged.

"They're not worth it. None of them."

"*You don't know that.*" Alex glared at him wildly. "Everyone hates me."

"No, no."

"And now . . . now . . ." Alex thought of the picture, of himself stripped naked, laid bare in front of the entire school. "You don't know *anything.*"

"I hate them too. Kurt. Tim. All of them."

"And I hate you," Alex spat.

"Alex, I—"

"You had no right to stop me."

"No right? I—"

"You ruined *everything.*"

Charlie just stared, stunned.

"I was going to do it." Alex looked at the wall longingly. "I was ready. Now . . ."

"Alex, you'll see—"

"I didn't ask for your help. Ever."

Alex got up, his legs shaky, and shoved Charlie so hard he fell backward into the dust. Alex stood over him. "I hate you." Alex opened his car door.

Charlie picked himself up. "Please. Please, let's just talk."

Alex tried the engine, and it turned over. "Everything that happens now is your fault." Alex's voice was so anguished, so weary and defeated, that it left Charlie chilled.

Alex put the car in reverse and drove off.

Charlie would never get up the hill and back into the car in time to follow Alex. His Goldz were at zero and the Game showed him nothing. He called 911 and gave them Alex's name and car. "He's going to hurt himself," Charlie told them. He called Alex's home number and left a message for his parents, but Charlie had no idea how to reach them at work. Then he climbed his way back up the hill—it was a lot faster on the way down. Peter was there.

"You could've helped me talk him down," Charlie said.

"I'm out of Goldz."

"No, with *him*. He listens to you."

"Not anymore."

Charlie felt himself crumbling inside.

I hate you, Alex had said.

Alex was going to kill himself, and Charlie couldn't stop it. He'd stopped it once, and it used everything he had. Now Alex was gone—Charlie couldn't find him, much less save him. The guilt tore through Charlie. *You don't want me in the group anymore. . . . I'd be better off gone. . . .*

"This wasn't my fault," Charlie said.

"I didn't say it was."

"Tim and Kurt did this."

"Of course they did."

How many other people had Kurt tortured over the years? Dozens, at least. Whom else would Tim crush—calmly, methodically—to keep his lousy place in the world?

"They have to pay," Charlie said.

Peter studied him. A moment earlier, Peter had felt lost, hating that Charlie had been the hero below, and in the Game no less. Now, seeing Charlie lost and reeling, Peter felt centered again.

"They *killed* him," Charlie said.

Peter's eyebrows raised. "What are you going to do about it?"

"You still have something on Tim?"

Peter nodded.

"It's good?"

"Yeah. It's good."

"And Kurt? You haven't put that video out yet?"

"Nope."

Charlie looked down at the savage skid marks in the dirt, far below them, where Tim and Kurt had sent Alex hurtling toward death.

This was the moment, Charlie realized. He'd always had that last thread, that connection to his old self, the voice in the back of his head. He *knew* he shouldn't do this. He *knew*, deep down, that it was his anger talking—or, no, not his anger, that was just another layer of excuse, rationalization—it was his guilt talking, and if he listened to that fading voice in the back of his head, he'd know that lashing out at Tim and Kurt was just a way to avoid seeing himself. But this was the moment when he went dark, when he knowingly snipped that last line to the old voice and let that Charlie go. You could mark it in a book.

"Let's ruin them. Let's destroy them and leave nothing behind."

Peter took a long slow breath, in then out.

Then he smiled. "Okay."

67 IMMOVABLE WALL / UNSTOPPABLE FORCE

Alex drove straight back to school—the last place Charlie or anyone else expected, straight down to the Tech Lab, where the 3-D printer was working away.

He knew Charlie had tried to call 911 to stop him from hurting himself again, but the Game had intercepted the call, so no one would be bothering Alex. It had kept Vanhi and everyone else at bay, too, so Alex could get back to the lab and finish what the Game had been guiding him through, step by step. Charlie was so sure Alex was going to hurt himself again, but that was the least of it. Alex had tried to do the right thing at the spillway, but coming out on the other side of that failed suicide attempt, having seen the wall come at him, having been ready for death and then cheated at the last second, he had found a clarity settling over him. The Game was right: killing himself was the easy way out. He would not disappear into anonymity, another loser gone and forgotten. He would leave a legacy. People would remember him, like the Friends of the Crypt, and shudder.

He took the new parts off the printer and hid them with the rest, waiting to be assembled. The DMT was kicking in. His suicide attempt had been rash, propelled by a jet fuel of shame and anguish, his dick pick spreading through the school, but it had given him an excuse, a way to bow out without letting the Game know he was scared to go through with the larger plan. But now he was glad

Charlie had stopped him. He should be thankful. This way was better. It would leave a mark.

He was in God's hands now.

Vanhi sat on the edge on the brick wall of the east lawn, her laptop open. The computers in the Tech Lab had locked her out. They kept replaying the kid cradling his shattered cat until she couldn't stand it. She tried the library, but those terminals blanked out one by one. Finally she grabbed her bag from her locker and logged on through her laptop outside, using a VPN and a mobile hot spot. But once inside the Harvard app, she couldn't touch it. Everything was submitted, time-stamped. Her beautiful essay and perfect GPA taunted her like models on a catwalk, inaccessible, locked.

She picked up her phone and dialed the admissions office.

The phone cut off midring and told her:

> You shall not pass!
> 10 Blaxx!!

She tried again, hitting Redial.

> You shall not pass!
> 1000 Blaxx!!

Her breath caught. She knew four hundred Blaxx was a hate brick through the window. What was a thousand? She thought of Kenny and his attack—a car nearly killed him over eighty-one hundred. She couldn't stop though. She knew she was being impulsive, frantic, but she had to make things right. She had to start with the application and unwind everything backward toward purity. Forgiveness.

She called again.

It rang twice before going dead.

She braced herself.

> You shall not pass!
> 100000 Blaxx!!

One hundred thousand? A queasy fear spread through her. It had jumped to *one hundred thousand*? In her haste she'd ignored the power of the multiples. What was she at now? Adding quickly: 101,010?

It was mocking her. She recalled her fight with Charlie.

You want the world to be black or white, ones and zeros.

That fucking twisted AI!

It didn't just want to step on her—it had to pull the wings off first.

But at some point she realized it didn't matter. Twenty-six hundred Blaxx had gotten Charlie a minor beating with a bat. Eighty-one hundred nearly got Kenny run down by a car. So what did it matter if it was one hundred thousand or ten million? Dead was dead.

So she dialed again because the only way out was through.

The phone rang and rang, and a sickening thought occurred to her. Were Blaxx transferable? Maybe she wasn't capped by the limit of her own misery. Maybe the bad mojo could spread to her parents, her friends, to *Vik,* who never sinned a day in his life?

She was about to hang up when a woman answered, "Harvard College Admissions Office."

Vanhi's phone read:

```
Don't do it.
Rat = Infinite Blaxx
Free Will!!!?
```

Free will. Vanhi thought about that.

I am Vanhi, goddess of fire. I can illuminate or I can incinerate.

Closing her eyes, Vanhi said, "I need to report something. Computer hacking in the admissions system."

After a brief pause the lady said, "Okay," more calmly than Vanhi would have guessed, as if she'd received this call before. "One moment please."

The call transferred, a series of clicks then banal music. Vanhi felt a steely resolve. She was proud of herself.

When the man answered, she took him through the whole story, and once it started, it poured out. She told him about the Game, the class rankings, messing with the essays and scores. The man listened patiently, with an occasional "Okay" or "Uh-huh." He asked Vanhi to repeat a couple things, and she could hear him taking notes in the background. He asked her to spell her name, repeat her address, and give her application ID number.

Finally, when Vanhi was done, the man said, "What I'm going to need you to do next is suck my dick."

Vanhi froze. She felt all the wind go out of her. She didn't even answer.

"You got that? Suck my dick. Suck it long and hard. Snitches are bitches and bitches are snitches. Know what happens to rats, fuckwad? Do you know? They get fucked and stuffed! Stuffed and fucked! Wanna get fucked and stuffed, rat?"

"No."

"Too bad. Too bad. It's out there, man. You already did it. See? You already fucked yourself. Got it, rat?"

The line clicked dead.

Vanhi stared up and down the long wall in either direction. She was alone, but she didn't feel like she would be for long.

68 ROKO'S BASILISK

Kenny had been researching all afternoon—philosophy, cognitive science—putting the pieces together. Now he met with Charlie and Vanhi upstairs, in a corner of the library that was the closest thing they could find to a dead spot, no computers nearby, no students with phones, a gap in security cameras. Not even a loudspeaker, which Charlie knew from doing announcements in his student council days could be switched into listening mode. They left their phones in their backpacks on a table downstairs, hoping the Game would assume they were studying quietly. They looked terrible, every one of them.

"We have to get out," Kenny said. "You, me, Vanhi."

Charlie looked between them. "Now you want to get out?"

"Yes," Vanhi said. "Why aren't you happy? This is what you wanted."

"It was. It is. But . . . the Game just saved Alex."

"Yeah, right after it drove him to it."

"That was Tim and Kurt."

"No, it was the Game *playing* Tim and Kurt. Trace it all the way back."

"I'm not sure quitting—"

"Give me a break," Kenny jumped in. "Two days ago you said—"

"I know what I said," Charlie snapped.

"But now you have a restaurant and an inside track to Harvard," Vanhi said bitterly.

"That's not it."

"The hell it isn't," Vanhi said. "Trust me, I've been right where you are. I get it."

"Look, you tried to pull us back," Kenny said. "Now it's our turn."

"It's not that simple," Charlie said. "Getting out is worse than staying in."

He told them about Scott Parker, his warning: the only way out was taking a life.

"What if there was another way?" Vanhi asked.

"There isn't. He said—"

"That's because he's a computer guy. You need a philosopher," Vanhi said. "It was Kenny's idea."

"What idea?"

"First you have to promise you're with us. If it finds out, we're done."

Charlie knew they were right to want to quit. But they were right about something else, too. The restaurant did matter. His dad was happier than he'd been in ages. . . . And now that Harvard was actually possible again, why *shouldn't* Charlie want that?

"All this time, you've been telling me to *want* things again. And now I do."

"Think about the restaurant, Charlie," Vanhi said. "Some guy didn't just decide to give it away to your dad all of a sudden. Someone suffered for that good luck. Did he deserve it?"

"Maybe he did. We deserved what we got."

"I tried to find Eddie," Kenny told him. "Trust me, Charlie, you can't live with this. I thought I could. It's not who I am. It's not you, either."

"We've all done things we regret. It's time to stop," Vanhi said.

"What have *you* done?" Charlie asked.

She couldn't bear to say it. She would fix it first, make it right. Then she'd tell him. Maybe then he'd forgive her. They heard a student walk by, talking on his phone, on the other side of a row of books. They fell silent until he was gone.

"Charlie," Kenny said, "we can't do this without you. I have the idea, but Vanhi can't code it fast enough alone."

"Please," Vanhi said. "I'm already toast. Infinite Blaxx. It's the only way for me."

Charlie stared at her. "Really?"

She nodded. He'd never before seen Vanhi look scared. She told him.

Fuck, he thought. *Everything was so good, for once.*

"Fine," he said. "On one condition. It's all of us together. No more secrets."

"Yes!"

"Okay!"

"That means Peter, too. And Alex, if we can find him."

Vanhi shook her head. "No way. We can't trust Peter."

"That's my price. We started losing the second we let the Game divide us."

"Charlie," Kenny said, "I know how you feel about Peter. But you have a blind spot here."

"No. No more jealousy. No more division. One for all, all for one."

Vanhi folded her arms. They faced each other; they were in a stalemate.

"He's a better coder than any of us."

They seemed uncertain, wavering.

"Look, this is about faith," Charlie said. "You said it yourself: We've all done things we regret. There has to be a second chance for all of us."

The three Vindicators stared at each other.

"One for all . . . ," Kenny began.

"Oh, shut up," Vanhi snapped. "Goddamnit."

Charlie grinned. "So what are we doing?"

Kenny took a breath. He looked around, to make sure no one was passing by.

"I think I know how to hack God."

69 PIECES

They had a plan. Charlie pressed through the crowded hallway. Kenny stayed in the library, prepping. Charlie would go find Peter, and Vanhi would get the gear.

As they split up, Charlie had taken her wrist. "Let's go together."

"Nah. I'm good."

"Vanhi, I've seen them, the other players. You haven't."

"Just kids."

"Not all. And the guy with the bat beat my ass. That car nearly ran Kenny over."

"I can take care of myself."

But she didn't look sure. It was fake bravado. How had he never realized that before?

"I know, but . . ."

"Charlie, we all have a job to do. Go do yours."

She hadn't stayed to argue, but she did touch his face tenderly before walking away.

On the way to his car, Mary intercepted him. He hadn't seen her all day, since the assembly threw everything off-kilter.

"Nice posters," she said dryly.

"I didn't . . . sorry."

"It's fine. We agreed to go our own ways. I didn't know that meant scorched earth. But, good for you."

"It's not like that."

She waved the topic away. "I want to tell you something."

He thought of the nasty text: *Next stop, Loserville!* "I can't. I'm in a rush."

"I want to tell you why I don't leave Tim."

Charlie froze.

"I owe you that much," she said.

Peter went to see Caitlyn. They met quietly in an empty classroom, where no one would see them, at Caitlyn's insistence.

"We won't have to hide like this for long," Peter said happily.

"What are you talking about?"

"I know what your boyfriend did to Alex today. It was horrible."

"It was."

Peter was surprised she agreed. "So then, maybe this won't be as hard as I thought." He pulled out his phone.

Without explanation or fanfare, he showed her the illicit video, Kurt and the other man, Dan, locked in gentle, urgent passion.

He watched her face. She didn't look away or flinch. When it was over, she looked up at him and didn't say anything.

"So?"

"So what?" Caitlyn wasn't angry or shocked or reacting in any way he'd hoped for. She seemed a little weary maybe, but with no hint of surprise or denial.

"Did you *know*?" Peter felt the ground shift under him.

She gave a little half shrug, staring at him.

"Did he tell you?"

"God, no. I doubt he knows how." She didn't say this cruelly. It sounded as if she meant it literally—as if Kurt lacked the vocabulary to explain himself.

"Then how?"

"There are some things you can't fake," she said mildly.

The thoughts were starting to connect for Peter, in a way that he couldn't live with.

"You mean . . ." He stopped and tried to frame it right. "You *knew*, and you still didn't choose me?"

She didn't put a hand on his or soften her voice or do anything to comfort him. Her life had been a series of hard edges, a monster visiting her at night. She slept with Peter because she wanted him physically, not any other way. She took him on her terms and felt no pity. He was seventeen years old. She'd dealt with far worse at twelve. Pity wasn't an instinct that came to her anymore. Even at Careloft, she brought strength, not sympathy.

"You chose a sham over us. Why?"

"If he's free, if he does something rash . . . Say people think I knew all along . . . or say they think I *didn't* know . . . either way, I won't be humiliated senior year. I've made it this far. My parents never loved each other, and they've been together thirty years. I can make it to graduation."

"Not if I put this out." Peter raised his phone.

"If you do, you'll never see me again." Her eyes were cold. "The world is what it is, Peter. Get used to it."

Vanhi walked alone through the parking lot. Her job was to run to her house and pick up all the old laptops she kept around to mess with and soup up. She would unscrew the Bluetooth ports and Wi-Fi cards, strip them down to their landlocked essences. No portals. No routes of entry. More than an air gap. A lockbox.

She shivered at her conversation with the fake admissions officer.

Rats get stuffed and fucked.

You wanna get stuffed and fucked, rat?

Everything vile and repellent, right there, in that call. Toxic masculinity. Or toxic electricity. She wasn't sure which.

I'm gonna need you to suck my dick.

Thanks, Game.

Gray clouds swept in, and Vanhi drew her jacket tight as the wind picked up. She kept a lookout for rat-stuffers and suck-my-dickers. The lot was so empty that anyone would have stood out, so the man across the street she noticed now did stand out.

Was he watching her? She couldn't tell. Charlie told her the Game was full of people spying on them.

Was he one? In the flesh?

His face wasn't visible yet but he seemed to be keeping pace with her but not looking at her. Just sort of moving in parallel, hands deep in his pockets. Why? Because it was cold? Because he had a knife? Was he looking for a rat to stuff and fuck?

She walked faster, and his pace picked up. She tried not to look at him. That was just slowing her down. Her car was fifty feet away.

The keys were in her backpack—fuck!

Why couldn't they be in her pocket?

Seconds mattered, and she'd have to rummage.

Being a woman meant feeling a tingling fear on the street every time, as if each man were a lottery ticket: friend, mugger, kind-heart, rapist.

But this was no ordinary day. And the man was definitely following her now because he was zigzagging, crossing the street at a weird time, only for her.

She swung her backpack around and fished out her keys without breaking stride. She had a keyless entry, but she put the old-fashioned hard key between her knuckles, letting it stick out like a knife. She would not go down, not today. Or if she did, it would be fighting.

The footsteps were evident now behind her, gravel crunching. How close was he?

No sense turning around. That would lose precious seconds.

She broke into a run and let her thumb click the doors open from ten feet away.

No penetration necessary. Waves and electricity.

I'm gonna need you to suck my dick.

No, I don't think so.

She felt a hand on her shoulder and she swung around and drove the key blade forward.

He knocked her hand away, but she put the other palm upward into the man's nose, feeling him buckle backward from the pain, and she got into the car and slammed the door, flooring the gas and ramming up and over the concrete hump in front of her parking space, hearing a grinding noise under her car but pushing ahead and leaving the man, knee down, in her rearview mirror.

70 EVERYTHING VIBRATES

Mary told Charlie everything.

In October of 2014, her brother Brian was turning eighteen. She couldn't believe it when he chose to spend his birthday on a double date with her and Tim. Brian was a kind older brother, if aloof, but they didn't hang out socially. After all, he was a senior, a god on campus who already had a full ride to A&M to play football, after which he would join the Marines. She said yes in a heartbeat. That night, Brian drove, with his girlfriend, Tracy, next to him, and Mary and Tim in the back. Brian had supplied the alcohol, and she remembered all of them laughing about something when the headlights blinded her and everything went black.

Tracy died instantly. Brian would die two days later. Mary remembered hazy patches from the crash, her parents at the scene, and her dad's lawyer, too, an important man talking in low tones with the policeman. And just like that, it all went away. The police report would reflect that the driver in the other vehicle had been intoxicated, above the legal limit. She never learned if that was true. He had died instantly, and his mother was an elderly woman who lived alone and had no resources to question anything. The police report declined to mention alcohol in the kids' car, or underage drinking, or Mary and Tim at all.

Her mom kept reminding her what a pointless shame it would've been to ruin their positively bright futures and unblemished records. She was devastated over the loss of her son, and she would gladly sacrifice a stranger's legacy for his.

Mary knew the irony of founding a SADD chapter in her brother's name. She didn't know what else to do. On the first anniversary, she'd found the address of the other driver and almost gone there. Her mom had stopped her. "They will take everything from us. They'll want money. There could be criminal issues with the police report—do you think that officer helped us for free? You will destroy this family. For what? Because you can't carry the guilt? That is the very definition of selfish." Mary had tried to push past her mom, who grabbed her, eyes welling with tears, begging her, "I have lost *everything*"—Mary didn't miss that word—"and you want to do *this* to me?"

Now, Mary looked up to see how appalled Charlie was, how much he hated her. "If I leave Tim, he'll tell everyone."

"That's crazy. And take himself down, too?"

"You don't understand him. He would in a heartbeat. I'm his destiny. He's got it all planned out. It would destroy my family. And that would be worth it to him."

"Call his bluff. Set yourself free."

She shook her head. "I won't. I may hate my family, but I won't hurt them more. I have to live with this."

"What if Tim wasn't a problem anymore?"

Mary shook her head. "Don't talk like that. I didn't come here for help. I just wanted you to understand."

Charlie nodded, then asked, "Did you ever get a text from Caitlyn, something about Loserville?"

She looked at him, confused. "No."

He nodded. He believed her.

71 ROBIN GOODFELLOW

Reeling from his conversation with Caitlyn, Peter had left campus. Now he was alone in his apartment, the one the Game had rented for him, with enough Goldz. Everything was transacted online. The Realtor loved the quick cash, and the paperwork looked right. He'd never know he was renting to a high school kid.

Peter had needed a place to stash his stuff. Sure, his dad was rarely around. But his version of parenting was the occasional random drug sweep when passing through town, and then there was hell to pay. As if that made up for months of absence.

Peter's newest toy was a $10,000 Voyan bathtub, seventy-two inches long with air jets and chromotherapy. The ceramic had a built-in warmer.

Peter knew Charlie thought he was directionless, but he had goals. He wanted to work on Wall Street one day. That was where smart money went to take dumb money.

He understood the way they thought on Wall Street. It was systems and anarchy. You played the system to achieve what anarchy used to provide: the power to take what you want.

Charlie thought if you worked hard and followed the rules, things would be okay. He should know better. But even cancer—that random leveler—hadn't shattered his naïve earnestness. He kept crawling back toward the light.

Peter saw Charlie approach, a dot moving down the hallway of the apartments.

Peter had installed a Qbit lock on the door.

Before Charlie could even knock, Peter swiped his hand in the air, and the door clicked. "Come on in."

Charlie walked into the dark apartment and saw what looked like a cauldron: a pool of bubbling water lit red from the inside, no other light in the room.

As his eyes adjusted, he made out the lines of the tub, sleek and modern, and saw Peter's blond hair slicked back and dark with water, his eyes obscured by sunglasses, Aziteks no doubt, one hand still above the waterline, wrist swaying back and forth in the air lazily, drawing commands in the Game.

"How did you find me?" Peter asked merrily.

"I got a lot of Goldz from the reservoir."

"That was supposed to be my big moment. I guess you lapped me again."

It was unnerving to hear self-pity from Peter. Charlie ignored it. "What is this place?"

"It's my pied-à-terre. You like it?"

"You want to put some clothes on?"

"Not really."

"I need your help. But first you have to be honest with me."

"I've always been honest with you."

"Are you a drug dealer?"

"Did Vanhi put that in your head?"

"Are you?"

Peter kept his gaze up at the high ceiling, invisible in the darkness. The red lights of the bath reflected off his Aziteks.

"I don't like labels, but, yes, I have occasionally supplied some narcotic refreshments to the free of heart."

"Why?"

"Social utility, at first. Then joy. A place in the great network of human need. It started at St. Luke's. I was coming in cold. An outsider. I needed a purpose. Turns out rich kids like drugs."

"The bag I gave Zeke. Was that . . . ?"

"Magic mushrooms."

"Oh, God."

"Relax. You didn't know."

But I did know. Why didn't I listen to myself?

"You gave Alex that Adderall?"

"And ayahuasca."

"Jesus. Why?"

"Because he asked. Because his life sucks. What's wrong with a little escape?"

"He's lost. He's doesn't know what he wants."

"Haven't you noticed by now, people are tired of you telling them what they need?"

"You were already playing the Game when you signed me up. Weren't you?"

"Yes."

"Why did you lie about it?"

"Because it was a game! I was trying to win. I mean, come *on*. I didn't know the stakes back then. I thought it was all just internet bullshit and fun. Stop looking for conspiracies."

"Did you make my dad get the restaurant?"

"No."

"Did you fake the texts from Mary and Caitlyn about me?"

"*No*. Jesus."

Charlie tried to read Peter. But Charlie knew one thing above all else. They wouldn't be able to pull off Kenny's idea without Peter. Vanhi might not trust him, but they needed him. It was a leap of faith. It wasn't clear they had a choice.

"Charlie, I never lied about who I am. I'm a fuckup. But I've never hurt you."

"I know. I don't care what you've done. We've all done things now. What I need to know is, Do you want a second chance? Do you want to be better?"

Peter took off his Aziteks. He held them up with one hand while he let the rest of his body sink down under the bubbling water, then he came splashing back up, hair dripping, slicked back. He might have had a hard time coming to St. Luke's as the new kid way back when, but it was hard to imagine, his body gleaming and his face so archetypally handsome.

"Yeah," he said, "I really do."

72 ANONYMOUS

Kurt was losing it. The fear had started creeping in when Charlie made that cryptic statement in the hallway: *How would you feel? If someone posted something secret about you?* The way he said it. . . . The way he'd looked at Kurt. . . .

What had he meant? What did he know?

After the fight with Charlie he'd gone to the old playground on Mockingbird, far from school, far from Tim, far from his father. He did his thinking there.

When the bell for fifth period rang, he was back on campus, waiting for Caitlyn outside her classroom. They went to the parking lot to sit in his car.

"There's something I have to tell you." He was normally so strong. Scary, even. The biggest and baddest. But right now, Caitlyn thought, he seemed scared. Broken. She thought of something Kurt had told her once, offhandedly—what his dad said when Kurt was little about what he'd do if he found out one of his sons was gay. It was a chilling comment, proof that even now the sunlight hadn't reached as far as people believed. But Kurt had relayed the story almost jokingly, like, *Can you believe he said that? Good thing he doesn't have to worry about that!* Yet the way Kurt had paused after telling her the story, in the dark one night, she'd known. On some level she'd always known.

Now he said, "It might come out anyway. So I want you to hear it from me."

Caitlyn realized she actually liked him in this moment. He was a better person, a little scared. She'd always wanted Tim, but Tim chose Mary, and Kurt was number two. You took what you got.

"It's okay." She took his hand. "I know."

"Know what?" Then he let go. "You do?" He nodded, as if that made sense. Of course she knew. "You won't tell anyone? If it doesn't come out."

"No. I don't think that would benefit either of us."

He nodded again. He rubbed a calloused large hand over his face, stopping to squeeze his temples, where his head was pounding.

"Still," she said gently, unusual for Caitlyn, "it might be time to see other people." She gave him a rueful smile. "It's not you, it's me."

Alex watched the 3-D printer dance in the air.

It was beautiful. Hypnotic.

The nozzle laid drips of material like toothpaste onto the heated bed, building 3-D objects one 2-D plane at a time.

It was like watching someone make a sculpture, but instead of carving it down from a brick of rock, it was being built up from nothing. This was creation!

The hand of the sculptor was replaced by the mindless nozzle, moving gracefully through space, blind and dumb to what it was making, guided by one simple command: here, not here; here, not here. And from that, you could build anything.

Alex had been staring at the bobbing head moving like a snake for so long he'd forgotten where he was or how long he'd been there.

As it finished each piece of the guts of his device, he placed them together, using the screws and pins he'd also printed. He had turned the Tech Lab into a one-stop death shop.

While the snake hose moved, and the printer licked its filthy tongue, the Game showed him verses and images, biblical and local mixed together.

And the LORD said, kill them all without pity or compas-

sion. Slaughter old men, young men and maidens, women and children.

It was like watching God's finger lay dots of fury, one real-life pixel at a time.

73 FUN HOUSE / MIRROR

In the car, Peter said, "I need to tell you something."

They drove toward Charlie's house, so he could grab his gear.

"Since we're doing second chances, I have one more thing to confess."

Charlie kept his eyes ahead. "Okay."

"My mom didn't die."

Charlie nearly drove them off the road, then the moment passed.

"She left. When I was really little. My dad told everyone she died. I'm sorry."

Charlie didn't say anything. He just stared ahead and drove.

"In a way, you're lucky. Your mom was taken. Mine wanted to go."

They stopped outside Charlie's house. "I'll be right back." He paused. "The stuff about Tim. Did you put it out there?"

Peter nodded.

"What was it?"

Peter laughed bitterly. "His parents are crooks. They steal from the bank they own. They drank and gambled their own money away. Imagine that, lucking into a family fortune, old money, and just blowing it."

"The dad steals?"

"Mom, too. There's enough there to put them both in jail and wipe out their bank accounts. Tim's trust fund, too."

"He beats Mary. Blackmails her."

"You don't have to convince me. Besides, I already launched. It's up to the Game now."

Charlie went inside, leaving Peter in the car. The wind whipped past Charlie as he made it to the door. His dad was home, taking a breather before the evening shift. He looked up. "When did you get glasses?"

"Oh. A while ago."

"We were packed at lunch. Full house, again. They've never seen the place so full. We're doing something right, Charlie."

He felt a crippling guilt then. His dad looked so happy. If the Vindicators' plan worked, it might all go away. All the secret machinations of the Game to make this happen, they might just cease. And if the Vindicators' plan failed, it was definitely going away. The Game would take Charlie's father down with a righteous vengeance. Either way, his dad would probably lose.

Maybe *that* was his place in the world.

Charlie startled. Behind his dad, a figure was watching. A man in a white porcelain mask and black cloak. Watchers, Peter had called them. Why was the Watcher here? What did they *do*?

"What's wrong?" his dad said, oblivious.

"Nothing."

Charlie felt more eyes on him and looked up. Another figure was on the balcony, staring down. White mask, dark eyes.

Now there were others, too. He could feel them watching. Something was happening.

"Charlie?" his dad asked.

A sign behind his father lit up, an old-timey bulb board flickering on and buzzing in and out, like some run-down corner of Broadway.

THIS WAY ⇨ it said, pointing him toward the stairs.

"I have to go," Charlie said, distracted.

"What, you just . . ."

"We'll talk later."

He left his dad standing there, baffled, a hooded figure on either side staring at Charlie.

CAN'T MISS a sign said at the top of the stairs, a vintage vaudeville finger pointing up.

☝

He pressed his way up the stairs warily, brushing past figures there, waiting for him.

The second floor of the house looked the same, no real changes through the Aziteks like in Peter's house or at school, vines and cobwebs.

A TV was on in the upstairs den, and the Game or the network or whoever showed him Hillary on the screen, smirking, saying, "Wipe it? What, you mean like with a cloth?" He passed her into his dad's bedroom, but it was dark and quiet and the stirring of figures was gravitating behind him, somewhere else. The image in the picture on his parents' wall, a framed museum-shop poster of *Starry Night,* his mom's favorite, quietly swirled, but everything else was unchanged.

He passed the hall bathroom and saw his reflection in a mirror.

He went back toward his bedroom and the TV had Trump on now, that shape-shifting lizard, saying, "I hope Russia can find those missing emails. . . . Those guys can hack. . . . I hope they find them!" A sign flicked on down the hall, burned-out bulbs glowing orange.

OVER HERE.

Charlie felt a growing dread. Too many Watchers were here, clustering around him. He could pass through them, but they stepped aside to make way.

He walked toward the laundry hamper, which now had a sign above it and an arrow, bulbs on the wall shimmering, pointing down.

DIRTY LAUNDRY

The Watchers were behind him. He tried to ignore them, but he looked back finally because he couldn't stand it and they were all there, white-glazed faces, featureless, appraising him. *I'm not your fucking toy,* Charlie wanted to scream, but he didn't, because he knew he was. "Don't open it," a voice said, and he knew who it was before he even turned around because his mother's voice was imprinted in his soul.

They waved her away and she disappeared, and Charlie didn't know if her words came from an independent intelligence, free of the Game with its own will as she had told him, or if the Game was speaking through her.

The Watchers wanted him to open the door, so he wouldn't. But that wasn't free will either.

Cursing, riddled with curiosity and anger and shame, he thought, *Fuck free will.*

He opened the hamper door.

74 CLOSED LOOP

What Charlie saw made him sick.

Not at first. At first it was fine. Nothing he didn't already know.

Inside the hamper, floating over the clothes, were emails back and forth between his father and the woman whom Charlie had met at the grand opening of Charlie's. Susan McAllister. She seemed like a nice lady, and as he flipped back through the emails, they were sweet, sometimes heartbreaking. Some were about how much Charlie's dad missed his wife, which felt like a weird thing to tell this new lady, but she was kind and tender and caring toward his father, which made Charlie like her even more. His bad feelings melted away. But as he kept flipping back through the messages, a strange thing happened. They didn't stop in the months right after his mom had died. They didn't stop when she was failing but still alive, near the end. They didn't stop in the year before, while she'd been sick and suffering. How far back did they go? Charlie felt ill. He didn't want to keep reading, but he did. He imagined his mom in her bed, desperate, in pain, while his father was out messing around. Charlie felt a rage beginning to boil in his blood. He kept flipping back. He knew these dates by heart. The surgery. The diagnosis. The tests. The symptoms. And before? *Before*. They went back even before. His fists were balled up. He thought of all the times he'd been there for his mom, his dad supposedly overwhelmed, supposedly hiding at work. Grieving. Torn up. Except he hadn't been at work, had he? He'd been out, out with her, fucking while Charlie was drowning, while Mom was dying. He felt a pulse ripple through what he had supposed was the reality of his life. He kept reading, going back in time, in inverse proportion to his fury. It was a lie, a lie, all of it. The sanctity of his parents' marriage. The dividing line of her diagnosis, between good and bad, before and after, paradise and hell. In his mind, his family had been sacrosanct, loving, well kept, *his life,* his foundation—until that horrible disease ruined everything. But what now? Now that it had always been ruined? Always been a lie? Never pure, never sacred, never the basis of his being, of right and wrong? Had she known, like some politician's wife standing weakly behind her apologizing husband? Had she known all those years she told him, *Listen to your father. Obey. Emulate.* And yet his dad was not just a feeble, weak man cowed by a terrible disease, but a fraud, a liar, a selfish bastard?

The voices were roaring behind him now, so much so that he couldn't think, he wanted to scream at them, but he was more blinded by rage at the moment and turned inward, deeper within himself, until the words appeared in front of him, the same ones he'd seen before, so simple, so black-and-white.

Do you love your dad? Y/N?

He swiped the words away and ran downstairs, past the figures in his way. He had to know, had to look into his father's eyes and find out, because it could be fake, it could all just be words on a screen, total fabrications. His dad was downstairs still, sitting at the table, and he turned and Charlie blindsided him.

"Did you cheat on Mom?"

His dad looked at him, sputtered, and his face said it all. He tried to muster a lie, a denial, but Charlie already knew. It felt like bitter dirt in his mouth.

"Charlie," his dad said, trying to stand up.

Charlie knocked past him, out the door, blinded with rage and betrayal. Peter was sitting in the car, oblivious that Charlie's whole world had shattered, and again the words popped up in his vision: *Do you love your dad? Y/N?* All he could do was be honest, ride the wave of his fury toward the only true thing he could say, and he reached up into space, the Watchers watching, his dad fumbling behind him, and he pressed his finger forward, marking *N*.

75 IN MY FATHER'S HOUSE . . .

The Vindicators met in the old darkroom because it lacked electronics, and because no one gave a shit about developing film anymore. Kenny had scoped it out as a true dead spot, but how long could they all be off-line before the Game noticed? Everyone was there except Alex, whom no one could find. Charlie looked horrible, his head buried in his arms in the dim light. He looked like someone had just kicked the shit out of him, but he wouldn't say why.

Kenny looked over his friends. Would they listen to him? Would they laugh him out of the room? They were the hard scientists, the coders. He was the fuzzy philosopher, just a half click away from his devout parents. But that's why his idea might work, he thought, because the Game was bred on theology. That was its base reality. If it meant saving his friends—even having a *chance* at saving his friends—it was worth risking their ridicule.

Kenny put a hand on the books in front of him—*Summa Theologica*, Bertrand Russell, C. S. Lewis—and took a breath. "After the car hit me, I was unconscious. I don't know how long. When I woke up, I had this idea. Almost like a vision," he added sheepishly. "All these things I'd been thinking about for years just kind of came together and made sense. When I was a kid, at church, I used to love this line from the Bible. John 14:2. 'In my Father's house are many houses.' I get it now, it's a metaphor. But when I was little, I took it literally. A house filled with other houses, like something out of *Alice in Wonderland*? Only God could do that."

Kenny's hands were shaking a bit. Vanhi put a hand on his, steadying him.

"I always loved things like that. Trying to imagine the impossible. Like what's bigger than the universe? Or what does a four-dimensional cube look like? There's this book, *I Am a Strange Loop*. I gave it to Charlie once. It's my favorite. Hofstadter wants to know, How does our brain create consciousness? How do these unthinking neurons—these little on/off switches—suddenly add up to something *aware*? He thinks it's like putting two mirrors facing each other. Suddenly a simple, flat picture looks like it goes on forever."

Kenny's eyes were wide in the dim light.

"But that's not the whole story. Hofstadter says consciousness needs one more ingredient. It's not just a loop, but a *strange* loop. It has to twist back on itself like an M. C. Escher drawing. A staircase that leads up, up, up, until all of a sudden you're at the bottom. Two hands drawing each other. See?"

Vanhi nodded gently. "I understand completely. You have a concussion."

Kenny shook his head and began again. "There's a riddle in Hofstadter's book. 'The barber is the one who shaves all those, and those only, who do not shave themselves.' So does the barber shave himself?"

Peter smiled. He loved logic puzzles. "If he shaves himself, he can't be the barber, because the barber only shaves those who don't shave themselves."

Kenny nodded.

"But if he doesn't shave himself," Vanhi chimed in, "then he'd have to be shaved by the barber, because the barber shaves all those who don't shave themselves. But that won't work, because he's the barber."

"Right," Kenny said.

"Maybe that's why God always has such a long beard," Peter said, grinning.

"Do you see where I'm going?"

"No," they all said at once.

"It's the set that contains all sets. Does it contain itself? Remember those spheres you programmed, Vanhi?"

"Yeah?" she said, more of a question than an answer.

"That was amazing. You programmed them out of thin air. C++, right?"

"Right."

"That blew me away. Perfect giant, rotating spheres."

"It was just triangles. You can build the whole thing out of very small triangles."

"I know that, in theory. But I don't know how to *do* it. I need you to do it."

"Do what?"

"I want you to make a bigger, heavier sphere."

"How big?"

"Well, that's the thing. Imagine you have a code that's self-aware. It has attributes. It believes certain things about itself, even if they aren't true. Even if they *can't* be true."

"That's sounds like every person I know."

"True. This is computer code, not genetic code. But same difference. It *thinks* it's God. That's what it's been told. That's wired into its deepest DNA. It can't be omnipotent—right?—because it exists in a simulation inside a physical medium. Fiber. Copper. Silicon. It has to follow the rules of physics. But it *thinks* it's omnipotent. It believes in itself."

"That's hackable," Vanhi said.

"I think so," Kenny agreed. "If you gave it a task that required all its resources, approaching infinity. Something it knows it should be able to do. Something that would appeal to its own sense of greatness."

She was starting to see.

"You need a paradox. The barber who shaves himself and doesn't shave himself. The house that contains all houses."

Kenny nodded. "Have you heard of the omnipotence paradox?"

"No," Vanhi answered.

"Saint Thomas Aquinas asked whether God was so powerful he

could make a rock that he couldn't lift." Kenny tapped on *Summa Theologica*. "C. S. Lewis wrestled with it. So did Descartes. If you take God seriously, it's a real problem."

Vanhi smiled. "You want us to program a sphere big enough to contain all spheres."

"Yes." Kenny grinned back. "I want us to trick God into lifting a really big rock."

Alex was putting the finishing touches on his device. It was larger than he expected. He was in a zone now, assembling, following the directions shining into his eyes. He had moved everything into the boiler room, the Game keeping him clear of his friends. He felt like a god himself, the way the Game let him move invisibly.

There was a last touch, which he fully endorsed. His father hated being called at work unless it was an emergency because the manager never let him live it down when he was caught off the sales floor. The Game had shown Alex a video of his dad groveling at work, to a boss half his age, and his father had the audacity to come home and beat *him*? Well, Alex was going to teach him a lesson in strength and power. Alex would never be pathetic like his father. Alex would never let his dad touch him again. Alex would destroy his father with righteous fire. His dad was the Lamb, not him.

When Alex spoke through the phone, the Game made his voice sound like that of Mrs. Fleck, the school counselor, and he read his script as it appeared in front of him. "Yes, we need to discuss Alex. He's really struggling. How about tomorrow at two P.M.? . . . I understand it's hard to miss work, Mr. Dinh, but this is very important. . . . Yes, yes, thank you for accommodating. We'll see you tomorrow."

76 ... THERE ARE MANY HOUSES

It was Charlie who broke the silence.

"It won't work."

"Do you have a better idea?" Vanhi shot back.

"No. But this is philosophical BS. No offense, Kenny, but it's angels on pinheads."

"Don't you see, that's the point. The AI was trained on angels on pinheads. That's all it knows. You don't have to take it seriously. It does."

"You have a bigger problem," Peter said. "Every virus has to penetrate the system before it can work. And this system is all about security. It's made by hackers, for hackers. They know every trick."

Kenny lit up. "Maybe that's it!"

"Oh," Peter said, as if that explained it all. "Cool."

"You said it. It knows every trick. We already hacked omnipotence. Now we just have to hack *omniscience*."

"This is some theological judo going on here," Vanhi said.

"Think about it. What's the blind spot for an all-seeing eye?"

Charlie looked up. "The belief that it's all-seeing!"

"Right. No eye can see itself."

"Mirrors on mirrors."

"Knowledge is data."

"Data has to be *stored*."

"Storage is finite."

"You can't fit *all* knowledge—the whole world, past, present, and future—into a box that's smaller than the whole world."

"Nope."

"But it *thinks* it's all-knowing."

"So how do you hack that?"

"You start with the *premise*," Kenny said.

"'I see all,'" Vanhi said.

"'Past, present, and future,'" Charlie added.

"That's it. That could be it!" Peter said.

"What?"

"Put yourself in the Game makers' shoes. If you had to defend the Game, and you had finite resources, you'd focus on the present, right, and then the future. Because the present is now. That's an emergency. The future is coming, so look out. But the past, well . . ."

"The past already happened."

"Right! It's already done with."

"So if you had to let your guard down somewhere, and you do, in a finite world, you'd do it there. In the past."

"Yes," Kenny said. "I don't have to defend the castle against attacks *yesterday*. They either already happened or they didn't."

"Oh, shit." Vanhi closed her eyes. "I had it. Then my head exploded."

"Had what?"

"An idea."

"Omniscience," Kenny said. "Omniscience."

"Past, present, future."

"I know," Peter said. "We need a time machine."

"Asshole," Vanhi shot back.

"No, I'm serious." Peter gave her an annoyed look. "We need to visit the past."

Kenny's eyes went wide. "He's right!" Kenny rummaged through *Summa Theologica*. Aquinas hadn't just wrestled with the paradox of the stone. Now Kenny remembered something about omniscience, too. He paged through the tome. Vanhi sat there, a hand on each side of her head against her cheeks, fingers through her hair.

Then Kenny smiled. "Everybody always worries about their own free will. If God's omniscient, how can I truly chose anything? Blah, blah, blah."

"Free will, blah, blah, blah, I like that," Vanhi said.

"But what about God's free will?"

Peter saw it. "If God can't be wrong, that means he's a slave to his own predictions."

Kenny snapped his fingers. "*Exactly*. If God says today it's going to rain tomorrow, then he *has* to make it rain tomorrow."

Peter nodded. "Because if he didn't, he would've been wrong."

"And he can't be wrong because he's omniscient!"

"But then he can't be omniscient and omnipotent at the same time."

"Except he is—those are two of his defining characteristics!"

Peter stood up. "So putting it all together . . . in a *simulation* of God . . ."

". . . that *thinks* it's God . . ."

". . . but can't defend every line of code every second . . ."

". . . in a vast code set . . ."

". . . you'd focus on the present and the future . . ."

". . . but not necessarily on what you said *yesterday* . . ."

". . . or even *years* ago . . ."

". . . about what would happen *tomorrow* . . ."

". . . but the *program* would be *bound* by those predictions . . ."

". . . or violate one of its central axioms . . ."

". . . which means that cross-checking against any past predictions . . ."

". . . might evolve as a feature of assumed omniscience . . ."

Peter smiled. "Our virus is a vector to the past. A date-stamped prediction inserted into old code with a spoofed timestamp."

Vanhi grinned from ear to ear. "We have to tell God that he knew yesterday . . ."

Kenny leaned in suddenly and pecked her on the forehead. ". . . that he was going to lift our rock today!"

Vanhi put a hand on either side of Kenny's head and kissed his forehead. "You're a genius!"

"Hey!" Peter held his palms up. "Don't I get a kiss, too?"

Vanhi gaped at him for a second, then marched right up and pulled his head in close. "For the first time I can remember, I don't feel the urgent need to kick your ass. Can we count that as a win?"

77 MIRRORS ON MIRRORS

They worked in a circle under the red light, their laptops linked in a tight intranet. Occasionally one of them would slip out to go online, hoping to keep the Game from noticing their absence. They found the formula for omniscience in *The Oxford Handbook of Philosophical Theology*:

> S *is* omniscient = $_{df}$ *for every proposition* p, *if* p *is true, then* S *knows* p.

But that just reminded them that the Game would almost certainly sense them hiding. When it was Charlie's turn to step out and check his phone, a message from the Game was waiting:

Where are you?

He didn't know what to say exactly, so he just said, *I'm here, just studying,* before slipping back in to help his friends.

They translated the logical proposition for omniscience into code. They created the vector, that innocuous bit of foreknowledge that would hide in dead code until its truth value was tested: they told the God Game that yesterday it had predicted that tomorrow at Φ P.M. it would run a piece of code with the signature comment of Φ, which would in turn require the software to do what only it could: create a sphere of sufficient size to contain all spheres.

They picked Φ because it was the golden ratio, something they thought would appeal to the Game's grandeur and belief that it had designed the universe: pyramids, galaxies. It was also an irrational number that went on forever without repeating itself, which meant the Game might enlist considerable resources being punctual and get distracted from the Trojan payload. Or so they hoped. They were making this up as they went. But the more rabbit trails that went on forever, the better their chances, they theorized. It looked something like this:

$$1 + \cfrac{1}{1 + \cfrac{1}{1 + \cfrac{1}{1 + \cfrac{1}{1 + \ddots}}}}$$

Ones all the way down. No zeros.

If all went well, Φ P.M. would translate to about 2:02:20 P.M., which gave them enough time to code and plant the vector and let it spread.

"It knows something's up," Charlie warned them. "Be careful when you go out."

"Maybe," Peter said. "It's got a lot of data to churn. It may not be focused on us."

"Did anyone else get the 'Where are you?' text?" Kenny asked.

No one had.

"Good," Peter said, "maybe we're still needles in the haystack at the moment."

Or maybe, Charlie thought, the Game was fully aware and just biding its time.

Peter and Vanhi took the laboring oars, doling out tasks to Charlie and Kenny, who were lesser coders.

"It's funny," Vanhi said as they typed. "All the gods in the Game are male. Have you noticed that?"

Charlie nodded. His eyes didn't leave the monitor, where the code was flying by in real time.

"There are so many goddesses in history," Vanhi said. "Isis. Arinna. Mazu. Aphrodite. But you never see them in the Game."

"They're all ancient," Kenny said. "Nobody worships them anymore."

"I think the Game's weighted by number of worshippers," Peter added.

"Or maybe it was just written by men," Vanhi said.

Peter shrugged.

"We're hacking that, in a way," Vanhi said. "It's very male to think you know everything."

"Like refusing to ask for directions," Kenny added.

"Yeah. 'I'm going to run the code because I said I would, damnit.'"

"I wish the world had more female gods," Kenny said.

"No, I'm done with gods," Vanhi replied. "We just need more ladies writing code."

It was Peter's turn to step out and go online to keep the Game feeling the Vindicators' presence. He checked the Eye of God, and what he saw broke his heart. Caitlyn was having a party tomorrow night, out at her parents' lake house. She'd emailed all the right people about it. Peter wasn't invited of course, but that wasn't the end of it. Kurt wasn't invited either. He was nowhere on the chain. But she'd sent Joss Iverson—Tim and Kurt's football buddy—a series of texts that made Peter's blood boil:

Ur so hot
    What about kurt?
what about him?
    Um ur boyfriend
Not anymore
    U 2 broke up?
yes . . . fair game . . . if ur man enough!
    oh don't worry bout that
come tomorrow night to my party
    im there

Joss was . . . Joss was Kurt. Kurt 2.0. Which was just Tim 3.0. Peter clinched his fists. *"Fuck. FUCK!"* Caitlyn had *told* him she wouldn't trade him for Kurt. But if Kurt was gone, if the path was clear, she *still* wouldn't pick him? Was he going to have to cut down every dumb fuck on the social number line from 1 to 1,000 until she reached Peter?

No, he realized. He wasn't even on the same axis. He was an outlier. An imaginary number. He would never, ever fit her mold.

Peter went into the Game, to the texts he'd been sending her at random times, even when they were together, so she'd never know it was him. He looked at one of his favorites:

U R Fat.

He knew this one hit home because he could watch her face through her phone on her camera as she read it. She would delete it, pretend to ignore it, then go to her mirror minutes later to pinch inches that weren't there.

He sent another of his favorites:

Small tits!

She typed:

Who are you? Leave me alone.

Peter knew tonight she would stare at her beautiful small breasts in the mirror. *It's me you see, when you look at yourself,* Peter thought. *I'm the man behind the mirror.*

Then he decided to torture himself.

He pulled up the audio of Charlie and Mary kissing in the woods. That was all the Game had for him on Charlie and Mary; he hadn't been able to find more yet, but it was enough. It was poison. That kiss ate at him as he listened to it over and over. He and Charlie were the same motherless losers who would've been kings in another place, a better world. Why was Charlie succeeding where Peter was failing?

He realized his eyes were tearing up, and that was off-brand. Mysterious handsome loners don't cry. Not at school. Maybe on their motorcycles going one hundred on the highway without a helmet, or in their girl's lap so she can think, *He only shows this to me.*

He wiped his eyes and thought of his mother, who'd told him, even back then before she left, "You've got a screw loose. Just like your father. There's something missing inside you."

She was right. Weakness was missing. He was done with tears a long time ago.

Vanhi said, "What's wrong with you?"

Charlie didn't look up from his computer. The code was soothing. "Nothing."

"Oh, fuck you." She grabbed him and pulled him into the long and empty hallway. "What happened? Spill it."

"I did something. That might hurt my dad."

"What?"

"I don't know. I just answered a question. Honestly I think." Charlie looked at her. "What's more honest—how you feel in the moment, when something's really happening—or how you feel later, when it's faded?"

Vanhi shook her head. "Maybe both are true."

"Can't be. Can't be yes and no."

"Charlie, what happened?"

"When I said I loved my dad, his dreams came true. What happens if I say I don't?" Charlie's voice was shaking. "I called him. I told him, 'Be careful.' I didn't even know what to warn him about." Charlie's voice broke.

Vanhi held him close for a moment, stroked his hair. "We're stopping this. The only way we know how."

"I know."

Vanhi wiped his cheeks. "I did something to you."

Charlie looked up. Vanhi was the last person on earth who would betray him. "I don't want to know."

"I trashed your Harvard application."

"*What?*"

"The one you said you didn't start. I found it. And I trashed it so mine would be better."

Charlie just stared at her.

She stared back, refusing to break eye contact.

"But I . . . but things were just starting to . . ."

"I know. The Game gave me the choice. And I took it."

Charlie nodded. "So did I."

"Let's destroy it. Let's tear it limb from limb."

"Okay."

He started to walk into the darkroom, but she pulled him back.

"We all suck, Charlie. You, me, your dad. That doesn't mean we're not worth loving."

"Okay. Come on. Let's get back to work."

"Soon. I have to get Vik."

"Let me walk you to your car."

"I told you, Charlie. I don't need protecting."

"Okay." He hugged her before going back in. "Okay."

But it wasn't okay. It wasn't okay at all.

78 BLACK HATTERS

Vanhi walked through the exit into the cold air. The wind hit her instantly and set her hair flapping back. The moment she cleared the door, someone grabbed her from behind. She saw broad arms close around her, draped in black.

Without thinking, she drug her heel back and down, and when the arms loosened slightly, she dropped to the ground and scrambled forward into a run.

The light was dimming fast as the sun went down behind the horizon, the dark blue sky veering into purple. The sodium lamps flicked on around the campus as she ran, no clear destination in mind, just trying to put distance between herself and the attacker.

Stay calm, she told herself. *You'll be fine.*

He's the one who better watch out.

She cut an angle, arcing around the side of the building so she'd be out of sight. She chanced a look behind her and saw a man in a white mask and a black hood coming at her. She didn't have her Aziteks on, so the figure was undeniably real.

She turned and ran.

She rounded the corner of the school, down the long strip that led toward the construction site and the portables. That was her best chance to lose him.

She realized her phone was a tracking device on her body. So were the Aziteks in her bag. She had a feeling that with her infinite Blaxx they would do her no good anyway. She had no Goldz left, there was no tool to buy, no app to run. In the Game, she was bankrupt. She tossed her phone one way and her glasses the other a few feet later. Then she went a third way, a narrow strip between two brown portables on risers. She turned sideways, pressed through the crawlway, and saw someone coming from the other direction, another man also in white mask and black cloak. She ducked back into the gap between the portables and crawled under the risers of one, coming out into the maze of temporary buildings, then dipping under some sawhorses that closed off a hard-hat area. She heard footsteps behind her, or maybe it was just the wind picking up, rolling loose gravel or rattling temporary signs on hinges. She found what she was looking for in a pile of scraps at the worksite—a nice hard pipe, a foot and change long, sawed off smooth on the end so the material shone silver while the outside was a nice tarnished rust. It felt weighty in her hand, and she practiced a swing. She kept moving because it was fairly clear now that she heard footsteps approaching, and one of the men came around the corner; he was ageless and faceless because he wore a porcelain mask. His hair stuck out in chunks over the top. He came closer.

Can I really do this? She abhorred violence.

Vanhi stepped back, keeping her eyes on him, sensing that the wall of a portable building was getting closer behind her. She wouldn't be trapped. She wouldn't feel afraid. Without warning she reversed direction and stepped forward. He had a knife in his hand and lurched toward her, not expecting the gap to close so quickly as she doubled back on him, then flawlessly she swung the pipe with both hands, winding up before he could notice and springing back a half turn to bring the pipe against his head. It made a cracking *thunk* noise— part head, part mask—and he went down in a crumpled heap. Vanhi turned and ran through another passageway between the temporary buildings, cutting left, then right, hearing footsteps on the gravel behind her again, crunching as they went. She came to a barricade and ducked under it, the only direction left to her, but within a moment she was cornered against a wall of dirt wrapping her in a U, the product of a long-gone excavator heaping dirt from a hole on the other side, which she couldn't see, for a project abandoned or at least frozen, a building that never made it out of the ground. So she spun back around, but he was there, another figure, this one upright and alive, knife pointed toward her in his hand clad in black leather.

"Rats get stuffed and fucked," he said.

Vanhi wasn't going down like that.

She started up the pile of dirt and got a good ways up, high enough to see the yawning hole below, but the dirt gave way under her feet and she tumbled back down the way she'd come, losing the pipe. He was on her, but she was fierce and kicked the side of his knee, bringing him down momentarily, long enough for her to get her fingers on the pipe. He grabbed and pulled at her legs, but she gripped the pipe and turned her torso, swinging. She landed a hard blow on his shoulder and he dropped her leg. Vanhi was up, ignoring the fear radiating all through her, holding the pipe like a batter. He slashed with the knife, and she hopped back and the blade swished by but missed her. She swung the pipe at the right moment but missed him, too.

"Go to hell," she spat at him. "Hide behind your mask, coward."

She swung the pipe the other way, but to her surprise she missed, and equally surprising was the way the blade went in before she even realized it, before she felt anything at all like pain. It just went in, like, surprise! She looked down at the improbable sight of the handle sticking out from her belly, and she thought, a little dreamily, *But I'm young!* The figure had let go of the knife, looking up from her belly to her face as if he was surprised, too. That's what Vanhi took with her, as she faded away. The strangely maternal observation that he didn't mean it.

79 FEAST OF PHOOLS

It was Charlie's turn for a break, but Vanhi never came back. He'd felt a nagging dread since the moment she left. The fear had stayed at a low churn for an hour or so. But now, with every passing minute, it was spiraling out of control.

Finally, he couldn't stand it and went to get his phone from his locker. As he got near and entered the combination, he could already hear it buzzing away inside, and his stomach churned. It was Vanhi's mom calling. He recognized the number and her voice and wondered if it was really her.

"Charlie?"

"Yes?"

"It's Mrs. Patel, Vanhi's mom."

"Is Vanhi okay?"

"That's why I'm calling you. Have you seen her?"

"She left to pick up Vik, over an hour ago."

There was an anguished silence.

"Mrs. Patel?"

When her voice came back, it was trembling. She was barely holding it together.

"She never showed up. She left Vik standing there with his teacher on the sidewalk. That's not like her, Charlie. She wouldn't do that."

"I know."

"Oh, God, do you think she was in a car accident?"

Charlie's heart sank. He remembered his steering wheel spinning against his will, whipping under his hands. "Wait. Hang on."

He ran to the parking lot. Sure enough, Vanhi's car was still there. But she was nowhere to be found.

"Her car is still here, Mrs. Patel."

"That doesn't make any sense. Where is she?"

"I don't know. Maybe it's good news," he lied. "It means she has to be on campus, somewhere. Maybe she just got distracted. I'll find her. I promise."

He prayed that was true.

He promised Vanhi's mom that he'd call as soon as he learned anything.

He tried calling Vanhi next, but it went straight to voice mail. He texted her:

r u ok?

No answer.

But then the Game wrote:

What are you doooooooooing?

He ran to the library, then the Tech Lab. It was empty, the lights off. He went to the Embankment. A lone couple were making out on the hill in the darkness, but otherwise it was abandoned. He interrupted them to ask if they'd seen anyone, and they looked at him as if he were crazy, a mix of annoyance and interrupted lust. Charlie felt despair setting in, infusing the fear. He ran back inside and looked up and down the long hallways. He could spend hours combing the school, going room to room. He could call area hospitals, but who knew if the Game would even let his calls go through? Every second he wasted meant Vanhi could be lying bleeding somewhere, or tied up in the back of a windowless van, speeding away. His imagination raced out of control.

There was another option.

He could already feel the burn of the hypocrisy.

How can I help you if you only believe in Me when you need something?

What was the old saying? There are no atheists in foxholes?

Fine. So be it.

He was a Deathbed Christian, then. That was fucking fine, because Night Cometh.

He put on his Aziteks, and the first thing he saw was:

> Congratulations!!!
> You Unlocked **Dirty Laundry** and ***PUNISHED THE WICKED***
> Righteous dØØd!
> TIME TO LEVEL UP

80 WATCHER

Charlie turned to find a giant face staring back at him, as wide and tall as his vision, a blank ghastly ghostface with shapeless features, no identity, no soul.

He'd seen the mask before, but now amplified, grotesque in its size and scale.

The eyes were black holes, empty and yawning.

The mouth was a straight line, neither smiling nor scowling, yet it managed to judge him with its lack of interest. The face saw through him, if it saw anything at all.

The effect set him back on his heels and he nearly stumbled into the lockers behind him.

"What is this?" His voice echoed up and down the hallway.

A hole opened in the face in front of him. It was like a tear in space-time, a portal into a new dimension, the mask opening to invite him in.

It was black and filled with stars. The Game told him:

You're a Watcher now, Charlie. You earned it.

The words echoed in his Aziteks.

"Where's Vanhi?" he shouted back. "What did you do to her?"

Come inside me.

"Where is she?"

Come inside me, Charlie, and All Will Be Revealed.

"If I'm a Watcher, can I see anyone?"

Yesssssssssssssss!

"Can I see Vanhi?"

I See ALLLLLLLLLLLL

He didn't want to go inside. It was another victory for the Game. Going higher, clearing more levels, didn't feel like winning.

Yet if Vanhi was inside, he would step through glass into a house of pain.

81 I AM A STRANGE LOOP

Charlie stepped through, and the world was black and starlit.

The true lights in the hallway switched off the moment he went in, leaving only the light of the Aziteks, which placed him in an abyss of stars rotating above him.

The ground below was an expanse of desert, windswept and barren. He could hear the soft thrum of water in the distance and saw the Nile, lush on either side for a few feet before the crops gave way to sand. Insects buzzed quietly in his ears, locusts and crickets.

Even though the ceiling was above in realspace, he saw in the darkness through his Aziteks constellations from his childhood, more vivid and jarring than they'd ever before been.

Leo, the Lion.

Cancer, the Crab.

Cassiopeia, the Queen.

A path lit up before him, a soft silk indication in the sand, guiding him where to go. He had no choice. Vanhi was missing, and there was no other way. He was tired of pretending there was always a clever solution to every problem, a way out that dodged the moral morass. Sometimes the only way was *through*, coming out bloody and tarnished on the other side.

Above, Perseus, the Hero.

Taurus, the Bull.

Libra, the Scales.

He followed the path as it went upstairs, in gamespace a soft dune that rose, rose, rose, to a higher plane of desert.

Above, Lupus, the Wolf.

Scorpio, the Scorpion.

He came to the third floor, clearing the top of a sand hill to see a pyramid rising above everything else in the distance, an illuminated eye at the top, a beacon, beams in the night. The desert was broader and wider than any school, but the path in realspace was the hallway stretching in front of him in pitch-blackness, lit in the Game as a walkway between two rows of miniature sphinxes facing each other in pairs, a flickering torch below each stone face.

It brought him to room 322, which appeared as a door in the pyramid.

He wondered, Maybe the Game *hadn't* been onto them? *Where are you? What are you dooooooooing?* Maybe it had been excitement—it was promoting him to a new level, it was *eager* to give him his reward. Maybe that's why it sent those texts only to him.

Or not. It didn't matter. All that mattered was Vanhi.

Inside, he came into a stone temple with a great golden scale, and ideas began to click in his head, fragments of conversation with Tezcatlipoca. *A great experiment whose end we don't know. The oldest question on earth. The Golden Algorithm. An algorithm for God.*

A book containing an infinite number of names was open on an altar before him. As he put his finger on it, the names began to flow by, ink scrolling across the ancient parchment.

Every moral system failed.

Maybe we could build something smarter than us to crack it.

Charlie touched the first name he recognized, Mr. B.'s.

The scale moved.

In one tray were Goldz, in the other Blaxx, coins piled on both sides. The Goldz sank lower, a slight surplus of goodness.

As with the Eye of God that Peter had shown him, Charlie could see things from Mr. B.'s life, down to his sad current moment sitting in a robe alone, watching TV as the TV watched him back. But what was new, what was available to Watchers, was the *scale*. The judgment.

A creeping suspicion hit him, and he reached out and tilted his hand in space over the balance, and it deposited Goldz and that side sank slightly lower.

I'm a guinea pig in a fucking morality play that stops when I'm dead?

Of course! Who else? Lab rats?

But why could *he* move the scale? Wasn't *God* supposed to be the judge here? *Something smarter than us to crack it?* A neural net? A deep Boltzmann machine? A tangled hierarchy?

"Why do I get to decide?" Charlie asked the Game aloud.

For the first time in this place, the Game spoke:

> God is invisible.
> Man is created in God's image.
> Ergo, the only way to see God is to see man.

It hit Charlie then, the brutal simplicity of the recursive loop he was caught in. The desperate failed experiment that was ruining his life, an algorithm tasked to find God that couldn't. Feed it a bunch of contradicting myths and ask it to spit out the answer, man creating God creating man creating God ... morality was outsourced to the Game, and the Game had outsourced it back, crowdsourcing the question of decency to the hive mind. It was as inevitable as it was hideous.

"You can't see yourself," Charlie said softly. He almost felt sorry for the Game then. "You have no idea who you are."

The Game didn't respond, if it heard him at all.

"Show me Vanhi."

The Game was silent.

"Show me Kenny."

> He is offline.

"Show me Peter."

> He is offline.

A sudden panic shot through Charlie—had he just given them away? Tipped it off to their hiding together offline? Had he just plucked the needles from the haystack and shoved them under the Game's nose?

Why are all your friends offline?

Charlie ignored the Game and asked, "Where is Vanhi?"

I am sorry. She is with me.

82 CONCEPTION

Charlie ditched his phone and glasses and ran down to the photo lab.

"It has Vanhi." he told Kenny and Peter.

"Is she okay?" Worry flooded Kenny's face. "Where is she?"

"I don't know. It won't tell me anything, and I'm a Watcher now."

Peter shot a jealous look—he alone should've been Watcher level among the two of them—then stuffed it down. "So we only have one choice."

Kenny nodded. "We have to destroy this fucking thing."

Everybody looked stricken. They didn't know if Vanhi was alive or dead. She *had* to be alive. They simply couldn't process the alternative. It was Not True. They all sank inward, burying their fear in nonstop coding, pressing harder, faster to launch their virus. They knew anything else would be futile—Vanhi's mom had already called the cops, but the Game would never let them find her, wherever she was. As the three coded, they did a good job of pretending not to be scared to death, although Kenny did run out and throw up in the hallway. This *thing*, this impostor god, it had to fucking die.

Alex knew there was only one thing left to do now.

He went home.

He wanted to see his mom. He'd see his dad plenty tomorrow. No question about that.

Alex found her on the couch, repairing one of his shirts, one of his favorites. She knew that. She was sewing with a fine red thread to match the color in the plaid.

He wanted to tell her, *Don't bother. I won't need it.*

Then he thought, *I can wear it tomorrow. I will carry a little bit of you with me.*

He was a bad son. He knew that. He had tried to make them proud. He never did. His mom deserved so much more, after all she'd suffered. Yet she loved him anyway. She couldn't stand up to his father, she couldn't stop the things he did. But she loved *him*. He did see that.

"What's wrong?" she asked without looking up from her needle.

I've come to say goodbye.

"Mom?" He didn't recognize his own voice.

"Yes?"

"I'm tired."

"I know, baby."

She put down her sewing and looked at him. "You father loves you. He's doing the best he can."

"I know."

"Is everything okay at school?"

They hurt me today.

That's what he wanted to say. But the shame was too great. Whatever she thought of him, he couldn't bear her knowing how bad it really was. She was weak, he realized, too weak to protect him. All the love in the world wasn't enough.

His mind was a house of pain, all exits locked.

He nodded, trying not to cry.

She swept his hair off his forehead. "Tomorrow will be better."

"It will," he said, and his heart broke.

An hour north, a man sat in the dark, staring at the message on his screen. He scratched his face out of habit and prayed for the message to go away, but it didn't.

He was a killer—well, a retired killer, to be fair, if there was such a thing. His story was a miracle. He'd gone into prison bad and come out good. Pure as Christ.

The Game didn't choose him by accident. It was curious about redemption. What were its edges and parameters?

The man had similar questions. Ever since his prison conversion, he'd wondered, Was God's grace really strong enough to wipe *his* sins clean? Who forgives murder in exchange for a loyalty oath? It sounded more like a mob boss than a holy spirit. But that's what the prison preacher was selling, so he was buying.

Beats hell, he figured.

All his sins, gone. There was the drug use, and the trafficking that had landed him in prison. There were the habits that drove him to meth in the first place. The websites he visited, for urges that society would never understand. The arrangements in strip malls he made to satisfy those desires. What was so wrong with wanting something pure? Something unspoiled? He knew the answer to that, but in the darkness the excuses glowed like angels. Meth had dulled those drives. Given him something new to crave.

But now he was clean in all ways. Released early for good behavior. He found a church. A charity paid to fix his teeth. He met a nice woman, and they got married, with—surprise!—a kid on the way. Sure, he sometimes went back to the websites that started it all. But almost every time he refused to click Enter. Even now, just before the message had come, he was saying no. That's how strong he was. He could face his demons and say no.

But the Game had turned everything upside down. It had started with an invitation, promising him what he wanted deep inside. Now it had blown up in his face.

His whole past was thrown back at him. Every transaction, every chat, every ad in Craigslist or Backpage, things no one knew, all tied together with a simple promise: *Do this one last thing, and it will all go away*. It was God's grace in a fun-house mirror: redemption, not through abstention but through one last sin.

But if you had to sin, a *last* sin was the best kind.

The man knew he couldn't trust this promise. How many times had he shot people after promising to let them go if they did what he asked? Now he was on the other end of the barrel, and he saw what they saw. There was no choice.

His wife called from beyond the locked door, "Come to bed!" That settled it. He was not going to trade clean sheets, a pretty wife, a kid on the way, for a prison cot and a sharpened toothbrush in the spleen.

So he took the clean gun out of the shoebox in the attic. *Why did I keep the gun? I could've thrown it in a lake. Did I always know this day would come?*

The next morning, he gassed up his car and looked at the photo of his target one last time, before he put a match to it, and wondered what the guy had done. They'd always done something. They always had it coming. Regardless, the guy was nothing to him. Just some asshole who owned a restaurant named Charlie's.

83 DRAGON'S LAIR

When the Vindicators stepped out of the darkroom the next morning, the loudspeaker was summoning Charlie and Peter to Mrs. Morrissey's office for the second time.

They were bleary-eyed and exhausted. They had all told their parents they were spending the night at each other's house, and the network of symmetric lies had worked.

Now, propelled by fear and desperation to save Vanhi (*If she is alive, she has to be alive*), they had coded through the night and their virus was almost ready. It was compiling now, and then Kenny would sneak off to a distant location and start it propagating through the system. By their calculations, it would take hours to burrow and spread and insinuate itself into the guts of the God Game, so that the eggs could hatch in enough places that the sweeper bots that read and reread vast libraries of dead code would, with statistical certainty, find the implanted memory. False memories of predictions past, an act of masturbatory confirmation: *What I said, is*.

The loudspeaker cracked off, and Charlie and Peter exchanged glances. Why would Morrissey be calling them now? The Game was making its move. They went to their lockers to retrieve their devices. Charlie prayed as he did that a message from Vanhi would be waiting, writing back to his text:

> r u ok?
>> Duh yeah quit being such a pussy

But no text was there. Just a million missed calls from Vanhi's poor frantic mom.

Peter came by with his backpack over his shoulder. "Ready?"

"Not really."

They walked down the hall together, toward the Dragon's Lair. The students they shoved past stared at them. One of them stupidly went "Ooooooo-ooooooh" while doing a tsk-tsk with her fingers. All the while, Charlie tried not to look up at the obscene number of posters of himself staring back down at them, as far as he could see down the long corridor.

As they walked, Peter whispered, "It's not going to work."

"What?"

"Our virus."

Charlie shushed him. Even with their devices buried in their backpacks, he was paranoid that everything was being heard.

"It already knows. Of course it knows," Peter said.

"How? We—"

Peter just smiled sadly. "It will see us coming a mile away."

"You don't have enough faith in us."

"You have too much."

Charlie had sat next to Peter all night, watching him solve problems in the code, just as he had saved them from hacking omnipotence without omniscience.

"If you're so sure it's not going to work, why'd you bother helping us?"

"I don't know, Charlie. I guess I'm trying to be more like you." Peter considered that. "It's not much fun."

They found themselves outside Morrissey's door.

"Glasses on," Peter said. "This is gonna be bad."

84 GRENDEL'S DEN

Elaine Morrissey sat behind her desk, looking grim. Mr. Burklander stood behind her, madder than Charlie had ever seen him. He looked betrayed.

"Sit down." Mrs. Morrissey's voice was barely restrained. It almost trembled.

Charlie and Peter took the two uncomfortable seats in front of her desk and glanced warily at each other.

"I have a student in the hospital."

"Vanhi?" Charlie blurted out feeling a ray of hope. Was she still alive?

"What? Why would Vanhi be in the hospital?" Morrissey asked, baffled. Vanhi's mom had indeed called the school several times already and spoken to the Game, who assured her that all steps were being taken.

"Alex?" Charlie tried again.

"No. What are you going on about? *Zeke*."

"Zeke?"

"Zeke Taylor. Overdosed on some kind of drug; they're not even sure what it was, it was so tainted. He's in a coma. He probably won't ever come out."

She paused, her eyes boring into them, waiting for them to say something. Peter just looked down at his hands, unconcerned, pleasantly aloof, the way he always was, which made people wonder, *Who is this guy? I want to know this guy. . . .* But this time it looked more sinister to Charlie. It felt like biding.

Morrissey leaned in. "And then after I go to the hospital and watch his parents cry over his ruined life, I get this."

She turned her monitor toward them, and Charlie watched her click on a file attached to an anonymous email that said, "Watch This!" He felt his stomach churn as he saw the video of them on the Embankment from just last week, Charlie and Peter lounging in the grass, talking. It was shot from above, from a security camera Charlie hadn't even known existed. Peter handing Charlie the crumpled brown lunch bag. Charlie walking it stupidly, innocently, across the grass (*He gave me half his lunch yesterday. I forgot mine*). Zeke looking up lazily, his long dirty-blond dreads and washed-out eyes (*Hey, from Peter*) (*Thanks, dude*).

"I'm alerting the police," Morrissey told them. "You killed that boy."

"No." Charlie shook his head. Peter put a hand on Charlie's wrist, as if about to remind Charlie of his Miranda rights. But he couldn't stop talking. "I thought it was a sandwich." He realized the moment it left his mouth how lame it sounded. His voice was desperate. "I didn't . . . I *wouldn't* . . ."

"Is that right?" the Dragon Lady said coldly. She pulled her phone closer, across her desk. Charlie couldn't process what was happening. The police were coming? For him? Just like that? Before he knew what he was saying, it came out:

"It was Peter's! He said it was food."

If Peter cared, he didn't show it. He didn't flinch or protest. He just stared down at his manicured nails benignly.

"Then how do you explain this?" Mr. Burklander asked.

Morrissey clicked on the second attachment, and another video came up. It was Charlie at Neiman's, buying the bracelet with his wad of cash.

"I guess we know where you got that kind of money," Mr. B. said.

"No."

Peter put another gentle hand on Charlie's forearm, but he swept it off.

"Those two things have nothing to do with each other!" And that was true! They were both crimes, apparently, just separate crimes. "I . . . I . . . made that money at my job."

Burklander snorted. "At the copy shop?"

"Yes," Charlie said, so desperately he felt pathetic.

He felt the wires tightening around him, curling like a vine around his chair, over his wrists and through his legs, across his neck.

Morrissey said bitterly, "We always knew Peter had a bolt loose. But *you*? You, Charlie?"

Burklander lost it then. "Goddamnit, Charlie. You ruined everything. You made an ass of me. Everything I did. All year. Trying to pull you back from the edge over and over. And you were doing *this*? You let me put you in front of *Harvard*? I knew you were lost, Charlie. I didn't know you were *gone*."

Charlie tried to answer. To tell him something that would wipe the heartbroken look off his face. Charlie came up with nothing.

Morrissey picked up the phone. She was dialing, then waiting as it rang. A rising panic came over Charlie. Was this the end? Would they frog-march him out the main door, in front of the entire school? Would he really go to jail?

His panic reached a fever pitch. The attacks had been scary. But he could fight his way out of those. This was the system, as invisible as it was ubiquitous. There was no one to punch back against. Two undoctored videos and the apparatus was in motion. His whole life over while he was still alive to suffer through it. Arrested, like Scott Parker. That couldn't be his path.

The picture on Elaine Morrissey's desk moved.

It was a photograph of her family. Three beautiful children around her. A grinning husband, his arms on her shoulders. The Dragon Lady was actually smiling in it.

Then the husband and children in the photo turned their heads and gasped.

It startled Charlie.

They were looking across the desk at another Elaine Morrissey—not the one on the phone, waiting for the district liaison officer to answer—but one on her back on the desk, her skirt hiked up.

Mr. Burklander was over her—not the real Mr. Burklander standing against the wall now, fuming, his eyes closed, but another Mr. B., plucked from another moment in time in this very room, just a week prior—his pants unceremoniously around his ankles, his white Costco boxers halfway down, hands on the desk on either side of his boss, in the very place where they were supposed to be adults guarding the well-being of children.

"Fuck me, Edward," said Elaine Morrissey's doppelgänger.

In the picture on her desk, the husband dropped his head in shame. The three children's mouths opened into identical cartoon O's.

"Fuck me, Edward," Charlie said out loud, before he even realized he was doing it.

"*Excuse me?*" Morrissey roared, her hand over the receiver of her phone.

"Fuck me, Edward," Charlie said, deliberately this time, across the Rubicon, driven by the sheer terror of prison.

Morrissey froze, her hand over the receiver. Ed Burklander opened his eyes and stared at Charlie.

"Right there." Charlie pointed at the spot on the desk where the phantom Ed and Elaine were now fading away, translucent ghosts still pumping in forbidden passion. "Right there, in front of the picture of your children?"

Now Charlie realized he was not just scared but *angry*. Because his mom was gone, but this mom was alive and treating her own family like garbage, just as his dad and Susan McAllister had done to him, screwing each other in secret while the real Mrs. Lake was suffering through chemo. All the rage and fear was now one indistinguishable emotion that he could only perceive as *forward*.

"Right there. And there. And how many other places?" The scenes were now flashing in front of his eyes, visible only to him. "Your house? At three in the afternoon." He looked at Morrissey. "Your *bed*?" He looked at Burklander. "Your *classroom*?"

They were all talking at once. Elaine Morrissey was saying, "How could you . . ."

But Burklander was fully enraged now, standing tall, coming toward them. "If you think, for one second, that you can blackmail us . . ."

"Ed," Morrissey said, "wait . . ."

"They are not going to . . ."

"Ed"—tears filled Morrissey's eyes—"you don't have a family. . . ."
Burklander stood right in Charlie's face.

"Ed, you don't have *kids*. . . ."

"I don't care," he said, eyes burning. "They will not get away with this."

"Yes, we will." It was the first time Peter had spoken, and he said it with his head still tucked down against his neck, calm and collected.

He stood up and stared at Mr. Burklander. The look in Peter's eyes was cold. Morrissey was right. There really was a bolt loose. His eyes were shining, but it wasn't from those mirror neurons that made people feel for others. The sparkle in Peter's eyes reflected inward, an illusion, mirror on mirror: infinite regress that was infinitely thin. Charlie wondered, Had it always been that way? Why was he seeing it now?

"You will sit down," Peter said to Burklander, raising a hand and pointing at him. "You will listen to your lady friend and keep quiet, about me, about Charlie, all of this." No fear was in Peter's voice.

"Or what?" Mr. B. didn't look like a teacher now. He looked like a grown man who'd had enough. Enough of kids. Enough of disrespect. He was one step short of rolling up his sleeves and pummeling Peter.

Charlie felt things spinning out of control. His anger had faded. He regretted immediately what he'd said to Mr. B. It was like his talk with Vanhi—what was real? How he felt now or two seconds ago? He tried to keep Peter from stepping toward Mr. B., but Peter shoved him back.

"Or what?" Mr. B. said again, a growl this time, stepping toward Peter. "You ruined Charlie. I can't fix that now. But you are done."

Peter moved his hand in the air. The arcane gesture was like a magus conjuring spirits, then he thrust his hand palm-forward and shot an invisible signal at the speed of light and Ed Burklander convulsed. His chest thrust back and his eyes went wide and bulged out. His implanted defibrillator went off like a mule kick. It sent him buckling to the ground.

His back arched up and he passed out.

Elaine Morrissey cried out and ran to his side, propping up his head in her arms. "Get help," she cried. "Somebody get help. Oh, Eddie."

"Come on." Peter walked toward the door, leaving Elaine Morrissey on the floor cradling Burklander's head and reaching back blindly for the phone above her on her desk.

Charlie tried to run toward Mr. B., but Peter grabbed him around the chest and yanked him back, with more power than Charlie realized Peter had.

"What happened?" Charlie yelled at him. "Is he okay?"

"He's fine." Peter dragged Charlie out of the room. "He just got a little pacemaker jolt. Happens all the time. Come *on*."

Charlie struggled to get away, but Peter was too strong.

Morrissey was dialing 911.

Peter caught her eyes. "You won't say another word about us, will you?"

She shook her head, terrified.

"*Go*," Peter said to Charlie, shoving him into the hallway.

Outside the office, Charlie spun on him. "*What did you do?*"

Peter wiggled his fingers in the air and said merrily, "I used the Force!"

85 ST. PAUL AND THE MAGICIAN

Charlie shoved Peter hard, his head hitting the column behind them. "We're done."

"Excuse me? Didn't you just come beg me to code your little virus?"

"You could've killed him."

"I saved your ass from jail. Remember?"

"There was another way."

"Was there now?"

"Maybe I should've gone to jail."

"Easy to say now."

"Fuck you, Peter. Vanhi was right. There's something wrong with you."

"Go back in there. Pick up the phone and call the cops. I won't stop you." Peter smiled, holding his arm out elegantly, inviting Charlie to turn himself in. "That's what I thought."

"We're not friends anymore."

"No, it's worse. We're brothers."

Charlie walked away.

"You think you're so high-and-mighty," Peter yelled after him. "You just don't have the guts to be honest about who you really are."

Charlie spun around and got in Peter's face. "I am not like you."

"No mom, shitty dad, handsome outcast, just a half click off from mattering. Yeah, we're nothing alike." Charlie started to turn but Peter grabbed his arm. "They will never give it to you. You have to take it."

"Keep telling yourself that." Charlie walked away, furious, because Peter was right. And what then?

"Take a look in the fucking mirror," Peter yelled after him, down the long hallway.

86 CONTROL/ALTER/DELETE

Alex sat with the bomb, in the hissing heat of the boiler room. He let his hands wrap around it, gathering his courage. The Game had whispered to him all night, as it had for the past several nights, introducing him to new intelligences who could fill in gaps in his understanding.

Christ sat to his left, whispering in his ear. The alchemist Hermes Trismegistus sat to Alex's right, explaining how his actions might seem cruel to some, but they would be understood eventually. All great plans were initially misunderstood, until the hidden meanings became clear with time. The alchemist transformed into his black-eyed alter ego, Thoth, who, carrying a lantern, would guide Alex's soul to the afterlife.

Freud was there, explaining that the most natural thing in the world was for a son to kill his father. That was the origin of religion, after all, in aboriginal cultures. Kill the father and replace him with a totem to worship. It both solves the problem and eases the guilt.

Alex closed his eyes and whispered to himself:

"For I have come to turn a man against his father.

"For I have come to turn a man against his father.

"For I have come to turn a man against his father."

"That's right," the Game said to him, stroking his hair, "that's exactly right."

"We'll ignite at a special moment," Christ said. Thoth drew it on the boiler with his finger, where the bloody pentagram once was, now a faint and distant memory.

Φ

"What does it mean?" Alex asked.

"It's a symbol I used, once," Freud said. "For something called the Project. How the brain makes consciousness."

"No," Jesus said, "it's the number of divine creation. The golden ratio."

"One point six one eight zero . . . ," Freud said. "Two oh two P.M."

"Just before school lets out," Christ said.

"And the building is full."

Thoth tapped the boiler.

"We'll fill the school with gas," Christ said.

"The explosion will be magnificent," Freud added. "A ball of fire."

"What about the good people in the school?" Alex asked.

"Did my Father worry about that with the Flood?"

"Are there any good people, really?" Freud put a hand on Alex's. "When the picture spread, how many people stood up and said, 'Stop this. It's unacceptable'?"

Alex couldn't bear to answer.

"No, they all laughed. Man is not a gentle creature. He desires to humiliate his neighbor, to seize his possessions, to torture and kill him. *Homo homini lupus!* 'Man is a wolf to man,'"

"You are not the Lamb," Christ reminded Alex.

"Rest," Freud said, "lie back and listen. There is so much left to know."

87 TABLET ON THE UNCOMPOUNDED REALITY

Kenny pedaled like a maniac. He hadn't ridden his bike in years. But it was all part of the plan. Low-fi. Off-line. No signals, no tracers. He wobbled at first but soon he had momentum, and muscle memory took over. He sailed through the traffic and found the back roads.

The plan was to go to the Oak Street Library southside. Far from their homes, unchecked internet access, no sign-ups, no log-ons. One of the last anonymous ports of entry they could think of. Every car Kenny passed made him flinch. Would this be the one to suddenly swerve, unbidden, running him off the road and into a ditch?

He linked finally onto the bike trails along the river and looked up, seeing the sun come in and out of view through the leaves. He felt alive and free and hopeful.

Miles away he came onto the roads, winding through a wooded back street until the Oak Street Library came into view. He kept waiting for something to happen—a transformer to suddenly surge and blow as he passed. A light to magically switch from red to green as he pedaled toward his own green light, sending traffic at full speed into him. It was all wired, available.

But he pulled up safely to the library, and the doors were old-school, not even automatic. The building was comfortably dilapidated. The signs in the kids section were cut out of construction paper. He could almost smell the Elmer's glue like paradise.

He had a panicked thought. What if the computers were so old they didn't even have a USB port? But they did. He pushed in the flash drive and copied the virus over, then launched it, following the steps Charlie and Peter had carefully laid out for him. Code spun on the screen rapidly. It was born. It was dividing and growing. Nothing about this birth was beautiful or sacred. But it was alive, and all he could do was hope.

Kurt Ellers watched the video. He was alone in the locker room, towel around his waist. He'd come to work out instead of going to geometry. When he got out of the shower, his phone was buzzing. The video was there, the one he'd feared since his run-in with Charlie Lake yesterday. *How would you feel? If someone posted something secret about you?* Kurt didn't know what the video would be, exactly, but he knew what it would show. And now it was real.

His first reaction was panic. How far had it spread? Who had seen it? What would his dad say? He thought of Caitlyn.

Kurt watched the video, fascinated. He hated certain things about it. He was fat, over his slabs of muscle. He had manhandles like an old man. That was inevitable—he ate like a beast to play like a beast. Other parts of the video were better than he would have guessed. The moment wasn't awkward or forced. It was deep and true. The passion was real. He loved the person in it. They'd met at conversion therapy. Kurt's father had told him he'd rather have a dead son than a gay son. Dan's father had offered to beat the gay out of him. Having pricks for fathers was their first bond.

Then Kurt realized all that would be over now. No more camps, no more preachers licking their lips as they told him to purify his thoughts. No more Seroquel or Prozac to fix his "distorted thinking." No more lies.

There was no hiding from this.

It was a bomb in the dollhouse of his life.

He would go to Caitlyn's party tonight. Of course he knew about it. She thought she could erase him just like that? Her boyfriend of three years just swept aside? He would do the one thing no one expected. He would show up, head held high. Not to claim Caitlyn. That was over. No, he would walk in because he was bigger and stronger than everyone else. And if anyone didn't like it, he would bring the pain. As if to say, *Sorry, motherfuckers. Some things haven't changed.*

Kurt recognized the name of the feeling that had come to him, once the shock and fear had worn off. It was liberation.

Tim was pushing Mary around, just before the call came on his phone. "You're letting him make a fool of you."

"Who?"

"You know who. Those posters. You put up, what, two? He's got a hundred."

"You're obsessed."

Tim smacked her hard across the face. "There is no escape plan. You are with me forever. If you so much as look at him again, I will tell everyone what your family did."

"You were there, too."

"I was a kid. Your parents were there, not mine. Your lawyer, not mine. Bribing police. Covering up their precious golden boy's dead reputation. I can destroy your whole world."

"I'm leaving you. I don't care what you do."

"I will hurt you, Mary. In so many ways."

That's when his phone rang. He glanced down and saw his father's office line. "Don't go anywhere." Tim poked a finger into her ribs. She grimaced with pain.

His listened to his dad's rushed voice and closed his eyes. Tim always knew this day might come. He'd heard bits and pieces over the years as his parents fought. They spoke in hushed codes, but he'd figured out enough: the money problems, stealing from the bank, the fear of getting caught. But now it was real: his dad was telling him to prepare.

His dad spoke quickly: *Yes, it was happening. . . . Yes, they'd planned for this. . . . No, it couldn't be on the phone. Especially not on the phone.* It was hard to hear his dad like this: he was tall, sturdily built with a large belly and broad shoulders, a deep, sonorous Texas voice, a banker-pioneer. Class and grit, all in one. It was hard to hear him in a situation he couldn't totally control.

Still, there'd be no shame in his dad going to prison. He wasn't the first CEO behind bars and he wouldn't be the last. His dad used to say, "No one gets rich without cutting a few corners." Rules were for little people. You planned. You took calculated risks.

So Tim went to meet his dad in a shady part of the city, and Tim was ready to do whatever was asked of him. He would be the man of the house now. His parents would try to flee. Tim would have to take care of his sister, and his mom, too, if a deal was ultimately cut to keep her free. But he couldn't help the creeping fear—what if he couldn't become his father? What if the world had changed and the old ways didn't work anymore? What then? Those were the only ways he knew.

He parked his Porsche blocks from where his dad told him and walked down a strip of pawnshops and payday lenders. Smart choice. His parents would probably leave right from here. Skip town and go where? . . . Mexico? Cayman? If they pulled it off, Tim might never see them again. A few locals stared at him, but he was big and tough and didn't give a shit and projected that, so he was left alone. He rounded the buildings into the alleyway and waited for his dad. But the people who came from the open end of the alley a few moments later weren't with his father. And they certainly weren't Feds either. Tim didn't know whom the fuck they were with.

There were three of them, with lead pipes, wearing hooded robes and white porcelain masks.

88 VIRUS/PLAGUE

By the time Kenny got back to school, the virus had had plenty of time to propagate, embedding itself into remote patches of code, implanting itself in the past, where no harm can occur because it's already passed. Unless they were right, alongside Thomas Aquinas and C. S. Lewis. Kenny locked his bike and met Charlie behind the Dumpsters as planned, where no cameras could see them, they hoped.

"Did it work?"

"I think so," Kenny said.

"How much time?"

Kenny looked at his watch. "Soon. It should be soon."

"Let's get back online."

When Charlie got his Aziteks out of the locker and put them on, he shuddered to see the halls swarming with players. There were avatars of all types, chimeras and characters from games and graphic novels and Watchers, too, moving among them in their masks and robes. They were everywhere, more players than he'd ever seen in one place. Blending in with the students, moving among them in the crowds. Was Peter right after all—did the Game know about their virus? Surely all these people hadn't gathered just to see their program fail? None of them seemed to be looking at him at all. Was something else happening? Charlie figured this many players would only gather to see something magnificent.

Kenny came up behind him, from his locker. "Hey." Kenny slipped on his Aziteks and yelled, "Jesus Christ!" In front of him, through his glasses, Charlie was white masked in a black cloak and robes.

"What?" Charlie had no idea what he looked like.

Kenny shook his head. "I forgot you were one of . . . them . . . now."

Charlie glanced down at his hands, horrified to see they were skeletal thin in black leather gloves coming out the sleeves of a dank robe.

Kenny gestured at the stream of players moving past them. "Why are they here?"

"I don't know."

"Should we follow them?"

Charlie nodded. He had an inkling of an idea, too horrible to let form.

Whatever was happening, word had spread far and wide, but it hadn't spread to him, and *he* was a Watcher, too, wasn't he? So why was this news being withheld from him?

"I know what the Game's about now," Charlie whispered to Kenny, as they climbed the stairs, following the rush of visitors moving virtually through the halls. "It's crowdsourcing morality, creating situations to see how players judge each other's choices."

"That's insane," Kenny said, as they turned the corner. "If that's how morality works, Donald Trump will be our next president."

The players seemed to be heading to the third floor. Charlie and Kenny ran after them, pushing past the students trying to go in the other direction. As the two made it through the crush of the stairwell, they saw the players moving in different directions, like eddies in a current.

"Where the hell are we supposed to go?" Charlie asked.

"That's it!" Kenny shouted. "Look!"

The goat, Azazel, was limping along the hallway, worse off than ever. He'd already been slaughtered and thrown on a pyre. Now he was charred and decimated, just a burned skeleton clacking down the hallway. He looked mournfully back at them, like, *Oh, shit, you assholes?*

"We should follow it," Kenny said.

"No," Charlie shot back. "I think it's a distraction."

"Trust me, the last time I saw it, it was important."

"Fuck, I don't know."

They followed the goat as he led them down the hallway, back to room 333, where Abraham had been. Azazel reached the threshold of the door and set himself down, spent, as if he couldn't bear to go inside and return to the scene of his ritual sacrifice.

Charlie and Kenny went in.

But instead of the art supply room Kenny had seen last time, on their Aziteks now it was dark and unadorned until floor lights came on abruptly with sound and music. The cheerful game-show melody had the occasional sour note, like a memory run through a meat grinder. The tune was a convoluted perversion of countless theme songs, the tempo slowing down and speeding up, an organ grinder distracted by his monkey. An announcer spoke as lights shone into their eyes, blinding them temporarily, spotlights lighting their stage, only the front row below them visible, porcelain white faces staring back.

The voice was both familiar and artificial. If real announcers were intentionally transhuman, this voice was their perfect amalgam, so generic it was every voice and no voice at once:

"Welcome, friends! It's time to play. . . ."

The title card came up before them, happy and bright, as if all life were a game:

WILL VANHI DIE?

The unseen audience cheered the name in unison.

89 LIFE METER

And there she was, suddenly, hooked up to beeping machines in a hospital room somewhere, filmed from above from the nurse's monitor camera on the wall. Her eyes were closed. The beeping on the machines was slow and steady. It kept her chest rising up and down.

Her name in type across the video feed said JANE DOE, AGE ~17–19.

Charlie felt a moment's relief just knowing she was still alive.

Then on the screen, Death appeared, a hazy pixelated character, cloaked and hooded. His skeletal hands held gardening shears with long blades, which he placed on either side of the real tubes running between Vanhi and the machines.

He looked at the screen and grinned.

Then he snapped the shears shut.

"Oh, no!" the crowd roared in unison.

The respirator shut off, and Vanhi's chest stopped moving. The machines around her went crazy, their screens flashing warnings and dropping vitals. But no alarms went off. No nurses came. The camera switched to the nurses' station, where they sat boredly, checking email and surfing the Web. The Game intercepted the alarm signals and squelched them before they reached the nurses, never to be heard.

The camera switched back to Vanhi. She was fading now, with a life meter over her head, ten little hearts in the top left corner, ticking down.

90 RED BULL/BLUE TEETH/ GREEN FIRE

Tim Fletcher faced the men at the end of the alley. There was nowhere to run. Behind him was a brick wall. He squared his shoulders and waited.

"What do you want?" he shouted, trying to show them he wasn't afraid.

The men began walking down the alley in their weird costumes, robes and masks like those of some freakish sex cult you read about in Europe. Satanists or tree worshippers.

"Who are you?" he yelled.

They marched closer, lead pipes down by their sides.

His dad should've been here by now. Were these thugs from someone his dad had cheated? Had they already taken his father?

"Where's my dad?"

How could he know his father had never called?

Through the eyeholes of their masks he now saw them gazing back. He tried to read their intentions, the way he would size up a defensive line.

The men got within a few feet of him and stopped.

They raised their lead pipes.

Tim braced himself for the pain. He was ready to fight.

Then the men paused.

As if waiting for something.

91 TABLET/SCROLL/
COMMENTARY

Vanhi disappeared, replaced with a screen that said LOADING . . . like an 8-bit horizontal scroller. Just before, the hearts on her life meter had begun dropping precipitously as the machines shut off and her chest lay still. Every heart would flash six times, then half would disappear, then six more flashes, another half gone . . . counting down to death that would come in minutes.

"Charlie, she's dying," Kenny said.

"I know."

Then the progress bar hit 100 percent and the game appeared, an old-school 2-D street-fighting game. The pixilated goons had white masks and iron bars and hooded cloaks. In the middle of their circle was a little digital version of Tim Fletcher, a caricature of his sandy hair and bulging biceps. His face was cartoonized from the football roster, same smug smirk. Vanhi's life meter was at the top left, still ticking down. Now Tim's was on the right.

For a moment, Charlie thought he was being asked to play the role of Tim, fighting his way out of the crowd, an interesting act of empathy.

But one tap on the icons at the bottom of his vision and all was clear. As he hit the button, the thug closest to Tim raised his pipe and swung through the air, hitting nothing—a little MIDI *whoosh* rang out. Charlie tapped the arrow, and the thug moved a step closer to cartoon Tim. The next blow would connect.

"It's too easy," Charlie said. "It's three against one. Unless . . ."

"You don't think . . . ," Kenny said, eyes wide.

"No . . ."

Vanhi's hearts were dropping.

"Charlie, we don't have much time."

"I know, but . . ." Charlie felt a sickening lump in his throat. "We don't *know* that there's any connection between this and real life."

"Why else would it be so simple?"

"We don't *know*," Kenny said. "But we *do* know Vanhi's dying, for real." Kenny looked at Charlie miserably. "We can't be sure we're hurting our enemy. But we know we're saving our best friend. That has to make it okay, right?"

"Not really."

"Yeah, me neither."

The goons stood around cartoon Tim, the only movement the steady, rhythmic animation of their breathing.

Charlie said, "We have to at least see . . . if it's even what the Game wants."

Kenny nodded slowly. "Okay. Once."

Charlie tapped again, and the pipe swung. *Thunk!* The little cartoon Tim buckled. A comical *wee woo woo woo* slide-whistled as he went down on one knee.

Tim's life meter went down. Vanhi's went up, the same amount.

"Oh, no," Kenny said.

"Don't touch it."

"Charlie, she's dying."

"I know. I said *you* don't touch it."

"We'll do it together."

"No. You already saved us once, with your swastikas." Charlie met Kenny's eyes. "Yeah, I know. That had to be for you. That's how the Game is. This has to be for me."

The men circled around Tim.

"Do you want money?" he asked. "Is that it? I can get money."

No answer.

"Then what?"

He didn't sound scared. He'd been on the other side of these circles, some victim in the middle. Everybody gets a turn in the ring, he told himself. But unlike that little coward Alex, who nearly pissed himself, Tim would fight to the death. And it wouldn't be his death.

"Come on, then." He closed his fists.

Then one of the men swung his lead pipe through the air, a few feet away, hitting nothing. It made a violent, whisking sound.

"Quick fucking around."

Then suddenly, the same man took a step forward, clearing the distance between them. He waited there, pipe raised.

"You bastard. Fucking do it."

An erratic pause—then suddenly, savagely, the man swung. Tim tried to dodge right but he was boxed in and the pipe landed squarely.

He felt pain blossom in the meat between his neck and shoulder. His vision flickered. He felt his knees weaken and went down on one. But he was strong. He rallied and lifted himself back up. He was Tim Fletcher, goddamnit. Two-time state champion. Another pipe cracked against his ribs, and he realized he might die.

What popped into his head was Mary.

Charlie was in a trance now. He had no choice. Cartoon Tim was fighting back. He even managed to wrestle one of the video-game villains down, and Vanhi's life meter dropped again, dangerously low. Kenny reached out and helped Charlie, pulling another hooded figure into the fight.

He gave Charlie a worried look. "For Vanhi."

"For Vanhi."

They could see Vanhi's life hanging in the balance. The hearts fluttered back and forth. Charlie gritted his teeth. He hit the button and the man took another swing.

And another.

And another.

Finally, it was too much for Tim to bear, and his little avatar went down and cradled on the ground as the blows kept coming. Charlie felt his gut clench as the life meter for Tim dropped low. Each blow helped Tim's hearts go to Vanhi's side, but how many would it take? How low would Tim have to sink toward his own death for Vanhi to survive? Another blow, with cartoon Tim cradled on the ground, Vanhi's meter closer to full, but every time Charlie paused, her hearts started dropping again rapidly, her machines still off. *Come on.* Another blow, Vanhi's life meter inching stronger, Charlie cringing as he gave Tim another blow, and then Vanhi's meter maxed out, flashing red and dinging, and the screen changed.

They could see Vanhi again, in her hospital room. Her machines roared back to life, and her breathing resumed, her chest rising gently up and down. Her vitals normalized. Death, the figure superimposed on her screen, lowered his shears. He walked away. The audience, unseen in front of Charlie and Kenny, applauded.

"She's okay." Kenny's eyes crinkled with relief.

The screen changed back to the cartoon street fight. Tim was flat on the ground. He still had half a heart left. His little form was breathing slightly, facedown against the concrete.

"Vanhi's okay," Charlie said. "We can stop."

"Yeah, we can stop." Kenny agreed, and they looked at each other.

"Why is it still showing Tim?" Charlie asked slowly.

"Isn't the fight over?"

But the same terrible idea had already occurred to them both.

"Is one of us going to say it?" Kenny said finally.

They watched that little cartoon character, barely breathing. Feeling no pain.

"'If you and your friends want to leave the Game, you have to take a life.'"

"'Human sacrifice.'"

"That's what Scott Parker said."

It would be so easy. Only half a heart left. And by appearances, he wasn't even conscious. Just one more click. One more press of the same button. He wouldn't feel a thing.

And they would be free.

The hooded men stood there, hovering over Tim, waiting for a command. As if reading Kenny's and Charlie's minds, a door appeared on the brick wall behind the action. The sign over it said EXIT.

"We still have our virus," Kenny whispered.

"If it works."

Kenny nodded. "How much more time?"

Charlie looked at his watch. "Ten minutes. Less."

But the EXIT sign began blinking over the door.

Fading away.

Charlie stared at Tim on the screen and tried to make himself angry. He thought about Mary's bruises. Tim smashing him against the lockers. Threatening Mary's family. Driving Alex to suicide.

There was no way the virus would work. It was a pipe dream. Charlie got himself angrier and angrier. Could he raise his finger to tap the button, just a tap, one more time?

"Charlie," Kenny said softly, putting his hand on Charlie's forearm. "No."

Charlie looked at him. "I wasn't going to."

"I know." Kenny nodded a little too much. "I know."

92 AUDIENCE PARTICIPATION

Everything had gone wrong at the restaurant. The electricity was out. The freezers were dead. The gas stoves wouldn't light. The phone lines were down. All Arthur could think was *Did Charlie do this somehow, some hacking trick, now that he knows what I am?*

Arthur met the maintenance guy, but there was no fixing this. They couldn't even figure out what was wrong. They tried plugging one of the freezers into the portable generator, but its circuits were fried. The entire dinner shift would be lost, and if the food spoiled, that would erase the gains Arthur had made so far. It was terrible luck, if it was luck at all—but then he thought about things he'd done and realized he deserved every bit of it.

After the maintenance guy left and Arthur sent the last waitress home, he heard the footsteps behind him, too late.

Charlie and Kenny were alone in room 333.

The street fight disappeared. Tim was gone. Vanhi was gone. All they saw now was the empty classroom. Not even an audience of Watchers to cheer them on.

The test was over. They used a spoofing technique to call 911 anonymously, telling the operator the street name that had appeared in the cartoon world where Tim was beaten. Maybe it would get him help. Strangely enough, the Game seemed to let them do it.

Kenny's watch went off: 2:00 P.M.

It was minutes to Φ o'clock.

"Get your laptop!" Kenny said.

Charlie opened the casing and popped the Wi-Fi back in. They texted Peter but couldn't raise him. By now, the virus had spread far and wide. It had implanted and opened the flaps of its Trojan horses. If it worked, they should be able to see into the back end of the Game, into the gearbox behind God's eyes. Charlie felt it suddenly. He looked at Kenny.

"There's no way this can work."

"I know." Kenny felt despair.

"Unless it does."

Kenny closed his eyes. He'd spent his whole life being a skeptic. Not a coldhearted atheist, the kind that takes pleasure in tearing down other people's dreams. He saw what faith did for his parents. He wanted it so badly but just couldn't lie himself into it.

But now he needed it. "Unless it does." He smiled. "You're my brother, Charlie. I believe in us."

They looked at the laptop, and it was working.

The great codex of the Game was churning in front of them.

By now, the gas from the boiler room had spread through the network of ventilation shafts coursing through the school like arteries. The Game had opened the pressure-release safety valves like flaps on an organ, piping the odorless carbon monoxide through the school. The building was full of students in the middle of seventh period. A few had begun complaining about headaches, but the bomb would soon go off, before anyone left. Once ignited, the bomb and the gas around it would create a sun, a spectacle of oceanic proportions.

It was time. Christ let Alex know, told him to be strong. The Game handed Alex a device lovingly crafted by the avatar of Sigmund Freud, a Victorian steampunk apparatus, all wires and alligator clips and a black-raised button ringed in polished brass. Its virtual wires ran from the controller to the actual bomb in realspace, which the Game would ignite with the real sparkbox in the boiler once Alex symbolically pressed the virtual button.

"We'll count down together," Christ told him.

Alex was shaking so badly he could barely stand. The images of Christ and Thoth and Freud were around him, but he misstepped, and they couldn't support him so he stumbled and was grateful no one was there to see.

"Be strong, be strong," the Game whispered over and over.

He knelt before the bomb and put his finger on the black plastic button, which looked like an old doorbell. It gleamed in the vacuum-tubed light.

"You can do this," Freud whispered.

"I'll guide you on the other side," Thoth said. "A great river, for you alone."

"You will show them all," Christ said. "They won't forget you."

Alex's finger began to push down. He could almost feel the virtual button lowering, the smooth domed plastic, when Christ said, "Wait."

Alex thought madly for a second that it was all a test, like Abraham and Isaac, that they would call it off now.

But instead Freud said, "Your father is late. We can't start without him."

As Charlie and Kenny watched, breath held, the atomic clock approached Φ o'clock:

2:02:17

2:02:18

2:02:19

It hit 2:02:20, and their eyes flicked to the code tracker.

They watched it light up.

The code was telling—daring—the God Game to create a stone so heavy it could not lift it. A sphere large enough to contain the set of all spheres. Assuring it that according to its own predictions, it would do so. In the sim, God would draw all resources from all corners of its botnet toward the task, causing an exponential memory drain that would arch toward infinity.

They felt very small then, and very foolish.

And then it worked.

They weren't sure what to expect visually, but the Game began to flicker. In one corner, they were watching the code executing itself. In another, Charlie's 3-D view in the school phased in and out, the players moving around the map fluxing. His chessboard was up, the pieces no longer black and white but various shades in between, battered and bruised. The screen locked and unlocked, fuzzed in and out.

This is it, he thought. Then, *Is this it?*

The code scrolled faster and faster.

"It's working," Kenny whispered.

Charlie squeezed Kenny's arm. Charlie was too nervous to get excited yet.

The map unfroze, then scrambled. More static. More pulsing. "Oh, shit," Charlie said. The code stream was accelerating to the point of being unreadable. He took Kenny's hand and put it on the hard drive. It was hot to the touch, almost burning. Together, they'd done *this.*

The lights in the room pulsed off and on.

It will suck power until it burns itself out.

The whole screen went black. Charlie felt a tentative hope spreading. The lights in the room came back on, and in the hallway, too, but the computers were dead. The Aziteks were dead, too, just blank, plain glasses now, the avatars in the hallways gone. Charlie and Kenny exchanged glances. Charlie picked up his phone and it was fine, but the text thread from the Game was gone. The hope sprouted, blossomed, spread.

Then a window opened in the middle of the laptop screen.

On a little cartoon hill with flat shrubs was a squat little God with a white beard and white robes. He hopped with each step. He was as flat and two-dimensional as the green landscape around him. He pushed a giant stone at the bottom of the hill, so infinitely large you could only see the bottom of it on the screen.

God waddled up to it, gave a little grunt, and worked his flat shoulders under it. The speakers chirped with animated sighs and heaves. God's knees bent, then straightened out, shoving the planetoid boulder until it started to roll up the hill. When he got near the top, it started to waver and almost roll back down, but then he gave a last shove and got it to the top.

He flipped it up onto his index finger and spun it like a basketball.

With his other hand, boulder still spinning, he raised his middle finger at the screen and jerked it up and down a few times, right at Charlie and Kenny.

God grinned at them.

The rest of the Game sprang back to life on their screen. The avatars filling the school. The dots swarming the map. Their virus, on the other hand, was gone.

The code bank was empty.

93 SISYPHUS

Alex's dad reached the school. He was running late, so he pulled too fast into a far spot and fumbled with his keys. The school towered in the distance, a vast tan building. He felt overwhelmed. For all Alex's troubles, what teacher had taken the time to call Bao in? The teachers had all written Alex off years ago. Bao couldn't say why it was happening now, so late in the game, but it seemed hopeful. It made him see his son a little differently.

He checked his watch and cursed. His manager had held him late, despite his pleadings that he had to meet a teacher for his son. It was humiliating, to be a grown man taking orders at sixty-five. Mr. Dinh wouldn't have argued with Alex about that. The thing Alex never asked himself was *why* Mr. Dinh subjected himself to such humiliation. For whom?

Bao half walked, half ran toward the front doors in the distance. The windows were filled with students counting down for the bell to ring. He imagined poor Alex, alone in those massive crowds, and suddenly felt such tenderness for him. He wished he could sweep his arms around Alex and protect him from the world.

But Bao knew he couldn't.

This was paradise, compared to what Bao had known. But it was all Alex knew, and it hurt just as bad, Bao realized now, seeing it.

So Bao Dinh went to find Alex and reminded himself to say something kind.

The virus was dead and the Watchers were everywhere, laughing now.

Their canned laughter, audience participation, was echoing in the Aziteks.

The Game showed the thousands of players who had come to witness the destruction of a school. Mr. Dinh was walking up the front steps, surrounded by them. Charlie and Kenny exchanged glances.

"Why is his dad here?" Charlie said.

"Is *that* why the players all came?"

"To see what? Is he going to hurt himself again? In front of his dad?"

"Or . . ." Kenny couldn't bring himself to say it.

But Charlie knew what he meant.

Everything that happens now is your fault, Alex had said, sending a chill through Charlie now. "He's not going to hurt himself. Not *just* himself."

"His dad?"

"Maybe more?"

Charlie shouted at the Game screen, "Where is he?"

The Game ignored him.

"You said I'm a Watcher now. You said I earned it. Show me where he is." The Game complied. It put the map on the screen and showed where Alex was.

The dot for his father was moving into the building. Whatever was going to happen was happening. They jumped up and went to the door, but it was locked from the outside. Charlie rammed against it and smashed it open, the lock bursting. They ran down the hall, passing the rooms filled with students, but ahead of them, the Game triggered one of the fire/panic doors the school had added last year, Wi-Fi enabled. The pins dropped and the heavy doors slammed closed, locking into place. Charlie rammed against them, but they were solid and he crashed off them.

"Come on," Kenny said. They ran back the other direction, but at the end of the hallway the Game triggered another safety door, slamming shut and blocking them in.

On their Aziteks, the Game said:

All Must Die

"Run," Charlie yelled.

A teacher came out from one of the rooms to check out the crashing noise, but they ignored her yells and ran back into 333. The Game sent overvoltages to lights above them, the fluorescent tubes bursting open with sparks. Charlie went to the window and opened it. The ground was thirty feet below them, but a Dumpster was below one window that might lessen the fall.

Kenny looked at him, gulping. "You can't hack gravity."

They jumped together, slamming into the top of the Dumpster, which buckled a little, absorbing some of the impact. They jumped off and ran for the basement. In the hall along the way, Charlie pulled a fire alarm, trying to warn the school that *something* bad was happening— *Get the fuck out!*—but the Game didn't let the alarm go off.

They ran down the basement hall to the boiler room and pounded on the door, yelling, "Alex, Alex, it's us."

On their Aziteks, the Game gave them an X-ray view through the door, a mocking tableau: in tears, eyes haunted and lost, cradled by Christ, Alex knelt before the bomb.

94 | ALONE

"Your father is here," the Game told Alex. "It's time." It spoke through the avatar of Freud, cold and aloof, eyes judgmental.

Alex cradled the Victorian box as Christ cradled him.

"It's your birthright," Christ told him lovingly. "No one can take it from you."

Thoth was standing now, silent. His black ibis eyes watched.

Alex told himself, *On Mars, there is no one to hurt me.*

Someone banged on the door.

"Alex, Alex, it's us," the voices cried. It was Charlie and Kenny.

Alex didn't answer.

"Alex, open the door. Don't do this."

Alex squeezed his eyes shut and covered his ears. He wanted them to go away.

"Submit yourself to God," the Game cooed. *"Resist the devil, and he will flee from you."*

"Alex, we can talk about this," Kenny yelled.

"Eloquent lips are unsuited to a godless fool," the Game hissed.

"We can help you," Charlie said.

"How much worse lying lips to a ruler!"

"Quit lying to me," Alex yelled.

"We let you down. I know it. I'm sorry," Charlie said.

"This isn't the way," Kenny added.

"*Pay no mind to the necromancers who chirp and mutter,*" Christ said.

"*You shame them,*" Freud told Alex. "*You are their totem and taboo.*"

"You're ashamed of me," Alex yelled through the door.

"That's not true," Charlie said. "We can be a team again. One for all, and all for one."

"*It's too late,*" Christ whispered, "*no one can serve two masters.*"

"It's too late," Alex yelled. "I have to do this."

"*Woe to the wicked! Disaster is upon them!*"

"They have to pay," Alex said.

"No, there are good people here, too."

"*I will put an end to all people, for the earth is filled with violence.*"

"All must die," Alex said.

"You're confused. You've been lied to."

"*They are the liars and the deceivers,*" the Game hissed.

"You're the liars," Alex said.

Charlie gave Kenny a desperate look. There was no getting through to Alex. The Game had cut off their view through the door—they were blind now, too.

"I've never—" Charlie stopped. "I did lie to you. Once. I did want you out of the group. Because I was a coward. Because I was afraid of what people would think of me. I was wrong about that, and I was wrong to lie. I won't do it again."

There was silence, for the first time, from the other side of the boiler room door.

"You *were* wrong," Alex said, with just a trace of connection.

Kenny raised his eyebrows hopefully.

"I know." Charlie felt his own eyes welling now. "I can be better. I *will* be."

Kenny and Charlie stared at each other, afraid to even breathe, waiting for Alex to respond.

"I'm sorry," Alex said finally. "It's too late."

The Game showed the view through the door again: Alex picked up the Victorian box and put his finger on the small black button.

"Alex, no!"

Kenny pounded on the door.

Alex's finger pressed into the black button, shaking.

The Game said quickly in Charlie's ear:

> Lie to him.
> Tell him his mother is here too.

The button moved inward, the metal couplings closing the millimeter gap between them, a spark forming. There was no time to think, but the Game's advice rang true—Alex's mom had always been kind to Alex.

"Your mom is here," Charlie yelled.

Alex stopped. He looked up at the door. "What did you say?"

"Your mom is here. She came with your dad."

"No."

"We saw her, in the lobby, with him."

"You're lying."

Charlie closed his eyes. "I'm not. She's here. Don't hurt her."

"Don't do this. Don't lie to me."

"I'm not." Charlie shook his head. "I swear it. On my mom's grave. She's here, Alex. She came for you. Don't hurt her."

Alex's eyes were wide. They welled with tears. A long, anguished moan came from deep within him. The box trembled in his hand.

"I never would."

He lowered himself to the ground.

The sprinklers went off, sending the students out into the streets—a gift of the Game, saving them from the gas they didn't even know was all around them. Charlie and Kenny banged on the boiler room door, begging for Alex to come out, and finally the door clicked open. But when they looked in, Alex was gone. The Game had led him out a back exit deep in the guts of the mechanical rooms, into a service hallway and out the delivery bay.

Charlie and Kenny pressed through the crowds outside. Charlie saw a text from his dad:

We need to talk. You didn't have to ruin the restaurant.

Charlie showed Kenny.

"It could be a trap."

"I know. But he could be in trouble. Can you look for Alex?"

Kenny nodded. "And Vanhi, too. She's at a hospital. I'll let her parents know." He put a hand on Charlie's shoulder. "Are you okay?"

"I think so. You?"

Kenny smiled. "I meant what I said. We're brothers."

Charlie nodded.

As Kenny left, Charlie turned to find Mary behind him.

Before he could speak, she grabbed him by both sides of the face and kissed him, in front of everyone. He was startled, and when she pulled back, she said, "Thank you."

Charlie was baffled. "Tim?" he said carefully.

"What about him?"

"Nothing. . . . Why are you thanking me?"

"You did this?" She grinned, nodding at the soaked students all around and giving his wet shirt a playful tug.

"The sprinklers?"

She smiled conspiratorially, as if they were in on the same joke. "I know what we said, and I meant it. But still . . . *this* . . ." She flashed her phone at him. "It's just . . . no one's ever been this nice to me. Not really."

Charlie looked at the text:

Sorry about the posters. Nothing a little rain can't wash away.

"I know what running means for you," she said. "And you did this anyway."

Charlie couldn't find words.

Not for the first time, he didn't know if the Game was rewarding him or mocking him. The algorithm was incalculable.

The water had washed away some of the concealer she'd used to cover up the red mark on her face. She didn't realize it yet, but the bruise was now exposed in two broad streaks.

He put a hand gently on her cheek, and she didn't pull away.

"Even if I won," he told her, "how would I know it was real?"

She looked at him like he'd lost his mind.

Then she stood on her toes and kissed him again, in broad daylight.

She didn't even stop when someone in the crowd held up a phone and snapped a picture.

95 THE GOLDEN TRIANGLE

Peter thought about the Game.

It was in charge. But it was open to suggestions. It delighted in them.

If you understood it.

And Peter understood the Game. He always had, before he even knew it existed.

Alas, poor Yorick! I knew him, Horatio, a fellow of infinite jest.

Charlie was always crawling back toward the light. Didn't he understand, the world wasn't getting better? It felt that way because the people in power wanted it to feel that way, to keep the little people running like hamsters on a wheel. No one would ever give a shit about Peter or Charlie. They would always be shut out, like Peter's dad, scrapping and hustling because the white-shoe firms wouldn't let him in. *Always have a game to play,* his dad liked to say.

The world would continue to be rigged against them, Peter knew, even if Charlie was too stupid to accept it. If they played by the rules, they would be crushed. The Game was made for people like them. But Charlie had made his choice, casting a dim light on Peter.

Still, Charlie had offered Peter a second chance, a chance to be better than he was. So he had to do the same for Caitlyn.

She hadn't hooked up with Joss yet. That was the red line. It wasn't too late.

She could save herself. He wrote her:

> Invite me to your party
> > go away Peter
> Take me. Not joss
> > R U reading my texts?
> its not too late
> > fuck off Peter its over

Well, there you had it. Second chance, done. *You deserve what's coming,* he told her in his mind. *I tried.*

But there was still the matter of Charlie. They were the same. They were brothers. Twins.

No mom, bad dad, jilted by the old world and the new.

Except . . . except Charlie *lost* his mom. Peter's *left*.

Except Charlie was getting the girl. Peter was not.

Except Charlie's dad was healing. Peter's was immune to salvation. *Why why why?*

Yes, he had changed Mary's texts before showing them to Charlie.

Yes, he had designed the Dirty Laundry mod, with the Game's permission of course.

Yes, he'd let the Vindicators code their stupid virus, even helped them, knowing it was a farce. Kenny hadn't had a vision—he'd been knocked out with his Aziteks on, the Game whispering in his ear the whole time he was unconscious, planting his dreams.

Yes, Peter had thought of the swastika challenge.

The Game had loved that idea, for the conflict. But Peter had another agenda. He *wanted* that swastika on the wall. He wanted Tim and Kurt to feel emboldened. He wanted Kenny and Vanhi to know, for every action there is an equal and opposite reaction. He wanted Charlie to see the world clearly so he'd know Peter had been right all along.

Peter could survive in a world of chaos. He could thrive in it.

But Charlie had made his choice. He wanted to be noble with Vanhi and Kenny, leaving Peter alone in the dirt, no dad, no Caitlyn, no friend, nothing. He rejected Peter, shamed him with his hopeless optimism. *Vanhi was right. There's something wrong with you.*

We're done.

"You made your choice," Peter said aloud.

He hit Enter on the new text:

We need to talk. You didn't have to ruin the restaurant.

"I sentence you to death," Peter said, telling himself he felt powerful.

96 WORLD'S FAIR

Charlie crept into the restaurant.

He knew it was a trap. But if his dad was there, he had to help.

The restaurant was dark and locked, a CLOSED sign in the window. His father's car was alone in the parking lot.

Charlie went around to the back and tried to peer in. It was pitch-black inside. He tried the door, and it was open.

The freezers were off. So were the washers. He listened for anything. The silence was total. He came around the corner and saw his father seated in a chair, bolt upright like a king, his hands and legs bound, his mouth gagged.

"Dad!" Charlie yelled, forgetting himself, running up to his father.

All his anger was gone as adrenaline took over. He forgot about every horrible thing his father had done. All he could feel now was love and fear. He tore at the bindings, trying to free his father.

Charlie felt the chill of premonition, the lizard brain warning him danger was near.

Something creaked in the main room.

Charlie worked faster on the ropes but it was hopeless. He wouldn't get one free before whoever was in the darkness arrived.

He heard the sound of glass crunching under a foot.

Charlie's dad begged him with his eyes, *Leave*. But Charlie went to the knife block instead, where he drew a long knife. The skin on his father's wrists had looked so thin, so much older and frailer than Charlie had ever noticed.

He turned toward the dark room. He put himself between his father and the unknown. His dad was trying to tell him something, but it was too late to loosen the gag.

He could wait for death to come to them.

Or he could step into the darkness and face it head-on.

97 BURNING MAN

"Where are you?" Charlie called, feeling his way through the dark, knife raised. Something creaked in the blackness.

"Here I am," a voice answered.

Something was very wrong with that voice. Charlie couldn't say why exactly—it was calm and pleasant—but the hairs on the back of his neck stood up.

He reached into the darkness and felt a wooden table in front of him. He was at the far row of booths, all a step up from floor level, along the rough brick wall below the neon signs that were now dark and silent. He eased down the walkway between the booths and tables, stepping backward, away from the voice. The ground creaked under his foot, and he cursed silently.

The voice was thin and nasally. He was a mouth breather. You could hear it in the dark. The low exhale, and the high sucking in, patient and reptilian.

"Here I am," he said again, sounding like an inquisitor, one accustomed to whispering in intimate spaces, threatening damnation, all the while a serpent unspooling between his legs, under his robes.

Charlie gripped the knife until his hand hurt. He had pulled it glistening from the wood block like a young Arthur testing his worth. He moved toward the voice, knife raised, and the blast was so unexpected that he didn't feel the bullet tear through his arm. It spun him around.

"Here I am." The voice was feral now.

Charlie realized he was on the ground. He had slid down the back wall. Things were slick and sticky behind him. He was leaking. Nothing good would come from this. His wound was burning with pain.

"Just a taste," the man said quietly, and it wasn't clear whether he meant Charlie's blood or his body. Charlie wondered where the knife had gone. It had spun out of his hand and landed who knew where. He reached in the dark along the floor, trying to feel it. He wondered if he could move enough to get back to the kitchen and shield his dad. He tried his legs, and they seemed to work. Could they hold weight? He used his good arm, his left arm, to reach behind him in the dark and find the table above. He gripped it and dug his heels in, and, yes, despite the slippery blood he found purchase and got his legs under him, so that he could almost stand.

There was another blast—a bullet hit the wall behind him, and a mist of brick sprayed around his face, stinging his cheek and eyes. He wondered, *Does he want to taste me alive or dead?* Which was worse? Charlie almost laughed, but he didn't because he realized that insanity lay at the end of that laughter. The knife, he told himself, focus on the knife. It's silver. It glimmers and shines. Fear was crippling, and he needed that image, that shining light. Chop this man. Chop his evil into bits and pieces. Save yourself. Save your dad.

He found the tip of the knife with his fingers.

Another shot rang out and he lost the knife and ran toward the kitchen with his head down, but he couldn't get there so he burst through the dark toward the bar. The wound on his arm screamed as he moved.

Two more shots went off. Charlie prayed someone was calling the police, but it wouldn't even matter if the Game just spoofed the calls. He ran behind the bar and felt for the liquor bottles closest to him.

When Charlie heard the floor creak across the bar, he stood and swung the bottle at the man. It connected with the man's head and smashed open, the smell of vodka burning in the air.

The man fired once and fell back, pained but not truly hurt. He gathered himself and crept toward the bar again.

When the man drew close, Charlie threw another bottle with all his might, and it missed and smashed somewhere behind the man, who was laughing.

How cute, the man thought, *how cute!*

He came forward again, still laughing, and Charlie cracked a bottle against the wall and splashed it over the man, the alcohol stinging his cuts.

The man was really laughing now; the boy's fear was sweet and desperate. Soon the boy would run out of things to throw. The man fired shots into the mirror over the bar, and glass shards rained down. But now he was tired of playing, it was time to kill the kid. He saw a light come on from the behind the bar, small and shielded.

"Call whoever you want," the man said, "we'll be done before they answer."

As he rounded the corner, Charlie finished typing the last commands of the Breath of God into his phone, which he locked onto the nearest cell, and the man's phone turned on in his pocket and began its infinite looping, feeding on itself and multiplying exponentially within the tiny lithium battery, just as it had for Kurt.

The man raised his gun and aimed at Charlie, a silhouette in the dark at the bar's gate. Then his phone ignited, and the small explosion lit the streaks of alcohol all over his body, and fire crisscrossed him like highways, zigzagging up and down while he stared perplexed until the routes converged and swallowed him up. The light was sudden and magnificent.

Charlie was surprised to see the man's face was shockingly normal, almost babyish. There was just a glance before the fire swirled over it from several directions and wound together, devouring him.

Charlie pulled himself up as the flaming body fell fast toward him, the bar going up in flames around them. Charlie's right arm hung uselessly. He stumbled over the bar and ran toward his father as the fire traveled beside him, gaining along the walls. He made it to the kitchen and dragged his father and the chair in tow with his one good arm, his strength momentarily superhuman with fear and love, and he got them out the door and into the cold night air, choking and gasping as smoke billowed out after them. He untied one bind with his good hand and his teeth, and together they got the rest off and backed against the garbage bins away from the building.

By that time, the flames had burst through the windows and were lapping out all four sides of the restaurant, wrapping the top of the building in tendrils until the whole thing was swallowed. Charlie's—formerly World's Fair—was done.

Miles away, deep in the country, Caitlyn Lacey's lake house was also burning down. Peter's revenge had only taken minutes to create. The rest—the metastasis—worked on its own.

He invited everyone to her small, intimate house party. Well, not everyone. A specially curated list of monsters: junkies, biker gangs, skinhead hooligans. You could never have done this in person without getting killed. But on the Web he could speak directly to them all from the safety of his home, in an instant. He posted:

> Rich Bitch secret party! Slutz & whorez! Secret lakehouse no cops no rulez!! Come / cum. Get crunked!

High school was a tangled hierarchy, he thought. He'd tried to climb it, but the hierarchy won. Time to tear the fucker down.

It had started slowly at first, a car here or there that didn't fit in with the Audis and the Beamers parked on the grass by the lake. You needed a map just to find the place. Peter gave them a map. The lake house was on *acres*. Anything could happen out here. Some motorcycles arrived, then more. A couple fights broke out, between the overconfident football crowd and the actual thugs. Then the real mayhem began—tatted party crashers flipping tables over and dumping desks. A chair through the bay window. Cigarette lighters on the curtains. A horde peeing on her dad's busted-open file cabinet and pouring alcohol over the mix.

Peter watched through their cell phones. Caitlyn was crying, her new boyfriend nowhere to be found. Had Peter done enough? Probably. But still, he couldn't help it. Just one last touch, for panache.

Your poetry sucks.

he texted her anonymously. He signed off—the Game had summoned him elsewhere, to the roof of A. B. Turner High, and he had to obey.

Kurt Ellers had come to the party, just as he promised himself he would. But it hadn't been so easy. He'd lost his nerve on the ride over, even turned around a couple times. So when he got there, people were already streaming out from the flaming house. Broken TVs and smashed chairs littered the lawn.

He moved through it all, against the throng of people escaping. He didn't see Caitlyn anywhere. He went into the burning house. He found her inside, pinned down by a toppled bookcase, unconscious from the smoke. A beam from the house crashed down in front of him, lighting his arm on fire. He batted it out and freed Caitlyn, slinging her over his shoulder. He took a blanket from the couch and draped it over her, shielding her against the flames. Another beam fell, singeing him savagely. He would be scarred for life, deep knotted tissue on his arm and face. He didn't stop moving until they were far away from the danger. He laid her gently in his passenger seat and drove her far away from there.

Though he didn't have the words to say it, what he felt was similar to what Vanhi had told Charlie, their friendship aching:

Just because I don't love you doesn't mean I don't love you.

98 THE FALL OF THE AZTECS

Alex stood on the ledge, fifty feet above the pavement, on the roof of Turner High. Downtown glimmered in the distance. The wind whipped past and chilled him, a sign of the winter he would never see. Legend had it that this was where David Meyer, founder of the Friends of the Crypt, had stood some twenty years ago, when his club was shattered and he was awaiting trial, his full ride to Princeton revoked and gone.

Alex was ready to follow suit, all the way down.

But unlike poor Dave, this wasn't a rash act of despair.

It was an elegant solution.

For once, he would be the hero, not the victim. Let's see how Charlie liked it, being saved. The shame of it.

Alex had summoned Charlie.

Come to the Roof of the school.—a.d.

Charlie would have to watch, to witness what Alex had done for him, so he could carry it with him forever. This was *his* idea, *not* the Game's, yet it would be a legacy better than any bomb. He felt proud for the first time he could remember.

Charlie arrived, his arm wrapped tight in a torn shirt, soaked with blood. He looked at Alex in shock, as if for a moment he'd forgotten everything about the Game and jumped straight from normal life to the roof of the school, wondering, *How did we end up here?*

99 THE GAME OF DEATH

Alex smiled from the ledge, hovering between life and death. "The key was always right there."

Charlie didn't speak. There was such an eerie calm about Alex, Charlie didn't dare.

"One for all, and all for one. That's what we used to say."

Alex lifted a foot, just for a moment, and seemed to waver forward. Fifty feet down, the darkness beckoned.

Charlie raised a hand, slowly—*Don't. Wait.*

"It was *my* idea. Not the Game's. I will be the One for All. I will free All for One."

Charlie took a slow, careful step forward. *Let him talk,* he told himself. *Don't startle him.*

Alex rocked back on his heels. "I know how you quit the Game. I know that's what you want. But you don't have the guts to do it. I'll do it for you. I made a deal. My life, to set you all free. And every day, you'll remember me. What I did for you."

Charlie stepped forward again, hand up, gently.

"I hurt someone, maybe killed them, at the restaurant. Let that count." Alex scoffed.

"A thug the Game sent? That's no offering. I'll save you."

Bad thoughts tried to fight into his conscious mind, bubbling up from the id. *Would it be so wrong? What is the alternative? Everyone dying, one by one, in the Game, like that hackers' thread? Or playing forever, losing our minds like Scott Parker?*

And Alex *wanted* to die. His plan made so much sense, it was so win-win, that Charlie started to question his own sanity. But he knew these were just greedy, impish thoughts from the id. He'd been through too much to claim they weren't part of him, but he shoved them back down in the vault where they belonged.

Charlie finally managed to speak, but it came out hoarse. "I'm sorry, Alex."

Alex just blinked.

"Come down. If you want me to owe you, that's how, because that's what I want. For you to come down."

"It's too late." Alex smiled sadly. "I'm too far away."

Did he mean the distance from Charlie to the ledge? Or to Mars? Either way, it was too far to bridge in time.

"I have to go now. Build me a totem."

"Why don't you finally leave him alone," a voice said from behind Charlie.

Peter was here. "The Eye of God sees all." He smiled.

Alex looked at Peter with a mix of awe and envy. He was the only one better at the Game than Alex. Peter had brought the Game to Alex—and the Game had given Alex's life its only meaning.

"You *apologize* to him?" Peter brushed past Charlie. "But you never give him what he asks. They're not worth it, Alex. They're not worth your sacrifice."

"They'll owe me. I'm the hero."

Peter smiled. "I know. But there's other ways to own them."

He moved so casually, so lovingly, toward Alex, that Alex was completely off guard when Peter grabbed him, pulling him back from the edge, face-to-face.

"They're my pieces, Alex," Peter said gently. "I can't let you set them free."

"I want to die," Alex moaned.

"I know. I'm going to give you that, too. And then the rest of us will play forever."

Peter lifted him off the ledge. Alex's eyes were wide, too spent to argue or struggle.

"Up and over, by my hand, not yours."

Peter was looking out over the rooftop when Charlie hooked his good arm around Peter's neck and pulled them backward, falling hard onto the gravel roof, Peter crushing him.

Charlie gathered his waning strength and rolled on top.

Peter looked up and grinned.

Charlie held him down and shouted into his perfect face, *"You did this to us. You brought the Game into our lives."*

"You should be thanking me," Peter growled back. "You were *nowhere*. A ghost. I gave you something to fight for."

Charlie smashed his fist into Peter's face. His own vision blurred. How much blood had he lost?

Peter rolled on top, grinning, blood on his teeth. "I hate you. You know that, right? I never lied about being a liar. You haven't known yourself a day in your life." He struck Charlie, and the stars blurred. "We were *brothers*."

"I'm not your brother," Charlie spat.

"Yeah. How's Daddy, by the way." Peter grinned. "I made that mod, too. 'Do you love your dad? Y/N?' Nice save, by the way! The Game loved it. Personally, I was betting on the meth head."

Rage exploded inside Charlie. He brought his good arm hard across Peter's perfect face, knocking him aside. "You did that to me? To my dad?"

"I got Caitlyn, too. And Kurt, no one will ever want to look at him again. Life is bullshit, Charlie. There's no fairness, no justice, unless we *make* it. Morality is an illusion, a social construct to hold back the masses while the hunters prey. When will you learn? When will you finally realize how wrong you are?"

Charlie did see it then. Peter was like the internet itself, a parentless creature, a trillion nodes connecting but nothing inside. Peter would never stop hurting people. There was only what he wanted and how to get it.

He put his hands around Charlie's neck.

"It feels good, Charlie, being who you really are."

Charlie managed to say, "I know. I was wrong."

"Yeah?" Peter loosened his grip slightly to let Charlie speak. "About what?"

He met Peter's eyes—those infinite, flawless blue eyes. "I thought you could be saved. You can't."

Peter's hand closed around Charlie's throat, and Charlie reached up, fingers through Peter's golden hair, and pulled him down hard, banging his head onto the roof. His eyes dazed. Charlie rolled on top of Peter and looked over in time to see Alex moving to jump.

"No," Charlie cried. He grabbed the back of Alex's coat and pulled with all his might, and Alex felt the roof leave him and saw the empty void below spring forward, then stop, still far away, as Charlie used a strength he didn't know he had to pull Alex back onto the roof, shoving him onto his knees toward the middle of the rooftop.

Alex was screaming, *"No, no, no, no."* It was pure rage. "You *can't. I'm the hero. The Game will never stop."*

Charlie said, "Yes, it will. The Game is over for us." He took Peter by the arms, pulling him up, still dazed. "And there are no heroes."

With the last ounce of his strength, Charlie cast beautiful, lost Peter over the ledge.

100 FILE SAVED

What does it mean to be saved? Is it a version of yourself from years ago, perfectly preserved, so that you can return to it one day, unblemished, no matter what insults have happened since? No matter the mistakes and errors and blows and sins?

Or is it the opposite: overwriting all past versions of yourself, so that everything before has been wiped away, leaving only the newest, latest version to go forward and sin no more?

Or is the simplest explanation true: that there is no such thing as salvation? Only a series of files, disjointed, slices of time that—when strung together—give the approximation of life. The way a flip-book gives the illusion of motion.

It would be comforting to think that there were hidden variables—that the universe was smooth and continuous, and not, at base, a series of right angles stitched together.

But Charlie didn't think anymore that was true. There *were* gaps. Rough edges. Every lullaby could be broken down into ones and zeros. Every landscape was at base a cloud of random particles. The real question was, Could you know that and still find the landscape beautiful?

Charlie awoke in the hospital to find Mr. Burklander sitting there, watching him.

"Don't try to move. You're still very weak."

Charlie wanted to ask, "How long have I been here?" but his throat was too dry.

Mr. B. filled a paper cup with water and handed it to him.

Charlie drank, and his eyes closed again for a moment.

"Your dad's getting some food. He'll be back soon."

"What happened?"

"To you?"

Charlie nodded.

"You're hurt."

"How did I get here?"

"You were on the side of the road. Out by Westbrook. Somebody called 911."

Charlie nodded slowly, trying to pull up the last thing he could remember.

Mr. Burklander held Charlie's gaze. "Peter was a bad kid."

Was.

"I don't doubt he was into some bad things, and maybe those things led to bad ends."

Charlie didn't respond. He just held Mr. B.'s gaze.

"I don't think you wanted those things to happen."

Charlie wasn't going to say anything, but then he remembered Mr. B. collapsing to the floor, his heart jolted from within.

Charlie was unable to control himself and his eyes welled up with tears. "I'm sorry."

"I know you are. You don't deserve to hear it, but I know you are."

They sat quietly for a while, then Mr. B. got up.

"I'll let you rest." He paused by the door, then decided to add something. "The older you get, you start seeing patterns. Maybe it's early dementia, who knows? Kids and their clubs. Hidden worlds. There's always more to it than we know. Anyway, story for another time."

Mr. B. gave one of those corny teacher's winks, but his face was far more weary than that. He left and let the door shut softly behind him.

Eddie Ramirez was at home when his doorbell rang, and Mrs. Morrissey was there. It was jarring to see the principal who expelled you at your house, but she came in and gathered with Eddie and his parents around the coffee table in their living room.

"The good news is," Mrs. Morrissey said, "that we can make this right. Kenny has turned himself in and taken full responsibility for the prank. He didn't intend for your son to get caught up in it. The consequences will be severe. He'll have to repeat his senior year, and of course this will affect his college applications. It will be a significant stain on his permanent record. At the same time, we'll make a full explanation to the colleges of Eddie's choice, and we'll make sure that they understand the expulsion has been fully expunged and withdrawn."

"What about scholarships?" his mom asked.

"It shouldn't affect any scholarships. We'll make sure of that. They'll know this wasn't Eddie's fault in any way." Mrs. Morrissey's smile tightened. "Now, if this resolution sounds acceptable, we do have these papers that the district's lawyers have asked us to share with you, releasing us from any lawsuits or things of that nature. If you'd like a chance to review with counsel of your choice . . ."

Mrs. Ramirez took the pen from Elaine Morrissey's hand. "This will be fine." Mrs. Ramirez signed away her anger and let a sense of peace—of intense relief—well up inside her.

Around the same time, Mr. Walker found an envelope filled with cash in his mailbox. He had no idea why. He couldn't know that Vanhi had sold her bass pedal, or that Kenny and Charlie had delivered the envelope to his tiny, boarded house in the dead of night. He couldn't even count the money. Later that day, Mrs. Morrissey would call and offer him his job back. It was baffling. All he could do was look up and down the street, seeing nothing out of the ordinary, marveling at a plan larger than himself that he could scarcely comprehend.

The funeral for Peter Quine was a small affair. His father was there, wearing sunglasses so it was hard to read his face. The obituary made vague references to Peter's troubled life, without mentioning his expulsion or arrest or suicide. Rather it just said that he had finally found peace in the arms of his Maker. The priest, who didn't know Peter and hadn't met him, was a little more direct, speaking of the troubles and temptations of today's youth, particularly online.

Charlie showed up, feeling strangely calm. His arm was in a sling.

He wanted to feel guilty. That would be the human thing to do. But in truth, he didn't. He felt guilty about a million other things. But for dragging a semiconscious Peter to the edge of a rooftop and casting him off—by far the worst thing anyone Charlie knew had ever done—he couldn't muster regret. In the moment, an upside-down moment to be sure, it had felt like the right thing to do.

Kenny and Vanhi were at the service, too. Alex was in a psychiatric hospital, getting help. He'd been diagnosed with depression and an acute psychotic break. Medications might help. Therapy, too. The Vindicators had gone to visit, but they didn't make it into the room. When they arrived, Alex's father was already in there, cradling him, singing a song in another language, but it had the universal cadence of a lullaby. "My boy, my sweet, sweet boy," he kept whispering between songs.

They couldn't reconcile the man in front of them with the man who'd sent Alex to school with welts and bruises, limping and broken. But that was another relic of the Game: they didn't even try. They watched quietly from a distance, then left.

After Peter's funeral, the small crowd dispersed without fanfare. Charlie, Vanhi, and Kenny walked together through the grave sites. Vanhi walked with a cane, to keep weight off her injury as it healed. In typical Vanhi style, she'd picked a silver-topped wolf's-head cane, which was, in her estimation, badass. They passed Peter's dad, standing alone against a tree, smoking a cigarette.

"You were Peter's friends?" he asked.

Charlie choked on the irony and couldn't find words.

Kenny said, "Yes."

"I don't know you," Peter's dad said. "I wasn't around much."

The Vindicators didn't know what to say, so they stood there awkwardly.

"Was he really that unhappy? You know, to do something like that?"

"I don't know," Charlie said finally.

"He was in trouble, at school," Kenny said. "I think that was it. I don't think he was unhappy most of the time."

The graceful answer seemed to give the dad some comfort. "I should have paid more attention. But, you know, he was always gonna do what he was gonna do. He had a will of his own." The man shrugged. He still had the sunglasses on, and his face was still unreadable. "Thanks for coming."

The Vindicators wound through the paths. The sky was bright and cheerful, an odd contrast to the graves. Charlie had told them everything. After the run-in with Peter's father, Vanhi said, "Charlie, what you did . . ." He tried to stop her but she said, "You shouldn't feel bad."

They didn't discuss it again.

After a while, Kenny said, "Should we do it now?"

Charlie and Vanhi nodded.

They pulled their Aziteks out.

"I peeked last night," Kenny said. "They don't work anymore. They're just blank."

"You mean clear," Charlie said.

Kenny laughed. "Yeah. Right. Clear."

One by one, they put their Aziteks on the ground. Together, they pressed their feet down, grinding them into pieces. Vanhi used her cane to crush her lenses.

Charlie kicked the remnants into the bushes.

"Okay." Charlie readied himself. "You sure you guys are up for this?"

"We should have done it a long time ago," Vanhi said.

"Yeah," Kenny said. "Let's go."

They wound together through the paths, until they came to the gravestone that read ALICIA LAKE. BELOVED WIFE AND MOTHER.

They stared at it, together. Vanhi wove her fingers through Charlie's hand. Kenny did the same on the other side. They looked for a while, without talking.

"It hurts every day," Charlie said.

"We're here." Vanhi nested her chin on his shoulder.

101 HOMECOMING

Vanhi withdrew her Harvard application. She applied again for regular admissions, this time with her real scores and essays. Three months later, she would receive an envelope in the mail, containing her rejection slip: *Dear Ms. Patel: This year Harvard received a record number of applications. We are very sorry to inform you . . .*

On that day, she would stand outside, no longer needing her cane, and feel okay. The world did not stop spinning. No one was hurt or gone. She would read the letter again, take a deep breath, then go inside to tell her mom.

Mary became student body president, after Charlie dropped out of the race. Caitlyn Lacey had won homecoming queen, and her new boyfriend, Joss Iverson, was king. People whispered that she'd gotten a "sympathy bump" because her lake house burned down. Talk about first-world problems, Kenny had said. Kurt was recovering. His life would never be the same, in ways both good and bad, although the balance between the two seemed to swing wildly from day to day. He hoped, no, he *knew,* one day that would even out.

The ashes of Charlie's restaurant were long gone. Insurance wouldn't pay to rebuild. The fire was too suspicious. Charlie dropped out of school and took a full-time job to help reopen the restaurant. His father had fought him hard on that, but Charlie refused to back down. Now the construction was moving along. Charlie and his father sat at the kitchen table, night after night, sketching out different possibilities for the new space. They fought over everything, but it was a mild, soft bickering.

Mary had come to see Charlie in the hospital. She fussed over his wound and kissed him gently. He told her everything. He learned that Tim would recover, but slowly. The Game had never delivered on Peter's attempt to expose Tim's parents, and their scheme went on. But Charlie figured Tim had suffered enough. Charlie hoped they got caught. But he wasn't going to do it.

The night the Vindicators were on the rooftop of Turner High, Mary had been far away, in a part of town she'd never been to. It started when she'd received the call about Tim. The police had found him, nearly dead, on a street in the Byerly neighborhood. She had no interest in seeing him. But she was compelled to go somewhere else. Her mom had tried to stop her on the way out.

"They'll sue. They'll want money. Everyone will *know*. You'll ruin us."

"Maybe." Mary's voice wavered. "Maybe not."

Her mother slapped her hard across the face.

Mary left. She drove to the address she'd memorized a long time ago.

An old lady answered the door. "I know you." She put a hand to her heart. "I've seen your picture in the paper. You poor girl. What my Sammy did to you."

Before she could say more, Mary held her and said, "No. No. That's all wrong. I'm going to tell you everything. And when I do, you can do whatever you want. All that matters is you know the truth about your son."

Inside, the house smelled of mothballs and tea. The old lady brought Mary a hot chocolate and sat her in a lumpy chair next to an end table with a lamp.

The old lady studied Mary, then hugged her and whispered, "You poor thing." She touched the bruise on Mary's cheek, which was hidden under makeup. "You tell me because you need to. And whatever it is, sweet girl, it will be okay."

The thing Charlie remembered most vividly from that strange time was coming home from the hospital and seeing his dad in the kitchen for the first time, right back at the table, as if they'd retaken their exact spots from their last, awful fight.

His dad had said the oddest thing: "Now you know. Are you glad?" It was the first and only time they spoke about the dirty laundry.

Charlie had wanted to forgive his father completely, right then and there. To say that it was okay that he had cheated on them, that he'd lied and disappeared and gone weak at the exact moment Charlie and his mom needed him most. Charlie wanted to believe that it was none of his business and that he would have been better off not knowing, so things could go on as they had before. But he couldn't say that and he didn't believe it and he saw his father now clearly. Charlie saw himself now clearly, too. One day his dad would die and be gone. It would be unbearable. Charlie wanted to believe in perfection, something pure and eternal, but he didn't and he couldn't, on this plane or any other. But he could be okay with that. They would still find redemption, both of them, but it would be in each other. Charlie wanted to say all this but didn't know how. So he hugged his father, harder than he had in years, hugged him and felt the stubble on his cheek and smelled his father's soap and put his fingers through his hair and cried and held him so, so close, because he was here, because he loved him, because he was real.

102 GÖDEL, ESCHER, BACH

In the darkness, Peter became aware. He felt weightless, floating. For a moment, he wondered if his consciousness had been uploaded to the machine. That was the only true immortality. If every neuron in his brain was mapped to a corresponding bit, it would be a perfect representation of his life, his memories and beliefs, his dreams and nightmares. Would that be him, a continuity of awareness? Or would his old self die, and this new thing would be someone else, disconnected yet seamless?

But it wasn't an electronic dream. He wiggled his fingers and toes. Every part of his body screamed with pain, but he was alive. He let his eyes open and saw the roof of the school high above him, then focused his mind on the sting of the net under him, taut thick cords of black nylon. His body was lashed where the real-world lines and nodes had torn into him on impact. The Game had foreseen all this, warned him, mapped out in an evolving stochastic web the possible outcomes of the rooftop confrontation.

Alex would jump, thinking he'd saved his friends, unless Charlie stopped him. Charlie would stop him, unless Peter interfered. If Peter interfered, Charlie would kill him, to save his friends from the Game. He would think it was noble even, although he wouldn't offer himself. The Game was retesting one of its favorite hypotheses: anyone is a murderer under the right conditions.

Peter had bet against the Game on that one, and it would cost him dearly in Blaxx. But he would recover, just as his wounds would recover.

It was child's play for the Game to calculate acceleration, to instruct other players on the height and tension in the net, so that Peter would hit just far enough above the ground to stretch down and smack the earth but live. Peter would hit the net because Alex would stand wherever the Game guided him. Had Charlie looked down from the roof, all he would've seen was Peter unconscious on impact, the black nylon invisible from fifty feet above. But the Game also predicted correctly that Charlie wouldn't even look—he would cradle Alex and carry him away.

Now, as Peter came to, Charlie and Alex long gone, he was laughing, partly because every inch of his body hurt, and partly because he knew he could now die and be reborn.

What was death, after all, but a police report in a system, which set in motion a series of events, boxes checked wherever appropriate? The Game would talk for the police to the principal, who was happy to learn the body was found and cared for before any media arrived. The Game would talk for the police to his father, who was offered the chance to ID the body by screen share since he was in Europe, before boarding a long flight back for the funeral. He accepted the policeman's thoughtful recommendation that cremation was the way to go here. The electronic charts would confirm the body was ruined, the DNA certain, the urn labeling the remains as Peter's delivered to the funeral home. Electronic signals would assure the right people that everything was accounted for, packaged, delivered, exchanged, disposed, departed.

The Game even provided a note, posted on Peter's social media, recalling his run-in with Morrissey on the drug charges: *You caught me. Better this than jail.*

And what if someone opened the urn to see what was inside?

It would be ash.

And Peter was free, to go anywhere, to be anyone.

Free within the Game.

He was laughing also because a new mod had occurred to him while he lay there. The Game would honor Charlie's deal, because

Charlie had—to the best of his efforts—offered a killing to the gods. The Game had stopped the death, but Charlie didn't know that. It didn't make Charlie any less a willing executioner, which was all the Game wanted to see.

But Charlie had only bargained for himself and his *friends'* freedom from the Game. Peter was already drafting the invitation in his mind, and the fun and games that would follow.

Do you love your son? Y/N?

Once, Peter had dreamed that if he couldn't have his own dad, maybe Charlie's dad would adopt him, too, be his surrogate father, but Charlie's dad had hated Peter instantly, leaving him once again in the cold—with Charlie, the favored son, always in the light.

A day from now, or maybe a month, Arthur Lake would sit alone in front of a screen, his loved ones asleep, and the Game would ask, *Would you like all your dreams to come true? You have a restaurant, yes, but would you like a second? A third? A new patio, an award, an empire?*

And the eternal loop would continue, filled with unwitting playthings tossed and turned by the whimsy of the fates—for amusement or sport or no reason at all—asking questions that have always been asked and expecting an answer.

ACKNOWLEDGMENTS

Thank you to my friends and family who took time from their busy lives to read and debate this book in its early forms and make it better, especially Jared MacDonald for keeping me tech-honest (all mistakes and artistic licenses are mine), Ware Wendell for keeping me Austin-honest (even in my highly invented Austin) and just generally honest (again, mea culpa), Atara Rich-Shea for spherical observations and collisions, Noam Weinstein for keeping me on waves and above the music, and Martin Tobey for reading the very first draft and pointing me in the right direction—you have a storyteller's eye. Thank you to Andrew Tobolowsky and Stephen Tobolowsky, who gave me biblical insights and anecodotes—spiritual, historical, archeological, and literary (all theological conflations and departures mine). A tremendous debt of gratitude goes to my indomitable agent, Jodi Reamer, and my delightfully sublime or sublimely delightful editors, Sara Goodman at St. Martin's Press and Rachel Winterbottom at Gollancz, who bring scalpels and mallets and know when to use which. You challenged me always to dig deeper and reach further, even when I didn't know I could. Jodi, you are a force of nature, and I want you in any trench I find myself. Thank you to their incredible teams, including Alec Shane and Jennie Conway—it takes a village to bring a book to life, and two to do it this nicely. Thank you to Dr. Charlie Miller and Chris Valasek, whose whitepaper, "Remote

Exploitation of an Unaltered Passenger Vehicle" was my research source for Charlie's hilltop car hack by the reservoir. As to the sign hack, I don't know who told a road sign in Dallas in May 2016 to comment that Donald Trump was a shape-shifting lizard, making national news, but it wasn't the Vindicators. Their other message was "Work Is Cancelled—Go Back Home," which brought a smile to my face, even if it wasn't true. Finally, my deepest thanks to my family. Writing a book is a lonely task that paradoxically can't happen without the support of everyone around you. This is a book about parents and children, and I am eternally grateful for my own in both categories. And most of all, thank you to Jude, for more things than I have room to list or know how to say. You didn't just read the book—you created the world that made the book worth existing in.

CREDITS

Danny Tobey and Gollancz would like to thank everyone at Orion who worked on the publication of *The God Game* in the UK.

Editorial
Rachel Winterbottom
Brendan Durkin

Editorial Management
Charlie Panayiotou
Jane Hughes
Alice Davis

Audio
Paul Stark
Amber Bates

Contracts
Anne Goddard
Paul Bulos
Jake Alderson

Design
Lucie Stericker
Joanna Ridley
Nick May
Helen Ewing
Clare Sivell

Finance
Jennifer Muchan
Jasdip Nandra
Afeera Ahmed
Elizabeth Beaumont
Sue Baker

Marketing
Tom Noble

Production
Paul Hussey
Fiona McIntosh

Publicity
Stevie Finegan

Sales
Jen Wilson
Victoria Laws
Esther Waters
Rachael Hum
Ellie Kyrke-Smith
Frances Doyle
Ben Goddard
Georgina Cutler
Barbara Ronan

Andrew Hally
Dominic Smith
Maggy Park
Linda McGregor
Sinead White
Jemimah James
Rachel Jones
Jack Dennison
Nigel Andrews
Ian Williamson
Julia Benson
Declan Kyle
Robert Mackenzie

Operations
Jo Jacobs
Sharon Willis
Lisa Pryde